ROAD

OF

WATERS

Written by
Eric Loren

Book 2
Ways of Camelot

Reader Hill
Yucaipa, California

Published by
Reader Hill
PO Box 490
Yucaipa, CA 92399
readerhill.com

Dedication

To my beloved wife. You are such a blessing in my life, enriching my days and filling them with laughter. Thank you so much. I will love you always.

Acknowledgments

I want to share my appreciation for the many people who helped to make this book a reality, including Irene, Traute, and Rena. I am also thankful for my fellow scriveners at the Writers' Gallery: Andrew, Joyce M., Judith, Ron, Robert, Cathie, Joyce L., April, and Michael.

All of you gave your honest critique and helpful suggestions. Thank you for your words of wisdom.

ONE

King's Haven

Thomas held Adele's fine hand in his, drowning in her beautiful blue eyes. A few strands of her long black hair waved in the light breeze. The newly-risen sun formed a halo around her head as they stood halfway down the broad stone stairway that led to the city's small harbor. He didn't want to let go of her hand. He wanted to keep Adele here in Camelot, but she was leaving in the evening.

She finally broke eye contact and gave him a fierce hug. "I must get on board," she whispered. "It will anger the others if they think I'm shirking my duties."

"There are only servant girls down there. The queen's other maidens aren't even here yet," he protested into her dark silken hair. He didn't want to let her go.

"I wouldn't be hugging you if they were."

Thom frowned. "Are they still calling you a whore just because Lady Ursula was so wanton?"

Adele pulled free from his arms. "Of course they are, for the silly things have nothing else to fill their days. When they aren't swooning over some pompous knight, they tease me about my supposed past. Don't worry, Thomas, I've endured much worse. Their words mean nothing to me. I'm just thankful to be under Queen Guinevere's protection, for they can't do much to me except gossip."

Thom had his suspicions that Adele was enduring more than just unkind words, but he didn't press the issue. By now, he understood how strong and determined Adele was; she intended to survive at the royal court in spite of the indiscretions of her previous mistress.

Dawn had fully lit the eastern the sky to a faint blue. He could hear the waters softly lapping under the King's Haven docks. The small harbor was the terminus of the Road of Waters. It lay within the walls of Camelot city, sheltered and almost still. The entrance to the harbor, known as the Water Gate, had already closed; it only opened at sunset for departing traffic and just before sunrise to let in arrivals. Boats taking the Road of Waters journeyed at night, following the glowing river through a maze of waterways. The galleys that had arrived a few hours earlier were still being unloaded.

Adele would be spending all day down here, getting a cabin ready for the queen, a whole day alone with those catty maidens. He wished he could spare her that experience. "Should I ask my master to intervene for you?"

"Levitanus has no clout at the royal court. They see him as some country bumpkin, no matter how powerful a magician he is. No, even if he spoke to the queen, it would not help me any. This is something that I must settle on my own." She came near again, stretching up on her toes and giving him a chaste kiss on the cheek. "Thank you for your concern, but I must handle this brood of clucking women on my own. I must either win them over or intimidate them into leaving me alone."

She will be their rooster soon enough, thought Thom, imagining Adele scaring the other maidens into obeying her. He doubted any of the others had Adele's skill with weapons. Maybe she didn't need his help, but he still wanted to offer it. He didn't want to see her in any distress, so he let it go. "I will miss you."

She smiled, her countenance open and trusting. He was amazed that someone so wonderful would be interested in him, a mere journeyman magician. He grinned back, though he doubted that his smile was as bright. Adele shone with beauty. He longed to linger here all day, but they both knew it was time from them to part ways. He wanted to let her know how much he loved her, yet the words caught in his throat, making him cough instead. She didn't seem to notice his difficulty.

They hugged one more time.

"Kiss her already!"

Startled, Thom looked over at a sailor clinging to the mast of the nearest vessel, repairing some line.

The man laughed. "Kiss her, boy, or I will."

Another sailor yelled out. "Come over here, pretty thing, and join me in my hammock. I get lonely during the day."

More sailors were looking at them now, laughing with their crewmates.

Flustered, Thom looked back at Adele, ignoring their audience as best he could. "Adele, I love…"

She put a hand over his mouth to stop his confession. "Please not yet, Thomas… It is too early for those words." She smiled to take the bite off her request. "You have my affection, but …"

This time he touched her lips to stop the words. He didn't want to hear the rest. Confused, Thom suddenly worried that maybe she saw him more as a sibling than as a romantic interest. Had he misunderstood her hugs?

Thom tried to kiss her lips but found only her cheek.

"You lost your chance!" yelled the first sailor. "A peck on the cheek is for your sister or your mum. There'll be no caressing or other fun for you, young wizard." The man had noticed Thom's journeyman staff.

More sailors laughed.

Thom reddened with embarrassment and anger. It seemed every man in the harbor was now watching and laughing at his awkwardness. He wanted to storm over and fight the lot of them.

Adele leaned close and whispered, "Pay them no heed. There's no other man that I want. Just you. I only need your patience, for I can't… I'm not ready to… I just need your patience."

He focused on Adele; his love for her so strong. But he fought to control his desires, realizing that wasn't what she needed from him. He wanted to kiss her passionately, to confess his love, and to ask for her hand in marriage, but he sensed that what she needed was his understanding. He suppressed his desire and offered her a sincere vow in its place. "My patience and my heart are both yours."

She gave him one more brief hug and then she was gone, hurrying to the dock where the royal galleys were moored.

Adele was correct in saying that his presence would cause more gossip, so he didn't linger to watch her climb aboard. He also knew that if he delayed he might be tempted to challenge those sailors after all, even if it would result in a terrible thrashing for himself. Thom realized that his true frustration wasn't with the rough rivermen. He just didn't want Adele to leave. So, instead of getting into a fight, he turned away and headed up the wide stone steps leading out of the harbor's basin.

The sun was rising quickly and he still had a long hike back across the city to get back to Clas Myrddin for a day of lessons, but he promised himself that he would be back to watch Adele's departure.

* * *

The king and queen left Camelot just after sunset. All three royal galleys went in their convoy: the Royal Lion, the Royal Ram, and the queen's Lovely Lady. Two other vessels went as escort to the king's boats, all of them filled with knights and servants. Numerous lanterns twinkled from the galleys' decks, giving the boats a golden glow.

Thom had slipped away from his duties to come down to the harbor and watch their departure. He stood at the top of the harbor stairway so that he could have a better view. He knew Adele wouldn't be able to see him, not on such a dark and moonless night, but he still wanted to watch.

He saw the five galleys cross the small harbor and approach the now-open Water Gate. A blue-glowing curtain of mist was all that he could see beyond the gate. Thom knew what that was: the mist formed within an archway, marking the entrance into one of the Ways of Camelot. The boats were entering one of Merlin's magical routes connecting Camelot to the rest of the realm. Thom watched as the boats disappeared through the glowing curtain of mist to start their journey down the Road of Waters.

River galleys were boats unique to the Road of Waters, with a short keel to avoid dragging the bottom and a large sail to catch the winds that steadily blew upriver. Since the boats traveled only at night, all of them had crew cabins where the men could sleep out of the sun during their stops at the various Waywaters along their route. The royal galleys were more ornate than most and a bit larger, but they still had the same shape as all the other boats in the harbor.

From what Thomas understood, King Arthur was headed for a parlay with

Mordred, his illegitimate son. The king's only offspring was bitter that he hadn't been named heir to the throne, but Arthur hoped to appease him with other titles and estates. Thom didn't know all the details of the coming meeting, but it must not be considered dangerous if the king was taking along his queen and her maidens.

TWO

Secret Truths

It was late by the time Thomas returned to Clas Myrddin, but Levitanus was still lingering over the fire when he entered his master's suite.

The wizard looked over from his upholstered chair, setting aside a mug of mulled wine. "I take it that the king and his entourage started their journey without incident. And your friend Lady Adele went with the queen?"

"Yes, sir," replied Thom, closing and bolting the door behind him.

"That is probably for the best, for I fear you are growing too fond of her. She is a lady now, Thomas, so it is expected that she will marry among the nobility, not a commoner."

Thom frowned as he walked over. His master was wrong in this, for he and Adele cared about each other.

"You disagree," noted Levitanus, motioning for Thom to take the other chair set before the fire. "I hope it works out as you dream it will, Thomas, but too often it does not."

He fell silent for a time, watching the flames as they danced, so Thom sat there looking into the fire as well. Then his master spoke again without looking over. "Being a magician is not an easy life. You are a student for decades longer than any other profession and there is no assurance that you will ever become a master of the craft. In addition, there is the constant lure of the dark side. Brother Francis was not wrong in all his accusations; the power of crafting magic can tempt all of us into doing awful things." He turned his head and met Thom's eyes. "We are tempted to use magic to kill or destroy. We are tempted to use others to get more power, even to kill to master magic. Even you will be tempted."

Thom shook his head, about to protest that he's no killer, but his teacher spoke over his protests.

"Even you, Thomas. We use magical plants and magical animals and magical beasts. But then we are tempted to use greater elements, to use powders made from magical beings. You realize the difference, do you not?"

"Of course," Thom replied. "A magical being is much like us, be they pixie or fairy, merfolk or dryad. They think, feel, and talk. They have a soul and dreams of their own. They are beings, even if they aren't human beings."

Levitanus nodded, "But they also have power intrinsic to them. Do you realize that they are necessary for any of the greater enchantments? Pixies died to create the Roads, as did some of the other magical beings. Their blood is very powerful and very alluring to a magician. Now for the Roads, every being volunteered to be blood-letted or even killed, but it still required that sacrifice to make it work. That is the dark secret of magic, that is what horrifies your friend the monk so much."

"You have killed pixies?"

He shook his head. "I was naive when the three of us came together for the crafting of the Ways of Camelot. It was Dalrake and Merlin who killed those who volunteered; I did not learn of it until after the deed was done. Nonetheless, I did not withdraw from the crafting we were doing. I continued with the work, for it was such a magnificent enchantment and to leave early would have endangered all that we had already crafted."

"Why would the pixies volunteer for such a thing?"

"Merlin was very convincing, offering them a refuge inside the enchantment, for they were a threatened people that were dying off. It is true that they and the dryads have thrived inside the Road of Leaves, just as the centaurs and merfolk have thrived inside the Road of Waters, and the faeries have on the Road of Clouds. Overall, we built a strong safe haven for Arthur, which allowed him to concentrate on wooing allies and conquering enemies. Without the refuge of Camelot, we would likely still be an island swarming with feuding little kingdoms. The sacrifice of a few helped bring peace and prosperity to so many.

"However, I do not like how doing such powerful enchantments brings out the worst in the magician. It changes you. It is why Dalrake left the guild with so many others, for they hungered to do ever greater magic no matter the cost."

"If you dislike it so, why do you still craft magic? And why take on apprentices like me?"

"I still believe that there can be just magic, the crafting of enchantments for just causes and doing so with full respect of those beings who are innate in it. Call me an old fool, but I think enchantments can be a boon for all, if done carefully and for the right reasons. It is still worthwhile training others in the craft, which is why you are my student. And you are now a journeyman, not an apprentice."

Thom ignored the correction and asked, "Does Merlin agree with you about magic?"

Instead of answering, Levitanus stood and motioned for Thom to do likewise. He led him to the far wall of the sitting room, richly paneled wall on which hung a series of large paintings that depicted the magical beings they had just been discussing. Levitanus walked up to the painting that depicted a centaur and lifted it outward, reaching behind it to do something. There was a click and suddenly part of the wall opened up to reveal a hidden room.

Motioning for silence, Levitanus handed Thom a candelabra from a nearby table and directed him to enter the long, narrow room. Following, he closed the hidden door behind them. On this side it was obvious, but from the sitting room it blended completely with the wood paneling.

"This room is known to only two of my past students and now you. I had it added when Clas Myrddin was built so many years ago. You can set the light on the shelf behind you."

As Thom set it down, he asked in a whisper, "Is this place shielded from magic?"

His master smiled. "No, this room is not lined in lead. That much lead would have been impossible to smuggle in here. It was hard enough to bring in the woodworkers to do this much without Merlin's notice. The only shielding is in those caches over there." He pointed toward oversized wooden boxes that sat on the floor beneath a rack of shelves. The crates reminded Thom of the sorceress' stash in the goat cart. He wondered how full they were of elemental powders and liquids. The shelves above the boxes contained an assortment of jugs, parchment rolls, bundles, and other containers, including two magician's boxes.

"You asked about Merlin," continued Levitanus. "It is best not to talk about him within his own house, for he doesn't appreciate criticism. Merlin is probably the greatest wizard this realm will ever see, but he is also arrogant and easily peeved. Try your best to remain unnoticed by him. To Merlin, everyone is either a servant or a foe. None are equals."

"He thinks you are beneath him?"

His master nodded. "He is that way even toward the king. It is hard to know which is greater: Merlin's power or his pomposity. When it comes to magic, he sees it as something to serve his plans, for he is convinced that his plans are always best. He hates Dalrake because the man disagreed with his vision, rather than being disgusted with Dalrake's abuse of magical beings for more power. To Merlin, we are all pawns to be played for his grand vision of a united realm where he is the benevolent guide to great prosperity and enlightenment. Especially among magicians, he expects his will to be final."

"If that is true, why do you remain in the guild?"

"That is a good question, Journeyman Thomas. Indeed, why do I remain?"

Thom waited, hoping for an actual answer but none came.

"You should also know this about the enchantments of Camelot and its Roads: Dalrake is still actively involved in maintaining the magic."

"Is he not Merlin's foe? I would think the sorcerer would have withdrawn from the enchantments."

Levitanus smiled sadly. "Dalrake opposes Merlin, not the magic. He wants it all to remain, just with him in charge."

"Cannot Merlin expel him from the enchantments?"

"That could not be easily done. The three of us have crafted layers onto these enchantments for so many years now, along with additions from various keepers and others. Every day, one or more of us are working on the magic to keep it going strong. To pull one thread from that tapestry could cause it all to unravel."

It seemed so complicated to Thom. He hoped they would never ask him to be a keeper because it sounded like a lifelong task, always mending and adding to the magic. Then another thought came to him. "What will happen when one of you dies?"

"None of us know. We have lost a handful of keepers over the years, and with each death tremors went through the Roads and the shield over the city, but eventually the enchantments settled back in place. I have no idea what will happen when one of us three are no longer there to maintain our original enchantments on which all of the rest is built."

Levitanus paused, looking around the narrow storeroom. "I wanted you to know about this room, Thomas. You have permission to take any of the supplies, including refilling your magician's cache of any the elements you have depleted. In the far corner is a money chest that you may also take from. I only ask that you give me an accurate accounting of all that's removed. You can also store any excess in here, like some of the money the king awarded you."

"You make it sound like you are leaving me behind."

"We may be separated, what with all the repairs needed on the Road of Leaves. Most likely, you'll have no need for any of this but I wanted you to know it was here."

Thom was touched by his mentor's trust in him. "Thank you, master. I will only come in here if the need is great. Your secret is safe with me."

"I know it is, Thomas. Now, take that candelabra and practice opening and closing the door. I want to make certain you know how to get in here."

It was easy to open from within, but after they stepped into the sitting room and let it close, it took some work for Thom to master the hidden latch behind the centaur painting.

Once Levitanus was satisfied, he announced that he was going to bed. "One last thing, Thomas. Tomorrow at midday, we are both to report to the magicians' council. I think they will be asking for our help."

THREE

Magicians' Council

At an hour before midday, Thomas followed his master down the carpeted staircase to the first floor. He wore the formal attire of his rank, the dark-blue robe of a journeyman. On Levitanus' advice, he left his magician's box and staff in his master's suite, as did the wizard. The door was sealed with a small enchantment that would hold it shut and warn Levitanus if anyone tried to break through. He had called it the Rabbit and Vine enchantment and it included powdered Blue Eared Rabbit and Fierce Tangle.

On the ground floor, Levitanus led the way to the open doors of the council room. Thomas was surprised at the crowd that meandered in and out of the chambers. Just before they entered, his master leaned close and spoke softly. "This is not the time to make purchases or to accept any invitations. Make no promises and do not share any information with anyone until the council convenes. Before the meeting starts, all these lordlings, hawkers, and hucksters will be escorted out. For the meeting, you will sit among the benches while I will be at the Founders' table. During that time, answer honestly but succinctly. No need to volunteer more than they ask, for Merlin frowns on excess chatter. Just remember to do as I asked."

Thom nodded, clearly remembering his master's warning the night before. He would do his best not to draw anyone's attention.

His master entered first and was quickly greeted by a servant who escorted him to the smaller of two tables on the podium. Levitanus soon had a full wine glass in hand and was surrounded by three black-robed magicians. Thomas felt alone as he moved further into the council room, keeping to the back wall and away from most of the activity. He wished he had something to drink himself, though nothing strong. It was just that his mouth was dry and his throat felt scratchy.

He leaned against the cool wall and watched the others bustling about. Nobles chatted in pairs and small groups; these were the patrons who gloried in having a magician at their court. They came here to be seen and to appear sophisticated, though they kept their women away out of superstitious fear that some potion or charm might be used on them.

Two merchants were trying to entice one of the council members with a sampling of magical powders. Thom could hear the rhythm of the elements from where he stood. He knew a few of the sounds- Bearded Nighthare, Western Tufted Marlet, Fire Berries, Azure Fireflies- but some others he hadn't yet been trained to recognize. Each had a distinct rhythm and beat, noticeable to anyone trained to listen with their inner ear.

A trio of musicians roamed the hall, strumming instruments and singing a ballad. Thom was uncertain if they had been hired to entertain or were trying to attract a patron. Likely unknown to them, their music seemed to play off the elemental rhythms coming from the exposed powders laid out on the councilors' table.

There were other magicians-in-training in the hall too. Two journeymen were talking with one of the wizards on the council. A trio of male apprentices huddled in the far corner, whispering as they watched. Nearby, a journeywoman listened to a lord telling some story. The magicians were easy to spot, for they all wore the formal attire of their guild: black for the masters, dark-blue robes for those of journeymen rank, and gray for apprentices.

Thom was acutely aware that most weren't raised to this rank until they were at least ten years older than he was. He hoped no one accused him of being a fraud, because he didn't know any journeymen-level enchantments to prove his worthiness of the new position. Frankly, Thom felt a bit like a fraud and it made him avoid the others of his new rank.

He stopped leaning on the wall and moved deeper into the room, still staying to the back and away from the various groupings. Eventually, he settled on the back bench in the hall, merely perching on its edge and still uncomfortable being here dressed as a journeyman. There were four rows of benches and people even milled around here, sitting and standing in small groups or just wandering the room. Thom saw a servant moving among those scattered on the benches and caught the man's attention. He asked for a cup of cider and was pleased at how fast the fellow responded. Apparently, a journeyman's robe offered some benefits, at least here in the guild house. He had just swallowed his first sip when Merlin swept into the hall, a pair of wizards behind him.

The greatest of magicians looked around the room and gave a slight nod when he saw that all of his fellow leaders were present. The white-haired man strode to his seat at the smaller table where Levitanus was already sitting. There was one empty seat between them and Thom suddenly wondered if that one had been intended for Dalrake. Merlin ignored those who tried to approach to make small-talk. He also pointedly didn't look toward Levitanus. Instead, he looked over the crowd and shouted out his first order. "Everyone out! If you are not of this guild then please leave, for this is no social gathering. The servants will offer refreshments in the west study if you want to linger at Clas Myrddin, but this hall shall be locked for our meeting."

The wizard paused to make sure everyone obeyed. When a nobleman tried to speak with him, he replied loud enough for everyone to hear. "Not now, Lord Roland. I mean no rudeness, but the king's business takes precedence over all else. Please join the others in the west study, if you wish, but you must vacate this chamber. Maybe we can chat later today."

The noble didn't look pleased with Merlin's dismissal, but he gave a slight bow of acknowledgment and left. Right behind him went the merchant that had been displaying the elemental powders. Apparently, he had made a sale because he had left behind three small pouches of powders that were throbbing to Thom's inner ear. It was so distracting that he missed where the guild guards had entered. He just suddenly noticed them politely herding all the others out of the room until only those in robes remained.

Merlin turned to one of the council members that sat at the larger table on the podium. "Thallud, could you please stow those powders? Their beat is distracting right now."

Wizard Thallud gave a nod and did so. Apparently, not everyone had left their magician's boxes behind. He poured the last of his new powders into a vial within his magician's box, stoppering it carefully. He then snapped shut the box. Once he closed the lead-lined lid of his box, the elemental sounds no longer throbbed in Thom's inner ear.

"Journeyman Thomas, check to make sure no one is lingering at the doors."

Thom was surprised to hear the great Merlin call on him. He hurried to obey, checking outside the great doors. He found no one outside except the guards on duty. He closed the doors and shook his head to indicate there was no one.

Merlin had already started his meeting, but he was also watching and gave Thom a nod of acknowledgment. The great wizard spoke of a war between magicians and sorcerers. It was mainly a discussion between himself and the five members of the guild council that sat at the other table. The council consisted of four men and one woman. Levitanus was mainly silent through all of this.

At times, Merlin or one of the council members called on some of the apprentices and journeymen to share their experiences. To his discomfort, Thom spoke quite often, for the attack on the Road of Leaves was a major part of the troubles. During his recent trip along that magical route to Camelot, Thom had walked into a trap meant to sever the Road and capture the queen. He and others had foiled the kidnapping and killed the sorceress leading the attacks, but the magical route was still heavily damaged.

Merlin also told of other problems, including assassinations and skirmishes among knights. The wizard concluded, "Those of the dark arts want to rule this land, but we cannot allow that. I want to restore the Road of Leaves, but that will demand most of our energies, leaving Camelot vulnerable. That is one of the reasons that the king left, though we claimed it was to parlay with his son. I wanted Arthur well away from here, for the sorcerers have already shown their interest in the capital."

"Are we sacrificing Camelot then?" asked Levitanus.

"We are outnumbered," replied Merlin, not answering directly.

"Then why bother repairing the Road of Leaves?" continued Levitanus. "Why give our enemies another route to the city? Leave it cut off, then we need only defend the other three ways to Camelot."

Merlin frowned at Thom's master, his disapproval obvious. "It is not just about the traveling route. Would you want to abandon all of those magical elements to our enemy? The Road of Leaves is one of our main repositories."

Levitanus raised an eyebrow. Thom knew his master well enough to recognize that he was angry. The old magician cleared his throat. "I am well aware of the Road's unique qualities. Maybe you have forgotten, but I helped to craft the original enchantment. I was the one who encouraged the dryads to settle at the Waycircles. I still say we should leave off the repair work until a calmer time. Stabilize the enchantments and then let it be for now."

"What say the rest of you?" demanded Merlin. "Do you also want to abandon the Road of Leaves?"

"I agree with Levitanus," said the lone woman on the council, "but we need to seal Narissa's opening."

The sorceress who had led the attack on the Road of Leaves had created a new entryway into the magical road. From what Thom had been told by his master, two wizards now stood guard over that opening to prevent anyone from sneaking through.

"That is a given," said Levitanus. "We cannot leave the archway active."

Two more council members nodded in agreement, leaving Merlin with less than a majority.

"So be it," remarked the king's wizard without calling for a vote, "but I still need everyone to help secure the Road of Leaves."

"That is agreeable," said Levitanus. "Do you need all of our underlings too?"

Merlin looked around the room at those listening in. "We will need the apprentices to support us, but I have a different mission in mind for some of the journeymen. I want Vivien and Thomas, along with Reginald, who is now watching at the Rowan Gate."

"What plan is this?" asked Levitanus. "Do not forget that Thomas was raised in rank only a day ago."

"Those three will go to the Isle of Mists, to assist Weston in defending the Road of Waters. Although your charge is new to the journeymen ranks, you must admit that he knows more about these attacks than most wizards. I do not expect any student to stand up against a sorcerer, but Weston can use their help nonetheless. Would you deny him the aid, Levitanus?"

Thom's master frowned. "Very well. Send them to Weston."

"Thallud, please send word to Reginald at Rowan Gate to join the other two at King's Harbor tomorrow at noon. Their galley will be the first out on the Road of Waters," said Merlin to one of the councilmen, then he turned to Levitanus. "You and I should lead the next party down the Road of Leaves, wouldn't you agree?"

Levitanus gave him a slight nod. "I will be at Rowan Gate, ready at dawn. Shall we go on horseback or foot?"

"Two days ago, a guide was thrown from his mount when the Road rumbled," stated Merlin. "His leg is mangled and the horse had to be put out of its misery and then dragged out of the enchantment. We walk."

"So be it," replied Levitanus. "I will see you then."

Eric Loren

FOUR

Parting Ways

The council meeting went for another hour but little else was done except for Merlin letting the council know his expectations of them while he was busy on the Road of Leaves. It was made clear that all magicians were to wear their formal robes when entering any of the Roads, as a way to assure the citizens that the guild was working to secure the city, but that the robes could be removed after entering since all were expected to work and that often meant getting dirty. When the meeting finally ended, Thom was hoping to discuss things with his master, but Levitanus sent him back to their rooms while the wizard went to arrange extra supplies for both of them.

When the wizard returned, he took Thomas to the secret room and had him refill his magician's cache. Levitanus added even more elements that were new to the journeyman, assuring him that he would be instructed on their use by either himself or by Wizard Weston. Then Thomas assisted with the replenishing of his master's cache, which had vials in every slot. He measured out powders and liquids he had never seen or heard before, one's so rare that his master cautioned him as he filled the vials to not overfill.

As they finished, Thom asked something that had worried him. "Master, is it wise of us to open these caches and expose the sounds of the elements? Will not other magicians hear it and deduce that this hidden room exists?"

Levitanus smiled. "You have been at Clas Myrddin a few days now. Haven't you heard such rhythms everywhere?"

Thom nodded, for that was true, especially from the halls where they taught classes for apprentices. (Classes he sort of wished he had been able to attend, instead of spending a decade isolated at a small cottage in the wilds.)

"Such sounds are expected from a wizard's suite, at least when that wizard is in residence. That is why I had you wait to restock your supplies until I was here too. Although you have my permission to come in here whenever you have need and to take any of the elements or other supplies, please do so with caution when I am not here as well."

"Do you expect us to be separated often?"

Levitanus put a hand on Thom's shoulder. "You are a journeyman now. This will not be your last trip apart from me. There will also be times when you are at Clas Myrddin and I am not. Just be cautious at those times, for most will see you as a mere apprentice due to your age, no matter the color of your robe. They might even bar you from my rooms when I am not here, considering them to fine for a student. If so, then you will have to be more circumspect in getting to the supply room. Tell no one about this room, even if Merlin himself were to command you. Is that understood?"

"Yes, sir."

"Good." Levitanus squeezed his should and then gave a firm pat on the back. "Let us get out of here and finish the rest of our packing. You will have the leisure of a morning stroll to King's Harbor, but I must leave very early to reach Rowan Gate by dawn's break."

As they stepped out, Thom asked about something else that concerned him. "When will I learn how to use my staff? I know it is meant to enhance the enchantments I craft, but I have no idea on how that is done."

His master closed the hidden door behind them. "Unfortunately, that is not something I can teach you in one night, young man. It is meant to be a puzzle at first. Your first task is to find a way to kindle the jewel set in the staff's head without hurting the wood around it. Learn that and you will be ready for the next lesson."

By the tone in his voice, Thom knew his master would entertain no more questions about that topic, so he asked if he could help him pack, but the wizard declined, so Thomas went to do his own packing. Entering the simple room that had been his while here at the guild house, he set his knapsack on the bed and then slipped his now-replenished magician's box to the bottom. On top of it he packed the cloth pouch that contained his mixing bowl and pestle. Next came his laundered clothes. Finally, he added a few snacks that would travel well: dried fruit, a wrapped chunk of cheese, and a small loaf of bread. There was always ample food set out in the sitting room, so he didn't have to ask the kitchen for extra. Even though they were going to feed him on the river galley, he wanted to make sure he had something palatable on hand. As a scheming child spying on tavern patrons to find a mark to pickpocket, he had often overheard York rivermen grumble about boat fare. Most likely the rivermen and passengers on the galleys plying the Road of Waters were better fed, but it didn't hurt to be cautious.

Lastly, he looked at the large pouch of coins and jewels he had received from the king as a reward for his help on the Road of Leaves. He realized it would not be best to take all of it with him on this journey, so he went back to the secret room and searched for a suitable container. He found a small empty strongbox and put two-thirds of his riches in it, setting it on the shelf next to the larger chests that held his master's money.

As he was exiting the room, his master saw him and gave a quizzical look. He explained what he had done.

"Wise choice. Even someone as street-wise as you can get robbed... not to imply that the Isle of Mists is a thieves' den. This way you will know that some of your fortune is safely stowed at the guild house."

"Thank you, sir."

That evening they had an early dinner in the sitting room and then retired to bed, though Thomas did not sleep well.

* * *

Well before sunrise, the two ate a simple breakfast and then headed out. Both had only a knapsack and a staff, but they left behind nothing outside of what was hidden in the supply room. Thomas saw his master to the stable gate where one of the guild's carriages waited.

"Founder Merlin will be down within the hour," said the driver as he helped the older man to be seated. "Something came up and he is a bit delayed. May I offer you a lap blanket, Founder Levitanus?"

"No need. I am used to the predawn chill," assured the wizard as he settled his knapsack at his feet and slipped his staff into the custom holder. He turned to Thomas. "Get going. You do not want to be here when Merlin shows up because he can be rather grumpy in the morning. Take your time and see more of Camelot, but be sure to arrive at the harbor by midday."

"I will, master."

"And Thomas, be careful on the Road of Waters. It is a route that shifts and shimmers. As you have already learned, not all magic is benevolent and not everyone is as they seem."

He assured his mentor that he would be vigilant. He would have lingered a bit more, but the wizard ordered him to go, so Thomas headed back into the guild house, being careful to avoid any of the other wizards who might be up this early. He would stay at the guild house until dawn, but once the main gates he would head out into the city. For now, he needed a place where he wouldn't be noticed. He settled on the library, picking a book on elemental beasts and sitting at a table near the still-darkened windows where a lamp was already lit. He half-read the book as he waited for the sky outside to brighten.

A pair of apprentices came in, most likely trying to get in some studying before their morning class. They kept their conversation to a whisper as they searched the shelves and then settled with three tomes at a table away from him. Thom paid them little heed as his thoughts wandered, the book in front of him also ignored. He had really wanted to find something written about the staff leaning against the table next to him. A magician's staff was meant to heighten an enchantment's effectiveness, but he had no idea how to utilize it nor even how to kindle the jewel's light. It was all rather frustrating.

Tired of pretending to read, he re-shelved the book he had and tried again to find anything that spoke about how to use a wizard's staff. He read a few passages about acts done with a staff, but found nothing to suggest how its jewel could be lit. By the time he gave up, the sun was in the window and the apprentices were gone. He put back the last book he had tried and went to retrieve his knapsack and staff. It was time to start his hike across the city to King's Harbor.

Eric Loren

FIVE

Two Companions

Thom came to the harbor about an hour before he was supposed to report. He found the correct galley, but they were still busy loading and had no time to deal with passengers. Rather than stand around the pier, he wandered over to a food stall and bought something to eat.

By the time he returned, another of the student magicians had arrived. She was a red-haired woman in her forties, old compared to Thomas but still attractive. He recalled that her name was Vivien. She stood to one side on the pier with her arms crossed, watching the final loading of the galley's cargo. At her feet lay a trio of travel bags and on her back hung a fine-leather knapsack. Her dark-blue robe announced that she was a journeywoman; her stance announced that she was growing impatient with the delay.

Thom was debating whether to walk over and introduce himself, when a carriage pulled up at the foot of the pier. Such transport was rare in Camelot, since mundane animals couldn't tolerate being inside the city's enchantment for long. Those who maintained stables for hire had to regularly take their horses out of the city to keep them happy. It was an added expense and duty that meant most of the city preferred handcarts for transporting goods. Only the rich ever bothered with horses, especially for carrying people, which is why it had had been such a treat to ride in the guild's carriage. The one that had just arrived was one of those rental carriages, pulled by a matching pair of black mares.

The driver set the brake, then came around and placed a step on the ground before offering his passenger a hand. A dark-blue robed man stepped out and looked around. As the driver struggled to gather the man's large assortment of travel bags, the magician strode down the pier with only his knapsack and staff. The man was probably in his mid to late thirties, which would place him about halfway through his journeyman years. As Thom recalled, the man's name was Reginald and he had been on duty guarding the Road of Leaves before Merlin reassigned him. Maybe that justified the carriage, but it didn't justify his smirk as he looked at Thom and Vivien.

Surprisingly, Reginald was surrounded by the sound of an enchantment. Thom's inner ear had picked it up as soon as the carriage pulled up and it had become more obvious as he walked closer. Thom only recognized some of the rhythms involved, for it was a complex form of magic. He wondered why the journeyman would be doing this so openly, even if only magicians could hear it. Was he simply practicing something his master had recently taught him?

Although he was curious what the enchantment was supposed to do, Thom held his tongue. It wasn't his place to be questioning a stranger.

Thom decided to ignore the bore and walk closer to where Journeywoman Vivien was waiting. As he approached, he took the time to study her. She, on the other hand, was doing her best to ignore everyone else as she looked around the harbor.

Vivien was old enough to be his mother, but her red hair showed only a few strands of gray. Her complexion was fair and almost flawless, with just a few, faint wrinkles at the corners of her mouth and eyes. Although he wasn't attracted to her, Thom judged her to be good-looking. He realized that the sailors were eying her, though none dared to make any suggestions like those thrown at Adele yesterday. Whenever Vivien looked toward any of the sailors or loaders, they quickly looked away, apparently intimidated by her being a magician. She made no attempt to talk to Thom, but actually took the effort to avoid looking his way.

Reginald came to a stop near them, having the driver place his half-dozen bags in a neat pile to his left. Beyond his orders to the driver and his paying of the tab, he said nothing. Thom gave him a slight nod of recognition, but it wasn't returned.

They had to wait on the dock while the captain and his mate oversaw the loading of the river galley's remaining cargo. Thom waited patiently, but the other two seemed perturbed by the delay. He found their obvious annoyance a bit entertaining.

Thom spent some time just observing the boat he would be traveling on. It seemed small and low in the water, though he could tell it was no smaller than any other galley in the harbor. It was just that Thom didn't like the idea of being trapped on a boat for days.

The galleys that plied the Road of Waters were unique in their design. They sat low and sleek in the water, with an upper deck at the stern just above the deckhouse with its cabins for passengers and crew. The galleys each had a huge sail for catching the constant winds that blew upriver as well as a row of oars. The boats didn't have a deep draft, for at places the river was rather shallow, but they still held a large load of cargo from what Thom could tell.

* * *

By the time the captain let them on board, the western sky was stained red and the evening star shone overhead. The lanky man stood at the end of the gangplank and gave them a look-over. "I'm Captain James and I welcome ya to the Starlight, magicians. The pilot asked me to remind ya to do no magic while traveling the Road of Waters, for we can't have any incidents like those that closed the Road of Leaves."

Thom couldn't help but glance at Reginald. Whatever enchantment the man was holding, he seemed unconcerned about the warning. Thom could see no obvious effect on anything, but his inner ear itched from listening to a rhythm that for some reason seemed a bit familiar, even though it was no enchantment he had ever done.

When the haughty man strode up the plank, he had no problem looking the captain in the face and nodding his acceptance of the warning. "I am Reginald. See to it that your men handle my bags with care, good sir."

He had left his luggage sitting on the dock.

The captain blocked the end of the gangplank. "The three of ya are passengers as a favor to your guild, so I'm not making any coins here. Ya do your own carrying; my men don't work for free."

Reginald pulled a coin bag out of a pocket in his robe and removed a handful of coins. He pressed them into the captain's palm. "This should satisfy your purse's hunger."

Captain James scowled but let the journeyman come aboard.

Thom heard Vivien mutter "boor," although he wasn't certain if she meant the captain or her fellow magician. She struggled a bit as she picked up her luggage. The three bags seemed heavy and awkward to hold, so Thom offered to carry two of them.

She raised a fine, red eyebrow. "I may not be as young as you, but I'm still quite capable of carrying my belongings." She then turned her straight back to him and strode up the stout plank while deftly handling her luggage.

He never meant to imply that she was decrepit; he was just trying to be polite. Although he could not tell much about her figure beneath the voluminous robe, she seemed neither portly nor emaciated and she handled the heavy bags with confidence. He certainly didn't think of her as old, just obviously older than he. He merely realized that she had far more baggage than he did and wanted to help.

Thom shrugged off her rebuff as he walked after her.

He had no need of any assistance himself. He had never even set down his pack and he certainly wouldn't pay anyone to carry it or his staff. When he stepped onto the boat, he gave the captain a sincere smile. "I am named Thomas, once of York."

"York? I sailed the Ouse a few times. Not bad sailing there, though nothing compares to the Road of Waters."

Thom nodded, although he had never sailed any river in his hometown. He had spent his childhood pilfering from shops and market stalls, not playing on the water. It was a childhood he would rather forget now. "Where do you want me?"

"Keep to the upper deck or go to your assigned cabin. Ya can linger at the lower rail if ya want, but only once we are clear of the harbor gates. It can get a bit tricky in the harbor, with all the other boats and the narrow gateway channel, so I can't have any of ya underfoot. Once we're across the lake, it's all oars and current as we travel down the Waters. Just keep out of the crew's way. We won't be using the sail until our trip back.

"Ya and the other man have the mate's cabin for this journey, while the lady gets our guest cabin. Should ya tire, ya can sleep in a bunk during the night, though the mate gets his cabin back when we anchor for the day. Leave no mess or ya lose your bed for the trip."

Thom thanked him and headed aft, taking the ladder up to where the pilot stood at the boat's tiller. As he understood it, on the Road of Waters the pilots weren't part of any crew, but were king's men. They served much like the guides on the Road of Leaves, leading people through the enchanted passage. Every boat that plied the Waters had a pilot on its deck to make sure the boat stayed on course and on schedule. Since the Waters vanished during daylight, if a galley failed to reach one of the Waywaters by dawn, it would be destroyed.

Vivien had apparently sought out her bunk already, but Reginald stood on the upper deck, still enveloped by magic. Thom looked over Reginald's chiseled features, which were lit by one of the boat's lanterns. The magical rhythm nagged at his memory, a deep thrumming that almost sounded sinister. Maybe he had heard someone crafting the same enchantment during his brief stay at the guild house; magic was often in use there.

Reginald startled Thom by suddenly speaking. "It must seem marvelous to you."

Thom frowned, unsure what the fellow was implying. "What do you mean?"

The journeyman smiled, but it only brushed his fine lips. "For a country mage like you, the Road of Waters must seem like a miracle, does it not?"

Thomas' master preferred a solitary life, as he collected and studied magical plants and insects. It meant that Thom had spent most of his apprenticeship with few human interactions. Thom visited cities only twice a year, usually to help carry the herbs and vegetables that Levitanus bartered to get other needed foodstuffs. He had never been to Camelot before this last trip, so he guessed that the title country mage fit him. However, he didn't appreciate the other's condescending tone. "I am just glad that the enchantment remains harmonious. I had a belly full of chaos on the Road of Leaves."

"Ah, yes. You were ever so heroic. I am surprised that they did not promote you to wizard as payment for your brave deeds. Well, you will just have to outdo yourself on this trip to win that rank."

Thom frowned, disliking this fellow more with each word he uttered. "I've no desire for any title that I haven't earned."

Reginald smiled and it almost seemed sincere. "Well said. When we reach Wizard Weston, you may have a chance to prove your worth to the rest of us. I hear the Isle of Mists can be a wild place, what with herds of centaurs galloping about and pixies underfoot. Should any of those beastly horse-men stampede toward us, you can send a whirlwind to blow them away. I look forward to seeing that."

Thom chose not to respond to the other's sharp tongue, although he wanted to. It seemed that neither of his companions had any respect for him. He wondered if anyone of his rank would, or would that not come until he was at least another decade or two older.

Road of Waters

The water gate rose just after sunset, revealing a stone archway over the channel on the other side. The archway held a curtain of bluish mist that hid whatever lay beyond it. With the opening of the gate, outgoing traffic started to slip out of Camelot. Three boats left, the Starlight being the last one.

The Road of Waters' enchantment sang out, no longer muted by the lead-lined gate. The wizards' work captured Thom's attention, just as the Road of Leaves had. The magic was extravagant yet intricate. He doubted that he would ever be able to craft such an enchantment even if he practiced for another fifty years, but it was fascinating to listen to the rhythms and sounds as they resonated within him.

"It certainly catches the ear, does it not?" said Reginald.

"The grand symphony of wizardry amazes me," confessed Thom. He had no qualms about admitting his awe, but he wondered if such a great enchantment intimidated Reginald. Maybe that was why the journeyman kept his own magic kindled. Thom just hoped his companion would finish his magic soon, for it would not be good to have the two enchantments clash.

Thom was about to insist that the man release whatever enchantment he was playing with, when the man spoke.

"It is time for me to retreat to the cabin. I have seen the Waters enough times."

Reginald strode off, still wrapped in an enchantment, before Thom could voice his objections. The captain had just climbed to the upper deck, so Thom dared not call after Reginald about using magic. That would upset the captain and his crew. So instead, Thom went after the other journeyman.

Reginald took the ladder down from the upper deck and then walked around to the larboard side of the deckhouse, to the mate's cabin. Thom followed, intending on insisting that he cease his enchantment before it endangered the rest of them.

But before Thom caught up with him, Reginald shut the door and released his magic. Thom still intended to go in and talk to the man, but he found the door already barred. He banged on it, but received no response. Not wanting to yell through the thick wood, he gave up and went back to the upper deck.

Thom stepped off the ladder just as the boat started to pass through the blue-glowing fog. He stood there, holding the upper deck railing next to the ladder, and watched as more and more of the galley vanished into the mist.

Eric Loren

SIX

Entering the Waters

Thom felt gooseflesh when the boat passed through the enchantment's boundary. The magic made his skin tingle even as his inner ear filled with the rhythms of the magical elements. He stared upward as the mist overtook them. Everything vanished in the blue fog and soon he couldn't see anything more than an arm's length away. He held up his arm, fascinated by the glowing droplets that formed on it.

The fog curtain wasn't much deeper than a galley's length, but time seemed to slow as they passed through. Although the enchantment's sound filled Thom's inner ear, all else became quiet. Even the oarsmen stopped their rowing as they drifted through.

And then they were out the other side, entering a small lake known as the Royal Waywater. Thom looked back and saw nothing of Camelot. Only the soaring archway and the glowing fog that lingered beneath it. To either side of the archway stood trees, tall and dark in the night. He couldn't see anything of the city walls behind the woods.

He wondered if it was even there.

* * *

The crew rowed the Starlight across the Royal Waywater. The mate had the drummer set a mellow beat, nothing too strenuous for the rowers. The men sat at their benches and pulled in near unison, propelling the boat smoothly toward the far side of the lake, where another archway led to the actual Road of Waters.

Thom moved to the starboard side, looking out at the passing shoreline. Merlin's work was an intricate symphony of magical elements, too complex for Thom to fully comprehend. The lake's shore was lined with Allgold Willows and Evergreen Elms. In the dark, Thom couldn't see the magical trees' distinctive colors but his inner ear caught their thrumming, so apparently each had been tapped to let their innate magic seep out. The trees screened off the surrounding countryside and also provided a magical anchor to this endpoint of the Road of Waters.

He looked down into the dark lake, a bit disappointed that it didn't glow but knowing that this was not yet the actual Waters. This was one of the havens that allowed travelers to survive through the day, when the glowing river vanished. He wondered if any magical creatures hid in its depths, but could neither see nor hear anything down there.

He gazed ahead, at the faint, bluish-white shimmer of their next gateway.

The magic inside that archway was like a steady downpour, an unceasing whisper in the background. He stared that way until one of the other boats tacked a bit and blocked the distant light.

He straightened when he realized that he was no longer alone at the rail. Vivien was beside him.

"I notice that Reginald has finally stopped playing with that enchantment. Where is he?"

"He has locked himself in our cabin," replied Thom.

"You know, I find him to be even more conceited than I remembered."

Thom agreed about the conceit. "Do you know our companion well?"

She raised a fine eyebrow. "Reginald cannot forget that noble blood flows through his veins; he befriends no one except other nobles and he is courteous only to his superiors. I am neither, and a woman as well, so I am no friend of his. No, I do not know him well and I have no desire to change that."

Thom nodded in understanding, but he thought the masters wouldn't be happy if they allowed personality to divide them. "No matter his lack of manners, he is our companion for this journey so we should strive to work with him. He must have some redeeming characteristics. Why else would the council choose him to accompany us?"

"Reginald is like the rooster who thinks the sun rises because of his crowing. He may fool the master magicians with all of his fawning but not I. I can see behind his mask."

Thom wouldn't be surprised if her assessment was correct, but it was dangerous talk. At least it was for someone as new to his rank as Thom. He decided to change topics. "What do you think awaits us at the Isle of Mist?"

"Work," she said, looking at the crew bustling around the vessel, "and not honest work like these men do, who follow their trade. I'll not have that privilege, for I am a woman. I'll be tasked with cooking or washing clothes or some other feminine duty, for most wizards are first an old man and then a worker of enchantments. Most likely, Wizard Weston will see me as a temptation or a distraction or a pest. He will not see me as a fellow magician." She met his eyes. "I am sorry for sounding bitter, but I've had to endure such treatment for many years as I've traveled as a journeywoman."

Her harsh words surprised Thom. As the son of a thief, he had always thought of himself as worldly, but it seemed that he had been rather sheltered during his time as a magician's apprentice. For all of his curmudgeonly ways, Levitanus treated women fairly. His master showed respect toward herbalist crones and vegetable sellers- which were the only women who regularly visited the man's country cottage- and that was the only example Thom had had for the last decade.

"You needn't stare at me so," she replied with a bit of bite.

"I didn't mean to stare; it's just that your tale surprises me." He paused to weigh his words. "Maybe this trip will be different. Maybe you will have the chance to show your skills as a magician."

She touched a dainty finger to the tip of her nose as she considered what he said, but then shook her head in disagreement. "I doubt that will happen, but I will endure what I must to reach master magician. The cost is worth it."

Thom didn't know what else to say, so he fell silent. Vivien stared at him for a moment, apparently waiting for some argument or snide remark. When he still said nothing, she gave him a nod in farewell and strolled off to where the captain and pilot stood beside the tiller arm.

He didn't want to linger up here any longer, so he took the ladder down to the main deck, finding it awkward to do so while carrying the long staff in his hand, and then made his way carefully past the oarsmen to the galley's prow. He wanted to enjoy what he could of the night. But, as he found a place at the forward rail, his mind began to spin about what lay ahead.

He wondered if the Road of Waters was at risk for an attack, like what happened to the Road of Leaves. That might be why the council decided to send him to the Keeper of this Road, but he wondered how he could help Wizard Weston; his successes on the Road of Leaves had been more from luck than talent. His two companions were far more knowledgeable, more skilled. Thom was acutely aware that he was a journeyman in name only. He hadn't even begun to learn any journeyman-level enchantments and now he was separated from his teacher. He doubted that the Keeper would have either the time or the inclination to instruct him, so that left him still ignorant- an apprentice wrongly dressed in dark-blue.

Eric Loren

SEVEN

Changing Course

The Road of Waters was known as one of the enchanted Ways of Camelot. Boats plied the route every night, following its glowing flow either toward the king's city or away from it. The Waters' far end was on the Thames, coming out across from Readingum. In between, the route shifted every night, sometimes crossing known waterways and other times seeming to create its own channels through the countryside. When it did follow normal waterways, its flow remained distinct- a glowing path among the dark waters. It was said that any night-traveler on those shared lakes or rivers would be unable to cross over. Like the Road of Leaves, there were only two entrances to the Waters. The magic even went overhead, filtering the sun and weather and keeping the route temperate.

Thom wondered if the boats outside would bounce off the enchantment's walls or if it just became harder to row as you approached, like fighting a strong current. He had heard from his master that items inside the enchantment would bounce off its unseen boundaries, pushed back toward the center of the glowing river.

Thom knew a little about the Road of Waters, but he had never experienced it. He was eager to do so and, when the Starlight finally entered the Waters' luminescent flow, he was amazed. They passed through another mist curtain and came out in a world of muted blue.

The river glowed, casting everything in its sapphire hue. The Waters' light was brighter than he had expected, lighting up the vessel's side and shining on his face and hands as he hung over the prow's rail. The glow went down the center of a larger river, creating a bluish watery highway for the boats to follow. To either side of the enchantment, the water was dark and mundane, seemingly unaffected by the magic running through it temporarily.

The light was neither steady nor even. As Thom stared across the river, he noticed the swirling and pulsations in the glow, revealing the currents and eddies of the Waters. Even more mesmerizing than the glow was the Waters' rhythmic beat. His inner ear caught its unique sound, reminding him of a waterfall in its continual rushing noise. But it also varied, waxing and waning in unison with the swirling color. Although most on board couldn't hear the magic's sound, he certainly did. The enchantment filled his inner ear with its steady beat.

"Don't stare too long or she'll pull you in," said a rough voice from nearby.

Thom looked around and spotted a sailor staring at him.

The fellow jerked his head toward the river. "The Waters has drowned her share of gazers. Look too long and you'll hear the whisper of her voice singing to you."

Thom startled, wondering if the man could hear the magic with his inner ear. Levitanus said that far more than the guild realized could hear magic if they were trained to do so. Had this man somehow learned to hear enchantments?

"Don't look so surprised," the fellow continued. "All rivers have a voice, but only the Road of Waters sings. Trust me, you don't want to hear her full song, so don't be looking at her too long. She notices those who stare."

A shiver went through the boat and suddenly the crew became more active. Someone sounded a bell on the boat ahead of theirs and an answering ring came from the Starlight, loud and clear. Thom asked the sailor what was happening.

"The Waters shift. It will do that often during the night. Right now, we need to bring the boats closer together or else we might lose each other for a time." The river boat shuddered again. "It might get a bit rough as the Road of Waters fights for a new path across this river. Looks like it might snake off to the right soon."

The sailor hurried off to other tasks as Thom clung to the rail. The magician looked out on glowing waves that crazily crashed into each other. The steady breeze had given way to fitful blasts of wind from all directions. The enchantment no longer sounded like a steady waterfall; it had a deeper and unsettling sound, like a giant drum struck slightly off-beat. The Road of Waters was unsettled, its magic sounding faster.

Thom didn't like the way the boat rolled and bucked, for it made his stomach churn. He tried to steady himself, to stop the heaving inside, but failed. Suddenly, he leaned over the side and vomited his last meal. He spewed until his stomach was empty and then endured a round of dry heaves. Not until the Road of Waters settled down into its new path, was he able to stop retching. He felt awful and his belly muscles ached.

It took some time before he dared move away from the boat's railing. When he did, he realized he needed to do some cleaning. He found the nearest rinse bucket and lowered it over the side. By the time he pulled the bucket up, the water inside was no longer glowing, no longer part of the enchantment they were floating down. He rinsed out his mouth and spat it over the side, and then washed his face. Thankfully, his violent vomiting had not soiled his clothing. He did, however, have to wash down the railing and a little of the deck. He cleaned while trying not to smell the stuff, for he feared the stench might trigger more retching.

He finished cleaning, put the bucket back on its hook, and then tried to enjoy their magical route again, now that the boat no longer rocked or bucked. They were moving down a narrower channel through a marshland of tall grasses. Their glowing route snaked through the wetlands, with no dry land in sight. Their route was so twisty that he couldn't even spot the lead boat. The river reeds and marsh grass hid it. Well, at least the Waters had calmed. He was thankful for that.

When their route left the marsh, the warning bells sounded again and Thom grabbed the railing. The Starlight shivered like a beggar in a blizzard and Thom could do nothing except hang over the railing as his stomach churned. He gagged, but only sour bile came up.

This time, the shaking wasn't as long and then the boat entered a meandering waterway with heavy trees on either side hanging over the flow. Thom's stomach calmed enough for him to notice the Waters' enchantment again. Even when he wasn't gazing at the glowing river, he was still listening with his inner ear to its song. He enjoyed what he could of the magic, but his rebellious stomach had taken some of the wonder away.

After another hour, he grew tired and decided to go to his assigned cabin. However, when he got there, he found the door still barred to him. Reginald ignored his knocking and sharp whispers.

Thom leaned close, pressing his ear to the wood, but heard nothing. Not even snoring. He also didn't hear any more magic. He stepped back as far as he could on that narrow walkway, his back pressed against the railing, and studied the door. It might give under a strong kick, but he dared not damage the mate's cabin. He considered banging harder and yelling, but that would attract the captain and pilot, who were on the deck just above his head.

Frustrated, he wondered if Reginald had done this on purpose or had simply forgotten about him.

Maybe he could make an enchantment that would catch Reginald's attention or even open the door. Thom removed his knapsack and knelt, rummaging for his magician's box in the tightly-filled pack. But before he pulled it out, he considered what magic might help. As he considered all the enchantments he knew or had seen used, he suddenly remembered where he had heard Reginald's magic before- on the Road of Leaves.

A shape-shifter's enchantment made that particular sound.

Thom's breath caught as he stared at the closed door. Whoever was inside was not Reginald; he might not even be a wizard.

He hastily closed his pack, swung it over his shoulder, and moved carefully away from the cabin. Whoever was pretending to be Reginald could very likely be a sorcerer.

Eric Loren

EIGHT

Long Night

Thom hurried around to the other side of the deckhouse, to where Vivien's cabin was. He quietly but insistently knocked on the door.

"Who is it?" she asked without opening it.

"It's Thomas," he whispered. "I need to talk with you."

"Come back in the morning," she replied.

"No. We need to talk now."

She finally opened the door, but didn't invite him in. She was still dressed and a lamp was glowing behind her. "This had better be important, young man."

"It is," he assured her. He looked around to make sure no one was near, even straining to see what he could of the upper deck, then blurted out his newfound secret. "I've finally recognized the enchantment that Reginald has been using. He is shape-shifting."

Vivien stared back, not saying anything for a moment. Then she nodded. "That explains his odd behavior- odder than usual for Reginald. Come inside. This is not something for us to discuss where others can overhear."

He came in and sat on one of the two bunks. She closed the door and then sat down across from him. "Are you certain of this?"

Thom nodded. "I heard that particular enchantment while on the Road of Leaves. Sorceress Narissa used it to hide her true self, posing first as a bricklayer and then as a lady. She killed her victims and then took on their visage. What should we do?"

"Do? I plan to do nothing but watch my back. Anyone capable of such an enchantment has far more knowledge than I. To confront him might result in our deaths."

"Shouldn't we tell the captain?"

"And endanger him as well? I think not. We should wait to confront the shape-shifter until we reach the Isle of Mist and Wizard Weston. Then there will be enough of us to overwhelm him."

"But what if he endangers the Road of Waters?"

One of Vivien's fine eyebrows rose in skepticism. "I do not think they will repeat that folly; the sorcerers are not fools. They learned their lesson after the defeat on the Road of Leaves. No, he will not attack the Waters. Most likely, he is a spy trying to escape the city. If so, he will want to avoid us as much as we want to avoid him."

Doing nothing felt wrong to Thomas, but he saw no alternative. Not without Vivien's help.

Just then, the boat started shivering as the Waters shifted its course. Thom's stomach reacted as usual and began heaving in response.

"Not in my cabin," protested Vivien, yanking him to his feet and shoving him out the door. "And do not sick-up on the walkway either. I do not want that smell permeating my cabin."

She slammed the door as he staggered to the end of the walkway and vomited off the back of the boat.

* * *

When both the boat and his stomach calmed, he hurriedly cleaned. He had become something of an expert at vomiting tonight and had kept both his clothes and the deck clean this time. He fetched the nearest wash bucket so that he could rinse out his mouth and then pour two buckets' worth of river water down the side of the boat to wash off any splatter.

Once done, he considered what he should do about the Reginald impostor. He decided to go along with Vivien's plan for now, unless he saw an opportunity to get the upper hand on the shape-shifter. He would wait and watch. But that left another problem. Where would he be sleeping? He doubted the sorcerer would let him into their shared cabin and even if he did, Thom wouldn't be able to sleep knowing that a shape-shifter was in the room.

He looked for a comfortable spot on deck to lay his blanket. But there didn't seem to be any soft place to rest, just grimy decks, stacks of barrels and hard crates. Having no other choice, he found an out-of-the-way niche between two barrels and sat down on the cold deck planks, leaning against a third barrel. He used his knapsack as a pillow and his blanket as a covering. It was an uncomfortable bed but he made do, and he rested there without ever really sleeping.

The Waters shifted two more times that night and each time Thomas had to rush to the railing as his stomach betrayed him. After the last time, he felt light-headed and his abdomen ached. It was well past midnight now and he felt exhausted. The river's breeze seemed chillier, especially with his damp clothing, and he longed for a real bed. Thom decided that he would have to find a softer spot, since it looked like he would be sleeping outside for the length of their journey. He would also have to find some way to protect himself from the sorcerer.

He considered crafting a Whisper of Warning around him even now, but was afraid that he wouldn't wake in time to stop the enchantment before they entered the next Waywater. If the magics clashed, terrible things would happen, so he risked sleeping without protection.

* * *

He woke an hour before dawn, stretching cramped legs. It took a moment for him to realize what had broken his fitful sleep, but then he saw the archway towering over the river. It sang a new song, a change from the previous rhythms of the Waters' magic. They were passing into a Waywater, one of the harbors where boats sheltered during the day while the Road of Waters faded until the next night. The stone arch soared over the waterway in an impossibly long curve, without support or pillar. Thom stared up at the approaching stonework and the cloud of bluish-glowing mist under it.

He stood and realized they had entered a side channel. The glowing waters had split and they were following a smaller flow directly at the fog. The cloud curtain floated down to rest on the water. He saw the other two boats in their convoy disappear into the shimmering mist, slipping under an arch that was twice as tall as the highest mast. A bit later, the Starlight passed into the fog as well and suddenly everything was covered by shimmering dew drops.

Thom lost sight of the craft and its crew, though he could hear their shouts and actions. They were heading back to the oars as the current slacked. Thom realized that the sailors were probably past being awed by the experience, having passed through such an enchantment hundreds of times just this summer. Glad that he had no duties, Thom slowly turned in the fog, feeling the dampness on his skin and hearing its subtle beat in his inner ear. The light was diffused, not really illuminating the vessel but giving a glow to the mist itself. The droplets that formed on his arm quickly faded into normal water.

The boat passed through the mist and came out in a calm channel lined by tall trees. Because the water didn't glow here, Thom could barely make out the two boats still ahead of them, their deck lanterns twinkling in the darkness. As the sailors rowed in pursuit, the quiet waterway began to widen to either side, the banks lined by tall reeds. And then they entered the actual Waywater, a still lake surrounded by a dense thicket of reeds and rushes. Thom overheard it called the Quiet Reed Waywater.

As the crew rowed the boat across the lake, Thom heard frogs and crickets among the rushes and he wondered what kind of magical creatures they were. Normal animals shunned the enchanted Roads to Camelot, but magical animals often took shelter within Merlin's work. Thom had not yet studied much about water insects or reptiles, so he was unable to recognize these by their calls.

In the center of the lake stood the Day Dock, where vessels could tie up while their crews slept. The structure spread like a wooden spider, offering docking on each of its eight legs. There were no buildings or lights on the Day Dock; it was just a simple, open refuge for the boats plying the Waters.

The Starlight's pilot aimed for one of the free berths at the eastern end of the haven. The other two boats were already abutting their chosen docks nearby, with men scampering to secure lines. There were another four galleys already there, tied at the more western berths- upriver traffic, surmised Thom. While he was watching the boats tie up, Vivien and Reginald joined him at the rail. Reginald was again surrounded by magic.

"So, what do you think of the Road of Waters?" asked the journeyman.

"I'm awed by the enchantment," admitted Thom, trying to act normal and not stare at the shape-shifter.

Reginald smirked. "Outshines the muck ponds your master orders you to wade into, I would think."

Thom was uncertain how to respond. He didn't like the man's mocking tone, but he tried his best to play the ignorant apprentice. "If you mean stepping into the water to harvest Wail Lilies or Turvond Cattails, then I've done my share. My master insists that I learn all aspects of the craft, from growing to harvesting to distilling the elements from magical plants."

"I believe it," said Reginald, looking to where Thom grasped the railing. "Even in this poor light, I can see the dirt under your nails."

Thom frowned but held his tongue. How was he supposed to react to ridicule? He didn't want the shape-shifter to realize that Thom knew of his charade.

"Have you no one else to mock, Reginald?" asked Vivien, sounding peeved. "Leave off with the young man, for he is barely out of swaddling clothes. And while you're at it, stop playing with magic. It is dangerous to do so while inside another enchantment."

Reginald laughed. "I am just having a little fun. The lad knows I am joking. As for my magic, I am only practicing some of the enchantments that my master has recently taught me. You need not be jealous, Vivien. Someday you will be good enough to learn how to craft the greater enchantments."

Thom suspected cruelty or arrogance behind the jibes, but didn't argue. He disliked this fellow, and not just because he was an enemy.

Vivien showed her displeasure by moving farther down the rail.

Thom considered following her, but his unpleasant companion spoke again.

"Well, it is time to clear out the cabin so that the mate can get his sleep," stated Reginald. "Come with me, young Thomas. I wish to talk with you while I pack up my belongings."

The man had some nerve, after barring Thom from the cabin all night. "I think not."

"You will come," said Reginald. He lowered his voice so that Vivien couldn't overhear. "Your master expects you to listen to me, just like he always expected you to listen to Hag Helena."

Thom's blue eyes narrowed. Hag Helena was a hedge crone who knew more about mundane plants than anyone else, according to Thom's master. How did the man know that Levitanus thought her worth listening to?

"Come," repeated Reginald, now stepping away from the lantern light and heading toward the ladder that led to the main deck and to the cabins. He didn't look back, but seemed to expect Thomas to follow.

Thom wavered a moment, then gave in. He followed the journeyman around to the larboard side and down the walkway that led to the cabins. Reginald didn't linger on the walkway, but ducked inside. Just after the cabin's door closed, Thom heard the man's enchantment end. He wondered who he would find inside. Was Reginald a sorcerer in disguise? Thom considered crafting his own enchantment, but pulling out his magician's box in the open would be too obvious. If the captain saw it, he might abandon Thom at the Waywater for endangering the galley. He decided to confront the shape-shifter without using magic. He debated between the sword that hung at his side and the long staff in his hands and decided that neither would be of much use in the tight space. The best he could probably do was to use the staff as defense to keep the man at a bit of distance. Better to move fast than to hesitate and become an easy target.

Taking a deep breath, he walked up to the cabin's door and boldly opened it, stepping into a narrow and dim room crammed with two bunks and a large storage chest. When he looked at Reginald, he noticed that his hair had changed color, to a silvery white. That made him pause.

Reginald had his back turned, his head slightly lowered to avoid the low ceiling. "Close the door, Thomas."

His voice had changed too. Thom knew that voice all too well, after getting lectured in that tone for over a decade. It was Levitanus' voice. "Who are you?"

The other man still didn't turn. "Step inside and close the door. Now."

Thom obeyed. He couldn't help it. He had spent too many years jumping for that voice. "Master?" he whispered.

The other man finally turned around. It was Levitanus, the man who had been training Thom for a decade.

"Where is Reginald? Is he dead?" asked Thom, thoroughly confused. During his adventure on the Road of Leaves, someone had died whenever another took their form.

"Do not be foolish. He lives. Taking the shape of another does not require you to kill that person. Does a mockingbird kill the bird it imitates? Does a Chameleon Ogre kill those it copies, except for its prey? Just because Sorceress Narissa killed people, does not mean everyone who crafts a Chameleon Mask murders their model.

"Reginald lives and is still at his duties guarding Rowan Gate; at least he will be there in three days, once he has completed another task. Merlin made sure he would be out of sight for a time so that our ruse would not be spoiled."

Thom was still doubtful. "Is it truly you?"

"Do you hear any magic around me? Of course, it is I." Levitanus sat down on a bunk and then motioned for Thom to bar the door. "Make sure no one can wander in here. I wanted you to know my true identity before you try something foolish. You were planning to expose my disguise to the captain, weren't you?"

NINE

Unexpected Companion

"Pardon, master, but I still don't understand. Why are you here?"

"Give it some thought, Thomas. Do you really think the king would take Guinevere to a parlay with Mordred? His bastard son hates the woman, fearing that she will give the king a legitimate heir. King Arthur has no plan to meet with Lord Mordred."

"I did wonder about that," admitted Thom, "but I thought Mordred gave some promise of safe passage."

Levitanus guffawed. "Nobles are no more trustworthy than robbers when they want something desperately enough, and you know how honorable thieves are. We will not be going anywhere near Sir Mordred."

"Then where are we going, master?"

"King Arthur seeks refuge along the Waters, for Camelot is no longer safe. There are traitors in the city and even in the castle." Levitanus sighed. "Camelot may fall soon and it will not be easy to win back."

Thom thought of the beautiful city and its namesake castle. He hadn't had much time to wander its streets, but what he had seen of Camelot was wondrous. He could not imagine the place overthrown or someone else sitting on Arthur's throne.

"Is Mordred behind all of this?" asked Thom.

"If Sir Mordred is involved, it is as a mere puppet for our true foes. The attacks on the Road of Leaves tell us who the enemy is; we fight sorcerers and not just some bitter bastard."

Thom had thought the defeat on the Road of Leaves would have discouraged the rogue magicians. Apparently, his hope was misplaced. He wanted to ask more questions, but he could tell that his master was done with answering.

Levitanus was gathering up the clothes he had discarded last night, cleaning up the cabin. "This could prove to be a trip even more dangerous than your walk along the Road of Leaves, but I do not expect any problems before we meet up with the king's vessels at the Isle of Mists."

When Thom tried to help pack Levitanus' things, his master stopped him. "As long as I am playing at journeyman, I will have to do my own chores. Go back out on deck and do what you can to appease Vivien. I want to keep my identity a secret for a while longer; if she learns of it, her demeanor will too obviously change. I want her to continue being her prickly self."

When Thom hesitated, his mentor made a shooing motion. "Go."

He had not been inside long, but came out to a sky already a pale grayish-blue. Dawn neared.

Vivien was quick to confront him, for she had seen the two men go into the cabin. She motioned for him to follow her to the upper deck. As Thom went, he quickly thought of what he could say.

She turned on him as soon as they were off the ladder. "What were you doing in there? I thought we had agreed to avoid the shape-shifter."

"I couldn't help it, for he wanted me to follow. Would it have been wise for me to refuse?"

"What did he want with you?"

"He told me that I could sleep in there tomorrow night, if I promised not to snore. He just wanted another chance to mock me for serving my apprenticeship out in the wilds, as he put it."

"Be careful," said Vivien. "This is not a game that we are playing, at least not a child's game."

"I will remember that." It was a game, thought Thom, just not the one she thought it was.

'Reginald' came up the ladder just then, preventing Vivien from saying any more. He smirked at them and sauntered near.

An awkward silence came over the three magicians.

Captain James spotted them and came over with the pilot. "A few more instructions for the three of ya. If ya want to join in on the crew's meal, ya can. It's nothing grand, but it is filling. Beyond that, I've not much to say. Do what ya want today. Walk the docks, visit the other boats, laze on deck, or hunt for mermaids. I don't care how ya spend your time, just don't wake my crew and be sure to be on board when the sun sets. I'll not linger for late passengers. Miss the boat and ya have to find some other craft to carry ya."

"And do not practice any magic," added the pilot. "You magicians must restrain yourselves while you are within Merlin's enchantment."

Thom resisted looking at his master, who was surrounded by magic at that very moment. Out of the corner of his eye, he saw Vivien give 'Reginald' a pointed look. None of them mentioned anything to the pilot though.

The captain nodded his agreement, not noticing their awkward looks. "Aye, no magic while on the Waters. We don't want this Road destroyed as well. I hear it was some foolish apprentice who caused all the disruption on the Road of Leaves."

Thom wanted to protest, to say that he was no fool. He'd been that magician's apprentice and he had certainly not been the attacker, but confessing all that would just raise the captain's suspicions. So Thom gritted his teeth and let the man slander his name.

"I know ya three are journeymen, but still ya must control your urges. I want no magic thrown about while on my boat."

Thom's master gave the captain a polite nod. "We will restrain ourselves."

"Good," replied James. "See that ya do."

"May we leave the vessel now?" asked 'Reginald.'

"As soon as the plank is set in place."

* * *

Once the gangplank was down, Thom's master strode off the boat. He didn't wait for breakfast, but seemed to have some mission to accomplish. Thomas didn't want to eat either, but he did long for a comfortable bed.

"Come on," said Vivien to him. "Let us see where he is going. I believe he is up to something." She stared after him as 'Reginald' trod toward the center of the Day Dock. "I want to find out why he was in such a rush to get off the boat."

Thom could imagine how angry his master would become if Thom spied on his actions. "You can follow if you want, but I'd rather not further antagonize him."

Vivien's right eyebrow rose in a fine arch. "For one who has been proclaimed a hero, you certainly are reticent."

Thom couldn't offer any defense without exposing his master's secret, so he just gave her another shrug.

"Well then, I will go alone." She strode off in pursuit, leaving Thom behind.

He was in a quandary. He couldn't convince her to stop this foolishness without revealing his master's secret, but if he didn't stop her then she would likely cause them grief anyway. Thom sighed and decided to follow her at a distance. He had no plan but he felt he had to stop Vivien somehow, for both their sakes.

Eric Loren

TEN

Magicians and Brothers

Thom walked along the wooden pier as the sun rose high enough to light the Waywater. The sunlight glared in his eyes and stretched long shadows from each boat that rested at a berth. His own shadow stretched across the planks and out onto the still waters. He wondered what magical creatures might be swimming beneath the surface and would have paused to peer over the dock's edge but he needed to catch up to Vivien. Somehow, he needed to convince the red-headed woman to leave 'Reginald' alone.

The three magicians marched along the wooden walk, Thom wanting to keep Vivien from catching the wizard well ahead of them.

The disguised Levitanus reached the center of the Day Dock and turned down another leg, heading toward another boat from the convoy. He didn't seem aware of them following, but that was only because Levitanus was focused on whatever was up ahead. Thom's master was prone to that; over the years Thom had often been forced to repeat himself to get the man's attention away from some project.

He tried to step lightly, but his boots were still loud on the wooden planks. If not for some rowdy sailors singing and laughter on the galley, Thom's and Vivien's footsteps would have been obvious.

Thom increased his pace.

As he pursued Vivien, he noticed that the Day Dock held an enchantment about it. The planks were normal, but the support beams underneath and the pilings that rose out of the water's depths all gave off a unique rhythm that he assumed was some type of magic meant to strengthen and preserve the landing. He would have liked to study it further, but he had a more pressing need- catching a headstrong woman.

When Vivien turned to march out to the other boat, she finally noticed Thomas. She frowned at him, then hurried her steps. The open area didn't allow for any hiding or stealth and she didn't seem bothered by that. The journeywoman walked boldly after 'Reginald,' making Thom wonder if she planned to confront Levitanus right now.

The thought caused him to speed up even more. He chased after her, afraid that she would storm onto the other galley and blurt something she would regret.

"Vivien! Wait!" he whispered sharply when he had nearly caught up.

She didn't even slow in response, but rather stayed focused on her goal.

He meant to grab her arm and stop her, when she suddenly stopped on her own. Thom staggered, almost running into her.

She ignored him. Instead, she stared at the other galley that Levitanus was boarding.

As he stopped beside her, Thom realized what had made her pause. Someone besides Levitanus was using magic on that boat. "Don't do anything rash," Thom told her. "There is much that you don't understand yet."

"That is obvious," she replied, not taking her eyes off the boat. "And now we know that there are two of them."

Thom was curious about the identity of the other wizard, but he had to focus on Vivien at this moment. "We should head back to our boat before they realize we're spying on them."

She frowned, but nodded agreement. Without saying another word, she turned and marched back along the planks.

Thom followed at a slower pace, glad to have prevented any confrontation but not eager to walk at her side. If he stayed close, she might begin questioning him again and he wasn't certain he could keep the deception going. So he let her get ahead.

As he reached the center of the Day Dock, he saw a monk waving and walking toward him from the third galley of their convoy. Thomas stopped and waited for the brother.

The monk was a giant of a man, his simple black robe a tent over his muscular frame.

Thom guessed him to be fifteen and barely out of his novitiate. He looked strong enough and big enough to lift a man over his head. Thom could feel the dock vibrating under the young man's heavy steps. He was glad the monk was smiling as he came close, for a scowl would be intimidating on such a large fellow.

"Are you Thomas, the magician's apprentice?" the monk asked.

With a nod, he admitted that he was, though he chose not to mention his recent promotion to journeyman.

"Very good. Can you come with me, then? Someone in the abbot's delegation would like to speak with you, discreetly. Will you come?"

Thom hadn't known that an abbot was traveling in their convoy. He wondered if it might be the abbot of Saint Barnabas, the monastery in Camelot where his friend Francis served. Maybe someone wanted to pass on a message from him. Thom would like that, for he had feared that Francis would be angry with him for refusing to abandon his profession. "I'll come."

"Good, good, good." The huge monk's smile widened. "Follow me, if you please. This way, please."

He started back toward the boat, looking back once to make sure Thom was following. The fellow walked with agility, in spite of his huge size. The early morning sun exaggerated all shadows, projecting a mountain of shade from the monk.

When Thom was led onto the galley, he noticed that almost all of the crew had already retired to their bunks, leaving only two on day watch and some passengers on the deck. He saw the abbot and a pair of monks on the upper deck, near the tied-down tiller. His over-large guide didn't take him up there however. Instead, the big monk led him to clamber among the cargo to reach a small clearing at its heart. Sitting on a crate waited another monk, one that Thom knew.

"Francis!"

The middle-aged man grinned. "It is good to see you, Thomas." He stood up and stepped forward to hug Thom fiercely.

Thom returned his friend's embrace, but then pulled back as he thought of a new worry. Levitanus would not be happy to hear that the magician-turned-monk was in their convoy. If that other disguised magician was Merlin, then it would mean even more trouble. "You shouldn't be here."

"I go wherever my abbot asks me to. Why shouldn't I be here?"

"I'm traveling with…magicians… who will be angry if they learn of your presence." It was a weak answer, he knew, but he didn't want to expose the secret identity of 'Reginald.'

Francis' sharp look showed that he didn't fully believe Thom's answer, but the monk didn't press for more details. "I realized the possible difficulties when I saw three of you marching across the docks this morning. Why do you think I sent Brother Bartholomew to fetch you?" He turned to the big man still looming behind Thom. "Again, you have my thanks, brother."

"Of course. Of course. I'm glad to help, Brother Francis." The big man smiled. "And, please, both of you call me Bart. I may be large, but I'm not big enough for a four-syllable name. Bart fits me fine; it's simple and straight-forward."

Francis nodded agreement to his fellow monk. "I'm sorry, Bart. You've asked me to use your nickname before and I hadn't remembered. I'll do so now."

Bart held up a huge sausage of a finger. "Ah, just one limit on that, if you please. The Father Abbot frowns on nicknames…"

Francis chuckled. "I understand, Bart. I'll not embarrass you before our superior." He paused a moment, then added, "Could you excuse us for just a few minutes, Bart? I need to talk about some sensitive topics with Thomas. Once done, we can all chat some more."

"Oh, I understand. Please excuse me." He withdrew from the niche amid the cargo.

They stood there in silence for a moment, then Francis sat down on a crate and invited Thom to sit on another. "I see that you are now a magician's journeyman. I'm sorry that I cannot congratulate you, but you understand why."

Thom certainly did. His friend had once been a magician's journeyman himself, before joining the monastery. When Francis had been forced to kill his master to stop the slaughtering of a village of fairies, it had caused him to renounce everything to do with being a magician. Understandably, he had a great distaste for magic, although he had been forced to craft his share of enchantments during their adventures on the Road of Leaves. The monk had hoped Thom would leave-off wanting to be a master magician.

Thom decided to talk about something else. "Why is the abbot traveling the Road of Waters now and why does he want you along?"

"We are on our way to join the king," said Francis. "I have my suspicions why my superior wants me here, but he hasn't explained his reasons to me."

"Do you know where the king is?"

Francis frowned. "Somewhere on the Waters, I would assume, for he departed only a night ahead of us. He travels to parlay with Lord Mordred. Do you suspect him to be somewhere else?"

Thom clamped his mouth shut, realizing that he'd almost revealed too much. He carefully considered his words, not wanting to lie to Francis but also not wanting to betray the confidence of his master. "It's just that my companions and I are also on our way to join the Isle of Mists. How will you avoid a confrontation?"

Francis shrugged. "That may be impossible to avoid. I'm no longer in the guild, so it no longer has any authority over me. Nonetheless, I will do my best to avoid your brethren for as long as I can. Yet they will learn that I'm here sometime during our travels and then the fun will begin." He smiled, but with a tinge of sadness. "Those of your guild take offense at my very presence, as if I smelled like a pig in a sty." He shook his head at their folly. "I doubt that the journeymen with you will give me much grief but, once we reach the king, I will need to face wizards too. They are more prickly about my abandoning the craft."

Thom wondered if his friend had recognized the enchantment wrapped around Levitanus. Hopefully not, since Francis tried hard not to use his inner ear. "Even though my companions are mere journeymen, you should still be careful. You should also know that there is another magician on the first boat in our convoy."

Francis nodded his understanding. "I will be careful."

They fell into an awkward silence. Thom wanted to confess all of the secrets he had learned, but knew that he couldn't; he had to leave his friend in ignorance.

Francis finally broke the silence. "Well enough about magic, for I hate the topic. Let's invite Bart back and talk about other things."

He called for Bart to rejoin them and the three of them lingered among the crates and barrels for a couple of hours, chatting about life. Francis had just brought a new load of books to the monastery's library and he told of the excitement there over some of his finds, so much excitement that one brother-librarian passed out and another fell off his stack ladder. Francis finished his tale with, "Who knew that dusty tomes could be so dangerous?"

Bart told of walking a circuit through a series of poor villages where he preached and gave aid as he could. Apparently, the children saw right through his intimidating size and saw the warm heart within, for they would climb all over Big Bart as soon as he entered a settlement. The stories lightened Thom's heart.

At Bart's urging, Thom shared a little about what had happened on the Road of Leaves, but would have downplayed his part in saving the queen and stopping the sorceress, had Francis allowed it. But the monk kept correcting him, making him admit to Bart his pivotal role. Thom said nothing of how Francis' knowledge of magic had been invaluable, for he knew that his friend wanted that kept secret.

* * *

When Thom finally left the monks, it was nearly noon. The day was bright and warm. He walked along the Day Dock's planks, heading back for the Starlight. Around him, the Waywater lay languid, its water deep, dark, and cool. He wondered what water creatures might be lurking beneath its sun-touched surface but saw nothing, not even a Sun Carp who were known for lingering just below the surface.

When he made it back to the Starlight, Thom searched for his master until he realized that Levitanus hadn't returned yet. He could have saved time if he had asked Vivien where 'Reginald' was, but he had no desire to try talking with her again so he avoided her cabin. Once certain that his master was still elsewhere, he found a shady spot on the main deck and took a nap, using his pack as a pillow.

Nothing much happened the rest of that calm day. The crew didn't stir until near sunset. Most of them slept jammed together in the pair of larger cabins assigned to them, through a few chose to sleep on deck. But when the day neared its end, they woke, stretching and yawning as they began their tasks. They prepared the galley for departure and then gathered on the main deck for a dinner shared with the passengers.

As Thom was taking his bowl of stew and heel of bread, he saw his master coming up the gangplank. He almost rushed over to serve him a meal, but caught himself. That would have been inappropriate, since they were pretending to be equals. Instead, Thom took his food and sat away from the others so that Levitanus could easily approach him, but his master never came near. Vivien also avoided him.

Thom ate and then moved to a spot on the upper deck that would be out of the way. He watched the sun set in a blaze of red and purple, while the evening star shone overhead. He took a deep breath of cool air and then looked at his nearer surroundings. The lake was now almost black, the surrounding reeds just silhouettes against the last of the day's light.

He looked across the Day Dock at the four boats that were heading upriver. As he understood it, the other convoy of galleys would be the first to leave and he saw that their silhouettes were already in motion. There was no wind here in the sheltered Quiet Reed Waywater, so the crews were rowing their boats away from the Day Dock. It seemed a tranquil scene- until he heard the first scream.

Eric Loren

ELEVEN

Frothing Water

The scream cut off sharply, followed by shouts and a great splash.

Thom saw the third boat slow as men left their rowing. Something large rose up next to the galley, something very tall, yet lithe. It towered over the deck and then came crashing down like a pine succumbing to an ax's final blow. Thom heard wood crack and men scream. Whatever it was, the thing seemed to be lying on top of the boat now, having smashed the rail and splintered the deck. The weight must have been great for the galley settled low in the water, leaning to the side. The thing was slithering across the boat now. Its head dropped over the far side, returning to the water, and the long snake-like body followed, sliding across the deck and pulling the boat lower.

It took a moment for him to realize that someone nearby was shouting his name.

"Thomas! Thomas!"

He finally heard and looked that way. His master pointed at him.

"Kindle as many Wizard Lights as you can and send them over there. I need to see this monster."

"Yes, master," he replied automatically, hurriedly pulling off his pack and rummaging through his supplies. He pulled out his magician's box and a mixing bowl. Crafting a Wizard Light was a simple task, one of the first enchantments he learned as an apprentice, but he still almost bungled it in his haste. He pried open his box, the elements inside singing out, and chose the right ones more by sound than sight. He sprinkled out the powders, spilling some on the deck in his nervousness. The powder made from Azure Fireflies left a sparkle on the rough wood, while the powder made from Meadow Dragon wings quickly drifted off despite the lack of a breeze. But Thom got enough of each into the mixing bowl, adding the crushed Glow Berries and then stirring them with his pestle until it sounded just right. He heard Levitanus ordering him to hurry up, but he didn't want to fail at this. When the mix seemed right, he spat into it and then added some water to form a paste.

Taking a small ball's worth, he put it in the palm of his hand and it started to glow. A Wizard's Light, cool to the touch yet bright to the eye. He willed the blue light to float over the water, toward the boat being attacked. Using his eyes and his inner ear, he kept his focus on it and brought the light to hover over the carnage. Finally, he saw clearly what was attacking the other boat. A sea serpent had thrown its weight across the deck and its long body was still slipping over and down into the water on the far side. Its greenish-gray scales glistened wetly in the Wizard Light. Men tried to slash and stab at the thing, but their attacks were no more than a nuisance to the giant monster.

Without letting go of the first light, Thom crafted another and sent it over too. Then he made a third and a fourth. He still had a bit of the paste left in the bowl but he was at his limit now. He made no more; juggling four enchantments was more than he had ever done. The four lights bobbed and shifted over the listing boat, as Thom did his best to keep them in place to illuminate the chaos on board.

The serpent's body still slid across the deck, but now its head came up again, rising into the night air and then crashing down on the deck a second time. With slippery speed, it raced across the deck, scattering cargo and men, to plunge back into the lake. Two coils crossed the deck now, creating more havoc as they slithered over. The galley groaned as it was pushed down by the weight of the serpent, near to capsizing.

Thom's master kindled a fireball that he threw at the beast with great accuracy, but the flames did little to the slick creature. Vivien flung fire as well, but her aim was not as good nor was her fireball as tightly wrought. The flames splattered off the serpent's wet skin, showering the boat and its desperate crew. Thom heard his master yelling for Vivien to stop. It seemed that none of their magic could help to slay the monster.

When the creature's head rose out of the water a third time, Thom sent his Wizard Lights straight at it. He missed with three, but the final one caught the serpent in the face. When the magical elements crashed into the magical creature, there was a small explosion, not much but it was right in the beady eyes of the beast. The serpent paused in its assault, shuddered, and then plunged back into the water without wrapping the boat a third time. Unfortunately, twice was enough to doom the galley.

As the sea serpent dove deep into the lake, its body tightened on the boat and yanked it lower. The central mast snapped with a loud crack, then the listing side dipped far enough down to let water rush in and fill its hold. Within minutes, the boat was gone, leaving only a few survivors bobbing among the flotsam on the still-disturbed surface.

Thom let go of the remaining Wizard Lights, too dazed to keep focused. In the renewed darkness, he could hear cries of help from the water but saw only vague shadows out on the dark waters. He expected that the other galleys would turn and help, but the first two were rowing hard for the archway out, while the last boat in the group swerved around the wreckage without slowing. He realized that fear drove the captains of the other vessels.

"Magicians! Report!" bellowed Captain James, gesturing emphatically. The Starlight was still at its berth but half of its securing lines were already loosened. The crew was in confusion, some wanting to heave off while others wanted to tie the boat tight again.

Thom gave a quick glance toward 'Reginald' and got a slight nod, so he hurried to face the captain. His master came over at a more dignified pace, while Vivien stalked across the deck in obvious agitation.

"What was that?" demanded James.

"Sea serpent," replied Thom, trying to sound confident even while his heart still beat wildly from the terror of what he had just seen.

"Where did it go? Is it dead?"

Thom looked to the others' approaching, uncertain what to say. He had no idea where the monster might be.

"It was stung by our enchantments," answered 'Reginald', "but it is by no means dead. The beast still lurks somewhere in the lake."

"How can we escape?"

Levitanus sighed. It was Reginald's voice but a mannerism Thom knew well. His master often sighed when having to share something distasteful. "The serpent will not strike the Day Dock, so your galley is probably safe while tied to its side..."

Captain James interrupted, yelling at his men to re-secure the lines. He then turned back to the three magicians. "Can ya tell where the monster is right now?"

"No, we cannot," replied Vivien, speaking up before either of the others could. "We can hear enchantments, but not magical creatures. You will have to tell your men to watch diligently."

"...but we cannot linger here too long," continued 'Reginald' as if neither had interrupted him. "Serpents are crafty beasts; it will find a way to get us away from the dock if it wants to capsize us."

"Shouldn't we offer aid to those thrashing in the water?" asked Thom.

The captain frowned, then looked to the pilot. "Ya are the king's guide for the Waters. What say ya?"

The man shook his head. "In all my twenty and more years of rowing and sailing this route, I've never seen its like. I know the Road of Waters, but I'm no expert on magic. I'd say listen to the magicians."

Captain James shook his head at his few options, then shouted for two men to climb the mast and be on the lookout for any sign of the beast. He sent three other men to prepare the boat's rowboat, before turning back to Thomas. "I'll only send the men out to rescue the others if ya go along. They'll want a magician at their side."

Thom swallowed, dismayed at the sudden turn. He wasn't much of a swimmer and that rowboat looked rather small, especially after it was dropped over the side.

"Well, magician, are ya going to help save those people or not?" asked the captain.

Thom saw no other choice, not with people still yelling for help, so he agreed.

He went to the galley's rail and leaned over, looking down at the men already climbing into the tiny rowboat. They carried ropes and poles, seemingly familiar with pulling victims out of the water. A rope ladder had been dropped down the side, but its rungs seemed narrow and the whole thing appeared rather flimsy to him. Nonetheless, he stepped over the rail and started down the side of the galley.

One of the men helped him into the rocking boat and he quickly sat down on a rough wooden bench. Two of them set their backs to the oars, while the third stood in the bow as lookout. They rowed away from the Starlight and out around the Day Dock, heading toward the jetsam.

As they headed toward the ruined boat, Thom noticed that the three galleys left from the upriver convoy were now passing under the archway. They had not stopped to offer any aid. The other two boats in the downriver convoy were still moored.

For the next hour, Thom and the sailors with him labored to pluck men from the lake. A rowboat from the abbot's galley joined them and Thom recognized Brother Bart helping to yank others out of the water. In the end, they rescued nearly half of the sunken boat's crew. A few more had swum to the Day Dock on their own and climbed out, but most of the rest had died with their galley.

As Thom and his weary shipmates returned to the Starlight with the last two rescued, a cry echoed. It was a warning yell from one of the men clinging near the top of the galley's mast. The sea serpent had just reappeared.

TWELVE

Meeting the Abbot

Thom made it back onto the Starlight without incident, as did the crew and the last two they had rescued. The serpent had surfaced, but not nearby. It had shown itself near the archway and was apparently heading out of the lake. The crew, upon hearing this, gave a ragged cheer. However, all was in chaos on the upper deck, as three captains now argued near the tiller. Thom walked over with caution, stopping at his master's side. 'Reginald' gave a slight nod, but quickly returned his attention to the squabble.

Thom soon grasped that the other two captains were insisting that the magicians be spread out between them. Captain James complained that they were his passengers so they should stay on his boat. Thom felt like he was the loot being argued over by a gang of thieves. Apparently, his master felt something similar and was no longer amused.

"Enough of this," Levitanus shouted, loud enough to be heard. "We will go where we choose to go. Give us a moment to talk among ourselves." Levitanus motioned Vivien and Thomas away from the others.

When they were far enough away to not be overheard, 'Reginald' gave his orders. "I want Thomas on the abbot's galley and Vivien on the other one."

"Who are you to give me orders?" asked the woman.

She still thought she was dealing with sorcerers in disguise.

"Do you really want me on that boat with my friend?" asked 'Reginald,' revealing that he was aware that Thom and Vivien had followed him when he went to meet that other disguised magician.

She pursed her lips in agitation. "Fine. I will go there."

"And you will be the one doing the magic, since that is what they will expect. They think our comrade on their galley is just an apprentice and I want them to continue to believe that. Your duty is twofold: protect the boat and protect our friend's identity."

"How can I expose someone who is unknown to me?" she asked.

"Nonetheless, do you agree to your duties?" pressed Thom's master.

"I will do so for now, sorcerer, but if either of you do anything to endanger us or the Road of Waters, we will expose your trickery."

"Neither of us are sorcerers, woman," stated Levitanus. "We belong to the guild; it is just that we must conceal our identities for now. Take my word for it; the council approves of our actions."

He stared at her, daring her to challenge his claim.

Vivien was not intimidated. "Well then, I will protest to the guild council once all of this is over. They will learn of your hubris, Reginald… or whoever you really are."

"So be it," said Levitanus, dismissing her anger. "Thomas, do what you can to protect the abbot and his entourage. They are on their way to join the king too, and will be his spiritual succor during what might prove to be a long stay on the Isle of Mist. I want the abbot to make it to Isles Waywater whole."

"I will do my best."

"Your best had better be truly that. Now, go to your assigned galleys while I talk some sense into these captains. We need to be sailing soon or we will not make it to the next Waywater, and I will not have us lingering here for another day."

He stared at the two of them until they obeyed.

* * *

When Thom came onto the river galley called Azure Nights, he was greeted by a slap on the back from Brother Bart. "You came! Thank you, thank you, thank you. When the captain said he would demand a magician for our boat too… well, we didn't think he'd succeed. Let me take you to the abbot and introduce you, Magician Thomas. I think Brother Francis is with him right now. Come with me, if you please."

Thom let the big man lead him to the galley's guest cabin. It was a well-appointed room, but still crowded with a pair of bunks and a clothes chest. It also had a low ceiling, preventing Thom from straightening after ducking through the small doorway.

Inside, he met the lanky abbot of the Saint Barnabas monastery. The nearly-bald man stood up carefully to avoid hitting his head on the cabin's low ceiling and gave Thom a warm greeting, offering his hand in welcome.

"Journeyman Thomas, it is good to finally meet you. I am Abbot Justin. Brother Francis has told me much about you. I must admit that I underestimated Captain Harold; I doubted he would be able to pry any of you magicians off that other boat. But I am glad that I have been proved wrong. And I am so pleased that you are the one joining us, since Francis has told me of your talent and bravery.

"Please, sit on the bunk next to Francis, for I cannot remain standing hunched over like this. You younger men are lithe enough, but my old neck and back are already protesting."

Thom sat where he was asked to, nodding at Francis as he did. The abbot settled on the cot across from him, while two more monks sat on the floor near the chest, squeezed into the narrow space so tightly that they were knee-to-knee and elbow-to-elbow. Five people in here made it stuffy and overcrowded, but the abbot didn't seem bothered by it.

Brother Bart stayed outside, closing the door behind him. Thom was glad that the large man didn't try to squeeze in here too.

"So, tell me, Journeyman Thomas, what do you know of my travel plans?"

Thom hesitated. His master had mentioned that the abbot was being sent to join King Arthur, but did the abbot know that? Did he know where Arthur was going?

The leader of the monks spoke up when Thom didn't. "From the silence, I surmise that you do know things and are uncertain what you can reveal. Enough with the secrets. Please tell me what you know." Abbot Justin folded his hands in his lap as he met Thom's eyes. His look spoke of determined patience.

"You travel to join the king," said Thom, deciding that much wouldn't be a real secret, "though I'm unsure why you came and not the archbishop of Camelot. Perhaps your presence is not meant to be well-known back in the city, since you left the night after King Arthur did."

"Perhaps," replied the monk superior, not really confirming anything. "What else do you know, magician?"

"I know that I shouldn't tell you about other people's secrets."

"You think me some magpie, who will shout your words to all who will listen?"

Thom frowned. "No, sir." He wasn't certain how to address an abbot. "I just know better than to betray another's confidence."

The abbot smiled and gave him just the slightest nod, then looked at Francis. "He is not as naive as you implied, brother. He knows how to hold his tongue."

Francis chuckled. "I never claimed he was a gossip, Father Abbot."

"True enough. Well, maybe I can share some things with you, Journeyman Thomas." The abbot looked at the monks sitting on the floor. "Please excuse us, brethren, but I wish to speak with the magician about more sensitive matters."

Both quickly stood and gave respectful farewells to their superior. Francis would have joined them, but Justin motioned for him to stay. When it was just the three of them, Justin continued, "Thomas, we sail into dangerous waters, and I am not speaking about the sea serpent. Do you know our final destination?"

Thom answered cautiously, "We go to the king."

"Yes, but that will not be on some parlay field near Oxford or Readingum. We will see nothing of Lord Mordred, no matter what people were told. No, the king will likely not even exit the Road of Waters. Instead, he will be sheltering inside Merlin's enchantment because Camelot is considered too exposed. It is thought that Arthur will be safer somewhere along this magical route, though after what happened to the Road of Leaves, I have some doubt. If the city falls, then we may become Arthur's court in exile." The abbot sighed as he considered his own words. "Spiritual advisor. That is a role I have no desire to fill. Merlin thought it would be too obvious for the archbishop to leave just after the king, so they chose me instead, but I know nothing of court intrigue. I hope you can do better in the role of magic advisor."

"There are others more qualified," demurred Thom.

"Ah yes, the other journeymen traveling with you, and there was a pair of wizards on the royal galley." Father Justin nodded acceptance of that. "In truth, I was surprised that the magicians' council sent the three of you without a master to watch over you... or did they?"

The abbot held Thom's eyes, almost as if he wanted to catch the magician in a lie. Thom chose to remain silent instead.

When it was obvious that Thom wouldn't answer, the abbot's lips turned up slightly, in a whisper of a smile. "Well, I really did not expect an answer to that question. Keep your guild secrets, if you must. So long as we can depend on you to help defend the galley, then you are welcome among us, Journeyman Thomas."

"Thank you, Father Abbot," he replied, mimicking how Francis had addressed his superior. Thom wanted to be on this man's good side, if at all possible. He was in no position to alienate such a powerful man.

There came a knock at the door. When the abbot called out, Brother Bart stuck his head inside. "The captain wants to see the magician, for it's time to leave the Waywater."

"Thank you, Brother Bartholomew. Tell him that Thomas is on his way." The abbot stood up, motioning for Thom and Francis to do the same. "We will talk more, young man, for I want to make sure you are aware of what we are traveling into. I know your ignorance during your last journey was vexing to you. I will not have you say that it was the Benedictines that withheld information from you this time."

Thom didn't look over at Francis, but it had been the monk who had kept the biggest secret from him while on the Road of Leaves. The monk hadn't wanted to admit that he had once been a magician in training like Thom and that he had renounced it after being forced to kill his master. Thom forgave Francis for keeping those painful secrets from him, but the abbot obviously knew that it had hurt Thom greatly when he had first learned of Francis' deception.

Thom stepped out of the cabin and walked around to the ladder, climbing to the upper deck. He headed for the captain, who hovered around the tiller. It was time to dare the Road of Waters again.

THIRTEEN

Merfolk

Thom met Captain Harold, a barrel-like man with just a wisp of hair on top of his head but plenty of it growing across his face. He greeted Thom with a crushing handshake and a warm smile, introducing him to the mate and the pilot. After that, the man turned serious. He swept his arms outward, as if to embrace his whole boat. "This is my beloved, the Azure Nights, and I will do all that I can to protect her. By coming onboard, you are volunteering to be a part of my crew, so you need to understand my expectations of all serving under me."

He paused until Thom nodded his understanding.

"I expect three things from you, magician," said the captain, counting them off on calloused, sausage-like fingers. "One, warn me of any magical dangers. Two, do your part to fight off any attacks. Three, never challenge my authority on my boat."

Thom agreed, though he didn't like that the captain was treating him like one of his hirelings.

The three vessels pulled away from the Day Dock, out into the dark lake. There were sailors keeping watch at the top of each boat's mast, looking for any sign of the sea serpent. The Azure Nights was rowed to the fore, heading for the archway exit. Like almost everyone else on the galley, Thom kept looking out over the water, worried about the monster. The only ones not looking were the men bent over the oars, working hard to speed the boat out of the Waywater.

The Azure Nights made it across the lake and under the soaring archway without incident. The other two galleys followed. But the first sign of trouble came when the archway mists thinned, revealing debris in the water. Watchmen hollered warning. The pilot cursed as he turned the boat away from some larger flotsam.

Captain Harold yelled "Take the run off! Drop the drag anchor!"

The crew stopped rowing, dragging their oars in the water to slow the galley. An anchor splashed into the channel to further slow the boat. It bought enough time for the pilot to turn them away from a half-submerged hulk.

Debris thickened around them and the captain responded by yelling, "Ship the oars! Pull in that anchor!"

The rowers pulled in the oars to keep them from tangling in the refuse. Others heaved in the anchor before it snagged on anything.

As the pilot maneuvered them around the crushed and sunken boat, the captain took a moment to look at Thom and demand an answer. "Where is it, magician?"

He knew what Captain Harold meant. The man wanted to know where the monster hid, but he answered honestly, "I don't know."

"Find it!"

Thom was listening with his inner ear, but that wouldn't help to locate a magical beast like the serpent. Innate magic didn't reveal itself unless such a creature was injured, or when killed and rendered down to its powerful elements. The sea serpent was hale, so there was no way for him to hear its magic.

Thom had to depend on his eyes and ears, just like anyone else on the galley, but he doubted the captain would be comforted to hear that. So Thom would do what he could to help. "I'll go up to the bow to make sure nothing lurks ahead of us."

"Do that, magician. I don't want my boat becoming the beast's dessert." The captain returned to his crew, ordering them to lower their oars again, now that the channel was no longer so choked with debris.

As Thom made his way to the front of the boat, he looked over the rowers' heads at the pile of crushed wood and sail they were passing and wondered if anyone had survived. He saw no one moving out there in the dark. Maybe the other galleys in the convoy had rescued them, but he doubted that. They had done nothing for the crew of the first galley the serpent sank.

* * *

The Azure Nights turned downriver, letting the current speed it up. The wind was contrary, for on the Waters the wind always blew upriver, so Captain Harold kept the sail down and the crew rowing. The galley was now in the Waters' main flow, along with the two boats following it.

Thom made it past the rowing sailors and up to the prow. He found Francis already there, so he walked up to him and leaned over on the railing at his side. The monk glanced over, but remained silent. The river's glow shone on Francis' frowning face, highlighting his sadness.

"How can I find this monster?" Thom asked after more silence. There was no one else he could ask, now that he was separated from the others of his guild. Francis knew so much more about magic, even though he didn't practice the craft anymore.

"Look and listen," said Francis. "Smell will not help you much. I'm told that they have a fetid breath, but that means it's already too close. There isn't much else you can do, Thomas. There are subtle sounds that will reveal magical creatures, but that is a skill that takes years of practice before your inner ear is sensitive enough."

"Do you think it's still nearby?"

Francis sighed. "It could be anywhere, although not nearby. That much I can discern. Maybe it followed the last two galleys upriver. If so, then I pity them, for the serpent seems bent on sinking any boat it can wrap itself around."

Thom stared out at the glowing Waters. He saw some of the debris caught in an eddy of the river's current. The debris swirled toward the boundaries of the enchantment, then rebounded back toward the boat as the magical wall repelled it. The wreckage came at them, but too slow to endanger the Azure Nights. They were past and moving faster than anything bobbing on the river.

He wondered if they could survive an attack out here on the Waters. What if the serpent hadn't followed the other boats? "Are there no fish in the river for that thing to feed on?"

"The Road of Waters is an enchanted way," said Francis, "just like the Road of Leaves. Animals and fish will avoid it, disliking the magic. There are other magical creatures within the Waters' flow, that is true, but they may be harder to catch than normal prey. Besides, I've read that water serpents find us humans to be a sweet delicacy."

"Did it wander in here by accident or did someone send it?"

Francis met Thom's eyes. "This beast was lured to enter the Road of Waters. That much is obvious to me. Sea serpents prefer the deep ocean, though sometimes they head up a great river like the Thames. But to swim up a narrow river like this? The Waters' magic might have made it curious, but I would think the river's shallowness would have kept it from entering. No, I think it's no accident that the monster came here."

The abbot and the captain walked up to where Thom and Francis still looked out over the bow.

The abbot spoke, "How many boats were destroyed?"

"One of the three who left the Waywater, Father Abbot," answered Francis, his eyes on some more debris that they were passing. The monk looked away from the wreckage and at his superior. "I think the other two galleys made it away, at least for a while."

"You think the serpent stalks them?" his superior asked.

The captain interrupted. "It's a cruel thing to say but I hope it does, for otherwise it's somewhere nearby."

"It seems to be nowhere near us at the moment, Father Justin," answered Francis. "Thomas does the best he can, but I don't think any magician can know for certain where the beast has gone."

Thom recalled that the abbot already knew of Francis' former life as a magician's journeyman, so he knew that the careful answer was meant for the captain. He listened but was still gazing into the night ahead and, just then, spotted a shadow on the Waters. Something moved quickly and quietly their way. "What is that?"

Captain Harold was the first to recognize what it was. "That's a good sign, I would think. It's a pixie boat. If anyone would know of danger close by, it would be them little folk."

"Are those swans pulling a rowboat?" asked Thom. He had heard stories of this, but had thought them just sailor tales. The line of great birds flew up the river, pulling the skiff behind them.

"Aye," replied the captain. "Pixies don't need sails, for they hitch their boats to birds or fish. It's the darnedest thing to see. Don't ask me how they tame their beasts, because I don't know. I just know that no human can harness a fish or tether a flock of birds."

As the boat came nearer, Thom could hear the swans calling out as they flew in a tethered line, pulling the slim boat and its two small passengers. When the smaller boat came up on their craft, it turned so that the swans pulled it alongside the river boat. The birds landed on the river and now the pixie boat floated downriver with the galley, the birds tugging it along just enough to keep it apace with the galley.

Thom could now see the couple distinctly, lit blue by the Water's glow. He could not tell the color of their elaborate tattoos, but each one had them on hands, neck, and face.

"Hail, boat. Why do you have your warning lantern lit?" asked the pixie man, his voice deep for such a small person.

Thom hadn't known the captain had lit such a lantern. He looked around and finally noticed the red light hanging from a pole not that far away.

"Two galleys were destroyed tonight by a sea serpent," shouted Harold to the small man, "and we aren't certain where the beast has gone. The two boats left in that convoy have continued upriver, so maybe it trails them."

"You do well to warn others, for the beast sank three other galleys farther downriver. However, do not worry any longer for we go to slay it now."

Thom was thankful that the captain didn't laugh at the little man's bold claim. Maybe the man had learned what Thom had, that pixies were great hunters despite their diminutive size.

Captain Harold offered a warning, though. "The monster is a hearty creature, not easily injured. We have three journeymen magicians in our convoy and they couldn't do it any serious harm."

The woman pixie hefted a spear. "They didn't have our poisoned weapons, and we are not alone on this hunt." She took the butt of the spear and beat it on the wooden boat five times. In response, six mermen surfaced.

Glowing water beaded off the merfolk's slick bodies as they surfaced. Their hair was long and strand-like, resembling seaweed in its thick unruliness. One of the mermen sang a query at the pixies in a beautiful tenor voice. The other five silently stared at the line of three galleys, their triton spears at the ready. The pixie woman sang a response back to the merman who had addressed her. They exchanged more words in the merfolk's musical speech, then just as suddenly all six dove out of sight.

"You send monsters to hunt monsters," noted Captain Harold. Thom was surprised to see that he had a bare sword in hand.

"Do not believe all the fables you hear about the merfolk," replied the pixie man as his wife stared after the mermen. "They prefer to leave your kind alone."

"Are you claiming that they aren't dangerous?"

The pixie woman turned away from the now-unseen mermen and laughed. "My husband said no such thing, foolish man. Merfolk do cause a certain… agitation among humans of the opposite sex. We pixies are better able to resist their allure, but you humans are easily swayed. Why do you think I signaled for just the men to surface?"

"You mean there are mermaids around us too?" The captain looked genuinely alarmed, making Thom suspect that there might be truth to the wild tales he had heard, of sailors jumping overboard in passionate pursuit.

"They have already moved on, past the third craft," stated the pixie man. "Your men are in no danger from our hunting party."

"Never understood their appeal," grumped Harold. "Hugging a mermaid must be like cuddling a carp, cold and slimy." He shook his head at all of it.

The pixies didn't respond. Instead, the little man pulled on the swans' tether to turn their boat. The pixie woman shouted out one more thing as they quickly moved away from the convoy. "Keep your warning lantern lit, but you are now safe from the sea serpent. We will not let it get past us to terrorize anyone downriver. Just warn those who are still heading upriver, for it may take us a bit of time to corner the brute."

"What if there are more sea serpents than just this one?" asked the captain.

"The danger is past; I cannot imagine more than one coming up the Waters," the pixie woman yelled back. "Just see to it that you warn any boats coming up river."

The captain yelled back that he would do so.

They all stood at the rail and watched as the birds rose into the sky and picked up speed, yanking the skiff against the current. They soon lost sight of the tiny boat and its occupants.

The captain and the abbot walked away from the prow, heading back to the pilot, leaving Thom and Francis to stare out at the blue Waters.

Thom wished he could have caught at least a glimpse of a mermaid, though he was glad none had lured him to jump over the rail.

"Do you know there are four different enchantments that utilize parts from the Night Swan?" asked Francis. He kept his voice low, even though there was no one close enough to overhear.

"They are said to have extraordinary skills in flight and sight," replied Thom, uncertain why the monk mentioned it. Magic came from distilling the elements of magical plants, insects, and animals. Usually, Francis avoided any topics like this one.

"And I've seen more than a dozen enchantments that use elements from merfolk."

Thom could only stare at him in shock. Who had killed merfolk to try such experiments?

"It is tempting to some magicians," continued Francis. "The merfolk can breathe underwater and race like a fish, not to mention how their voices are able to lure in the opposite sex. Eight of those enchantments used merfolk tongues." Francis stared at Thom for a moment, the Water's blue lighting making his features look harsh. "The lust for power can lead to terrible behavior, like justifying murder. That is one of the dark secrets of your guild and you need to face that truth, my friend."

Thom couldn't hold the other's stare. Instead, he looked out over the glowing river and tried to reconcile what Francis said with what his master had taught him.

His thoughts swirled in a jumbled mess.

FOURTEEN

Dead Magician

They made it to Pine Isles Waywater without any more surprises. Thom was glad, but only for that. At the insistence of the captain, he had stayed up all night on guard for any magical attacks. The whole time he had listened with his inner ear to the Road of Waters' rhythmic sounds while staring out at their glowing route. It was exhausting work although he did no physical labor.

The boat shivered and rocked six times that night as the Waters sought out new routes, and each time Thom's stomach heaved in response. At first embarrassed by his stomach's betrayal, he tried his best to hide his seasickness. He grabbed the nearest water bucket and washed the worst of the stains from his robe. He splashed off the deck, refilled the bucket, and then moved away from the nearest lantern. He didn't want the sailors to see his stained and wet robe, though they must have heard him being sick. He couldn't even look at Francis, even though the monk showed nothing but sympathy toward him. He had been told that he needed to wear his robe only for their departure, but with all the troubles he had felt it best to keep it on as a reminder to the crew. Now he was having second thoughts about changing.

By the second bout of vomiting, Thom's stomach was empty, yet he still retched violently. By the third time, he no longer cared who saw his heaving. He didn't care about much of anything, except wanting his stomach to calm. He just wanted to get to their next stop.

Francis provided him company for a few more hours, but then he retired to his bunk. Thom stayed up, enduring the duty given him by the captain. He kept to the prow and the crew avoided him. They probably wanted to avoid the smell lingering around the journeyman.

He hadn't asked Francis anything more about dark magic. But he was thinking about it- at least he was whenever the galley calmed enough to let him do any thinking. Was his friend right? Did every magician face a constant temptation to find greater magical elements, even when that meant killing a magical being? The possibility chilled him.

Around midnight, the Azure Nights passed a group of five boats heading upriver and the captain gave them a warning just as he had promised. Other than that, they encountered nothing else that night.

It was a few hours before dawn when the crew rowed the galley up the side channel to the next refuge. By now, Thom leaned heavily on the boat's railing, tired from a night of watching and vomiting.

He stifled a yawn as the boat entered a still lake littered with small islands. They rounded one forested spit of land and the Day Dock came into view. The dock sprawled over a tiny islet, offering berths on either side of the rocky speck of land. The Azure Nights headed toward the closer berths, with the other two river boats following after. By the time the galley was secured, the eastern sky already hinted at a coming dawn.

Thom yawned again.

When the crew gathered for their sunrise meal, the abbot and his entourage of six monks joined in. Thom also sat down to eat, though it was hard to get his stomach to accept anything. He avoided the fried bacon and greasy tubers, keeping to unbuttered bread and a small pear. The crew members were used to working nights and were jovial as they ate. The abbot's men acted more subdued, but Thom wasn't certain if that was due to the early hour or because the sailors' constant profanity offended their ears. Thom made no pretense at being social, for he was just too tired. He simply ate what he could and tried not to doze off in front of the others.

When Captain Harold offered Thom the second bunk in his cabin, he gladly accepted. Not wanting to offend the man's nose and lose that precious bed, Thom discreetly stepped aside and gave his robe a more thorough cleaning. Better a wet robe than a soiled one.

As the sunlight flooded the Waywater, most of the crew headed off for their beds. Thom followed the captain to his cabin, stifling another yawn. He was far behind on sleep.

* * *

Thom woke to a banging on the door. Still exhausted, he turned over in the bunk and pulled the blanket over his head. But the knocking continued and then Captain Harold bellowed out to know who was disturbing his sleep. As the captain opened the cabin door and confronted whoever was outside, Thom tried to recapture his dream about kissing Adele. That didn't last long, for Harold stomped over and yanked the blanket off.

"She wants you," he said gruffly.

Sleep befogged, Thom's dreams mixed with reality. He wondered how Adele got onto the boat. When he sat up, he saw that it was Vivien instead. The redhead had her arms crossed and was staring at him through the open doorway.

A bit self-conscious, Thom pulled on his trousers and his boots. She didn't look away or respect his modesty. Instead, her fingers started tapping with impatience.

When he turned his back to fasten his trousers and to pull on his shirt, she whispered her exasperation. "Get dressed and make it quick. You act like a flighty lass trying to protect her virtue. Have no fear, you oaf. I have no designs on you." She snorted. "You are young enough to be my son and homely besides."

Thom almost protested that Adele didn't think him ugly, but he held his tongue. Instead, he pulled on his still-wet robe and then gathered his belongings.

He quickly folded up his blanket, secured it to his pack, and then hefted all his possessions to follow her.

As he ducked out the door, she said, "You need not bring all that, but hurry up. They are not used to waiting on others."

Thom didn't have to ask who "they" were. Vivien had been on a boat with a disguised wizard. By her tone, he suspected that she now believed that these two who were shape-shifting were actually from their guild.

They crossed the deck in bright midday sun. A lone sailor on watch gave Thom a nod but didn't approach.

Vivien said nothing more until they disembarked from the Azure Nights. Only then did she look over her shoulder to glare at him. "You could have told me they were wizards. Do not deny that you already knew about that and left me to think the one pretending to be Reginald was a sorcerer."

"I would rather not receive their wrath," Thom replied, still hesitant to even name Levitanus.

Vivien turned back to the wooden dock in front of her, but he could hear the anger in her reply. "Well, you certainly have earned my wrath. Think of that, Thomas, for you will not always have a wizard nearby to protect you. I never forget those who have belittled or betrayed me."

"I didn't betray you," he protested. "I only obeyed the commands of a master. You would have done the same."

He doubted that his argument did anything to mellow her anger, for she pointedly looked away and strode down the wooden pier.

They walked along the docks in silence, only their boots making any noise. He was surprised when she marched past the last boat in their group, but said nothing. Vivien led him onto the rocky isle at the center of the Waywater's docks, taking the wooden stairs two at a time in spite of her shorter stride. He hurried to follow.

The islet had a wide-spaced, evergreen forest growing on it, but it was mostly exposed stone. The stairway climbed up to the isle's peak and then descended to the landing used by galleys going upriver.

Vivien surprised him again when she didn't start down the stairs on the other side. Instead, she deftly climbed over the pathway's railing and started along the isle's narrow spine, past a mixture of mundane and magical evergreens, all of them straight and dark. He was curious, but dared not try to talk to her again.

Their footsteps seemed loud in the silence away from the boats.

It wasn't until they came to the end of the promontory that Thom saw their goal. He looked down at a small cove hidden from the boats moored to either side. There waited Levitanus, no longer holding on to his disguise. With him were the other wizard and a mermaid half out of the water. At the magicians' feet lay a human body.

Vivien stopped when she saw the cove, but it wasn't the corpse that surprised her.

"Who is that gray-hair in blue?" The wizard that had been pretending at being an apprentice wore gray, so she meant Levitanus.

Thom saw no reason to keep that secret from her any longer, not if his master had abandoned his disguise. "That is Wizard Levitanus, who pretended to be Reginald."

Her gray-blue eyes widened. "Your own teacher? So two Founders have been hiding in our convoy." She shook her head at the information. "I can only assume that you also knew it was Merlin pretending to be the apprentice. You should have confided in me, Thomas, rather than let me make a fool of myself in front of them."

He hadn't known that the other fellow was Merlin, but he realized he wouldn't be able to convince her otherwise.

Without another word, she turned and started down the steep slope to where the master magicians stood.

Thom sighed and followed.

A narrow path appeared, winding down to the cove. Thom wondered what creature made it, for he doubted any humans ever took the time to explore the islet. It would have to be a magical beast or being, but he saw no evidence of what or who had done this.

The masters looked over when Thom and Vivien reached the rocky beach. Out of habit, Thom hurried his step to get to Levitanus' side. Vivien lengthened her stride in response, making it almost a race.

"Thomas, you took your time getting here. Come over and look at this body. You should as well, Vivien."

He accepted his master's mild rebuke, knowing better than to argue. He stepped up to the corpse and examined its condition. The dead man was wet, the body bloated and the gray hair an unruly, stringy mess. Thom couldn't tell what the man's rank had been, but the hands showed no obvious callouses. The oddest thing about the body was that it had been stripped of all outer clothing. It lay there in soaked and drooping underclothes, undignified, like debris washed ashore.

Thom looked briefly at the naked mermaid, realizing that she must have pulled the corpse from the lake. She was half-woman and half-fish, her powerful tail still swishing beneath the water even as she sat on a rock near the shore. Her pale arms seemed too thin to have carried the dead man all the way onto the pebbly beach, but she must have. He couldn't imagine either of the masters laboring to do that. Her midnight-black hair still dripped as it trailed over her upper body, but the hair didn't seem bedraggled. The long tresses were her only covering and didn't hide much of her pale skin.

He tried not to stare at her exposed breasts, but to focus on her eyes. It was a struggle to do so. He couldn't seem to catch his breath and he felt overly warm. After a moment, his eyes drifted down from her water-colored eyes, drawn by that barely-hidden bosom.

Thom cleared his suddenly-tight throat and forced himself to look back at the dead man. It took another moment for his eyes to focus on it, then he noticed the lack of clothes again. It finally triggered a recent memory of something that had happened on the Road of Leaves. Thom looked at his master, new apprehension filling his heart. "A shape-shifter?"

Before Levitanus could respond, Vivien blurted out her concerns too.

"Masters, who was this?" She asked with more respect than Thom had ever heard her use.

Levitanus answered Vivien first. "This was the Wizard Bradig, who until yesterday had been accompanying King Arthur. We suspect that he has been replaced by an enemy now. Thomas seems right in that guess."

"What of the king?" she asked.

Merlin motioned toward the mermaid, who spoke for the first time. Her voice was a beautiful melody of sound. "We saw the human king go sailing. At sunset his boat left, without further life theft. However, at his side stood one who looked to be a twin of this man."

Her actual words didn't register with Thom. Instead, her melodious voice captured him. With just those few words, she exerted a strong pull on his emotions. She had said nothing alluring… she wasn't even looking at him… but her magical powers were still overwhelming. He suddenly wanted her. In spite of her being half-fish, he hungered for her. The power of her innate magic startled him. Even though Thom knew why he felt as he did, he couldn't stop the emotions.

Levitanus coughed, tried to speak, and then coughed again. His behavior was so unusual that Thom stared at him. The older man appeared flushed as he concentrated on the mermaid.

His master finally spoke. "Thank you for retrieving Bradig's body. We would not have known of his death otherwise."

She gave Levitanus a slight nod, her lips curving into the slightest of smiles. They were lips that needed kissing, thought Thom.

"Can your people take the corpse back into the water?" asked Merlin. "We cannot have others learning of this and the galleys will pass within sight of this cove when they leave this evening."

"We have no desire for your ire, magicians, but we would rather not have it back. It fouls our fine abode."

"Understood. I ask only that you keep it hidden until tonight and then your people can let the Waters carry it away or you can drag it back out onto the shore."

She nodded again, her smile fading. "We will do this, but only because you are the Builder. Have you more to ask? For we must school our thoughts on how to do what you require."

She is too fair to frown, thought Thom. He wanted to tickle her or amuse her somehow.

"I have no other requests of your people," replied Merlin.

She slipped from the rock and back into the water. Thom watched her lithe movements, fighting the desire to jump into the cold water after her. He even took two steps in her direction.

"Thomas, resist your urges," ordered Levitanus. "Come to my side. Now."

Only the habit of obeying his master stopped him. He shook off the mermaid's allure, just as he saw four others surface around her. It was hard to turn his back on the magic, but he did. His feet seemed leaden as he moved toward Levitanus, yet each step was a little bit easier. Out of the corner of his eye he saw Vivien smirking at him, enjoying his weakness.

"What do you want, sir?" he asked of his master.

"I want you to stay dry," said Levitanus, "and I was worried you would dive after her. The temptation of mermaids can overwhelm even the strongest of men."

Merlin sighed. "Even us old men are aware of it. And you needn't feel so smug, Vivien. Mermen have a similar effect on women." The great wizard used his booted foot to shove the corpse, moving a leg so that the body lay in a more dignified position.

"Sir, why do you want it to remain hidden?" asked Vivien.

Merlin looked up. "Because I do not want my enemies to know that I am aware of their plots. Now it is time to leave, for we need to get back to our boats before anyone grows suspicious."

"The two of you go ahead," said Levitanus, waving Thom and Vivien away. "Merlin and I must prepare our disguises before returning."

Thom was tempted to linger when he noticed that the mermaids were swimming toward shore, but he really didn't want to lose all self-control. He nodded to his mentor and walked away from that place of death and desire.

FIFTEEN

Some Secrets Revealed

Thom hiked the narrow trail behind Vivien. He tried talking to her, but the red-headed woman didn't respond. They climbed back over the railing and onto the Day Dock's wider path. Vivien didn't even look at him; she just marched back toward her assigned boat. Thom let her go, for he would rather have silence than hear more accusations.

When he returned to the Azure Nights, he found Francis waiting. As Thom strode up the gangplank, he weighed what he could reveal to his friend while still being discreet. He came close and whispered to Francis. "Tell me, who was Orem and what did he warn you against when we stood at the Royal Oak gate?"

Francis had once asked him a similar question during their travels on the Road of Leaves. It had been the monk's way to ascertain whether Thomas was real or merely a shape-shifter.

Thom hoped the question would be enough to give his friend a warning that shape-shifters were about again. He didn't want to be too direct, for he still needed to guard the identities of the two disguised wizards.

The monk frowned, understanding all the question implied. "Bricklayer Orem accused me of begging for coins and warned me of his tightly-closed purse." He paused a moment to collect his thoughts, then added a careful question. "Why would you worry about such things now?"

Thom whispered back, "This island has a hidden cove; I was led there to see a body on its pebbly beach. The dead man had been a wizard in the king's entourage."

"That isn't good. Are you certain it was a repeat of the Goat Woman's trick?"

The Goat Woman was the name they gave Narissa, the sorceress who had led the attack on the Road of Leaves.

"Someone saw another who looked just like Wizard Bradig on the royal galley as it departed last night."

Francis looked skyward. "God protect us; the strife continues." He looked back at Thom. "May I tell my abbot? He should know of the king's danger. Do not worry about his tongue wagging, for he is a discreet man."

Thom considered. His master would not be happy to learn that he had already revealed this much to an outsider, but he trusted Francis. Maybe even almost as much he did his own teacher. If Francis vouched for his superior, then Thom would rely on his friend's assessment. He gave a slight nod.

"Thank you, Thomas." Francis put his arm across Thom's shoulders.

He let the monk guide him across the deck to where the abbot stood near the prow. The rest of the monks, including big Brother Bart, sat on the first few oarsmen benches, listening to his morning teaching. The elderly abbot had an open scroll in hand and was reading from the Psalms, adding commentary as he shared an exegesis of the text. Francis stopped behind his brothers and waited patiently for his superior to acknowledge him. Abbot Justin finished his lesson and invited the men to contemplate it further, then he stepped away, motioning for Francis and Thom to follow.

"What is it, Brother Francis?"

"Thomas has chilling news. The king is in grave danger already."

The abbot took a deep breath. "This is sooner than I had expected. What can you tell me, young Thomas?"

Thom told as much as he dared. He spoke of the dead man and about a shape-shifter replacing him. He didn't say anything about Levitanus or Merlin.

Abbot Justin shook his head at the news. "Well, I hope we can reach the king before anything worse happens, but I do not think there is any way to travel the Waters at a faster pace... is the Road of Waters in danger too?"

Thom hadn't considered that. He hoped not. "I hear no disturbance in Merlin's magic, but we are isolated in this Waywater."

The older man turned to Francis. "Are you of the same mind, brother? What do you hear?"

Francis frowned. It was obvious that he didn't appreciate his superior asking him to use his magical talent, even if it was nothing more than listening with his inner ear. When he took too long to answer, the abbot pressed him. "What do you hear, Francis? Are the enchantments whole?"

"You ask me to practice forbidden arts," protested Francis.

"I ordered you to use the skills God has blessed you with," corrected Justin. "I do not ask you to practice sorcery or witchcraft. I gave no demand for you to kill another to release magic. All that I ask is that you listen. Do not become squeamish now, Brother Francis. There are lives at stake, maybe even the fate of the kingdom."

The abbot waited for his answer.

Francis grimaced but complied. "The Waywater enchantment sounds fine, Father Abbot. I cannot hear the Road of Waters from in here."

"Do either of you know of a way that we can communicate with the king or speed up our travels? He must be warned of this."

"I do not," said Francis.

Thom shook his head. "I know of no way to send a message ahead or to change our pace on the Waters."

"What of your magician companions?" asked the abbot.

Thom paused. How could he say anything, in spite of the fact that the creator of the Waters was among his fellow magicians? He didn't want to lie, having sworn off deceit when he left his childhood of thievery, but he couldn't reveal others' secrets. He chose to give a cautious answer. "All of my companions are more skilled than I, but I cannot speak for them."

The abbot raised an eyebrow at Thom's answer. "Well, I would suggest that you make certain all of them understand the importance of this."

"They know," replied Thom. "All of us saw the body."

"You hide something, young Thomas. Who leads the magicians? Maybe I should talk to him."

Thom almost laughed at the absurdity of it. "Everyone knows that Merlin heads the guild… but of those with me, I think they would tell you to seek out Reginald as the most-likely spokesperson. He is on the Starlight, the last boat in our group."

"Very well. I will see if he is more cooperative." The abbot shook his head. "I do not understand your hesitancy in committing the others to the king's aid. Do you suspect a traitor among your guild members?"

Thom gave no answer. He froze at the thought of the abbot ordering 'Reginald' to this boat and lecturing him on the duties of magicians. Levitanus wouldn't be pleased.

Francis intervened. "Father Abbot, less than a week ago Thomas was a mere apprentice. Maybe he is uncertain of what he can promise in the name of his fellow magicians."

"This is no time to worry about offended sensibilities." The abbot looked over at the monks still sitting on the deck. "Brother Bartholomew, come to me please."

When the huge monk came over, the abbot gave him orders. "Go to the Starlight and retrieve the magician's journeyman known as Reginald. Be forceful about it, brother, for I hear he is a pompous one who might balk if you are too polite. I want him before me within the hour. Go."

As soon as Bart left, the abbot turned his attention back to Thomas. He pointed a bony finger at the magician. "You do not seem to understand how precarious the situation is, young man. The king is in mortal danger and we will do all that we can to help him. Arthur must be protected, for without him this kingdom falls. We cannot return to the dark years of war and famine."

The extended hand caught Thom's attention. The abbot's hand was clean, its nails trimmed, yet that was not the hand of a pampered man. He saw callouses and Thom realized that the abbot labored with his hands, beyond holding books or pointing at magicians.

"Are you even listening to me?"

Thom finally met the watery blue eyes that made Justin seem a simple-minded man. Those eyes lied about the abbot's nature. Thom was embarrassed at having been distracted.

"I hear your concerns, Father Abbot, but I cannot be of any help. There are far better men to defend the king."

Justin cocked his head to one side. Suddenly, those blue eyes seemed piercing. He opened his hand and extended it farther, taking hold of Thom's shoulder. "I think you are a good man, Thomas of York. The king needs good men like you."

Thom was uncertain how to respond.

* * *

Brother Bart was soon back with Reginald. When the abbot explained why he had called for him, the disguised Levitanus looked over at Thom. "So, my fellow journeyman has been tongue-wagging, has he?"

Thom flinched but made no excuses.

"You planned to keep this a secret from me?" asked Abbot Justin.

"This is a guild matter. It is none of the church's concern."

"I am the king's spiritual adviser now…"

"Then worry about his soul. Leave magical things to our purview." The two locked eyes, neither giving in. Finally, Levitanus added, "We are doing all that we can to protect the king, Father Abbot. Not all magicians have twisted to the dark arts. You need to trust us in our expertise."

Levitanus looked over at Thom. "You will answer for your loose lips, Journeyman Thomas. I am sure your master will not be pleased when he hears of it."

With that, the wizard turned his back on them and left, never bothering to ask the abbot's permission to withdraw.

As soon as 'Reginald' was off the boat, Francis stepped in front of Thom. "Who was that? Another shape-shifter?"

The monk had heard the enchantment surrounding Levitanus.

Thom spoke carefully, "He calls himself Reginald, a journeyman in the magicians' guild." He dared not say any more.

"What are you talking about?" asked Justin, now confused.

Francis answered without looking away from Thom. "That man was wearing some magical disguise. He is not who he appears to be."

"He is one of the master magicians," Justin quickly deduced, "for the man's arrogance was more than just an act. Their wizards often think of themselves as the same rank as high nobility. But which one was he?"

"He might be a sorcerer," warned Francis.

"I think not. Young Thomas would have warned us. No, 'Reginald' is most likely one of the men sitting on the magicians' council. Do you know who he is, Thomas?" The abbot stared into Thom's eyes and seemed to find something there, for he nodded. "I see that you do but cannot tell. I will respect that and I will let your fellow magician cling to his secret for now, but I will not let him go before the king in disguise. Do you understand?"

Thom nodded.

From then on, the abbot avoided the topic of the disguised magician traveling with them, but he did try to tease more information out of Thomas. Justin asked about ways to expose a shape-shifter and how to protect the king from such people. The abbot was able to coax even more from Francis, learning how difficult it was to make such an enchantment and what it took to make the disguise look so believable. Thom hadn't known about the need for a strand of hair and a drop of blood from the victim.

When it became obvious that Thom was growing overly tired, the abbot dismissed him back to his bunk for a few more hours of sleep. Thom readily obeyed, drooping as he lumbered back to the captain's quarters. Thankfully, the door wasn't barred so he slipped quietly in and dropped onto his assigned bunk, fully clothed.

In spite of his worries, Thom slept soundly until Captain Harold shook him awake.

"Get up, magician. We are under attack again."

Eric Loren

SIXTEEN

Second Serpent

Thom woke to a heaving boat. His stomach instantly protested.

As he moaned and turned over to face the captain, the man yanked on his arm. "Get up, magician! The sea serpent is back and has already wrapped itself around my boat."

He became aware of men screaming and wood cracking. Thom sprang from his bunk and grabbed his pack, for his magician's box lay nestled inside. He didn't bother with his staff, for he still didn't know how to use it. He ran after Captain Harold, out to the chaos.

The serpent's body was slithering across the boat directly in front of him, its slick body slipping by quickly. The beast wasn't coiled over the boat; instead, it crossed a corner of the stern and its weight caused the vessel to tilt that way. Water sprayed over Thom as the beast's body slithered past.

Sailors crowded the narrow walkway, trying to stab the monster with spears and docking hooks. Thom heard more trying to do the same on the upper deck, but its hide was too thick and slimy. Thom saw one man lose his footing and slide down the tilted boat toward the monster. The fellow tried desperately to grab something, but failed. He was sucked under the monster and lost from sight.

"Magician, do something!" yelled Harold. "My boat is sinking."

Thom had to prepare before he could use any magic. He looked around for a safe place to kneel and open his knapsack, for he didn't want to lose his footing and slide under that beast. He decided against going back inside the cabin because the serpent's coil could easily shift and smash that fragile refuge. Instead, he pushed his way up the canted walkway and around to the front of the deckhouse.

The captain chased after him. "Where are you going? Do you flee like a coward?"

Thom replied as calmly as he could, even while swinging his pack off his back and starting to search through it. "I need to prepare an enchantment before I can use it. Magic isn't something I can just pull out of my pocket and toss willy-nilly."

The man was not appeased. "Well, see that you get your magic ready or we will all be swimming soon."

Thom nodded his understanding but concentrated on his work as he knelt in the shelter of the cabin house. He opened his magician's box and quickly pulled out the vials of elements needed for a Wizard Light: powdered Azure Fireflies, powdered Meadow Dragon wings, and crushed Glow Berries. He poured some of each into his mixing bowl and then began stirring the elements together, adding the proper amount of spit. Using his leg to pin the bowl against the cabin wall, he hastily stowed his magician's box back among his dirty clothes in his knapsack and then turned back to his concoction. He had mixed enough to make three Wizard Lights; he just hoped that would be enough. While holding the mixing bowl in one hand, he shoved his magicians' box back into his knapsack and resecured the top flap, but left the pack sitting at his feet.

As he stood again, Thom formed a Wizard Light. In his eagerness to help, he forgot to put on his pack. He looked over the deckhouse at the huge beast slithered over the deck but didn't bother releasing the glowing sphere yet. He waited, hoping the monster would raise its head out of the lake soon. Instead, the sea serpent apparently dove deeper, for its length tightened on the boat and yanked it down.

He was thrown against the cabin house. His pack and his mixing bowl spun away, slipping around the cabin's corner and racing down the slanting deck toward the monster and the water now rushing over the rail.

Thom yelled out as he lurched after his belongings, stepping away from the sheltering cabin wall. He slipped on the steep slope of the deck and fell, sliding after his pack. The sailors who had crowded the walkway earlier were now gone, most likely swept overboard, so there was no one to catch him. He dropped the Wizard Light he was holding as he desperately tried to grab something to stop himself. He spilled into the lake just as the monster slipped off the boat. Behind him the boat surged upward, freed of the beast's great weight.

Flailing in the water, he grabbed hold of some flotsam- a barrel bobbing in the churning water. Around him, Thom heard men shouting for help. Suddenly, the serpent's tail burst up out of the water and then plunged downward. It created a whirlpool that sucked much after it, including Thom. He lost his grip on the barrel and was pulled down.

The wet darkness consumed him.

When his descent into the deep ended, Thom had no idea which direction was up. It was too dark down here, for something clouded the usually-clear waters. He spun around, trying to get his bearings. He hungered for air.

Suddenly, someone grabbed him from behind and yanked him to the right.

Startled, Thom opened his mouth and tried to fight free. Precious air escaped, bubbles floating off to the right as well. He was able to look over his shoulder and saw that a merman had him. Why was he pulling him away from the docks?

Thom motioned back that direction, but the merman shook his head and indicated that they were going to the right. With his powerful tail, the magical being swept Thom through the water.

Water filled Thom's mouth now and he wanted to scream for air. He doubted he could survive long, being dragged through the deep, but he was too weak to break out of the man's solid grip. Just when Thom thought he could endure no longer, they burst through to the surface.

Completely disoriented, Thom nonetheless gasped for air.

Eric Loren

SEVENTEEN

Horns at Sunrise

The merman who rescued Thom deposited him on the Day Dock's planks before going back for some of the dunked sailors. With his face pressed against the wet wood, Thom coughed up water and swallowed air. He was still lying there when his master found him.

"You live? That is good." The old man rolled Thom over and stared at him. He wore his 'Reginald' disguise again.

Embarrassed, Thom struggled to sit up. Levitanus offered no aid but watched carefully. When the effort caused a coughing fit, Levitanus gave him a few hearty thumps on the back.

"You swallowed foul water, poisoned by serpent blood and whatever was in the galley's cargo, so spit out as much as you can."

Thom's stomach roiled as if in obedience to his master's suggestion. Too exhausted to move, he vomited all over himself. Levitanus stepped back to avoid the splatter.

Once clear of the danger, Levitanus ignored Thom's continued heaving and looked out onto the lake. His master said, "The serpent still fights against the merfolk, but I think this one will die soon. Vivien helped, sending a fireball down the beast's throat. She might yet prove herself worthy of a master rank, despite her temper."

Thom paid little attention to his master's musings. He felt too wretched to care. The vomiting had stopped, but his stomach still heaved like a rowboat caught in a winter gale.

"How is he, Journeyman Reginald?" Thom recognized Brother Bart's voice. He looked over as the monk knelt beside him.

"Alive," replied his disguised master. "The oaf swallowed plenty of foul water though. Maybe you can offer him some kind of tonic or tea."

"I will do that," said Bart, helping Thom to his feet. The monk didn't seem bothered by Thom's wet and filthy condition.

"Good. You seem to have him in hand, so I will see where else I can offer aid." Levitanus then wandered off, saying nothing further to Thom.

Bart waited until Levitanus was well away before speaking. "Brother Francis asked that I come to you. Let us get you back to him, for he is skilled with medicines." Bart shifted his grip on Thom and then led him back to the now-upright boat.

* * *

Thom sat on a crate, leaning against the deckhouse and wrapped in a borrowed blanket. He was still sipping the rich tea that Francis had brewed, one swirling with odd aromas and a sweet yet savory taste. It seemed to help with his unruly stomach. His friend sat beside him, keeping him company.

He heard that five sailors died in the sea serpent attack, making him even more thankful to be alive. He realized how close he had come to drowning. Some of the crew told of witnessing mermen riding the serpent as they sunk their trident spears into its side. From what the man had seen, the merfolk finally killed the monster.

The other boat captains sent over sailors to help clean and repair the Azure Nights, so that it would be ready to sail by sunset, for the pilots were adamant that no boat should linger in the Waywater overnight. The men worked hard, not finishing until the last sunlight faded to red.

All of the river galleys left together, for no one wanted to linger here. The Azure Nights came last in line. As the crew rowed the boat toward the Waywater's archway, Thom saw the bloated serpent floating near the exit. Four mermen swam near it, holding up vine ropes and signaling the boat. Captain Harold ordered his men to the ready and they caught the thrown lines. Soon, the boat was towing the carcass out.

Thom shivered at the sight even though the monster was now dead. He looked away.

Francis had stepped away from him for a time and now he returned, carrying something familiar. "I believe this is yours," he said, holding out a wet knapsack.

Thom took it gladly. "Where did you find it?"

"They recovered it on the deck, wedged against the railing. You should check your magician's box to make sure the powders haven't mixed. That could be a dangerous thing."

Thom hurriedly did so, untying the knapsack's flap. He pulled out soaked clothes and laid them aside. He found his magician's box intact and let out the breath he didn't realize he was holding. Carefully, he opened its lid and looked inside. Elemental sounds whispered to his inner ear.

"Check the vial of powdered Golden Mouse," suggested Francis as he listened to the whirl of sounds with a slightly tilted head.

Thom did so and found the powder in that vial to be wet. The powder was spoiled, already mixed with lake water and who knew what else; that was a shame for he had never used the powder for an enchantment yet- he had received it from his master only a few months ago.

Thom carefully checked every other vial, but found all properly sealed. At Francis' suggestion, he took the vial of ruined powder over to a water bucket and rinsed it out, then poured it all over the side of the boat. The powder dissipated quickly, becoming harmless in the vastness of the lake.

* * *

It was already three hours after sunset when the two convoys left Pine Isles.

Road of Waters

The line of boats passed through the mists of the archway and up the side channel to the Waters' main flow. There the group separated; five galleys turned upstream, sails billowing as they caught the constant wind, while the other three rode the current downstream. The crew cut the carcass loose and then the captain ordered them back to the oars so that they could put some distance between the boat and the bloated thing. The other two boats also sped up.

Thom couldn't help but stare after the serpent body. The thing floated close to the Road of Waters' boundary and then seemed to carom off it, floundering back to the middle of the flow. He soon lost sight of its dark form, but he couldn't shake the memories.

He was expected to keep watch but he was too worn out to be very attentive. When Francis volunteered to help, he gratefully thanked him. The two sat on a crate and watched the glowing waters together. Thom dozed off a couple of times, but the monk never complained.

Thom only vomited once that night, which was an improvement. Either the Waters' shifts were becoming smoother or his stomach was finally adapting to the boat's motions. As he wiped his chin, Thom was grateful that Francis chose to ignore his weakness.

* * *

Thom was fighting off sleep, his head nodding. It took a moment for him to notice when the pilot finally turned them up another side channel.

They reached Jagged Lake Waywater unmolested. It was a long and narrow refuge, surrounded by steep hills. Judging by the enchantment's sound, Thom could tell that the hills were included in the magic. At least they were up to the highest ridge. He wondered about the far slopes and asked Francis, who had stayed up with him through the long night.

"I'm not certain what lies over the ridge," confessed the monk, looking up at the rocky heights. "That's a steep climb, so I doubt anyone has bothered to explore it since the masters crafted the enchantment decades ago. Who would dare such a hike and risk being lost or left behind? Besides, I don't think any river pilot would allow a boat to anchor anywhere a person could find a suitable path. Our assigned Day Dock is beneath a cliff. There is another Day Dock across the lake for the traffic that heads upriver."

Thom yawned. It was a gaping yawn, causing his eyes to scrunch closed and his jaw to ache. He had a hard time reopening his eyes. "Well, I would love to have some good solid ground beneath my feet no matter how steep the slope."

Just then, the boat lurched a bit, startling Thom awake. He looked around, worried about another attack, but it was nothing of the sort. The crew had let the boat coast through the archway but were now rowing again. Some had been off-beat in their oar strokes; that was all. After three pulls they were back in rhythm, but Thom's queasiness had returned. He listened to their labors, trying to ignore his rebellious stomach.

"Settle in, boys," ordered the mate behind the last pair of rower benches. "Nice even strokes. We aren't racing the other two or else I'd be whipping you now."

Thom expected some snide reply to the whipping comment, but the men were focused on their duty.

"Ease up on starboard oars. We're rounding the headland now, boys. Just a bit more and you can start cuddling your pillows for the day."

The Azure Nights followed the other two boats around a rocky point and the Day Dock came into view- a floating platform at the base of a steep cliff. They docked without incident and then the men gathered for the communal meal. Thom ate two of the biscuits and a spotted pear, but he passed on the sausage and the chunks of ham. He sat with the abbot's party but didn't really listen to their banter. Instead, he gazed up at the high hills that were just starting to brighten with the sun's first caress. His thoughts drifted in half-sleep until a horn sounded, then he caught more of the conversation around him.

"Brother Francis, what is that sound?" asked large Bart.

"The centaurs are blowing on brass horns," replied Thom's friend. "Their kind likes the steep hillsides of this Waywater. I do not know if the call is in celebration or warning but it has nothing to do with us. They call out to each other. I have heard it before when traveling through here."

"Centaurs? So they are real too?"

"Yes they are, but I would rather not meet any. It is said that they are surly and quick to take offense at our kind. They see us as something only half-formed, hampered with just two legs."

Thom scanned the nearest slopes but couldn't spy any of the illusive beings.

When the meal was over, Thom went to his assigned bunk in the captain's cabin and gratefully curled up on the bed. He fell asleep within minutes.

* * *

Thom finally captured the uninterrupted sleep that he so desperately needed. He woke at sunset to the quiet stirrings of Captain Harold and lay there for a moment longer, enjoying the peace. When the captain stepped out, Thom sat up and noticed his wrinkled and stained clothes. He had been too tired to do more than remove his robe but now regretted it. His shirt looked awful and his trousers not much better. There was an aroma about him too, an unpleasant odor.

He retrieved his knapsack from the floor and looked inside for a change of clothes, but realized that everything was still damp from yesterday's dunking. The sleep-wrinkled clothes would have to do, for at least they were dry. He retrieved the dark-blue robe strewn at the foot of the bunk and held it up. It looked worse, even though he had used water to rub away most of the stains last night.

He sighed, realizing that he would have to wash all of his clothes and find some place to hang or lay them to dry. He would have to get it done before the sea sickness overpowered him. He put on the wrinkled and dirty robe, deciding to avoid others as much as he could. He would rather not embarrass himself.

As Thom moved about the cabin, he felt aches and pains that he hadn't been aware of yesterday, bruises from the serpent attack. It promised to be a long night, even if there were no more attacks. Frankly, he would rather just linger in bed a few more hours, but his stomach was growling. He didn't want to feed it, since he would just be vomiting it all back up later, but his belly was insistent.

Settling the pack on his back, he opened the small door and ducked out into a golden evening. Clouds hung overhead like pinkish-orange cotton balls scattered across the sky. Thom walked over to the railing and looked out at the calm bay that had sheltered them for the day. It already lay in shadow, but sunlight still sparkled on the center of the lake, out past the headland. The hills on the opposite shore of the narrow lake were in sharp outline, casting long shadows.

"Excuse me, sir, but you are wanted."

Thom turned to find the overlarge Brother Bart speaking. "Who wants me? The abbot?"

Bart nodded. "Yes, Father Abbot is one of them but the group also includes the captain, the pilot, and your fellow magician. The one called Reginald."

Thom had the sudden concern that Levitanus might be reclaiming him now, and not so that he could continue his training. His master probably worried that Thom's tongue had become too loose and wanted him close enough to control.

Bart motioned for him to follow. "They have already gathered near the pilot's tiller and I don't think any of them are used to waiting. Sorry for rushing you, but please hurry."

Thom strode around to the front of the deckhouse, avoiding the sailors scurrying about to get the boat ready to sail. As he climbed the ladder to the upper deck, he realized that they hadn't waited for him at all. Instead, the four were already deep in conversation. Troubling conversation. The fact that the mate stood nearby to make sure no others tried to listen was not encouraging.

"...should we row over and offer help?" asked Captain Harold.

"I doubt any still live," stated Levitanus, his disguise failing to hide his confident attitude. "We would only be offering ourselves up as a second meal to the pair."

"Where did all of these serpents come from?" asked the abbot, sounding angry. "What twisted magic is this and why would Merlin allow it to disrupt the Road of Waters?"

Thom hesitated to stand among those three, so he stopped next to the pilot who was a step back from the others. He was glad that he wasn't the topic of conversation but their words were still troubling. Had there been another serpent attack? He looked over, but the other two boats in their convoy seemed whole.

"I cannot answer for Merlin, but I doubt he is permitting this," replied Levitanus. "The herding of so many sea serpents into the Waters says that we magicians have powerful enemies now. Sorcerers are arrayed against the guild and they have been planning their attacks for some time."

"You are worried, Magician Reginald?" asked the abbot.

"I would be a fool not to be," was the reply.

"You said the monsters won't attack the Day Docks," said the captain, "so that leaves us two options. We can either hunker here where we can flee to that dubious shelter or we can try to slip out of the Waywater without attracting their attention. Can you magicians tell us where the serpents hide?"

Levitanus grimaced. "Magical creatures are not so easily found. One of the beasts was wounded when the pair shattered the other boats. Thomas can find that one easily enough, but the other is much harder to locate."

Thom heard his master's hint and concentrated on the magical rhythms around him. It took a moment, but he finally picked out the odd thudding sound, almost like that of a giant heart, from somewhere beneath the Waywater's surface. The sea serpent was far off, but that didn't comfort him much because he had seen how fast the creatures could move.

"You can sense the monster right now?" asked the captain, looking at the two magicians in turn. "Close?"

"Across the lake," assured Levitanus, "but it will not linger over its kill all night. The two will take a little time to break open the wrecks and find all the men to eat, then they will move on. We should flee soon."

"What do the other captains say?"

"They are making ready for a stealthy retreat," said Levitanus. "If you choose to stay, you will be alone, for we magicians will go with whoever is traveling on."

Thom was surprised at his master's forceful tone. He sounded like a wizard, and not like a mere journeyman. He hoped his teacher wasn't endangering his disguise by ordering others around.

Harold grunted. "I don't see much of a choice. I'll leave with the others."

Levitanus nodded and then turned to leave, but Abbot Justin held up a hand. "A moment, journeyman magician. What will keep the serpents from following us down the Waters?"

"Nothing. Even if we successfully sneak out of here, they might still come after us. The feeding habits of a sea serpent are not within my ken. Maybe you know how many humans it takes to satisfy a serpent's hunger, but I do not."

"Will we be safe at the Isle of Mists?" asked the pilot, speaking up for the first time.

"Oh, I doubt that, river pilot. The sea serpents may not want to hunt there, for the merfolk and their poisoned triton spears are thick in that area, but there will be other dangers. There are always dangers in this world." Levitanus swept the group with a stern look and then walked off.

* * *

The boats pulled away from the Day Dock an hour later, with the rowers taking extra care to use steady, even strokes. Thom stood next to the pilot and the captain, eating the last few bites of a chunk of bread. He had avoided the richer fare offered at their meal. As he stood there, his focus was on the one serpent that he could hear. He had no idea where the other one was lurking. Thom was just about to tell the captain that the beast wasn't reacting to them when the serpent moved. He strained to listen to the song of its innate magic, thinking it might be his own fears. But no, the sound was growing louder. Closer.

Thom grimaced as he looked toward the north. The wounded serpent was coming across the lake, although he could not see it with his eyes yet.

"What is it, magician?" asked the captain.

Before he could answer, the sea serpent sped up. It was now racing toward them.

"It has heard us and it's coming our way," answered Thom. He pointed toward where he thought it was and, at that very moment, the monster breeched the surface. All saw its huge head in the distance before it dove deep again.

Eric Loren

EIGHTEEN

Jagged Lake

"Row!" yelled Captain Harold to his gawking crew. "Hard at it! Put your backs into it, boys, if you want to live to see another sunrise." He then ordered the drummer to beat a faster pace. The boat jerked some as the men struggled to get into rhythm, but soon the Azure Nights was leaping forward across the lake. The other two boats also sped up.

"Where is it now?" demanded the captain.

Thom pointed to where he guessed it to be. "It sounds like it's nearly halfway across the lake."

"Have you found its twin yet?"

Thom shook his head. "I have no idea where the other serpent hides. Maybe the two beasts are racing side-by-side, but I can only find the wounded one."

The captain swore.

"I will try harder," Thom promised, though he was uncertain what he could do.

At first, their boat was ahead of the others when it rounded the headland. But the pilot, at the captain's insistence, kept the boat closer to the shoreline instead of aiming directly for the archway exit. The Starlight didn't follow; it took the shortest path out, directly across the lake. The third boat followed the Starlight. Thom wondered if the wizards were going to finally reveal their power now, for it seemed a deliberate confrontation.

Abbot Justin came walking over with Francis. "They are being overbold," he said as he gazed at the other boats.

Captain Harold glared at him. "Keep out of the way, Father Abbot, and don't distract the magician. I need him to concentrate on those monsters."

Thom wanted to ask Francis if he knew of a way to spot the sea serpents, since the monk had once trained to be a wizard. But he held his tongue, for he didn't want to betray his friend's trust. Francis had renounced that past and didn't want others to know of it.

However, the abbot knew of Francis' former life and seemed to know of Thom's need, for the elderly man led Francis close and then stood so that the captain wouldn't see any whispers from the monk. The monastery leader acted oblivious toward Captain Harold's continued glares, apparently confident that his high rank would stop the captain from doing anything rash.

"Thomas, can you hear the other one?" asked Francis in a low whisper.

Thom kept his eyes on the lake as he put a hand over his mouth to cover a pretend yawn. "I cannot. Do you know how?"

"Warn the captain that it hides directly ahead of us. He needs to turn the boat toward the others."

"Where is it?" asked Thom, looking ahead and trying to hear any sound from the magical creature.

"There is no time to teach you now. Trust me. Order him to turn immediately."

Thom needed no more urging; he had no desire for another encounter with the beast. "Captain! The second serpent is lurking ahead of us. We need to turn toward the other boats now."

Harold cursed again. "Hard turn, men! Starboard, hard pull! Larboard, ease off those oars for three beats."

The pilot needed no urgings, but was already wrestling the rudder over. The Azure Nights leaned as it turned and then straightened.

"Oars all in. Dig that water, men. Drummer, up your beat."

They began racing toward the other boats now. From overhead, a sailor clinging to the mast shouted a warning. "Captain, I see it. It just lunged toward us and it's picking up speed quickly. Whitewater to the starboard."

"It's coming right at us," said the pilot, looking that way.

Thom saw a coil of the serpent crest the surface as it sped toward them.

"Check your swing, pilot. Keep that rudder straight," ordered Harold. "Don't turn maiden on me, fluttering across its path to flip our skirts. We're not flirting with the thing. Keep our prow aimed at the others."

The pilot glared at the captain, but straightened the rudder nonetheless.

"Thomas, who is on the other boats?" asked Francis in an urgent whisper. "They start enchantments that are beyond anything I have ever seen or heard. What wizards have been hiding on the other boats?"

Thom finally realized what Francis meant. Apparently, Merlin and Levitanus were crafting some great enchantment because he could hear the elements being stirred and blended. He wasn't certain of all the sounds, but he recognized five of the magical powders by their distinct rhythms and noted at least three others. Thom had never mixed more than three magical elements together. He couldn't imagine what it took to craft something so complex.

"They make something with fire and water combined. Who are they?" asked Francis again.

Thom dared not reveal too much. "There are two wizards among us, but I'm forbidden to reveal their names."

The abbot grunted and Thom realized that he had been listening.

Francis raised an eyebrow at Thom's refusal. "Well, warn the captain that they are about to release something bright and loud. Most likely some kind of fire that can burn underwater."

Thom did so, warning the captain just as a huge fireball formed in the hands of someone on the Starlight. It was Levitanus, his gray hair now revealed. He had let go of his disguise to work this magic. The fireball grew ever larger as his master shaped it with both hands and then held it over his head. He threw it into the lake, at the fast-approaching, wounded serpent. The fireball roared and then exploded as it plunged into the cold water. For just a moment, Thom could see and hear the flames underwater and then there was a great explosion with water shooting into the sky.

"Thomas! We are getting too close to the other serpent," whispered Francis with urgency. "Tell the captain to stop our advancement or else we will get caught in the fireball that is about to be tossed."

"Captain, we need to stop or else we will come between that fire and the other serpent."

The man didn't question Thom's words; he immediately yelled at his crew to stop the boat. "Square the oars!"

The sailors instantly stopped rowing and plunged their oars into the water to cause a drag on their progress.

It was not enough and Captain Harold realized it. "Hold her hard! Half-beat, drummer."

The men began to row in reverse, fighting against the boat's movement. It was a dangerous move and four sailors fell off rhythm and clashed oars. Men cursed and moaned. Two oars shattered, but at least the Azure Nights quickly lost her speed.

Merlin threw his fireball and it roared across the boat's prow to crash into the lake nearby. The fireball plunged deep, lighting the water's depths until it exploded next to the serpent's head. The explosion threw the galley sideways and soaked everyone as lake water flew skyward and then rained down.

Thom tumbled across the deck as the starboard rail rose high in the air. He hit the pilot in passing and sent that man sliding too. When the boat rocked back upright, Thom was pressed against the far rail and the pilot was missing.

"Man overboard!" roared Harold, taking hold of the tiller. He called out to the mate. "Bill, have them fish out our pilot."

Thom looked into the still-choppy lake and spotted the pilot treading water. Feeling guilty, Thom considered jumping in after the struggling man, but the captain called for him.

"Are the monsters dead? Where are they?"

As Thom returned to the captain's side, he realized that he would no longer have Francis to help him. The monk was assisting a now-injured abbot.

But, as he listened, Thom found that both serpents were easy to hear, for each one was now injured and leaking not only blood but also their innate magic. "They have fled, nursing their new wounds. One heads toward the other shore while the other snakes it way toward the lake's far end."

"Did either receive a mortal wound?"

Thom wasn't certain, but neither seemed to have bled enough. "I think not. We should leave while we can."

Harold nodded and then yelled again for his men to get the pilot fished out.

When they finally had the dripping man on deck, the captain ordered the men back to their rowing and took the rudder's tiller himself. The pilot let him as he went to change into dry clothes. Thom would have done the same, for the man would be on duty all night and it was already growing chilly.

Thom was glad that he wasn't soaked this evening, for it promised to be another uncomfortable night even if the sea serpents stayed away.

NINETEEN

Fog Town Harbor

All three boats made it out of the Waywater and onto the Road of Waters. Men stopped rowing when the mate ordered it and they let the current carry them downriver. This time, the Azure Nights was in the center of the convoy. Thom spent the night at the prow, for he didn't want to be on the upper deck where the captain and pilot would witness his seasickness. He was resigned to vomiting every night until he could escape this restless Road, but he would rather not have an audience.

Around midnight they came upon a line of five boats heading upriver, their sails full of the steady, magical wind. Words were yelled between decks as the boats passed, with the captains shouting a warning about sea serpents, but the other flotilla kept going. Thom hoped they survived.

The river galleys followed the meandering Road of Waters until two hours before sunrise, when the Waters flowed beneath a triple set of archways. Captain Harold had called Thom to the upper deck, wanting him closer. Thom had complied reluctantly. Although he hadn't soiled his garments any more this night, he knew he wasn't the sweetest smelling fellow on deck. He was determined to wash his robe more thoroughly as soon as they anchored for the morning.

"This will be the last night," the captain stated. "We make it through tonight and we can have a good rest at the Isle of Mist."

"We are already halfway through the Road of Waters?"

"Isles is indeed the center rest on the Waters, and I haven't longed to see her this much in many a year. It will be good to lay into a proper harbor."

Thom was still on the upper deck hours later, when they came to the Isles Waywater. This refuge had two gateways onto the river according to the captain, one at either end of the large lake. The convoy chose the upriver entrance. Thom wondered if any pilots ever chose to bypass the stop, but doubted it.

They turned down the calm side canal and a triple-set of archways came into view. He was glad to see the shimmering fog that hovered like an ethereal curtain over the canal's expanse, marking the end of their harrowing trip.

Thom was standing next to the pilot and the captain when the boat passed into the glowing fog. He lost sight of the mast and everything else that was farther than an arm's length from him. The other two men became mere shadows among the blue-lit mist. Thom lifted his arm and watched as the glowing droplets settled on his sleeve and faded to mere moisture.

The fog curtain was thicker, hanging beneath three arches this time and, instead of ending, it grew darker and more ominous as they passed through-losing its glow. Thom didn't understand what was happening, until Captain Harold yelled out. "The clouds are thick today. Sound the fog song, Bill."

Someone began to ring a bell at a slow pace. Listening carefully, Thom could hear similar ringing both ahead and behind them. They had come out in the Isles Waywater, but the lake was befogged.

"I hate it when the fog is so eager to hug us in welcome. I'd almost rather be smothered by one of those fishy mermaids," grumbled the captain. "To the oars, men. Mate, make sure to set the drummer to a steady and slow beat. Keep her on course, pilot. I'd rather not join Dreaming Emily in her wet bed. After all that we've endured, I just want to reach Fog Town and drown in some ale instead."

Thom had no idea who Dreaming Emily was but he dared not ask, not with everyone focused on making it safely through the fog. He just stood there quietly and listened for any magical danger. The Waywater's song was a steady background, but so far he heard nothing else.

"Len, how high does this fog go?" shouted Harold to the man clinging to the mast somewhere overhead. "Is it just a skim on the lake or does it climb high?"

"We are deep in it, Captain. The clouds are so thick that I could pee on 'em and stain 'em yellow."

"Don't be sending any golden rain on us or I'll have you castrated, you ill-begotten spawn of a hedgehog and a carp."

A few of the rowers chuckled, proving that they had overheard, but Thom didn't hear much else from them. The fog encouraged whispers instead of shouts, especially since men had to listen for the other galleys' tolling. A pair of sailors hung over the prow and watched for anything up ahead.

They had rowed for a time when they heard some shouts from the boat in front of them. In another minute the reason became obvious when a watchman shouted out, "Ware larboard."

The fog thinned a bit and Thom saw a half-sunken hulk on the left. They neared it and then passed by, almost within an oar's reach.

"A bit close, pilot," said the captain. "We almost followed the Starlight to Emily's bosom." He spoke calmly yet Thom saw the stiffness in the man's stance.

The pilot said nothing in return.

"I could really use that drink now," Harold mumbled. He looked over at Thom. "Any monsters hiding in this cloud soup? Did those sea serpents follow us in?"

"The Waywater seems calm, but who knows what might be lurking in the depths beneath us?" answered Thomas. No matter how much the captain wanted it, he couldn't answer with any greater certainty. He simply knew too little about water magic. "I will keep listening."

"You do that, magician. Shout out if something seems amiss." The captain shook his head and mumbled something too low for Thom to hear, but the pilot grunted in agreement. He suspected the man had complained about Thom's lack of talent.

The trio of boats moved across the fog-shrouded lake. Although there was a current here because the Waters flowed through, it wasn't enough to keep to the pace the captains wanted. So the men rowed. There was also a headwind, but it didn't do much to shred the fog; it simply sped up everyone's soaking.

Apparently, the pilots were used to the Isles Waywater being foggy, for they kept the galleys together without getting too near.

It was one of the prow watchers who yelled out about their next obstacle. "Lily lights closing in on starboard, Captain."

Harold swore and then yelled out orders, "Rowers, ease off on larboard for two beats. Help the pilot get her aimed down the channel."

Once their course was corrected, the captain turned his focus on the man holding the tiller. "Your fellow pilot on the Starlight is staggering like a drunkard on this approach."

"The fog's thick," replied the pilot, neither defending nor defaming his comrade on the lead boat.

The captain shook his head and then shouted to his crew again. "Mind the oars, starboard. You hit one of those stinking things and I'll have you scrubbing the deck while the rest of us enjoy our stay in Fog Town."

Thom looked off to the right and saw a glowing field of lilies, its green light faint in the fog. The lilies bobbed in the Starlight's wake and that disturbance must have caused the plants to release their stench, for suddenly it smelled like a thousand farts. Thom gagged, covering his nose. He heard many of the crew coughing.

"I swear, James did that on purpose," groused Harold about his fellow captain. He waved his hand in the air, trying to get the stink away.

From the rancid smell, Thom knew these were Sweet Lilies but he knew little else about the floating pads. Within another year or two, his master would start teaching him about the magical plants in the ponds near the cottage; so far Thom had only needed to recognize which ones to pick for his master's work. He hoped Levitanus didn't make him harvest these awful smelling things. Thom couldn't imagine what useful elements could be distilled from such a disgusting weed.

The fog thinned a bit and lightened with the coming of dawn. Thom realized they were very close to a rocky, forested island- the Isle of Mists. As the pilot corrected their route to the center of the channel, Thom noticed the darkness of another island to their left. One of the sailors named it the Isle of Trees.

They were heading for a settlement halfway down the Isle of Mist's shoreline: Fog Town. The day lightened to a dreary gray as they moved between the two islands. The fog lessened and now Thom could see the other two boats easily, but most of the shoreline to either side remained a shadowed uncertainty. He saw more patches of Sweet Lilies glowing eerily near the shore, but the boats were far enough away to avoid the stench. They rounded a bend in the waterway and Fog Town port came into view: a bay with a dozen river boats moored at its docks.

The captain spoke up, "Looks like some galleys have taken refuge here. I wonder if they've heard of the monsters haunting the Waters." He grunted. "It would've been nice if someone had shared that bit o' news with us. Have you ever seen so many boats at Fog Town?"

"Not I," admitted the pilot.

"Well, bring us in as close to the settlement as the pixies allow." Harold nodded his head at the trio of swan-pulled dinghies that were heading out to meet the newly arrived boats. "I know they want no bribes, but tell them we have urgent news for the harbor master. I'd rather not be jumping too many canals, but we'll have to be reporting about the beasties we met."

Thom had heard of Fog Town's maze of canals but he couldn't see them through the haze. From this distance, the town seemed a jumble of wooden structures along the bay's edge, before the land rose into the foggy hillsides beyond. He moved to the rail, where he could stand and study the hamlet more carefully.

As a pair of pixie guides led the Azure Nights into the bay, more of the settlement became visible. Thom could now see that the nearer buildings were actually on the bay, perched on stilts, reminding him of long-legged water birds wading in a marsh. Between the buildings ran narrow channels, knifing into the town's shadowy depths. Wooden walkways spanned the gaps between the buildings, serving as aerial roads for the people milling about bayside.

Thom looked up when he heard loud quacking. A flock of Blue-Winged Ducks flew past, heading toward the far end of the bay. Except for their color, they didn't look any different from any other water fowl. Unlike a normal port town, there were no seagulls or pigeons swarming the boats, but then there were no fish catches getting hauled ashore either. The Road of Waters had neither, for normal animals avoided the enchanted way.

Following the mate's instructions, the rowers lifted their oars to let the boat glide the last few yards, not dipping them back in until they were needed to help slow the craft. They docked at a short pier that led to an impressive wooden building. A half-dozen pixie boats were tied up here, the swans paddling under a neighboring dock as they did whatever water fowl did.

Thom noted that the other vessels in their group were tying up three docks over.

"You outdid yourself, pilot," remarked Captain Harold, not sounding totally pleased. "We couldn't get any closer to the harbor master's office unless we swamped those cockleshells."

As the crew tied up, the abbot and his monks appeared on deck. Francis and Bart came over to Thom. The two were dressed in simple monastic robes, rough and faded black in color. But each carried a pack and a walking staff. They set their packs and staffs down nearby and then joined Thom at the rail.

"Something is wrong with Fog Town," said Francis to Thom. "It seems too quiet, as if the whole settlement holds its breath."

"Will we find trouble here?" asked Thom. He and Vivien were supposed to disembark and join the Wizard Weston. He wasn't even certain that they would still be doing that. All the intrigue and secrets had him confused. Were they now traveling on, to join the king wherever he was going?

Francis frowned. "Trouble is already here. Usually, you can hear active magic in the settlement. It is a favorite spot for your fellow magicians; they often come here to gather magical elements and then try a new enchantment." Francis stretched out his hand and swept it across their vista of the town. "But no one is experimenting. I hear nothing beyond the Waters itself and I mistrust such a change. I just hope it will not be as terrible as what we faced on the Road of Leaves."

"I still cannot believe half the tales I've heard about that adventure," said Bart, who had been listening to their conversation. "Do you really think we are facing that much danger again?"

Francis turned to his fellow monastic. "Yes, Bartholomew, it looks that way. Whether we stop here at the Isle of Mists or sail the lower Road of Waters, I think we'll face more attacks. Now you needn't raise the fears of our brethren, Bart, but you should know of this. Father Abbot insists on you being involved."

Bart grimaced. "I love Abbot Justin, but he will not forget what I was trained to do before taking my vows to the Lord."

Thom gave him a puzzled look but didn't ask. The look was enough to loosen Bart's tongue more.

"I trained as a warrior, though I fled it because I… detest killing." His voice faded to a whisper on those last two words.

Thom couldn't imagine this man as a knight or soldier. He was huge, but Bart seemed far too humble… too quick to apologize.

"Bart was the younger son of a noble," added Francis when the other monk didn't continue. "His sword skill and archery talent are unsurpassed, but he kept pulling back from making the killing blow, even if it was just a mock killing in a tourney." Francis reached out and put a hand on the other's broad shoulder. "Bart has a warm heart, not a killer's coldness."

"If only my father had been so understanding," muttered Bart. He sighed, but then he pulled Francis close and hugged him, his hugeness enveloping the other. "That is in the past though. I have a new family now- my brothers of Saint Barnabas."

"It is good to see camaraderie among the brethren," said Abbot Justin, walking up on them. "Are the three of you ready to depart?"

The two monks nodded in near unison as they let go. Francis pointed to where their knapsacks rested against a crate.

The abbot glanced at the packs and then turned his attention to Thom. "Do you have a change of clothes?"

Thom nodded, though confused at the question. "I do, Father Abbot. Why do you ask?"

"I suspect that your comrades will want you in less conspicuous garb." He didn't explain any more, but turned to Francis instead. "You have been through Fog Town far more than I have, Brother Francis. What is wrong with the town? It seems off kilter to me."

"The magic is subdued here…"

"Damaged?" interrupted the abbot, his gaze sharpening with concern.

Francis grimaced. "No, Father Abbot. The Road of Waters is sound. That is not what I meant. It is something else… There are usually many other enchantments active here at Fog Town. Magic from lesser magicians. I can hear but two right now, very distinct due to the absence of the usual noise."

"Magic used inside another enchantment? But they tell everyone that other magic is forbidden while on the Waters," replied the abbot.

"Yes, they do say that, but the guild brings their students here to train them on water enchantments since there is no lake or river in Camelot. Every other time I have been at the Isle of Mists, I've heard magic crafting along the isle's shoreline. The guild even maintains a collection of shelters along the coast for students that need a dry area to work out of the constant cloud drip."

"Is the lack of magic the only thing wrong here? Am I developing an ear for magic in my old age, that I sense its silence here?"

Francis shook his head. "No, there is a general stillness over the settlement, even with the harbor so crowded. Usually there are hawkers at the dock to greet every boat that arrives. We should also be hearing music and laughter from the nearest saloons, for they are just over there. Something muffles Fog Town besides its normal mists."

"I feared as much. Arthur leads us into trouble, as is his wont. God knows, that man does seem to revel in mischief and warfare. I think he was jealous of Thomas' exploits and now seeks out the most troubled area on the Ways of Camelot so that he can find his own adventure." The abbot shook his head and grunted at the prospect. When the others stared at his bold words, he added, "Oh, I say nothing that I haven't said to Arthur's face. There is a reason why he doesn't seek me out as his spiritual counselor more often. I'm too sane. The archbishop is far more the romantic, encouraging the king's exploits and calling them great deeds fitting for a great ruler. I just call them childish games and foolish risks." He wrinkled his nose. "Maybe Arthur chose me for this journey so that he could drag me into one his escapades."

Another grunt showed the abbot's feelings about that idea.

Thom felt he should explain that this was more than just some quest or tourney. "There are deeper concerns here, Father Abbot. The attack on the Road of Leaves was carefully planned by sorcerers and most of them have not yet been found. Maybe the king is seeking refuge…"

"Inside one of Merlin's enchanted ways? Hardly. That is not our king's bent.

He does not hide or retreat. No, he plays the bait, hoping to lure the sorcerers into attacking. It is another foolhardy scheme, but this time I and some of my brethren have been dragged into it. And now you have confirmed more to me, Thomas. King Arthur had no intention of just passing through the Road of Waters; he is planning to linger in here. Probably right here at the center of it."

Thom was crestfallen. He had once again let his tongue wag. His master wouldn't be pleased upon learning of it.

"You think the king offers himself as decoy?" asked Francis, frowning.

Justin sighed. "Arthur would not think of it in such terms nor would he sit there idly as his knights and magicians fought for him. If battle occurs anywhere near him, he will draw that pet sword of his and charge into the thick of it."

"Here come the other magicians," said Brother Bart softly, pointing to where three people strode toward them along the docks.

Thom saw that the other boats' captains and pilots were nearby, having stopped outside the harbor master's building. Captain Harold and his pilot were there, too. The magicians were walking past the group, heading for the Azure Nights.

The three weren't dressed in their robes anymore, but the two wizards had on billowing capes with deep hoods that hid them from any curious passersby. Merlin no longer pretended to be an apprentice, but openly carried a magician's staff that only journeymen and masters owned. Thomas could hear the magic still around Merlin and Levitanus as the two came closer. A step behind them walked Vivien, her red hair and fair skin emphasized by the dark brown dress she wore.

Since none of them was dressed in robes any longer, Thom hastily took his off and stuffed it into his knapsack. He pulled out a well-worn cloak in its place.

"Do you think they will let us go with them?" asked Francis of his superior.

"I will insist on it," stated Justin. "A master magician might be able to deny an abbot's order but these two play at being journeyman and apprentice, so I will use their disguises against them."

Francis chuckled. "Neither one will like that."

"True enough, but I promised that I would serve as Arthur's counselor on this trip and I intend to keep my word." Justin paused to look at his two underlings, then he flicked his fingers in the air at both of them. "Francis, raise that cowl over your head now. You too, Bartholomew. I want both of you to remain covered while we are traveling with these overly sensitive magicians. I would rather not upset them needlessly."

Merlin would be more than just upset when he found out about Francis, thought Thom. The great wizard might retaliate by deserting all three monastics.

Eric Loren

TWENTY

Crossing Bridges

Justin was right; the wizards grudgingly gave in to the abbot's authority, letting Justin and the two monks accompany them. The abbot grudgingly agreed to leave behind the other four monks, though Thom had the impression that the man had intended to do so regardless.

It seemed that Justin was the better bargainer today. Thom wondered if the abbot would have been so bold if he had known that Merlin was one of the men he had confronted.

The four magicians and three monastics left the boat and headed to a building next to the harbor master's office. It was a low-ceilinged building meant for people much shorter than humans. Merlin rapped on the bright-yellow door. When a young pixie woman answered, he asked to see one of the elders.

She gave a slight nod and then closed the door, leaving them out in the cold.

As they stood out there, the fog came back, its tendrils brushing them with cool droplets. Finally, a white-haired pixie came to the door, his face lined with age and highlighted by elaborate tattoo swirls in dark red ink.

"What do you want of me?" His voice was deep for such a short fellow—only the height of a ten-year-old. But Thom had grown accustomed to pixies while traveling the Road of Leaves and wasn't particularly surprised at encountering a child-sized man.

Merlin touched the edge of the hood he wore just as he let go of his disguise. The sudden ceasing of magic's rhythm around Merlin was obvious to Thom and apparently the pixie noticed some change too, for he tilted his head as he gazed into the shadows of Merlin's hood.

"No names are to be spoken, elder, but I think you recognize me."

The small man frowned. "Indeed, I do. Why are you here?"

"We need to get to Haven House quickly."

The pixie elder raised a white eyebrow, causing his forehead tattoos to wrinkle on that side. "Then you had better stop dawdling at my door and start hiking. You have many miles to cover."

"Do I not deserve better than your insolence?" asked Merlin pointedly. "The galleys that carried us are continuing downriver. We need pixie boats to carry us around the isle."

"I do not disrespect you. We no longer sail to the far side of the isle, for it is too dangerous now. If you want to reach your retreat home then you must get there overland."

"Are the sea serpents infesting this Waywater too?"

"That would not keep us away. No, it is sorcerers that we wish to avoid." The elder looked over at Levitanus. "I would suggest that you and that other one cease with your extravagant use of magic. There are many around who can hear such things and not all are friendly."

"They are here already? How many?" asked Merlin, stepping closer.

The pixie looked up at the master magician with a steady gaze. "Why not ask the Wizard Weston? He has seen far more than I, for the Dark Ones have been avoiding Fog Town. Stop filling my doorway and get on with your hike. You, of all people, have no need for a guide. And before you ask, none of my kind will go with you. Our duty is to help defend the Road of Waters and it is not at risk; this is some feud between you human magicians. My people will keep their distance from your squabbling, for our innate magic is too much of a temptation. Some of us have already paid the ultimate price just this week." He paused, almost daring Merlin to argue with him. When the wizard didn't reply, the pixie ended their conversation. "May your travels be swift and uneventful... though I doubt either will be the case." He closed the door, not waiting for any parting words.

Thom expected Merlin to bang on the door after such disrespect, but the wizard remained calm. He looked over at Levitanus and they exchanged a nod. Thom's master raised his hood, letting go of the disguising magic. 'Reginald' was gone.

Thom noted their interaction even while his thoughts came back to what the elder had implied. Someone was killing pixies to render them into magical elements. It made his stomach turn. Thom didn't look toward Francis but he knew the monk would consider this more proof of magic's evil. Thom wasn't certain that Francis was wrong; he just doubted that renouncing the use of magic was the correct response to others' cruelty.

Merlin turned to face all of them. His features lay hidden within the deep hood of his cloak but he still pulled it down a bit more, exposing an aged hand. "This changes much. I had not expected the danger to be imminent. Father Abbot, you should return to the boats with your brethren. I cannot protect you..."

"It changes nothing, magician," replied Justin. "I know that we walk into danger but I have given my word to the king. I am determined to reach his side and serve as his counselor, for he will need good advice- especially now."

There was a moment of silence as the two stared at each other, two strong-willed men used to commanding. Thom had expected the abbot to back down, but it was the wizard who finally looked away.

"So be it," said Merlin, "but anyone who falters will be left behind. I have no time to coddle the tender or the timid."

"Lead on, apprentice. We will keep up." By his tone, the abbot made it clear that he knew the magician was not the lowly person he had pretended to be.

Merlin strode off without another word, taking one of the wooden walkways that led deeper into the town. Everyone else followed, as the mist thickened even more.

Thom walked behind Levitanus and Vivien, just in front of Justin and the monks. He was tempted to slow down and let Francis catch up, for he wanted to ask the monk so many questions, but he resisted. There were just too many secrets in this group, but the one secret he wanted to respect was Francis' desire to remain unnoticed by the other magicians.

So Thom concentrated on the town around him as Merlin led them along its planked ways and over numerous bridges. He saw others, but never nearby. It seemed the townsfolk wanted to avoid such a large group of strangers, choosing to cross to the other side of a channel or to take stairs to one of the second-floor walkways. Thom gazed into some of the open shops they passed but no shopkeep tried to lure him in. He saw a pair of produce boats pole by in the hamlet's channels heading downstream to the harbor, but the vendors didn't call out their wares. It seemed that no one wanted to attract attention. Maybe they were making a delivery to some warehouse rather than selling as they moved through the settlement.

He wondered what kind of people would choose to live in this misty place, for it had all the burdens of living in an enchantment without the sunshine and bustle of Camelot. These humans would still have to travel out of the Road of Waters regularly to avoid becoming strange, and they would be dependent on river galleys for all trade and transport. It seemed a dreary place to call home.

The fog grew thicker, settling between the buildings and hovering over the water channels they crossed. Thom pulled his cloak tighter and lifted its hood as everything became damp. He walked in silence, as did the others.

Merlin was crossing another bridge when he suddenly lifted his hand to signal a stop. He looked to the left, up the canal, and whispered something to Levitanus. Thomas heard Vivien ask what was wrong.

"Quiet, woman," rebuked Merlin in a whisper, "and train your inner ear better. Someone is starting an enchantment."

Thom strained to hear, but caught nothing. He heard some shuffling behind him and looked back. Francis was leading the abbot and Bart to shelter up against a nearby shop. Maybe Francis' hearing was more sensitive.

Thom would have followed them but he knew better than to make any disturbance when two masters were concentrating.

Finally, he heard something- a new rhythm of magic forming. An enchantment was being crafted, but Thomas didn't recognize it. The fog shredded, wisps caught in a sudden wind. The stiff breeze made Thom swallow nervously, for he remembered the disturbing winds of the Road of Leaves. But he heard nothing wrong with the Road of Waters' magic.

"Hurry!" ordered Merlin, finally looking back at the others. "Cross the bridge and get up that stairway."

He didn't wait to see if anyone complied, but strode quickly off the bridge and to the wooden stairs that he had indicated. Levitanus gave Thomas a commanding wave and hurried to follow. Vivien lifted her long dress and scurried over the bridge.

Thom chased after them, rushing onto the bridge. As he crossed over the canal, he looked up its length. The wind now blew so hard that his eyes watered. He noticed that the water seemed lower but he could hear a rumble a few blocks away- heard it with both his ears and his inner ear. He slowed as he tried to understand what was happening.

"Keep running!" yelled Francis.

Thom realized that the three monastics were charging past him.

"Run or drown," shouted Francis, again urging him onward.

Thom ran, although he still didn't understand what was happening. The four of them made it over the bridge and onto the stairway just as that rumbling turned into a roar. Astonished, Thom looked down the stairway, over the monks' heads, to see the bridge now gone and a wall of water charging down the canal. He quickly turned back and hurried up the last few steps as the building they were on started to shiver.

"Use no magic," snapped Merlin to the others. "They cannot find us as long as we keep our talent unused."

"I think we should keep going," stated Justin, "for this structure groans from the water's pressure."

Merlin was already moving, following the second-floor walkway past closed doors and across a narrow bridge to the next building on that block. As Thom followed, he heard the first building creaking and cracking under the water's pressure but it didn't crumble. The second-floor walkway continued until the block's end, but then they were confronted with a wide gap. Thom joined the others at the railing to look down at another flooded canal, muddy water rushing past at a furious speed.

There was no way over to the far side. The water had washed away the bridges and lower walkways. It now crashed against the buildings that lined the canal. Thom watched as it ripped away a door on the building across the way and poured inside, to bubble out a window and flow on, now cluttered with someone's belongings.

The building at their backs creaked and then Thom heard a loud snap and their perch suddenly crumbled. Thom and the others plunged toward the ugly flood.

TWENTY-ONE

Rushing Water

Thom grabbed the railing with his free hand then wrapped his other around it too, barely holding onto his staff, as the walkway dropped five feet and then came to a jarring stop. Just as he took another ragged breath, the whole thing began to sway outward and tilt them toward the roaring waters. When it stopped this time, Thom was staring straight down at the flood. He heard the waters roar, someone yelling, and the walkway cracking. His own voice was scared out of him.

The walkway began to move again, swaying to the side and then dropping straight down.

Cold water rushed over Thom as he clung to the railing. He tried to shout and inhaled water instead. He could see nothing in that muddy flood.

The walkway held together for a moment, bobbing to the churning surface. Thom gasped for breath in the spray-filled air. He was aware of others clinging to the railing as well but he wasn't sure who they were. Desperate, he looked around for a way out of the flood, but saw only churning water. The still-standing buildings blurred as the waters rushed him past.

He was going to die now, never making it to master magician. He was going to die and Adele would never hear of it.

The walkway swirled into an eddy, up a side canal, and then crashed into another building. It rammed a still-clinging bottom floor walkway, ripping open the side of the building. Thom lost his grip and tumbled over the railing, into the soaked ruins of someone's bedroom. Sputtering, he staggered to his feet as the water swirled through the room. Surprisingly, he still had his staff in hand and knapsack on his back. Wild-eyed, he looked around the dingy place. He saw that Vivien had also been knocked off and was now getting to her feet nearby. He saw none of the others.

The walkway began to move again, sliding along the side of the building and crushing more of the wall as it moved.

Thom considered leaping back onto the thing, for he feared that water would sweep in after it left and flush him out into the flood.

"Don't do it!" yelled Vivien, as if reading his thoughts. "Can't you hear the change in the magic?"

Thom gave her a puzzled look, before realizing what she meant. The enchantment that had been driving the flood was now over. In his panic, he hadn't noticed.

He didn't try climbing onto the still-moving walkway. It slid past and then ripped away, swirling off in the flood. Water rushed in after the blockage cleared, but not any higher than his ankles. He and Vivien were able to resist its pull.

Soon the water level dropped, leaving behind just puddles and drips.

"Do you think anyone else survived?" asked Thom, now able to think beyond his own life.

"Let us look around," she replied, stepping carefully around the ruins of a wardrobe. She seemed dismayed by the wetness all around her and yet acted unaware of her own bedraggled appearance.

She kindled the jewel set in the head of her staff, illuminating the soggy room in a greenish light, but it only showed that there was no one else with them. Thom tried to sense how she lit her staff but failed, just adding to his frustrations.

He followed her to the edge and looked out at the ruins beyond. The canals were nearly to normal level, although debris cluttered the flow. He saw nothing of the walkway they had been riding on, except for a section of it still jammed into a room to their left.

"I think we can climb down to the ground over here," said Vivien, as she leaned over the side.

Thom followed her gaze and saw a possible path, though he was unsure of the building's soundness. He looked over his shoulder, wondering if there might be another way out of here, but saw no doors or other openings. Apparently, this had been a one-room domicile. When he turned back, Vivien was already climbing over the broken side. Seeing no alternative, Thom followed.

The ground was a muddy mess along the canal bank and under the building. Like many of the structures in Fog Town, this one was elevated above the ground and now water lingered in the darkness underneath it, a small lake around its support posts. The building loomed over Thom and Vivien, broken siding dangling in the air and rubbish and mud plastered on everything. Water dripped everywhere.

Thom nearly fell as he slipped and slid with each step. "Can you see any of the others?"

"Hello!" shouted Vivien, looking up at the damaged place.

A few faces peeked from the wreckage, but no one from their group. None of these locals called for help nor did they ask if the two strangers needed aid.

"We will need to search them out," said Thom, debating if he should climb back up and search other damaged rooms.

"Or go on without them," noted Vivien.

Thom stared at her, shocked.

She shrugged. "You need not glare at me. Unlike you, I was not close to any of them and a search will most likely be just a futile delay." She sighed when Thom's stare didn't lessen. "Well, maybe we can look for the masters. We will need someone to help us find our way to the king. But be forewarned, if we find anything, it will most likely be a corpse."

Thom frowned at the thought but gave her a slight nod anyway. "I think we should start up there." He pointed to where a segment of walkway still dangled from the side of the building.

"It looks ready to break free," Vivien replied. "Can you climb up without getting under it?"

"I think so." Thom trudged through the mud to a pile of debris. With caution, he climbed up the soaked boards until he was high enough to grab hold of the studs that had once supported this building's walkway. He pulled himself up and now stood on two of those splintered ends. He was within reach of the walkway remains but he didn't dare touch it.

He leaned over to look through the gap where the wooden promenade had torn into someone's abode and called out for the others. "Hello? Master? Francis? Anyone?"

He heard nothing and saw no movement except drips of water, but there was an open doorway at the back of the exposed room. He wondered if anyone had retreated deeper into the building and was looking for a safe way to climb inside and investigate when he heard someone call his name.

"Thomas."

He leaned outward and looked up. Francis stood on the building's roof.

Thom grinned with relief. "Is everyone with you?"

"Only the abbot."

"How did you get up there?"

"We found a passage from the room we crashed into."

The monk looked over as Justin came up beside him and also looked down.

"There is a stairway on the far side of the building," the abbot said, gesturing to his right. "I just investigated and it seems sound."

"Then we will meet you at the base of those stairs," yelled out Vivien, entering the conversation. "Come back down here, Thomas, so that we can get going."

"What about the others?" Thom asked.

"Let us reunite, then we can plan our search together," suggested Justin.

* * *

When Thom and Vivien arrived at the stairway, a crowd had gathered to share tears and stories. But the locals avoided the strangers. A few grudgingly answered questions from Father Justin and Francis, but the clerics learned nothing about their missing companions.

For the next few hours, they searched through the ruins. They were able to help two people pinned under wreckage, but they found no trace of the others.

Francis suggested that they search downstream, so they went through the remains of two more buildings before reaching the next canal. It took some maneuvering to get across, since the bridges were all washed away in this area, but they finally paddled over on some floating debris.

They didn't find any of their lost companions and were chased off by some angry residents who accused them of being scavengers, so they had to hurriedly cross a second-floor walkway that had survived. The third block had far less damage.

It was here that they finally found two of them: a worried Bartholomew sitting in protective watch over Levitanus, who was lying on his back among the rubble of what had been a dock under one of the tall buildings.

Thomas hurried to the wizard's side.

Levitanus' eyes opened and he lifted his head, reaching out for Thom's hand. "Help me up."

He did as told but still asked, "Are you hurt, master?"

Levitanus grunted as he stood, leaning heavily against his student. "My injuries will not kill me."

He pushed off Francis' attempt to inspect his ribs and then stared hard at the man. "You! So that is why you kept your hood up." Levitanus glared at Justin. "My companion was right; you are troublesome, Father Abbot."

The abbot shrugged. "Yes, Francis concealed his identity, but you did the same, master magician. I recognize you, Wizard Levitanus, even if we have rarely crossed paths at Camelot. Besides, Brother Francis is no longer one of yours, so you have no say over where he goes. He is here under my protection."

Thom's master grunted his annoyance. "Do not use my name, for some sorcerers are gifted at listening for such things." He looked over at Vivien. "Where is our other companion?"

"We have not found him yet," she replied.

"That is not good." He pushed away from Thomas to stand on his own, though he needed two brace himself against a pier. "We will need to search him out."

"Pardon my bluntness, magician, but what if your companion is dead?" asked Justin.

"Then we have failed. Not only will the kingdom fall but the city and its Ways will unravel."

Justin frowned. "So that is the identity of your disguised partner," he deduced, without saying the name aloud.

"Maybe we can find him by using the right enchantment," said Vivien, removing her knapsack and starting to open it.

Francis stepped near and lightly restrained her small hand. "Please do no such thing, journeywoman. Any magic use will bring us to our enemy's attention. Your missing magician lives and is well for now."

She yanked her pack away from him. "How can you declare that, monk? Has God given you some miraculous insight?" Her snide tone announced her doubt of that.

Francis ignored her sharp tongue and simply answered her question. "I know because the Road of Waters' enchantment is still whole and hale. Listen to it, Journeywoman Vivien, and tell me if I am wrong."

Vivien might be easily offended but she was also an intelligent woman; she proved that by pausing and doing just as the monk said. Thom did likewise and found no faltering in the enchantment. It kept a rhythmic hum in the background, faint but strong.

Levitanus grunted again. "The outcast is right. He must still be alive, for the enchantment shows no strain."

"Well, what shall we do now?" she asked. "It could take days to find one man among the flood damage. Can we delay reaching the king for so long?"

Thom's master sighed, then pointed at him. "Help find my staff in all this rubble. I sense it nearby but I cannot see it and Brother Bartholomew was unable to spot it. I will need to lean on it as a walking staff. We have many miles to go and time is short." He turned his attention to big Bart. "You look strong and able, monk. Can you find your way back to the pixies' elder house?"

Bart nodded. "Yes sir, I think I can… I mean I will go… um, I mean if the Father Abbot allows it I will do as you bid."

"The abbot will not object, for this will speed up our leaving. Go fetch at least one of the elders back here." Levitanus paused, expectantly. When Bart still hesitated, he made a shooing motion at him. "Go, monk. Get me a pixie elder."

Bart still hesitated until he received a nod from his superior, then he set off.

Before he had gone too far, Levitanus called out after him. "One more thing, monk. You have my thanks for digging me out. You are a good man and most certainly a strong one."

Bartholomew gave a quick glance over his shoulder but kept going. Thom thought it was a look of surprise.

"Why are you still standing there staring after that monk? Find my staff, Thomas."

Embarrassed, he nodded to his master and started searching through the rubble. While he searched, he heard the others still talking.

"What is your plan, wizard?" asked the abbot.

"The pixies will have to find my companion and see to his care. We do need to get to the king, for danger is pressing in on him from all sides."

Thom could tell by his master's tone that he wasn't pleased with the situation.

"You and your monks can help the pixies in their search…"

"I think not, magician. The three of us are going to King Arthur too. We will either walk at your side or we will be chasing your heels. Leave off your pride, Lev… wizard. You might find that we can be of help."

His teacher said nothing, but Thom could imagine that Levitanus was scowling.

* * *

Thom finally found his master's staff and wiped the worst of the mud off it. As he made his way through the rubble to where the wizard now sat, he noticed that Brother Bart was approaching in a trio of small boats filled with a half-dozen pixies and the monks they had left behind at the river galleys. As Thom neared the ruined docks from behind his master, he saw the abbot draw close and he overheard their brief conversation.

"It looks like you will get your monastic searchers after all," noted Abbot Justin as he leaned over the sitting wizard.

"Are any of them part of the League?" asked his master, looking up at the monastic.

"Only Bartholomew, and he is going on with us. The others would not be good candidates. And before you ask, I haven't been able to convince Francis to join."

Levitanus grunted. "That's not surprising, considering his strong opinions."

"Why do you think we were thrown together on this trip? Do you think someone suspects something?"

"At the royal court and at the guild house, people are always scheming or worrying about the plotting of others. However, I do not think any of them have put us together."

"May it stay that way a long time," replied the abbot, straightening up.

Thom realized he might be accused of spying, so he purposely stepped on a brittle board and then spoke out. "Master, I finally found it."

Levitanus looked over his shoulder. "Good, and just in time. The brother has returned with the pixies."

The abbot smiled toward Thom but then moved to greet his returning brother.

Levitanus accepted his staff back, running his hands down its length to check its soundness. Once satisfied, he used it to get to his feet and then limped toward the arriving pixies.

As Thom followed him, he wondered about the League they mentioned and why monks were in some kind of secretive group. His master wasn't particularly religious, so why was he interested in something the abbot was organizing? Thom had never seen a monastic at the cottage and when he had traveled with his mentor there had been minimal interaction with any clergy. He also wondered if the two had wanted him to overhear their conversation and, if so, why?

Levitanus thanked the pixies for coming and even welcomed the additional monks, then suggested they move up out of the muck.

The pixies agreed, tying up their crafts on what remained of the dock and then they all took a wooden stairway up. As Thom helped his master maneuver the stairs, he noted that in this area it looked like the flood hadn't made it above the first few treads.

At the first level they found all as it should be. From this height, Thomas could see that the flood had roared down just one channel, causing only minimal damage to the neighboring waterways. It had been definitely directed along the route their party had been using.

Thom shivered and it wasn't just because he was soaked and muddy.

He listened as his master and the pixies talked. Surprisingly, his master openly admitted it was Merlin who was missing from their party and asked the pixies to help find him. He used his name only once, but at least that secret was now revealed. The pixies agreed with the plan.

"Elder Trovaro, we must be going, for I fear our king needs us," Levitanus stated to the pixie leader. "If the enemy is so bold as to flood a city, then they are either cruel or desperate, or maybe both. Whoever attacked us might not have known who was in our party, but they knew we were magicians."

The elder nodded at the dirty staff, to which the wizard clung. "Even Fog Town's people noticed four jewel-topped sticks passing their doorways. The lack of robes does not hide you when you parade with such things. They must be like war banners to the sorcerers, showing your position from afar even when they are not kindled."

"Most likely, but you know very well that the staffs help us with our crafting. However they found us, they knew we had arrived and wanted to stop us. At least none of us died, but I am not so certain about all the townspeople. Look at the damage." He let go of his staff with one hand and pointed at the mess that was in the canal below them. "Please help the townspeople to dig out their people and do your best to aid the other magician. See to his needs and let him know where we have gone."

"You know that we will," replied the older pixie. "Those affected along these flooded canals are our neighbors. As for your companion, he will be found and helped on his way. You are certain that he has sustained no serious injury?"

"He is likely as bedraggled as I am, but I doubt much worse. He is certainly not dead or else we would hear it in the enchantment that surrounds us."

"We will find him if he is still in Fog Town, but have you considered that maybe he is hale, angry, and in pursuit?"

Levitanus nodded. "Yes. That would be like him, to charge off without us. That is another reason why I do not want to linger here. The searching needs to be done, but it will take some time to wade through all this muck and each hour means more danger for King Arthur."

"We will do the work. Go on and warn that headstrong king who was so foolish as to bring his battles onto the Road of Waters."

Eric Loren

TWENTY-TWO

Keeper of the Waters

The six travelers didn't make it past the outskirts of Fog Town that day because they were all soaked and shivering. Although Levitanus was anxious to get to the king as quickly as possible, even he had to admit their limitations for he was limping badly. They stopped for the night at an inn on the hamlet's edge, a simple establishment that most likely catered to traders who came out this way to trade with loggers and farmers who worked the land that sloped up from Fog Town. The inn had only five small rooms and two of those were already occupied, but it was dry and relatively warm. They washed clothes and themselves, ate a hearty stew, and bedded down for the night. The tiny rooms went to Levitanus, Abbot Justin, and Vivien. Thom and the two monks had to settle for the hard floor of the common room in front of the fire. Their clothes hung on lines above their heads. It seemed that it was a common practice on the Isle of Mists to dry clothing indoors, for the innkeeper already had the hooks set in the walls and needed only to bring out the coils of clothesline and stretch them in place.

In the early morning, before the other two guests were even awake, they had a hot breakfast of porridge, ham, and warm tea. The three monastics spent a few minutes in quiet prayer, but they must have shortened their usual morning devotions, because they were ready to go when the others were, helping to take down hanging clothes and pack. Soon, the six were out the door into another damp day. The dawn had fitfully arrived, barely lightening the gray sky as they started their march across the Isle of Mists.

They had been on the road for less than an hour when they all heard horn calls from somewhere higher up the island's slopes, and then answering calls from even farther away. All of them looked to Levitanus for an explanation.

"It is the centaurs' normal morning challenges and greetings. There are many of them who live on this island. You will hear such horn blows most mornings and evenings."

"Is there any message in what they are sounding?" asked the abbot.

Levitanus nodded. "It does not translate directly into words, but I would say that this morning's notes were typical. They tell others where they are and tell them to keep away from their chosen pastures. It is like a greeting and warning combined."

They walked on and, at first, the clouds stayed higher, letting them see the lands around the dirt road they followed. They passed tilled fields and thick woodlots. However, by mid-morning the mists swirled around them, obscuring much. The worked lands gave over to the wilds of dark forest made shadowy by the incoming fog.

They had been quietly walking for about a few hours when a screech echoed through the woods around them. It was a sound that Thom remembered from his harrowing trip along the Road of Leaves and it made him shiver. The sound brought them all to a stop.

"What was that?" asked Bart.

"A griffin," replied Vivien, "but they usually hunt at dawn or dusk. Something sends it out during the day."

"Someone drives the beast," said Francis in a soft voice. "They push it to hunt, most likely for us."

"What do you know of griffins, monk?" demanded Vivien in a whispered yet accusatory tone.

"Thomas and I fought one not long ago," he replied.

Her intensity turned on Thom. "You certainly have many secrets, journeyman. You fought a griffin and lived?"

"The others with me did most of the fighting," he replied. He didn't want her to think he was a braggart as well, but he also didn't want to admit how the dying griffin collapsed on top of him, nearly suffocating him with its weight. "Pixie hunters brought it down with arrows dipped in dryad poison."

"Well, we have neither pixie hunter nor dryad poison," stated Levitanus softly but adamantly, "and griffins hunt by sight and sound as well as scent. Keep moving, but no more talking until it passes."

The master magician walked on, still using his wizard's staff heavily as a walking staff but moving better than he had yesterday. The others followed, trying to be as quiet as they could.

When the griffin cried out again, the sound was farther away. Still, they did their best to make no noise as they hiked onward. By the next call, they knew it had missed and was flying away from them, toward another part of the forested isle.

"Well, we are safe from it for now," declared Levitanus in a normal volume, motioning for them to keep moving.

* * *

Near midday the heard centaur horns again. Closer this time.

Levitanus to listen more carefully, then suddenly said, "We will change directions at the next crossroad. We must go north."

"What is this, sir?" protested Vivien. "That is not the usual land route to Haven Home or the Keeper's house."

"You detour us?" asked the abbot. "Is that wise, when you have been saying how urgent it is for us to hurry to the king's side."

"I need to seek out the Road of Waters' keeper, and he is on the move. That is all that I will let you know, Father Abbot, for this is guild business. We go north."

Abbot Justin didn't argue any further but his countenance showed his disapproval.

Thom was close enough to the monks to overhear what Francis whispered to the abbot. "The centaurs warn of danger. There was more in their calls but I'm not that adept at their horn language."

Thom looked from them to his master and back. There was just too much secrecy on this trip.

* * *

They hiked for a half-hour more before finding a crossroad, then Levitanus led them northward. The fog lifted to a gray overcast, but there wasn't much to see, just trees in all directions. Thom did spot a few magical plants but there was no time for harvesting anything. He could guess their destination: the home of the Wizard Weston, Keeper of the Road of Waters. He wondered if the wizard had pixie servants like Wizard Cruthen had on the Road of Leaves.

The trail twisted and turned, eventually crossing a ridge. The trees thinned on a particularly steep slope and revealed a cove below them, one that was upriver from Fog Town. Thom had just caught a glimpse of the water when Levitanus motioned everyone to a stop. Soon it was obvious what had caused him to pause. Hooves thundered toward them.

"I hear horses," said Bart.

"There are no horses on the Road of Waters," corrected Francis, "except aboard some of the boats. No, you hear centaurs coming our way."

"Shouldn't we run?" asked Bart. "Maybe we can elude them among that dense thicket over there."

"They have our scent," said Levitanus. "It would do us no good to flee. We will wait here and see what they want. Do nothing to provoke them."

Thom hoped it wasn't to collect his head on a spear.

A herd of eight male centaurs came into view, crashing through the underbrush- at least Thom thought they might be called a herd.

The horse-men rushed at them and encircled the group, their hooves kicking up dirt and grass. As they raced around the humans, the centaurs twisted their upper bodies and aimed their bows at the trespassers. In response, the humans pressed together, back-to-back, in a tight knot within the milling circle.

One of centaurs sounded a horn, painfully loud from this close, bringing the huge beings to a halt. They targeted the humans, bows steadily aimed at the trespassers. Each centaur's lower half was that of a powerful horse, standing as tall as the greatest dray horse that Thom had ever seen. The human torso towered up from that, making even the shortest centaur at least twice Big Bart's height.

Levitanus threw back his hood to reveal himself and began to yell at the huge beings, motioning for them to move on. They apparently didn't understand. No bow lowered; no horse-man turned. When he gave up on his unheeded commands, silence descended on the small clearing.

Thom noticed that the centaurs' eyes were dark and steely. They didn't seem to blink or look away. One in particular- a curly-haired, auburn-coated centaur- had his eyes locked on Thom. It made the journeyman very conscious of his every move, not wanting to provoke the archer.

Another horn sounded, from among the woods this time, coming closer with each blowing. Thom heard an enchantment begin in that direction, but was too rattled to clearly hear what it was. The centaurs seemed to be waiting for this other one to arrive.

Suddenly, a human came running out from among the trees- a man in dew-stained clothing, his long white hair flowing behind him as he raced toward them. He cupped a fireball in his upheld right hand, the flames brightly lighting one side of his face while leaving the other side in shadow. In his left hand was the long horn he had been sounding.

Thom wondered how the magician kept his unruly hair from getting too close to the fire.

"Weston! Call off your guards!" bellowed Levitanus.

The man didn't slow or extinguish the fireball. He yelled back in the breathless voice of someone who had been running a long while. "Who are you?"

Levitanus cursed. "You know me, you wild-haired wretch. We journeyed together in our youth. Look at me, you dolt. You know my visage and, if you do not call off your horse-men, you will also know my anger."

Wizard Weston slowed to a stop and studied the humans carefully. Thom had the distinct feeling that he was listening for any magic in use.

"Weston…"

Thom clearly heard the warning in Levitanus' voice but he wondered if the other magician heard it too. It became clear that the man did, for he dropped the fireball, letting it sputter out among the dew-soaked grasses. He raised his horn and blew a series of short blasts.

Instantly, the centaurs responded. They lowered their bows and most of them turned and raced off in different directions, some heading up the trail while others went down. A few others headed off into the woods. Two remained though, moving closer to Weston.

"Why are you not in your home?" asked Levitanus. "Does something stir along the Waters?"

The other laughed, a cold guffaw of cynicism. "You are not that naive. You are well aware of what stirs here, since you and Merlin most likely provoked some of it. I wish you had aimed the Dark Ones elsewhere. Why not back at the Road of Leaves, since it was already disrupted?"

"The king chose this ground," replied Levitanus.

"Since when does Arthur make any choices without Merlin's nod of approval? Merlin allowed my Waters to be disturbed. For that I will not forgive him."

"I sense no mis-beat in the enchantments' rhythms. My inner ear is not as sensitive to its beat as yours, but I should be able to hear something…"

"Oh, stop your word games, Levitanus." Weston's tone spoke of his anger. "You are as much a part of this magic as I am. You can feel it inside as well as hear it."

"Weston!"

Thom had never heard his master issue such a sharp one-word rebuke.

Weston paused, looking over the group. "I spoke of something better left unsaid. What of it, Levitanus? Monks will not understand such words." He then pointed at Thom and Vivien. "Are those other two merely journeymen? Well then, they heard a hint of something a bit early. That is all."

Thom was confused about what they were implying. He looked to see if Vivien understood and realized she was listening intently. Apparently, she grasped something about this inner feeling that the wizards spoke of.

"You are a fool, Weston. I do not worry about them. You spoke too freely in the presence of the Rogue."

"The wizard killer? Here? With you?" Weston looked worriedly at Thom and then at the monks.

In response, Francis lowered his cowl and Thom realized that the two wizards had been talking about his monastic friend.

"It was not a wizard I killed, but a sorcerer," replied Francis. "I also have a name, Keeper. I am known as Brother Francis now and I no longer care for the guild's petty secrets. Besides, I am well aware of the inner feeling of the greater enchantments. The wizard revealed nothing new to me."

"Why do you bring him here? Especially now."

"I brought him," said Abbot Justin, speaking up for the first time. "The Road of Waters is free to anyone. The guild never banned him from any of the Ways."

"Maybe we need to rectify that," grumbled Levitanus.

"I think not, wizard. He is a brother at Saint Barnabas so he needs to be able to travel the Ways. How else could he get to our home in Camelot?"

"Let him join some other monastery. Such a troublemaker should not be anywhere near the king's city."

Thom didn't like what his master was implying about his friend. Francis was neither rogue nor troublemaker. He was just a man who had renounced the guild and his training as a magician.

"I am not your priority now," said Francis. "What are your fears about the Waters, magician? Is it ready to unravel like the Road of Leaves?"

Weston frowned at Francis' question. When he answered, he directed his words toward Levitanus. "The Waters are sound, but so much inside of the enchantment is stirred up. Sea serpents have been lured inside; dangerous magic has been used. Worse, someone has been harvesting elements without permission."

"Poachers again?" asked Levitanus.

Weston shook his head no. "This is too wanton to be some mere collector. Some magician or sorcerer is stealing, stockpiling their box with very particular powders."

"So that is why you have left your abode? To hunt them down? That might not be the wisest course to take."

Weston gave a short laugh. "I am not that foolish, Levitanus. I am fleeing. Too much trouble is heading toward the Isle of Mists and I cannot risk getting caught in all of it. I will go elsewhere to concentrate on maintaining the Road of Waters."

"What have you heard?" asked Levitanus.

The question implied two meanings to Thom: rumors and the magical whispers heard only by an inner ear.

TWENTY-THREE

Across the Isle

The Wizard Weston, keeper of the Road of Waters, looked over his shoulder like a frightened boy. He seemed to take comfort in the nearness of the two centaurs. He turned back to his fellow wizard and finally answered Levitanus' question.

"Sorcerer Dalrake and his allies are coming. This is war, Levitanus. It has finally come. It will be magician against magician, to the rue of all."

"You have seen them? Where are they?"

"I have not seen them yet, but Dalrake sent me a message, delivered by crow. He orders me to step aside or die."

Levitanus stepped close, face to face with his comrade. His countenance darkened in anger and his words came out in sharp bites. "You obey him now?"

Weston took a step back and raised a hand in pleading. "No, I do not. I assure you that I am still loyal to the guild… It is just that my first duty is to the Waters. If something happens to me, then the enchanted Way will start to unravel. You, of all people, should know that."

"So you run." Levitanus' tone dripped with contempt. "You go to the other enchantment focal?"

Weston looked at the others in the group, hesitating. He looked around the clearing. Finally, he gave a slight nod, though he still didn't look back at the other wizard.

Thom had no idea what an enchantment focal was, but then he was barely past his apprenticeship. Maybe he could ask his master about it later, but he doubted Levitanus would answer him beyond another riddle. Francis might be more open, but the monk detested talking about magic. What about Vivien? He looked at her, considering.

She noticed his attention and frowned at him.

No, she wouldn't answer his questions either. Thom sighed.

"I had hoped that you would aid us in crossing the isle and getting help for the king."

"I will speak with the other Keepers, but I cannot offer more direct aid for I will not neglect my duties."

"Your responsibilities are well known to me," replied Levitanus, "and I do not ask you to neglect them. Convince the centaur mares to bring the herds to our side."

Weston shook his head in refusal. "They rarely come to even the most urgent of calls; I cannot linger here waiting for them to come. It is too dangerous."

Levitanus stepped close to Weston again, ignoring a warning sound from one of the centaurs. "Run away then, but remember your duty to the Road of Waters. Now is not the time to neglect any of the enchantments. No matter what happens with the sorcerers, keep the Waters whole."

Weston met the other's stare and nodded again. His reply was barely above a whisper. "I will."

Levitanus thrust out his hand. "Give me your horn. You choose not to help, but maybe some of the herds will come to my call."

Weston frowned but handed over the long horn he held.

"Go now. Run away, Weston. Your fear creates a stench in the air." Levitanus dismissed him, even turning his back on the wizard.

Thom watched the Keeper's jaw tighten and his eyes blaze with anger, but Weston did not lash out. Instead, he turned away too, motioning the centaurs near and talking softly with them. One of them handed over his horn to the wizard, then the three of them ran off into the woods, the centaurs keeping to a mere trot for the wizard's sake.

"What of Thomas and I?" asked Vivien. "The council ordered us to join Weston. Are we to chase after him?"

"No," replied Levitanus. "That was just a ruse, as you certainly have realized by now. The real plan was for you to help protect the queen while Merlin and I join those around the king."

"And what of him?" asked Vivien, indicating Thom.

"I insisted on bringing him because he is in dire need of more training."

Vivien nodded. "At least someone finally admits it. I've never seen so young a journeyman."

"He is just starting the road you have almost completed," said Levitanus, "and it will not an easy road for him, so leave off your jealousy. Journeywoman, I would rather you focus on ways you can protect the queen and her ladies. Consider what enchantments you can use and when it would be appropriate. You are a magician and almost a wizardess, you know the importance of proper focus."

"My apologies, Founder," she replied, lowering her eyes in contrition.

He nodded and then said, "We will have to pick up our pace now, after this worthless detour. I thought Weston was in imminent danger, not that he was fleeing."

He turned to Thomas. "I will need you near, should my injured leg cause me to stumble." He handed the horn to him. "I will sound this tomorrow, when we are well away from the Keeper. No centaur stallion-man would come near to such a craven man, let alone a mare-woman."

Levitanus then turned to the others. "I want to make it across the island's spine before nightfall. We need to get to the king."

Before anyone could reply, the wizard set off, back up the trail they had just come down. With the aid of his staff, he set a strong pace.

The rest of the day they hiked through a wild land absent of any people. It was quiet, without any bird calls, squirrel chatter, or insect buzz. Unnaturally quiet. Thom was very aware that they walked inside an enchantment, a place scorned by non-magical life. Only plants thrived in here, both mundane and magical plants.

Levitanus used the day to test him, having him name the various magical trees, bushes, and flowers they passed.

The quizzing felt odd to Thom, considering all that had recently happened. His master acted like they were back at the country cottage and he treated Thom like he was still just an apprentice.

Thom answered as well as he could, feeling embarrassed whenever his master rebuked him publicly for missing something. Thom doubted that Vivien would have made any of his mistakes. Nor Francis, though Thom doubted that the monk would have answered with anything but silence. But none of them said anything about his lessons even though everyone in the group heard them.

The trail wandered and twisted to avoid crossing the main pasture lands of rival centaur herds, according to Levitanus. They had barely started down the isle's far side by the time evening's darkness forced them to stop.

Levitanus was noticeably limping by now, after such a long hike, but he didn't complain. He just suddenly called them to a halt and assigned evening duties to almost everyone. Only Levitanus and Justin, the two oldest in their party, took a much-needed break to watch.

Bart and Thom gathered wood which Vivien sparked to flame with a stone and flint. Francis did the cooking.

After the meal, Levitanus led Thom and Vivien away from the monastics to share a few words in private. Thom couldn't see his facial expression in the deep darkness, but his words were strong and harsh. "The two of you are to be careful around the Rogue. Do not give ear to any of his ramblings. Is that understood?"

"May I ask why, master?"

"You certainly know why, Thomas. He has betrayed the guild."

"Master, is the monk a sorcerer?" asked Vivien.

"No, not that. But he knows too much about us and our craft and he hates everything that has anything to do with magic. The monk is dangerous. Avoid him."

Thom felt his master was being unfair toward his friend and tried to defend him. "We would never have stopped the attack on the Road of Leaves without his aid."

"Francis helped us greatly there, but do not be lured in by his kind tone or friendly demeanor. In his mind, there is not much of a difference between wizard and sorcerer, between a well-crafted enchantment and the bloody butchery of magical beings. He detests it all."

"But there are only six of us hiking over this island," protested Vivien. "Will it not be obvious that we're avoiding him?"

"I do not care if he is offended. What I do care about is the two of you becoming too friendly with him and then slip up in front of others. They will not be as tolerant as I am. Trust me, you do not want to be known in the guild as a friend of Francis."

"That seems rather harsh," complained Thom. "He has been nothing but helpful to me."

"Nonetheless, he has been declared anathema by the council. If you associate with him and Merlin finds out, you will be tossed from the guild. Do you want that? I think not. So, please give me your word that you will not talk with him. Either of you."

"I give you my word," said Vivien readily.

Thom was a bit slower, causing his master to glare at him. Reluctantly, he spoke up too. "I promise not to talk with Brother Francis."

In the darkness, Thom couldn't see Levitanus' expression, but he still felt it; Levitanus was slow to nod acceptance of Thom's vow, most likely doubting its sincerity.

* * *

The next day their path climbed over a rocky ridge. Even though there was a break in the trees as they scampered over the rocks, the mist shrouded any distant horizon. Instead, they saw only gray in every direction. Listening, Thom could tell the Waywater's edge wasn't that far away, but just by looking it seemed that the fog went on forever.

Francis tried to talk with Thom then, as they stood on top of the rocks, but Thom ignored him. It hurt to turn his back on his friend, but he couldn't disobey his master or jeopardize his place in the guild. He hurried his step to get away from the monk, keeping close to his master as a way to discourage any more attempts at conversation.

At their midday break, someone else sought him out. Vivien. Levitanus was out of sight at the moment, having gone among the trees to relieve himself. Thom was sitting on a damp rock when she came to stand over him.

"Tell me, why is the monk so feared by the wizards?"

Her commanding tone grated on Thom, but he didn't want to lose this opportunity to talk with her. He motioned for her to join him on the boulder, even scooting over to offer her the spot where his trousers had already absorbed most of the moisture.

She hesitated until she saw that he wouldn't answer unless she did, then she daintily sat down next to him.

"Francis was a journeyman once, at the cusp of becoming a master magician, when he was forced to kill his master after that one turned sorcerer." Thom went on to tell her more of what Francis had reluctantly confessed to him. He told her about the monk's hatred of magic, of his renouncing it all and joining the monastery. He also told her about how Francis had been forced to use his knowledge again to help them save the Road of Leaves.

When Thom finished, she was silent for a time, just staring off into the woods. Finally, she looked over at where Francis sat with Justin and Bart. "He is truly named Rogue then, though certainly not a failure. I could almost respect such a man for his convictions. Almost. But how can he live, hearing magic all around him but never crafting any of it? How can he renounce such power?" She shook her head and then looked over at Thomas. "Thank you for sharing."

With that, she stood and walked away. Levitanus had stepped back into the clearing, so she walked toward him.

* * *

The trail twisted for a while and then dropped into a ravine to follow a creek downstream. Levitanus had to go slower as their path became rougher, but the others dared not leave the wizard behind. He was their guide now that they had lost Merlin.

Twice more, Francis tried to talk with Thom and the journeyman was forced to be rude to him. When Francis tried to grab his sleeve, he pulled away. When the monk stepped in front of him, Thom walked around without meeting the other's gaze. He felt terrible doing this, but he had given his word to Levitanus.

Someone tried to talk with him a third time, laying a hand on his shoulder. He almost pulled away without looking behind him, but realized the hand was too large to belong to Francis. He turned to find Brother Bartholomew confronting him.

"Pardon me, Journeyman Thomas, but how has my brother offended you?"

The question surprised him. "Francis has done nothing wrong." He gave a quick glance past Bart's large back to where Justin and Francis walked toward them. Thom turned and kept walking, for he didn't want either of them to catch up, yet he didn't protest when Bart fell in at his side.

"Forgive my bluntness, but if he has done nothing wrong, why do you shun him?"

"My master has ordered me to avoid Francis. I am not allowed to talk with him."

Bart made a tsk-tsk sound. "And people say that I serve a demanding master. The Lord has never told me to turn my back on a friend. I am sorry for you, Thomas. It must be hard to obey such unjust orders."

Bart's words made Levitanus sound like a tyrant. Thom disagreed. He knew that his master must have a good reason for his orders, but he felt that Bart wouldn't be convinced by any attempt to argue otherwise. So instead, he asked the monk to explain the situation to Francis.

"I will tell him about your vow, but I do not think it will sooth his pained heart. He misses your friendship."

Bart's word cut to Thom's soul. He wanted to renounce his promise, to run up the trail and embrace his friend and beg forgiveness. However, if there was one thing that had been ingrained into Thomas during his many years of training as a magician, it was obedience to his master. So he controlled his feelings and just gave Bart a nod of thanks.

The monk stopped Thom to give him a hug and then let him walk on. Bart lingered on the side of the road to let Justin and Francis catch up. Thom didn't look back, but hurried his gait to catch up with Vivien and Levitanus.

TWENTY-FOUR

Centaur Call

They never saw the sun that day, just the gray skies overhead that sometimes dropped down to send swirling mists among the trees. Late that afternoon, while they were passing through a dark thicket of birches, they heard magic. Well, all except Bart and the abbot heard it; those two were deaf to such things.

Someone was crafting an enchantment in the distance. Thom recognized some of the elements being used but not the final enchantment that came into being. He looked to his teacher but realized he wouldn't be getting any explanation from Levitanus. The wizard was staring into the distance, as if he could see through the trees.

"It begins," he whispered, just loud enough for Thom to overhear. "I hope we can reach you in time, Arthur."

His master turned to him. "Hand me that horn, Thomas. It is time to call the centaurs, even if it forewarns our enemy."

As he took the extended horn, Levitanus looked at the monks that had been walking behind them. "You should take your brethren farther down the trail, Father Abbot. I will be magically enhancing my horn blast and it might attract another attack. You will be safer if you keep your distance."

The abbot nodded his thanks and led his two followers past the magicians, continuing along the trail. All three of them had become more taciturn, most likely in reaction to Levitanus' declared anathema on Francis. Thom watched them pass with sadness. He wanted to talk with his friend, to hear his dry humor and gain from his wisdom. But that was now forbidden.

Levitanus now concentrated on the students with him. "Vivien, does your magician's box contain the elements needed to craft a Tarn's Call?"

She nodded, swinging her knapsack off her shoulders.

"Wait to open the vials until I order it, for I want to limit the revealing of our position to the shortest time possible," warned Levitanus. "Thomas, get your mixing bowl ready, along with the necessary mundane elements. You are to stir the powders quickly but thoroughly. Pause only long enough for me to add my spittle. The magic must be attuned to me, for I will have to be the one to sound the horn."

Levitanus held the horn in his left hand as he leaned heavily on the staff in his right. He needed them to be his hands for the mixing.

Vivien quickly retrieved the appropriate elements, handing them to Thom.

He mixed them as quickly as he could, adding the mundane elements as directed since this was a new enchantment to him. He was very aware of the noise the elements made.

He held it up for his master to spit into it, then finished the blending. When the mixing was done, Levitanus leaned his staff against the crook in a tree and dipped his hand into the watery paste. He smeared the enchantment on his lips and the horn's end.

The wizard paused a moment to gather his breath and then sounded the centaur horn. Its voice was greatly enhanced, echoing in the inner ear as well. He blew a series of short and long blasts in some code known to the horse-men.

Thom guessed that the clarion call would have been heard by anyone on the island who knew how to listen with their inner ear. The sorcerers would know where to look now.

"Must we wait here for the centaurs?" asked Vivien.

Levitanus grunted, handing the horn back to Thom and accepting the staff his student had retrieved. "No, the centaurs will easily track us. It will be best for us to catch up to the monks and move on before any sorcerer tosses a fireball in our direction. Thomas can tell you about their fondness for fire."

Vivien gave Thom an odd look; he wasn't certain whether it was curiosity or doubt.

* * *

The first dozen centaurs found them two hours later. They charged down the trail and nearly trampled the humans, turning at the last moment and speeding past. Dirt splattered on Thom as he jumped away from their sharp hooves. The twelve galloped on a few more yards and then turned sharply and blocked the road. They drew their bows.

Levitanus kept walking toward them; Thom and the others followed. The wizard didn't stop until the centaurs were towering over him, then he planted his staff into the damp soil and looked up at the lead centaur. The jewel at the head of his staff glowed now, like a warning lantern.

"Do you honor the vow?" asked Levitanus.

The centaur snorted, a horse-like sound. "Our lead mare-women made the vow with Merlin, not you."

"You do not recognize me as one of the refuge makers?"

The horse-man just stared down at the far shorter magician.

"Do you know who I am?" asked the wizard, his voice even more demanding.

"You are Levitanus," blurted out one of the other centaurs.

The leader glared at the one who spoke out and the offender bowed his head slightly to show his contrition and submission to the lead centaur.

"At least one of you has more sense than a steed chasing rutting mares," replied Levitanus.

The insult was obvious, comparing them to mere horses. The lead centaur's head whipped around and he aimed his bow directly at the wizard's chest. Thom saw that the arrow's tip was darkened by some liquid and wondered if it was dryad poison like the pixies used.

"Honor your vow," ordered Levitanus. He seemed unafraid of the certain death pointing his way.

None of the centaurs replied, but a few pawed the ground in agitation.

"Honor it or you shall be banished from this refuge."

The lead centaur kept up his silent threat but some of the others looked disturbed.

"Wyndo, we cannot face exile," one of them whispered harshly at their leader.

"What will the stallion-men do if they learn that we refuse a maker's command?" another asked. "What would the mare-women decree?"

Wyndo reared up in an awkward move that he couldn't sustain as long as a simple horse. It looked almost comical to Thomas, but he saw how the other centaurs gave their leader fearful looks.

"Enough!"

His forelegs dropped back to the ground with a thump. His eyes were daggers aimed at Levitanus. "Why do you do this to us now? Do you intend for us to kill the invading men and so earn the wrath of another three generations? We had to seek this damned refuge of yours for that very reason, as you well know. We have no desire to anger humans again."

Thom wondered what the centaur meant about invading men. Was there some army entering the Road of Waters?

"Your kind made a vow. You must obey." Levitanus' tone said that he would not allow any excuses.

"What do want from us? We will not endanger our mare-women…"

"Honor the vow." Thom's master didn't offer them any concessions. Thom was very familiar with his teacher's demands of unconditional obedience, but he wondered if the centaurs would ever be humble enough to give in.

To Thom's surprise, the lead centaur lowered his bow and bowed his head to Levitanus. Suddenly, the wild stallion became domesticated. The other centaurs also lowered their heads in submission to the wizard.

"Good," pronounced Levitanus. "Now tell me, where is this army of men you mentioned."

Wyndo frowned. "We thought they were leaving this Waywater when they left Fog Town, but their boats have turned and now are heading up the island's far side. They move in this direction."

"They head to Haven House," declared Levitanus. "When do you think they will arrive?"

The lead centaur let out another horse-like snort. "Do I look like a naiad or a merman? I am no expert on boats."

Levitanus waited, both hands resting on his staff now, and raising an eyebrow.

"Possibly by sunset," conceded Wyndo. "From what I have heard, the boats are heavy laden and so the sailors are slow in their rowing."

Levitanus nodded his acceptance of the centaur's guess. "We will not be able to reach Haven House in time then. We will have to ride."

Silence followed that statement. If Thom had understood correctly, his master wanted the centaurs to let the humans mount their backs. He hoped the centaurs refused, for he couldn't imagine himself being able to ride such a being without reins or saddle. What would he hold onto? How could he maintain his seat when even an old nag was nearly too much for his limited equestrian experience? Oh, he hoped that the dozen would refuse.

Wyndo shook his head. "You ask something unnatural. It is not done."

"I ask only out of dire need. If that army reaches Haven House before us, then King Arthur will likely be killed."

"Why should the death of a human king concern us?"

"It was out of his affection for Arthur that Merlin made these Ways. It is for the king that we magicians sacrifice so much of our attention to maintain the Roads. Should the realm fall, what will become of the Ways?"

Wyndo looked over his shoulder at his followers. "You may ride Stavion, but the other humans will need to follow on foot."

Thom hoped his master would accept that compromise. The indicated centaur, who looked to be the youngest of the group, stepped forward.

"All of us must ride," replied Levitanus.

"But they are not makers of the Roads," protested Wyndo.

"Two of them are magicians. I will need them to assist in protecting the king."

"Then leave behind the three men in dresses."

Levitanus hesitated. Thom had the impression that his teacher was considering it. He wondered if Levitanus would let him stay behind too if he promised again not to talk with Francis. He dreaded the thought of trying to sit on a centaur.

But Levitanus didn't want to leave anyone behind. "No, they must also ride. King Arthur would not want them left behind."

Wyndo looked on the verge of refusing, when Francis added his plea. "We humbly ask your permission to ride, Centaur Wyndo."

Some of the centaurs snorted with surprise. More than one whispered "the Defender."

"So that is the scent that teased my memories," said Wyndo in obvious surprise, looking more closely at Francis. "You are now reconciled with the others, Defender? You have returned to their herd?"

Francis shook his head. "No. I am no longer part of the magician's guild, but we gallop in the same direction and there is a storm brewing at our flanks. We have the same wolves howling on our trail. Will you honor us with your strength and speed? Without your aid we cannot reach the king in time."

Wyndo stepped back. "I will not impose this burden on my brothers without their agreement. Let us talk for a moment."

The centaurs withdrew down the trail to discuss what was being asked of them. When they returned, six of them presented themselves for mounting. Wyndo was one of them and stopped in front of Levitanus. The youngest centaur, Stavion, stopped in front of Thomas.

The journeyman swallowed his sudden fear.

"We offer our backs, but only if all swear to secrecy. No one is ever to know of this, neither centaur nor human, for it is a very humiliating thing that we are about to do. Do all of you so swear?"

The six humans each gave their promise to tell no one, swearing a solemn vow to God. Thom wondered if centaurs worshiped the Lord too. Whether they did or not, they accepted the vow.

Eric Loren

TWENTY-FIVE

Ride through the Forest

"Watch where you place your hands and feet, human," warned Stavion as Thom approached his side.

"How should I climb onto your back?" he asked, uncertain. There was no stirrup to help and the centaur was taller than any horse he had ever ridden.

The horse-man gave a snort of derision, then pointed at a boulder nearby. "Climb up on that rock and then onto my back. I will give you a hand up."

Thom did as told, leaping from the rock to the centaur. The being caught his arm and kept him from tumbling over the other side. Thom found the centaur much wider than a steed too, with his legs stretched awkwardly as he settled across its girth. He set his staff behind his left knee and into the crook of his arm, unsure if he could keep ahold of it if the ride turned rough. In front of him was the human-like back upon which hung the centaur's quiver of arrows. "Where should I hold on to keep from falling?"

Stavion looked over his shoulder with contempt. "Lean forward and place your arms around my upper torso. Reach under the quiver but do not push it to the side. I will keep my bow in hand so that it does not slap you in the face."

Once all the humans were mounted, the centaurs moved out. Three of those without riders galloped ahead to serve as scouts while the other three unencumbered took the rear guard.

Thomas almost yelped at the sudden speed that Stavion attained. He leaned forward, next to the quiver of arrows, and squeezed the centaur's chest in a fear-filled clutch, but the horse-man didn't protest. They raced down the trail, the trees just a blur to Thom. He noticed Vivien on a centaur in front of him but he dared not sit up to look around for the others. He heard the centaurs around him though, and even a short laugh of awe from Bart.

They had barely gained full speed when Thom heard another sound, the griffin's screech. And this time the monster was somewhere much closer. He felt that he should warn Stavion. "A griffin is near!" he yelled against the wind of their passage.

"I am aware of that, human," Stavion replied without looking back. "My people are not as ignorant as your kind. Griffins are more than just legends to us. Some of my herd have even fought one before."

Thom almost protested that he had fought one too, but he doubted that the centaur would believe him.

The horse-men tried to outrun the huge predator, but the griffin could fly straight while the centaurs had to follow the twists of the trail. When it became obvious that the griffin would soon be on them, Wyndo called them to a halt and ordered the humans to get off. "We must be free to use our bows, unless you magicians plan to use your powers against the monster."

"It is best that we do not," replied Levitanus. "More magic will just bring more attacks."

"So I thought," replied Wyndo. "Then keep to the trees while we kill it."

While Thom and the others hurried for cover, the centaurs raised their bows to point at the sky, ready for their target to appear.

The griffin swept overhead, screeching its fury and hunger. Arrows flew, some hitting the beast, and the screech turned into a cry of agony. But the monster that was half eagle and half lion was too powerful to succumb to just a few poisoned shafts.

The trio of centaurs that had been serving as a rear guard caught up with them just as the griffin came at them again, it swerved and swept down on the trio of centaurs, raking them with its claws. It even lifted one, straining at the weight, and then dropped it from a tree's height. The centaur hit the ground hard. The other centaurs shot more arrows and this time it was enough to stun the monster. It faltered in its flight and then spun away, crashing into the trees. Five of the centaurs raced after, to make sure it died, while the others gathered around the three who had been attacked, including one that was now down on his side.

Thom's stomach turned as he saw Wyndo slit the throat of the one who had been thrown to the ground. It was a mercy killing to end the centaur's agony, but it still seemed harsh.

The five who had gone after the griffin soon returned to report it dead. The eleven remaining centaurs then gathered around their dead comrade and sang an impromptu song of praise for his life. It was not a long ceremony of tribute and then they were done.

There was no labor to bury or burn the body. They just left it and returned to the humans. Thom wondered if that was how they usually handled death, or if there would be more rituals and remembrances later when they were back with their full herd.

Wyndo sent three back out as scouts and then ordered everyone else to get moving too. Soon, Thom was clinging to Stavion again for a wild gallop through the forest.

The stamina of centaurs was apparently greater than that of horses, for Thom noticed no slackening of their pace as they hurtled through the woods, following the narrow path down to the island's far shore. He wished that they would grow tired, for then they would slow down. As it was, Thom's heart raced and his hands became slick with sweat as he clung desperately to Stavion. The centaur's gait was jolting and he kept making sharp turns as he followed the winding trail. Thom nearly fell off three times from Stavion's sudden shifts, but the centaur reached back to steady him. The last time, however, he did scrape his shoulder on a passing pine branch before the centaur got him righted.

The path finally broke out of the woods at the island's shore. The centaurs followed its sharp turn southward and continued on.

When he dared, Thom could look to the side and see a bit of the Waywater before it vanished into a fog bank. He tired of the mist, hungering for some fresh summer sun. As if his thought offered a challenge, the fog swept in to hide the water and most of the trees around him. Soon, Thom and his centaur mount were wet from dew, yet Stavion hardly slowed as the weather worsened.

Thom was surprised but thankful when the centaurs finally slowed, for he saw no change in the foggy forest around them. He was about to whisper a question to Stavion, when he heard Wyndo order silence and whisper a warning. "Wizard Merlin's dwelling is near, but something is not right. The Lala birds are silent, and they usually warble loudly when the mist is this thick. What do you think, wizard? Why are they quiet?"

The question was directed at Levitanus. Thom had never heard of Lala birds, but they had to be magical creatures to thrive inside an enchantment. His master would know what to make of it. Thom couldn't make out his master's whispered response, but Wyndo reacted by ordering four centaurs to scout ahead. Wyndo then asked the humans to dismount.

Thom dropped off Stavion and almost gave his flank a pat of thanks then realized that would be highly inappropriate. Instead, he faced the centaur and gave him a slight bow of submission as he had seen them do to each other. "Thank you for your assistance, Stavion. I am in your debt."

For the first time Thomas saw a centaur smile, but it wasn't a friendly smile. "I agree, human. You are in my debt and someday I will ask you to repay it. Now remember your vow to tell no one of my shame in offering you my back to ride. No one, whether human or magical being, is to learn of this shameful act."

"I will keep your secret," he promised, holding the centaur's gaze.

Levitanus called for him but Thom hesitated, still looking at Stavion. He found the centaur's stare to be stoic and wondered what he thought of humans.

Levitanus called out again, adding Vivien's name this time.

Stavion motioned that he should go.

Thom nodded in response and did so.

Levitanus took his student and the journeywoman away from the others to prevent anyone from overhearing. "The centaur leader is correct. There is trouble here, though I hear no new magic being crafted. I suspect that sorcerers are already watching Haven House."

"What of the shape-shifter?" asked Vivien. "The one the merfolk said was in Arthur's party?"

"Let us hope that he hasn't revealed himself yet," said Levitanus. "If he has, then we might be too late. I would think they have placed him inside just to kill the king."

"What are we to do?" asked Thom.

"We wait as the centaurs reconnoiter. If all seems well inside the compound, then we will hurry inside before the enemy's army arrives."

"Master, I have been wondering something about the centaurs," confessed Vivien suddenly.

"What is it? Ask me your question."

"Where are the female centaurs? Will they not come to your horn call?"

Levitanus raised an eyebrow in amusement. "One came, just not within our view. Centaurs have their peculiar customs. Their females prefer isolation, avoiding each other and outsiders, while the males run in herds. It is somewhat the opposite of horses, where usually one stallion rules a herd. Their lead horse-woman is nearby, but she chooses to stay out of sight."

The females dominate. Thom found that intriguing. A quick glance at Vivien revealed a slight smile of approval.

* * *

When the scouts returned, one of them brought back another trio of centaurs. Whoever these three were, they caused a stir among Wyndo's group. They appeared older to Thom, though there was no gray in their hair or coats. Their human faces seemed more weathered though, more experienced. The trio spotted Levitanus and trotted up to him. Wyndo came up behind them, looking nervous.

"Why did you call?" demanded one of the new centaurs.

"I summoned you as part of our pact, Horadius," replied the wizard. "Surely you remember that agreement, since you were one of those who signed it."

"The treaty is for defense of the Ways, yet I sense no attack on the Road itself."

"The attacks are imminent and will be concentrated on Merlin's Haven House nearby."

Horadius stomped a hoof like an impatient horse, his tail swishing at non-existent flies. "You try to involve us in your human disputes."

"King Arthur is in danger."

"Why is that our concern? Do we call for you when there is a dispute between lead mares?"

Levitanus grumbled with frustration. "Do not play word games with me, centaur. If Arthur falls, then the kingdom does too. He has no heir besides the bastard Mordred, who has already allied with dark arts practitioners. If the king is killed, then the sorcerers will take over and the magicians' guild will be no more."

"Petty human squabbles," sniffed the centaur, stepping closer to tower over Thom's master. "All magicians bleed us. What does it matter if we are cajoled into it or simply hunted down? Either way, many of our people are butchered to make your magic."

Levitanus glared up at Horadius, apparently not intimidated by the other's far greater size. "At least we ask. At least we allow you to choose who will live and who will die."

"Dead is dead."

"Are you refusing the call? What will your mare think of that?"

"We gallop in unison; she supports my decisions."

Centaur and magician glared at each other. No one else dared to talk.

"Not all are as hesitant as you to heed a call, Horadius. Flee or fight, centaur, but make your choice. I have no more time to chew the cud with you like two heifers at pasture." Levitanus looked over at Wyndo. "What do your scouts report? Can we make it through to Haven House?"

Wyndo looked nervously at the elder centaurs before answering. "The gate is not blocked, but some humans hide among the woods above the compound. Another half-dozen linger near the shoreline, just out-of-sight of the dock fort. Most likely they await the arrival of the boats from Fog Town."

"Do you think we can reach the house before any can craft an enchantment against us? I hear no elements being mixed."

"You will have to run fast, humans, for we will not be going into that compound with you," replied Wyndo. "Our kind does not like being corralled."

"Are you turning away from your duty too?"

"I said no such thing, magician. Do not trample the very waters you want to drink from. We will serve from outside, where our speed and our long bows can most help."

Levitanus stared at Wyndo for a moment, causing Thom to wonder if he would refuse the offered aid. Thom realized that his master had carefully avoided saying anything about their recent ride. His master finally nodded his acceptance of Wyndo's offer and then turned back to Horadius. "And what of you? Will you honor the treaty or gallop away?"

The two centaurs who were in Horadius' group pawed the ground in anger, raising their bows and aiming at the magician for his insult. But Horadius did not move, nor did he speak. He simply glared down at Levitanus, trying to intimidate him.

Thom's master didn't flinch or look away.

Finally, the lead centaur spoke. "I will not let you saddle us with your human disputes, but I also cannot allow those others to gain the upper hand. We will honor the call, but only so far as it deals with Dalrake's followers. Leave us out of your battles for the Camelot throne. King making is Merlin's love, not ours."

TWENTY-SIX

Haven House

They didn't run the whole distance to Haven House, but instead left the path to prowl through the forest until they were within sight of a high hedge. Thom could only see the rooftops and trees beyond the thick wall of greenery. One gateway burrowed through the hedge, but a stout-looking gate shut that opening. To either side of the gate, the hedge rose higher. It took Thom a moment to realize that those were vine-covered towers from which guards could watch any who approached. Thom had thought they were going to some rustic cottage, but Merlin's retreat home looked more like a fortress.

A wide and open meadow lay between where they stood and the hedge wall. It was midday, but the overcast skies kept out the sun's brightness. Nonetheless, Thom kept to the tree shadows, as did the others. The grassy slope dropped toward the riverbank where a long dock poked out from behind a wooden palisade; he could see the royal galleys moored there, but no people. He looked in the other direction, upslope to where the trees started again. He saw nothing of the people hiding there.

Looking back at Haven House, he considered the distance. It would be a long run and he wondered how his limping master would do. He guessed that the elderly abbot would also have difficulties.

The centaurs left them there. Levitanus waited until they were gone, then motioned Thom near. "You will have to help me this last stretch, Thomas. Vivien, I will need you to listen carefully as we sprint this last stretch. Call out if you hear any enchantments being crafted."

He gave no instructions to the monks, leaving that to their abbot. If Justin gave any orders to Francis or Bart, Thom didn't hear. Instead, the abbot nodded to the wizard to let him know that they were ready.

Thom offered his master an arm to hold onto and then they were off, hurrying across the uneven terrain through wet grasses. Levitanus stumbled twice, but Thom kept him from falling.

"Someone mixes over that way," yelled out Vivien, pointing upslope, toward the eastern edge of the field. Thom saw no one, just fog and forest beyond the meadow.

"What specifically do you hear?" demanded Levitanus.

"Phoenix tongue, Spotted Pine oil, Azure Fireflies, and Crested Black Eagle feathers."

Even Thom knew what that would create. Fireballs. He looked nervously past his master, but still saw no one.

Levitanus made an effort to go faster, though it was still not a full run.

The first fireball arched through the air with a crackling roar, but missed. It shattered when it hit the ground, scattering flames over a large area, although the grass was too wet to burn for long.

The others were getting ahead. Thom tried to help his master along, but Levitanus could go only so fast.

When the second fireball came sizzling in their direction, Thom eyed its path and knew they were in trouble. He yanked his master to a stop and tried to cover him as the fireball crashed into the grass directly in front of them. Flames scorched Thom's clothing and bit his exposed flesh, but he didn't catch on fire.

Levitanus pulled free of Thom's attempt to shelter him. "We need to keep moving or the next one will land right on top of us."

"Should we craft an enchantment to protect us?" asked Thom, expecting that his master would know of something that could ward off the flames.

"There is no time," he answered, yanking Thom onward.

They ran in pursuit of the others, going through the burnt area rather than around the still-smoking grass. The gate was now nearer, but it was still shut tight. Thom could now make out shadowy figures watching from the towers on either side of the doorway, but he couldn't tell if they were humans. He coughed from the smoke, his eyes watering. His arm had suffered a burn right where Levitanus now clutched it, but he did his best to ignore the searing pain. There was no time to shift his master's grasp or to avoid the worst of the smoke. They needed to get to shelter as quickly as possible.

Because the smoke obscured so much, Thom heard more than saw the next fireball. The enchantment pulsated as it raced their way. He expected the worst, gritting his teeth in anticipation of burning alive.

But the sorcerer had chosen a different target since the smoke had hidden them. Just as Thom and Levitanus stumbled free of the burnt area, they saw the fireball land among the others. Vivien and the monks dove away from the explosion, but they were still showered in flames.

Surprisingly, all four rose to their feet, although Brother Bart had to yank off his robe when he couldn't smother its burning hem. Standing there in only his underclothes, he stomped out the last of the flames and then pulled it on again. By the time Bartholomew was dressed, Thom and Levitanus had caught up with them and they ran on as a group.

As the six entered the dark tunnel through the hedge, the gate finally opened, but only enough for them to barely scrape through. As they passed through, Thom realized that there was stone wall hidden in midst of the thick hedge and that the gate was in that wall. Once they were all inside the gate, a knight slammed it shut and dropped two crossbars back in place. Another knight gruffly ordered them to keep moving, for the hedge was on this side of the wall too. Before them was a tunnel of green that they trudged through.

They stumbled out into a small square surrounded by high walls. Here the late-day gloom was deep, making it almost like evening. More knights were on the ramparts looking down on them, but none had their weapons drawn. Another, smaller gate opened on the far side of the square and King Arthur strode through, accompanied by four of his knights.

"You are late, and where is Merlin?"

Levitanus let go of Thom's arm to offer the king a proper bow. Thom belatedly joined him, almost forgetting his manners.

"We had some difficulties, your majesty. Merlin will be here a bit later. May I ask where I might find the two magicians that accompanied you, sire?"

The king frowned. "That is something else you will need to explain to me. They have both vanished. Are you magicians deserting me?"

"We would not do such a thing. There could be other reasons for their disappearance. Might I suggest that we discuss all of this in a more private setting? Your enemies have large ears."

The king's frown deepened. "Very well. Come with me to the solarium. You too, Father Abbot."

Arthur turned and marched back through the smaller gate, his four knights following behind.

Levitanus handed Thom his knapsack, taking out only his master's staff. "Tell the pixies to prepare a room for me in Merlin's wing. Leave my things there, except the clothes. Tell the pixies to launder those."

Soon the wizard and the abbot were gone. The knights on the wall also disappeared. The two magicians and the pair of monks were alone now.

Thom couldn't talk to the monks, so he stepped toward Vivien. She ignored him, though. Instead, she headed for the small gate too.

Francis gave Thom a long look but didn't try to approach. Instead, he whispered to Bart and sent the large man over.

"Good day, Thomas. I have been asked to give you a warning. Actually, three warnings." Bart paused to recall Francis' exact words. He raised a finger as he recited each one. "Remember who the mermaids found. Second: Some nights are very dark, so keep a light ready." He raised his third finger. "Finally: Not all magical beings will side with magicians in the coming battles." Bart frowned. "I don't fully understand all of those words, nor do I like how ominous they sound, but you should heed them. Francis is a wise man, no matter what your teacher has told you."

The young monk gave him an apologetic smile and then returned to Francis' side. The two then walked through the gate, into the compound.

Thom lingered for a moment, alone, then followed.

Eric Loren

TWENTY-SEVEN

Encountering Adele

Thomas passed through the inner gate that the others had already taken. The gate opened to a covered walkway. On one side of the brick path lay a fragrant herb garden; to the other side was a garden of magical shrubs. Thom would have liked to linger there, for he noticed specimens that he had only read about, but he knew better. He had no way of knowing how long Levitanus would be with the king. So Thom stopped eying the plants and hurried his step. He followed the walkway to an ornate door that already stood open for him. An elderly pixie woman waited for him there.

He greeted her and asked where he would find Merlin's wing so that he could deposit his master's belongings in his assigned room. Thom half-expected the woman to refuse his request, for he was just a journeyman, but instead she just nodded her understanding and guided him through the compound.

As they walked through the reception hall, Thom wondered about this compound of buildings surrounded by such a large, hedge-covered wall. It was no fortress or keep, but more like some of country estates he had seen from afar while traveling with his master. He wondered if this was Merlin's private retreat, a refuge in the midst of his own enchantments. He also wondered why it was built on the Isle of Mists with all its dreary weather, rather than on the Isle of Sun on the Road of Leaves. Judging by the size of this reception hall, it was built on a grand scale, but it was also almost empty. There was no one else here because apparently Vivien and the monks had already been escorted on to their rooms.

The pixie led him out another door, revealing a thick wood in the center of the compound. She led him through just a corner of it, but he soon lost sight of the hall they had just left. They walked beside a stream that meandered through a series of tranquil pools. Thom caught just a glimpse of a naiad, but then she dove from sight. He would have stayed a few minutes to see if the being would resurface, but his guide didn't pause. He had no choice but to keep going, following the pixie over a wooden bridge and then into another building.

After passing through a confusing series of hallways and rooms, they finally came to Merlin's wing. The knight standing guard at the closed door stepped in front of Thom and blocked his way.

"No humans are allowed to pass, by orders of the king."

"I just want to deliver my master's belongings to his room, sir knight," explained Thom. "Levitanus is a wizard."

The knight crossed his bulky arms. The lord looked to be somewhere in his twenties- young and in his prime. His eyes were a steely blue and not friendly at all. "Your master cannot pass this way either. The king has forbidden this wing to all."

Thom could smell the oil that the knight had used to care for his metal shirt and the sweat from having to stand guard for hours in a stuffy hallway while wearing a hauberk and leather armor. The knight's bare head was damp and his blond hair darkened and a bit matted from lack of bathing. There was a wine stain on his sleeve and bread crumbs caught in the crannies of his shirt's ringlets.

Although the knight didn't look very tidy, Thomas knew his own appearance was much worse. He wished he had taken the time to change into his journeyman's robe, no matter how wrinkled it was from being crushed at the bottom of his knapsack. Maybe then he would have garnered more respect.

"Hand them to me," said the pixie woman, holding out her small arms. "I will make sure that his belongings are placed in his assigned chambers."

"If she is allowed to pass, then why can't I?" asked Thom of the knight.

One eyebrow rose with annoyance, but the armored lord said nothing.

Thom looked away, fearing that the knight might take offense at his gaze too. His eagerness to obey his master had made him too bold, for this was a lord before him. Thom was suddenly very much aware of his commoner past, of being the son of a thief. He shouldn't even be in the same room as a mighty man like this.

He handed over Levitanus' knapsack and the centaur horn to the pixie, telling her of his master's wish for clean clothing. He was still a bit reluctant and realized that there was another reason why he had wanted to deliver his master's things to his assigned quarters. He had wanted a peek into Merlin's private area, something he had never seen at Clas Myrddin. Well, that curiosity would remain unsated for now.

The knight let the pixie pass inside, keeping his attention on Thomas. When the journeyman didn't leave fast enough, the knight gestured with his hand. "Away with you. I tire of your ugly visage."

Thom frowned at the insult, but dared not argue with a man so heavily armored. Instead, he gave an obedient nod, avoiding any eye contact that might be construed as arrogance, and turned quickly away.

He trudged back the way the pixie had led him, soon getting turned around and coming to another guarded door. He didn't bother to approach this knight, for the man's over-doublet announced what lay beyond. He wore the colors of a queen's protector, so that would be the women's quarters ahead. Adele was probably inside there, but Thom would never be allowed to pass through.

He hurried on, not wanting to anger another knight, but his thoughts were on what lay beyond that blocked door. He was so distracted that he turned a corner too quickly and ran into one of the queen's women.

Thom stumbled, trying not to fall on top of the lady he had just knocked to the floor. Embarrassed, he stuttered an apology and offered her a hand up.

The young lady sat on the tiles and glared up at him, refusing his offer. "How dare you! The queen will hear of this."

Her female companion laughed and only then did Thom realize there was someone who had witnessed his offense. He looked over and had another surprise. It was Adele. Thom reddened with embarrassment.

"He did not purposely charge into you, Lady Tessa. Here, let me help you to your feet."

The fallen maiden accepted Adele's tendered hand and was soon standing again. She inspected her gown and became more outraged. "Dirt. There is dirt on my gown." She turned to Thom, her eyes now blazing with anger. "I will make sure that your master hears of this. What knight do you serve, boy?"

The maiden was younger than Thom, but she called him boy because she understood that he was just a commoner.

Thom hesitated to answer, for his master would not be pleased to learn that he had roughed up one of the queen's attendants, even if by accident.

"Out with it. Who is your master?"

Thom looked briefly at Adele, who was still smiling, and then at the furious Tessa. "I am a journeyman under the teaching of Wizard Levitanus."

"You are an oaf and I will tell your master that. When he hears how you have ruined my third finest dress, I am sure he will send you packing."

"Come now, Tessa. It is most likely not ruined," argued Adele. "Let us hurry back to the queen's rooms and have one of the servants clean your gown before the stain sets."

The offended maiden agreed, but first wagged a thin finger in Thom's face. "I will speak to your master and to the queen. You will be banished from court, for even here in the wilderness there are standards of decorum. The nerve. Now, get out of our way."

Thom hastily stepped aside, pressing up against the far wall even though it was a wide hallway.

Adele took Lady Tessa's arm and escorted her onward. As they passed, Adele met Thom's eye and graced him with a quick smile and a wink.

He just stood there, looking after them, his thoughts a dizzying mix. He was overjoyed to have seen Adele again, but furious at himself for tripping over the Lady Tessa. As they disappeared around the corner, he followed far enough to watch Adele a bit longer. She was whispering something to the other woman, probably trying to calm her. Thom admired how gracefully Adele sought to soothe her companion. He was still staring after them when Lady Tessa raised her voice to complain to the knight at the end of the hallway.

Thom stopped gawking and ran away.

* * *

It took some time before Thom dared to slow down and by then he was helplessly lost among Haven House's labyrinth of rooms. This would not do, for he needed to get on with his other duties. He finally found another pixie that he could question. This one was a younger male, carrying a tray of covered food.

"Excuse me, but do you know where my assigned sleeping quarters are? I've just arrived with Wizard Levitanus…"

"Sleeping quarters? Good luck with that, my friend. We have enough trouble preparing food for this royal horde. Haven House was not meant to be a garrison or an inn." The pixie eyed Thom and apparently noted his shabby appearance. "You might end up sleeping in the gardens like some of us servants. Many of the best spots are already taken, but there are still a few places where you can shelter out of the night's drizzle, under an eave or beneath a wide tree. I would suggest you stake your place now, while there is enough light to find a decent spot."

Thom didn't like the pixie's suggestion, but realized that he needed to take care of some other essentials first. "Where can I find a privy? And where should I go for a bath? Surely not the courtyard's stream…"

The pixie shook his head at such a thought. "I would say that the servants' baths are your only option, though go now while they are in little use. The knights have taken over half of our wing, grumbling the whole time that our furniture does not fit to their overlarge size. They will not tolerate any of us using the facilities in their sight, so I would think they would toss you out as well. So hurry to it before the next shift change. You will find the servants' wing beyond the large dining hall."

He pointed Thom in the right direction.

Thomas found the privies and did his business and then located the bathing rooms. There was no time to launder his clothes and he had to wash himself quickly, worried that he might be interrupted by some outraged lord or by a servant sent from Levitanus. The water was still warm when he stepped out of the tight wooden tub. He used one of the clean towels stacked in a corner, dressed in his rumpled journeyman's robe, and then pulled the tub's drain. Throwing his knapsack over his shoulder, he hurried back toward the heart of the compound.

He wanted to be easy to find when his master called. Levitanus would be doing so very soon, for time was running out. He headed for the main section of the largest building, the one from which Merlin's wing angled off. As he entered, he passed a pair of pixies who were lighting the oil lamps against the coming night.

TWENTY-EIGHT

At the Hedge Tower

Thom found out that the main building at Haven House had a Great Hall fit for a king and now a king was presiding over it. There was no dais or throne, but someone had set a large armchair at the far end of the room and cleared all the other furniture away. Candelabras on either side of the chair created a pool of bright light in an otherwise dim room, further emphasizing the seat. Thom spotted King Arthur sitting there as soon as he entered, in spite of the crowd milling about. No one was talking with the king and he seemed to be lost in thought as he stared at nothing in particular.

Some men seemed to be waiting to talk with the king, lingering at a respectful distance until their sire deigned to wave them near. Thom's master wasn't among that waiting crowd.

It took a little longer for him to locate Levitanus. His teacher now wore his black master's robe, so he had found his belongings. He was off to one side, talking with a pair of burly knights. Their conversation seemed tense, as did many others around the room.

Knowing better than to interrupt, Thom took a moment to look around and see who else was in the large hall. He was a little disappointed that the queen wasn't here with her entourage, for he wanted to catch another glimpse of Adele. The only women he saw were a handful of pixie servants and Vivien, also dressed in her magician's robe. She stood apart from everyone else, arms crossed as she surveyed the crowd. He considered whether he should approach her before trying to get Levitanus' attention. He had just decided he wouldn't bother trying, when Vivien spotted him and headed his way.

She frowned at his wrinkled wardrobe but what she said was, "Wise choice, putting on your robe. That is about the only way we can get any respect from this crowd."

Her appearance seemed much fresher than his, though her knapsack was still over her shoulder. She wanted to keep her box of elements close, as would any magician. Thom replied, "What is happening? Have they told you anything?"

Vivien sniffed in disdain. "Speak to a woman? Hardly, except when they are trying to flirt and this crowd has no interest in a mere journeywoman. I haven't been able to get your master aside to learn more. From what I have overheard, they expect the sorcerers' party to arrive within the hour. As for the missing magicians, both are apparently gone. No bodies. No sound of magical disguises."

Thom hadn't even thought of listening for the distinct sound of that enchantment. He still wasn't thinking enough like a magician, even after ten years of training. He had actually been doing his best to ignore the sound of magic because it was a constant background noise while inside the Road of Waters enchantment, like the non-stop sound of a waterfall, though more complex. He brought his thoughts back to what was in front of him- a temperamental journeywoman. "They haven't spoken to me either, beyond ordering to keep away from the Merlin's rooms because the king is using them and telling me to find some place outside to call my bed for tonight."

"Not even a room for you?" She sounded a bit offended for him, which he appreciated.

"I was told to find a tree or a wide eave. It seems that the king's party has taxed the estate's limits."

"They should at least offer you a rug in front of a fire. This ramble has enough rooms under roof, but the king's men would be offended to give up any of that to a mere commoner, even one in the guild. They gave me a pixie bed among the servant women."

Just then, a pixie man stopped in front of them. "Excuse me, but your fellow magician has sent for you."

They both noted that Levitanus was still absorbed in his conversation. Nonetheless, they thanked the servant and went over. The wizard looked over when they neared, directing the two knights' attention toward them.

"Here they are now. Thomas and Vivien."

"I will take the boy," said the older of the two knights, though he frowned at Thom.

"I think not," replied the younger one, crossing his arms. "I want no woman at the Lower Gate with me. She will run at the first attack or faint at the sight of blood. She will join you, Sir Talion, for your post is less likely to see any action. I will take the scrawny fellow."

The two glared at each other for a moment, but then Talion nodded his submission. He obviously wasn't happy, but the other knight must have outranked him despite his youthfulness. "As you say, Sir Walton."

"Come on then," said Walton to Thom, motioning to a side door.

"Just a moment, please," interrupted Levitanus. "Please give me a moment to instruct them- alone, if you will, sir knights."

The two men acquiesced, walking toward a human servant holding a tray of wine glasses.

Levitanus eyed Thom and Vivien. "Do either of you need any elements to refill your box?"

When both stated that their supplies were fine, he continued with a few warnings. "If you did not realize it when we came in, the hedge around Haven House is Knife Heather, so it will resist most attacks- hard to burn and nearly impossible to slash through. Try to keep any fire off the roofs and do not craft any enchantments that might interfere with the Road of Waters. We are some distance from the magic's wall, but you still need to be cautious.

"Now, the pixies will be joining us in defending Haven House, so be appreciative and respectful toward them. As for the knights, they may be pompous but they do know how to fight, so endure their idiosyncrasies." Levitanus paused to get a nod from Vivien. He didn't seem concerned with Thom. "I do not have much else to say, for I have no idea what our enemies plan. If you are in dire need of help, send word to me at the Heather Gate and I will come to your aid as soon as I can."

With that, Levitanus dismissed them.

* * *

Thom marched behind tall Sir Walton. Although the knight wore heavy armor, he set a fast pace across the compound- so fast that Thom had to hustle to keep up with him. He realized that he and the knight were not that far apart in age, but he felt like a mere boy as he chased after the noble.

From the great hall, they went through a series of sitting rooms that were only barely lit and empty of occupants. When they walked past an open pair of large doors, Thom was awed by the vast library that lay beyond. He almost forgot his duty, slowing to stare at the many tomes lined up on the shelves. Even the guild house in Camelot hadn't contained so many volumes. He smiled when he noticed Francis reading in the far corner under a pair of bright-burning lamps and almost turned in, but Sir Walton ordered him to hurry up.

Francis looked up at that moment and gave him a slight nod.

Thom nodded back, but then quickly turned away. He increased his stride to catch up with the knight.

They exited the building and came out at the top of a hillside garden behind the Great Hall. The knight strode under an arbor, taking a paved path that snaked downward. Thom was offered no time to appreciate the view; he had to hurry after, through a series of terraced gardens that were lush with plants and trees.

He was once more tempted to slow his steps as he recognized many of the trees and shrubs they passed. These gardens were not ornamental, though they were easy to admire. The plants all gave something back to Haven House, be it food, medicinal properties, or magical elements.

Thom saw a pair of pixies returning late from harvesting plums on one of the terraces. In spite of pending battle, the two had obviously worked diligently and had full baskets strapped on their back. They waited politely on the side of the path to let the big humans pass. Their calm demeanor encouraged Thom.

Sir Walton let the slope speed his gait, forcing Thom to again lengthen his stride to keep up. They crossed a series of small bridges spanning the same stream that meandered through the compound's inner courtyard. Here it sped up as it dropped through a series of short waterfalls, pausing only briefly in small pools, as if to catch its breath before another small plunge.

He caught a glimpse of another naiad, but she quickly vanished from sight as she dove into a dark pool.

Sir Walton led him past the last of the gardens and under a rose-covered arbor, coming out at the perimeter hedge, tall and impenetrable. The path followed the hedge wall for a time and then came to the Lower Gate. This entrance had two towers guarding it, too; the knight led him under the right-hand one. In the shade stood a wooden ladder that led up to the tower's perch. The knight quickly climbed, ignoring the creaking rungs. Thom waited until the man's metal-tipped boots were clear and then followed.

They climbed through a hatch and came out to a covered perch where two other knights and three pixies stood guard already. The tower room was open on all four sides. The tower walls came to Thom's chest but there was a ledge all around that cut that height in half so that pixies could easily see out. The three pixies were already standing on that ledge, peering over the walls in three different directions. The pair of knights also watched.

Looking west, Thom saw through the darkness that the meadow that rolled down to the Isle of Mist's shore. The long grassy slope led to the shoreline and the dock where the he could barely see river boats waiting- most likely the royal galleys that bought the king and his party. There was a tall, narrow wooden fort beside the dock, behind a high wooden wall that also protected the dock. He wondered why there were such fortifications on an island inside one of the guild's greatest enchantments, but then he had heard that centaurs could get rather combative during mating season so maybe the walls were meant to keep them from doing anything rash.

Turning and looking back up the slope, he could barely see the glow from the Great Hall's lights. The thick gardens hid all the rest of the compound. His attention was pulled back to his nearer surroundings when Walton spoke.

"This will be your post, magician," said Sir Walton, indicating the tower. He pointed down the meadow at the shoreline. "Try not to destroy the king's boats, for he will want to use them when it is time to leave. And do nothing to that fort down there, for the galley crews take refuge there. The palisade was built to fend off unfriendly beasts that might come out of the woods; hopefully, it will also do well against any attack by our enemies." The lord pointed to one of the knights on watch. "That is Sir Byron; he commands this tower, so you will obey his every command. Is that understood?"

Thom gave a hesitant nod.

Sir Byron gave him a stern glance, noticing Thom's pause, but then returned his attention to the land outside the compound. The noble casually held a long bow in one hand, his full quiver propped against the tower's wall within easy reach. Thom wondered how much the man's armor would slow his movements. More importantly, he wondered how great a distance the man could shoot. It would be best to kill any sorcerer before he could complete an enchantment. Thom would tell the knight as much, if he ever asked for his opinion.

"Sir Byron speaks for me, so he is not to be questioned," continued Sir Walton. "For that matter, you will obey any command from one of your betters.

We know warfare, magician, so you must heed our orders. Your duty is to let us know if anyone tries any magic."

Thom nodded again, not bothering to explain what he had recently endured on the Road of Leaves. He doubted the knight would believe him.

Someone hailed Sir Walton from the gate's other tower and the noble shouted back that he would come over. He left without another word.

Thomas stood there for a moment, not certain what to do next. The nobles were ignoring him, but then one of the pixies jumped down from his perch and walked over. An older fellow. He was the most gaudily-dressed pixie Thom had ever seen, in blue-and-green checkered trousers, bright red shirt, and yellow cape. A forest green cap sat jauntily on his gray-haired head. The pixie stopped directly in front of him and extended a small, wrinkled hand.

"I am Prince Dorthos of Clan Brythoni."

Thom noted that the man's hand was intricately tattooed with red ink. His facial tattoos only covered the left side and were a little interrupted by his many wrinkles. He was a sinewy man with a firm hand grip. This was the first time Thom had met any pixie royalty and was uncertain how to address him. "I am pleased to meet you, my lord. My name is Thomas, a journeyman of the magicians' guild."

"Are you Thomas the Road Saver? I had heard you were only an apprentice."

Thom blinked, mouth agape, confused by the title.

"Were you the one who killed the sorceress trying to destroy the Road of Leaves?"

"I was one of those who fought her, yes."

Prince Dorthos nodded. "So it is you. I am glad to have a hero among us. It might inspire others." He glanced meaningfully at the knights but they were paying him no heed.

Thom didn't consider himself a hero and he certainly was no Road Saver. He had a part in killing the sorceress, but other magicians labored to restore the Road. He muttered his objection, "I only did what had to be done. So did all the others who helped…"

"Do not be overly humble, lad. If I declare you a hero, then you are. I am a prince of the pixies, so who will dare argue against anything I declare? I, Dorthos the Daring, proclaim you a hero."

He beckoned the other two pixies over. "Meet Thomas the Road Saver. Show him proper respect, boys, for he is a mighty warrior-mage. Maybe I will hire him as my court magician when all of this is over."

Thom didn't know how to respond to that, so he did his best to ignore it. He looked around and also listened for magic, then he sat down heavily on a bench that ran along the back wall. He was so tired from this already-long day. Dorthos sat next to him and continued talking, sharing about his pixie clan and their settlements along the Road of Waters. Most of it he only half-heard in his weariness.

He spent the whole night in that tower, with minimal rest. As darkness settled in, Sir Byron had his men take turns sleeping on that back bench. He grudgingly let Thomas sleep a bit too, but because there was no other magician, he allowed no more than two hours slumber at a time and even woke him twice more when a skittish soldier thought he saw some movement. By the time dawn came, Thom still felt tired. Food was sent down from the kitchens: still-warm biscuits, fruit, cheese, and cider. The nobles complained about the lack of meat but they ate heartily nonetheless. Thom ate methodically, too tired to really enjoy the quality.

The waiting and watching continued into the morning. Whenever Thom sat down, Dorthos would come over to tell him more stories. For a lord, the pixie was rather gregarious toward a commoner like Thomas, but then maybe pixie nobles weren't as haughty as human lords. He certainly enjoyed talking at Thom even though the journeyman was too tired to be much of a conversationalist.

The knights began fretting about why the enemy had not struck yet. Sir Walton came over twice to ask Thomas if anything were happening magically. But nothing was. There were no new enchantments. There were no troops movements. They didn't even spot anyone spying on them.

Around midday, Thomas once again sat on the bench to rest his feet. Soon, Dorthos joined him and began sharing about the pixie rituals for marrying someone from another clan. It involved a mixing of tattoo colors and other details that Thom quickly forgot. He endured the talking for an hour, then felt that his ears needed more of a rest than his feet, so he stood and walked away from Dorthos, pretending to want to look out over the land but really just wanting to get away from the constant talking, at least as far away as he could in that small tower.

Dorthos followed, but then suddenly swerved to the other side of the tower as if he had heard something. "To the ramparts, boys. They are trying to sneak up on us" He rushed over to the tower's wall and pulled himself up so he could look over its lip.

Thom would have followed but one of the other pixies laid a restraining hand on him. "Do not believe everything you hear from Dorthos. He is a strong warrior and a good man, but often he says things that are only true to himself."

"He lies," said the third pixie bluntly. "We have no princes among our people. We call him Dorthos the Deranged, for he is as mad as a foaming hound."

Thom was stunned by their statements. Why had they let him believe otherwise for all those hours?

"He means well, though. It was good for him to have someone to talk to, someone who accepted him as he is"

"And it was good to have him talking to someone else besides us," added the other pixie. "Dorthos can be rather enamored with the sound of his own voice. By the way, I am Torien and this is Zandron."

"Hurry, boys. To the ramparts," ordered Dorthos, waving his bow at them, an arrow already notched.

"Do you let him have dryad poison for his arrow tips?" whispered Thom to the other two.

"Of course, we do," replied Zandron. "He may be crazy, but Dorthos hits the target at a greater distance and with more accuracy than anyone I have seen."

Thomas just hoped the insane pixie kept his arrows pointed in the right direction.

Sir Byron looked over his shoulder and caught Thom's gaze. "To me, for the enemy nears."

He hurried over. It seemed Dorthos' warning was not imaginary after all.

Twenty armed men stood at the edge of the clearing, looking up at Haven House. They stood there, studying the defenders even as Thom and his companions watched them. They made no attempt at subterfuge. Thom saw no new boats on the shore, so they must have landed elsewhere.

"They stay out of our range," complained Dorthos. "Should we take the battle to them? Let us charge out the gate and hunt them down like they do to us."

"You will do no such thing, you addled pixie," ordered Sir Byron. "We are here to defend the king. Your kind has pledged to do so, or have you already forgotten."

Dorthos frowned at the man. "What do you take me for? My people will honor our vow. Your suggestion that we storm the enemy is bold, but I say that we will stay at this post. Do not try to argue me out of it."

Byron shook his head at the other's confusion. The second knight muttered something about a dancing tongue.

Thom returned his attention to the enemy. Another group had come out of the woods, including two in black robes, a tall noble in burnished armor, and a bannerman carrying a limp blue flag.

"Can you make out the banner's emblem?" asked Sir Byron of his fellow knight.

"I think it is Lord Mordred's two-headed eagle."

Byron swore. "The rabid pup has come to challenge his sire." He moved to the side of the tower that faced its twin and then yelled across to it. "Lord Walton, Mordred has come against us."

Their leader leaned out of the other tower to respond. "I have already sent a runner to inform the king. What does the magician say about Mordred's pets? Are they brewing some awful spell down there?"

Byron looked to Thom for an answer.

"They have not started any enchantments," replied Thomas. He heard only the magic of the Road of Waters.

"Nothing, my lord," yelled Byron to his superior.

"Well, tell the magician to keep you informed."

* * *

The first attack did not happen at the Lower Gate. Thom was the first to realize that, when he heard new enchantments from the direction of the Heather Gate. He yelled a warning over to Sir Walton as he listened to new magic being mixed and released. Soon, the others saw smoke rising from that direction. Haven House was burning.

TWENTY-NINE

To the Great Hall

Thom stared at the smoke, worried as he heard more fireballs being created and thrown toward the compound. He looked back to where Lord Mordred and his small force had gathered and realized that they had slipped back into the woods. He glanced to Sir Byron for guidance, but the knight was still staring after the vanished party.

"What happens, Thomas?" asked Dorthos. "Do those with Lord Mordred work any magic?"

Thom tried to listen specifically in that direction, but the noise behind him filled his inner ear. "They may be mixing something, but the only active magic that I hear is from the attacks at the Heather Gate."

"So they might be brewing something down there too?" asked Sir Byron in a demanding tone, having overheard.

He admitted his ignorance. "I cannot tell from here. There is too much magical noise already coming from the battle at the Heather Gate." He pointed in the opposite direction, where the smoke had become obvious. He considered how he could find out about the sorcerers with Mordred. "If I were closer to them, then I would know for certain."

The knight paused, but then shook his head. "No, I doubt that Walton would allow me to open the gate for you."

Thom realized that Sir Byron had been weighing whether to send him after Mordred and his sorcerers. He was relieved that the knight wasn't going to ask that of him, for he was more concerned about what was happening uphill, at the front gates.

"Byron! Order that magician down here."

Both of them looked down the ladder and found Sir Walton standing in the shade below. A young squire was with him.

Thom didn't wait for Sir Byron to add his command, but hurried to descend the rungs.

"You are being asked for, lad," stated Walton. "You need to help protect the king in the Great Hall. This squire informs me that the Heather Gate has been breached and one of your fellow magicians injured. Our forces had to abandon the hedge wall and retreat beyond the Entry Hall because the building already burns."

Thom realized that he didn't know who had been assigned to that gate: Vivien or his master. He confronted the squire to get an answer. "Which magician was injured? The older man or the woman?"

The young man didn't reply to Thom directly, but instead looked to Sir Walton as he spoke, "It was the older man, the wizard, who was hit by the fireball. The pixies do what they can to tend to his wounds."

Thom caught his breath in sudden worry for his teacher.

"That is not good, for he was our only wizard. I thought it was the arrogant woman who had been hurt. I would rather lose her or you, journeyman," admitted Walton with a glance at Thom. "No offense meant, lad, but you cannot be as capable as your master." The knight seemed to consider how this additional news affected their cause. He looked back up the tower ladder. "Byron, I want you and one of those pixies to escort the magician lad to the king's presence. I do not want anything happening to him while crossing the compound. We have too few magicians on our side as it is."

Byron came down with Dorthos the Deranged. Thom didn't protest the inclusion of the crazy pixie; his thoughts were on reaching Levitanus as quickly as he could. He also worried about Adele's safety. Haven House was falling so quickly that he wondered if anyone would survive.

* * *

Byron took the lead and set a fast pace, with Thom following on his heels. The squire also joined them, striding right behind Thom. Short Dorthos came last, having to run to keep up. Thom only hoped that the insane pixie didn't shoot one of them in the back by mistake.

Although the Great Hall was the nearest building to the Lower Gate, they had no direct path, only the twisting route that Thom and Walton had followed to get here. They hurriedly climbed that slope, anxious to get to the king. Thom was also anxious to see his master; he hoped Levitanus wasn't gravely injured.

As they passed through the gardens, Thom saw nothing of either the pixies or the naiad. As they climbed, he realized that it was already past midday. He wondered what else would happen this day. When they came to the top of the gardens, the stench of the fire filled Thom's lungs. He couldn't see the flames yet, but smelled the blazing building and the pungent odor of the burning hedge. The young squire coughed from inhaling the acrid smoke.

"The cook has burnt something," complained Dorthos, coughing too. Thom wasn't certain if the man meant that as a joke or was just confused. Either way it was ill-spoken, so he gave no reply.

The Great Hall was now in front of them, still whole although smoke swirled about it. Thom could hear the sounds of battle from somewhere beyond the building but no one was in sight except his companions.

They hurried to the hall's nearest door and found it barred. Sir Byron banged his fist on the stout wood and yelled for entry, but no one opened it.

"How long ago did they send you for us, squire?" demanded Byron of the youth. "They should have been expecting us."

The squire bowed his head in submission but still spoke out in his own defense. "I swear that I came to the Lower Gate as directly as the path allowed, with no delays. That is the very door I passed through and it was unbarred when I left not long ago."

The knight harrumphed, sounding unconvinced. "How shall we gain entry then? The other doors will be just as likely sealed now."

"Follow me," announced Dorthos, leaving the pathway to thrash loudly through the dense shrubs between the hall and the gardens.

"Get back here, you crazy little man," ordered Byron, but Dorthos either didn't hear or just ignored him as he slipped around the building's corner.

"Should we follow?" asked Thom. "He may know another way in that isn't barred, like a servants' entrance."

Byron grunted in disgust, but set off after the pixie. Thom and the squire came right behind him.

The greenery pressed hard against the corner of the Great Hall, but once they were around to the building's western face the shrubbery thinned. Nonetheless, the bushes had been trimmed to about the height of Thom's chest and were numerous enough to create a maze for shorter folks like Dorthos. They would probably have lost the man if it weren't for his bright clothing. As it was, Sir Byron spotted the pixie among the shrubs and shouted for him to stop.

Dorthos finally listened and waited for them to catch up.

"Try not to be so loud, sir knight," he said as they came close. "We do not know who holds the hall now."

"You think our enemy has won their way this far?" asked Byron, showing new concern.

"We will not know until we spy out the hall. Come now. The servants' entrance is not far."

The foursome pushed their way through the shrubbery until a simple door came into view. It was barred, but that didn't deter Dorthos. The pixie rapped on the stout wood in a certain rhythm, to which someone responded with a short series of knocks from the other side. Dorthos looked over his shoulder at the rest of them and smiled. "They want to know who is with me. I will have to improvise names, since none of you have knock-names yet."

Dorthos eyed the knight and then gave a sequence of knocks. He looked at Thom and gave a different series of long and short raps. He gave the squire the shortest knock-name, a mere four knocks.

Thom wondered what sort of nicknames the madman had given them, but he didn't have time to ask. The door opened and a party of six pixies urged them to enter quickly. As soon as they were inside, the door was closed and barred again. Most of the pixies on guard had somber countenances, but two were grinning as they let Sir Byron pass.

"Is the human king still alive?" asked Dorthos.

One of the guards replied. "He is. You will find him in the grand assembly room." The man turned toward Thom. "Are you truly the Road Saver, or is that one of Dorthos' imaginings?"

"I am Thomas of York, journeyman under the Wizard Levitanus. I have no other titles. If you are asking whether I was one of those involved in the battle to save the Road of Leaves, then yes I was, but so were many others."

"So Dorthos named you rightly. You have our thanks, Road Saver. Although none of Clan Brythoni is inside that enchantment, our two brethren tribes are. We would have lost many if that magic had collapsed."

"I would not have won my way through to battle the sorceress without the sacrifice of numerous pixies." He would have stopped there to honor them by listing their names, but Dorthos was already hurrying on so Thom had to keep going. Instead, he recited their names silently to himself, recalling how they gave their lives to rescue the Road.

There were not many servants' passageways in this building, but Dorthos stayed with that route as far as he could. They came out in a room just off the assembly room, surprising the queen and her ladies. The pixie had picked a poor exit, for strange men appearing among the noblewomen caused an uproar. A woman screamed, another tried to assault Sir Byron with a lit candelabrum. As the knight fended off the brass and flickering flames, another woman came at him with long knitting needles. A third yanked open the far door and called in the guards who were just outside.

It would have turned into a melee, had not the queen and Adele quickly interfered. Thom was glad that they both recognized him.

Once that was all sorted out, they were quickly ushered in to see the king. As Thomas entered the large hall, he saw his master lying on a makeshift bed. Abbot Justin and Francis were kneeling over him, as was the king's medic. He caught a glimpse of his master's face and it was ashen under the soot stains and blood smear. Levitanus looked like a dead man.

THIRTY

Fallen Wizard

Thomas started toward his fallen teacher, but Sir Byron grabbed his wrist. "No. You will see your king first."

He would have pulled free, but Dorthos also put a hand on him. "I will go to check on your fellow magician," he assured Thom, "and I will yell for you if the man is near death." The pixie pointed to his own chest. "The king will not deny me, for I am his noble brother. Go to Arthur while I inquire about your injured companion. I assure you that I will call if you are direly needed."

Thom hesitated, not sure if he should find assurance in the mad man's rambling. Instead, he found more comfort in knowing that Francis was already at Levitanus' side, for the monk was wise.

Sir Byron yanked him again and this time he didn't resist.

King Arthur stood in the middle of the hall, arguing with a huge knight who seemed just arrived from the battle. The knight had removed his helm, revealing sweat-soaked brown hair. Blood and soot stained the knight's doublet. As Thom neared, he could make out the man's heated words. "You cannot go out there, my sire. Seeing you would embolden our enemy, for they will do anything to kill you. They shout their challenges even now, merely at catching sight of your banner. Better that you stay hidden and let us fight them off. Even better would be for you to withdraw to the boats."

"I will not flee. This ruse was meant to ensnare the sorcerers, not to entrap us." Just then, the king spotted Thomas. "You! Where is Merlin? You magicians have brought us to the edge of ruin."

Thom stared stupidly at the king, uncertain what to say. He had no idea where Wizard Merlin was; he knew that the great magician still lived, but only because the Road of Waters remained hale.

"Answer his majesty," ordered Sir Byron.

"Speak up, lad," added the sweaty knight who had been arguing with the king.

All three were staring at Thomas.

"I do not know what's happened to Merlin; I only know that he still lives. We last saw him in Fog Town, before a flood swept us apart."

"Can you not call for him with your magic?" asked the sweaty knight.

Arthur replied before Thom could, "Nay, Lancelot. They have no magical call for their brethren. They are not hounds to come running to a horn call."

"Wish they were," muttered the knight. "My dogs show more loyalty and sense."

"I do not like this," said the king, focusing on Thom again. "Your masters have abandoned me. The only one who remained was Levitanus and now he is of no use." He stepped closer. Thom lowered his gaze so that the others wouldn't accuse him of being disrespectful, but it was hard not to stare back. "What has the magicians' guild plotted? Where are all the other wizards?"

"I know nothing of any plot," said Thom forcefully, still looking down. "I merely obeyed the order to join two other magicians on the boats that came behind yours. I thought you were going to a parlay with Lord Mordred."

The king took hold of Thom's chin and lifted his face. "Keep nothing from me, young Thomas. We need magical aid or else we will be overwhelmed."

He met the king's blue eyes. "I have told you all that I know, sire. The only other wizards that we encountered were the dead one from your entourage and the Wizard Weston, who serves as the Road of Waters' Keeper."

"I could go to retrieve this Weston," suggested Byron.

"No," said the king, without letting go of Thom. "We cannot risk the Keeper. If harm came to him, the Waters would collapse around us. No, I think this young man is our last hope. He rescued Guinevere and saved the Road of Leaves, now he will have to defeat our enemies again."

"He is barely raised to journeyman," protested Lancelot. "You are right that he is our last hope, but he cannot possibly defeat so many sorcerers. However, he can slow their conquering of Haven House and buy you time to retreat to the boats. You must flee, sire. There is no other choice."

Arthur let go of Thom's chin and whirled to confront Lancelot. "I am no coward. You ask me to run without ever letting Excalibur taste any blood. You treat me as if I am an old man, Lancelot."

"I do not question the strength of your arms or the sharpness of your blade, sire. I know you thirst for battle, but they offer no honorable engagement; they kill from a distance. They are hurling fire at us. What can a sword do against a fireball?"

"Better to die facing my foe than to get an arrow in the back."

Lancelot was clearly frustrated. "If we linger here arguing much longer, the fighting will sweep around us. For the sake of your queen, I beg you to retreat to fight again another day."

"May I offer a compromise," suggested Sir Byron. "The king and the queen could fall back to the Lower Gate, ready to flee to the boats if the worst occurs. You will then be near enough to offer us your leadership, sire, while gaining some safe distance from the fighting."

"Will you do this, Arthur?" asked Lancelot.

The king hesitated, misgivings plainly written on his face, but then finally nodded. "I will withdraw as far as the Lower Gate, but I will not run for the boats." He turned to Thom. "You must defeat them again, Thomas, as you did on the Road of Leaves. Your king commands it of you."

Thomas swallowed at his sudden fear. "I...I will do all that I can, your majesty."

The king held his gaze for a time, then motioned for him to go. "You are needed elsewhere. No matter how good the woman magician is, she cannot hold them back alone. Lancelot, guide him to where the battle rages." He looked at the knight who had escorted Thom. "Byron, you will lead us to the Lower Gate. Let us gather the queen and her ladies and get them moving first, then we can leave in a more orderly retreat."

Arthur looked past them to where the lone squire waited. "And you, lad, shall go with Lancelot and Thomas to witness how badly we are losing. When Lancelot releases you, you shall return and offer me a full report. It eats at me to be kept from the battlefield."

With that, they were dismissed to their duties. Thom begged for a moment to see how his master fared, which the king granted. So he rushed to Levitanus and asked about him. His breathing seemed ragged and pained. His eyes were closed. Someone had washed his face, but new blood was seeping from a gash on his cheek. They had ripped his robe away from a burnt arm and an herbal paste coated the worst of the wounds.

"He lives, but it is serious," said Francis. "He certainly will not help anymore with today's fighting."

"Is there any magic that can help him? Teach me the enchantment and I will do it."

Francis shook his head. "Magic cannot force healing, my friend, but I will do what I can with my herb knowledge."

"And we will pray over him," added Abbot Justin, "for God's mercy."

Neither sounded very encouraging. Thom wanted to linger longer, but Lancelot was already motioning for him.

"We will stay with him," assured the abbot. "Go do your duty, Thomas, and we will do ours. We will do all that we can to relieve his suffering, not only keeping death at bay but doing what we can to see him on the path to full recovery."

"Come on, magician," ordered the knight. "I can now hear the fighting through the walls. We must go before our men are routed."

He looked again at the man who had been his master for a decade. Tears threatened to overflow his eyes. He cleared his throat and asked one more thing of Francis. "You will not hold a grudge against him, will you? I know you detest the guild, but he has been a fair master to me…"

"Thomas, I would never shirk in caring for another, no matter their profession. I will do all that I can to help your teacher."

"Thank you."

* * *

Lancelot and Thom hurried from the hall, with the squire at their heels. They had taken less than a dozen steps outside when a fireball flew over their heads to land on the Great Hall's slate roof.

Eric Loren

THIRTY-ONE

Desperate Stand

Thomas ran faster as sparks cascaded off the roof. He heard the squire cry out in pain as some sparks rained down on him, but the youth kept up with them. They ran over a small stone bridge and into the building to the left of the Great Hall. Sir Lancelot was avoiding the central gardens with its wandering paths and series of pools; going through the North Hall was most likely more direct.

Thom hoped the knight was making the right choice, for this building was already smoldering. He feared they would find fire blocking their route or too thick smoke, but the noble wasn't about to change course, so Thom had no choice but to follow. They ran through smoky rooms that were abandoned. He could see nothing of the enemy yet, but he could hear the magic being mixed somewhere ahead. It seemed that Vivien and the king's knights were making a stand on the far side of this hall, closest to the Entry Hall and the Heather Gate beyond.

Sir Lancelot knew where the fighting was without having to ask Thom what he heard, for the knight headed directly toward it. Thom didn't protest the nobleman's choice, though he was soon coughing as they hurried down increasingly smoky hallways.

They had gone only halfway through the building when a fireball came roaring down a corridor at them. Thom heard it before they could see anything through the smoke and shouted a warning, diving through an open doorway. Lancelot and the squire raced in at his heels, just as the fireball flew past, careening against the walls as it went.

When Thom peeked out, the hallway tapestries and furniture were on fire in either direction and the smoke was quickly thickening. He could also hear another fireball being crafted. He turned back to the knight and the squire. "We need to find another way out of here. There is no way we can go back."

"Can you not conjure up some rainstorm or sudden flood?" demanded Lancelot. "Drench the flames."

"I have little knowledge of water enchantments," said Thom, "and the sorcerer is crafting more fire even as we speak. We must flee and find some other way to confront the invaders."

"There is another door," said the squire, pointing at the far wall.

Sir Lancelot looked ready to argue until the second fireball sizzled down the hallway. The flames crashed into the door frame and splashed onto the room's carpet. They could feel the heat now as the carpet began to smolder.

"Go," ordered Lancelot, pushing the squire toward the far door.

Coughing, Thom followed them. Beyond the door was another hallway. They ran down it, checking side rooms for an exit until they found a way back out to the Haven House central gardens.

Thom gulped clear air as he staggered out, thankful to still be alive even if they had gotten no closer to the Heather Gate.

"This way," ordered the knight. "Quickly. We are too exposed here."

He led them at a run into a copse of birches. Thom's staff snagged on a branch as he passed under the first line of trees, causing him to stumble against the tree trunk. He pushed off the rough bark and kept going, for Lancelot hadn't stopped once they were among the trees. They pushed through to one the garden pools, skirting the silent waters as they tried to get closer to the enemy.

They were pushing through tall grasses at the pool's edge when Thom heard with his inner ear another fireball heading their way. He yelled out in warning, throwing himself to the ground and covering the back of his head with his hands. He heard the others drop as well, but dared not look. The fireball skimmed the grasses and crashed into an elm beyond the grasses, showering the men with fire.

Thom screamed in agony as he caught fire. He tried to extinguish the flames by rolling, but the grass was burning all around him.

Just then, a wave rose out of the tranquil pond and crashed over them. Thom was slammed against the ground by the water's weight. He gasped and water filled his mouth. Just as suddenly, the water poured off him, flowing back to its home. The wave had extinguished the flames and left him thoroughly soaked.

Thom sat up, sputtering water, and looked over his body for any remaining fire. Nothing burned, though his cloak was singed and his skin pulsed with pain on the back of his hands and arms. They were red, but he hadn't suffered any terrible burns.

"I thought you said you couldn't work water magic," stated a soaked Lancelot, his voice sounding smoky.

"I didn't do that," replied Thom, looking around for Vivien, for he guessed that it was she who had saved them. He spotted her on the other side of the pool, among some pines and pointed her out. Some of the knights were with her. "There is the one who rescued us. We should hurry to her side."

Lancelot nodded and led them in that direction. When they arrived, Lancelot didn't go to Vivien but to one of the knights. It was Thom who sought her out.

"Thank you for dousing the fire," he said sincerely.

She gave him a quick glance, but her focus was on a building at the far end of the compound- the building that stood next to the Heather Gate. Thom could hear some kind of magic being mixed over there but he couldn't recognize the particular enchantment.

She finally replied, "You should have been able to do that yourself. It was a basic enchantment that any competent journeyman would know."

The words bit. Thom was very aware of his shortcomings; he was a journeyman in name only. "I am certain my master will rectify my ignorance as soon as he can."

Vivien nodded in agreement without ever looking at him. "I should think so, for Wizard Levitanus is very competent."

Before he could reply, he was distracted by a surge in sound- a throbbing pulse that caused his ears to itch deep inside. He stared in the same direction as Vivien. "What magic is that?"

"Something to do with wind. Look, the trees at that end of the garden are whipping wildly." She turned her attention to the knights with her. "Windstorm coming! Grab hold of something solid or you will be tossed like a pixie at a throwing contest."

A whirlwind swept through the courtyard, shredding bushes and stripping trees as it came at them. Thom hurriedly hugged a nearby pine, pressing his cheek against its rough bark, but then realized that Vivien wasn't doing the same. Instead, she was hurriedly trying to pack her magician's box. He let go of the tree and went to her, kneeling to help store the glass vials and stow her mixing bowl. They didn't finish in time.

Eric Loren

THIRTY-TWO

Fire and Smoke

The whirlwind pushed Thom over, the glass vials in his hands lost in the tumble. He struggled to get up on his hands and knees. Something flying through the air struck him and he fell over again, sliding across the ground and into a bush. He grabbed the shrub's gnarled base as the wind tried to carry him off. A wind-whipped branch scratched his cheek.

Vivien cried out as she too was shoved sideways. Thom saw her fall, slide, and then cling to a slender tree trunk with one hand while still trying to keep a grip on her knapsack with the other. Although he could no longer see much because dirt and leaves filled the air, he heard others cry out, their voices shredded by the howling winds.

The enchantment didn't hold long, dissipating before it could damage the Great Hall. As the magic faded so did the wind, and silence fell over the central gardens.

Thom pushed the offending branch out of his face and just lay there for a moment. When he finally sat up, he saw Vivien struggling to her feet, clutching a wounded wrist. She no longer had her knapsack or her magician's box. Thom could hear more magic being crafted and knew he didn't have much time. He pulled out his own magician's box and called for Vivien, who was examining her hand. He might be too ignorant to fight the sorcerers off, but she probably wasn't.

"Can you mix something with my supplies?" he asked her. "Some way to deflect the attacks or strike back?"

When she didn't respond, he looked over again. Her eyes showed panic as she staggered toward the underbrush, looking for her missing pack. She didn't seem to be aware that he was talking to her.

His inner ear picked up the sound of fireballs being crafted again.

Desperate, Thom started mixing a response. The first thing that came to mind was a Twist of Air, an enchantment that he had never tried himself but had learned under Francis' guidance. He filled his bowl with the powdered Snow Hummingbird feathers, Saber Leaf Dandelion seeds, and powdered Midnight Petrel wings. To that he added the mundane elements of water and his own spittle to attune the magic to his bidding.

Following Francis' example, his last step was to smear some of the potion on his lips and hands so that he could guide the brewing breeze. A small whirlwind rose from the mixing bowl, one different than the windstorm that had just struck them- and certainly much smaller. He directed the swirling air with his hands and then blew it into motion, sending it to intercept the fireball that was already racing in his direction. He didn't know how he could use air to deflect the firestorm, but he had nothing else. He urged the little whirlwind forward with hand motions and breath, not wanting the enchantments to collide directly overhead.

He directed the spinning air toward the rhythms of the fireball, although he couldn't see it yet through the thick trees. When the two enchantments crashed together, he was glad he wasn't within its sight. The magics shattered on collision, deafening and blinding as they exploded. Winds whipped in every direction and fire rained down.

Thom had been too closely connected to the Twist of Air when it exploded and it left him stunned. It was Vivien that brought him back to his senses with a slap across his face.

"Come out of it, Thomas," she ordered. She was about to slap him again but stopped when he raised a hand in protest. "That was a foolhardy move. Daring, but foolhardy."

"I couldn't think of anything else to do," he argued, "and you were in no shape to help."

"I am ready to help now," Vivien replied. She had apparently come to grips with her loss. "I have no magician's box. May I borrow some of your elements to craft another enchantment? Already, one of the other sorcerers is preparing to attack us again."

Thom willingly let her use his supplies, for she knew so much more than he did. He needed her if they were going to slow down the attackers. "How many are against us?"

She replied even as she inspected his cache of vials. "There are three sorcerers and I do not think I can stop them. I told Sir Lancelot to get the king out of here, for it is only a matter of time before they kill me." She held up a vial and gave him a surprised look. "For one fresh out of an apprenticeship, you have some potent elements. That is good."

He tried to explain how both Wizard Cruthen and Levitanus had insisted that he take many of those, but it was obvious that she wasn't listening as she set to her mixing. She stirred together the powders of Phoenix tongue, crushed Azure Fireflies, and Crested Black Eagle feathers, along with Spotted Pine oil. She then added the mundane elements of oak pollen, black powder, and lamp oil. She lifted the mixing bowl close to her face to add her spittle, in an almost dainty move so unlike Thom's usual loud spitting.

He watched and listened as she mixed, for it was a new enchantment to him though it nagged at his memory somehow. She then coated her dampened hands with a powdering of white sand, almost like a baker coats his hands with flour to keep the dough from sticking to his fingers. It was not until she scooped her hands into the resulting goop and starting forming a glowing ball that he realized what it was. A fireball.

She threw the fire, sending it arching through the air toward their enemy. Its magic gave it flight as it soared over the smoldering gardens toward the Entry Hall. At almost the same time, a sorcerer flung a fireball at them. The two flaming spheres passed each other in mid-air.

Thom nervously watched the fire racing toward them. Vivien also traced its path. He almost raced away, fearing it would fall on them, but Vivien's calm demeanor kept him in place. The fireball crashed into the lush garden nearby but didn't touch them. Bright flowers vanished in flame and green trees blackened into sudden torches. He could taste the acrid smoke as it made his eyes water. Somewhere, among the smoke and trees, the king's knights were fighting against Mordred's soldiers.

Thom knew it was his turn to craft magic against their enemy, but his thoughts skittered. He remembered fighting the fire sorcerer at Oak Vale Waycircle. It had taken poisoned Pixie arrows to bring down that one and he had no Pixies to help him here. He almost asked Vivien where they were- even Dorthos the Deranged would have been a help- but he doubted she knew or cared where the small people hid. Maybe they were keeping the king safe.

Memory of his struggles on the Road of Leaves reminded him of something else he had done. Rummaging among his mundane elements, he found the three he was looking for and poured them into the palm of his hand. He stirred them with his finger, not bothering with a mixing bowl, and then ran over to the nearest flames, tossing them onto the fire. Multi-hued sparks shot out and then billows of dark smoke rose. A smelly, eye-stinging smoke.

"What are you doing?" she demanded to know.

"I want to hide us or the next fireball will kill us for certain." He ran back over and gathered up his magician's box, shoving it back into his knapsack and slinging the pack over his shoulder. "Come along. We need to move and then attack again. We will only stay alive if we keep them guessing about our location."

He expected her to resist, but Vivien apparently saw the wisdom in his idea. The two of them fled down a winding garden path, moving closer to the still-untouched South Hall.

The next fireball wasn't aimed at them. It fell on Arthur's brave knights. Thom heard the agonized screams of men dying aflame; he was glad the thickening smoke hid the awful sight from him.

Thom stopped beside another of the many little pools in the courtyard. He dropped his knapsack and knelt over it, pulling out his magician's box with nervous hands. He had thought of a magic that might help at least distract their enemy. He didn't know how to mix it but he knew the elements needed, so he found the correct vials and laid them out for Vivien. "Do you know how to craft a Cloud of Mist?"

"How will that help us?" she asked.

"That smokescreen will not be enough to blanket the courtyard, but adding a fog will help."

She still looked doubtful, but did as he asked. As soon as she unstopped the first vial, the sound of the magical element revealed their position. That sound almost killed them.

THIRTY-THREE

Wizard Lights

Vivien created the proper mix and poured it into the nearby pool. A fog rose, quickly hiding the still surface and rising ever higher. It was not a magic that you could just release, not without quickly dissipating, so she had to concentrate on it, directing the fog as it overflowed the pool and filled the air. That was Thom's error, because that meant they had to linger at the edge of the pool, making them an easy target. He packed up his magician's box and waited anxiously as she concentrated on directing the fog to mix with the smoke he had caused earlier.

Thom heard the next fireball arching toward them and hesitated, not wanting to distract Vivien from her work., but he quickly stuffed his cache of elements back into his knapsack and shouldered it. When he realized that the fireball was coming straight toward them, he shouted a warning and threw himself at her, tumbling both of them into the deep pool. They hit the water just as the fireball exploded around them. Thom felt a scorching heat and then cool waters extinguished it. When he surfaced, the pool's bank was on fire. The thick fog couldn't hide the angry glow or the crackling sound of the flames.

Vivien also surfaced beside him, her red hair now lank and stringy. He could barely see her even though she was less than an arm's length away due to the fog, but there was fire in her eyes. "You nearly killed us!"

Thom had no response. Instead, he started swimming to the pool's other bank. He swam blinded by the thick fog, but it didn't take very long until he found a half-sunken log and pulled himself out of the water.

He offered Vivien a hand but she ignored it as she also used the log to get out.

Around them, the garden lay half-hidden in mist and smoke. It was not as effective as it had been in the dark canyon at Twin Hills Waycircle, but it would keep the sorcerers from spotting them easily. "We can move closer to them now," he suggested. "Maybe we can get near enough to strike at them directly."

Vivien chuckled and shook her head in amazement. "You are a bold one. Yes, let us charge them."

Her tone sounded almost sarcastic but she followed when Thom pressed through the woods to the nearest stone path and then led them toward the enemy. He saw nothing bold in his plan; to him, it was their only hope to slow their enemy's advance. He wanted to buy enough time for the king and queen to escape. For Adele to escape. He doubted that he would live to see another dawn, she might as well make it count.

Thomas avoided the area where he could hear the fiercest fighting, leaving the walkway to skirt another of the pools. It was slower, pressing through the shrubbery, but he was no knight to get into single combat, let alone try walking through a melee.

They did no magic as they approached.

* * *

Close to the Entry Hall, the smoke and mist thinned to just a haze in the lowered light of evening. Thom and Vivien were able to creep up on one of the sorcerers, guided by the sound of the magic he was mixing. As they hunkered behind elderberry bushes, they watched him craft a fireball and send it sizzling off into the gathering night to crash among Arthur's knights. Thom could hear another one mixing somewhere off to the left, out-of-sight from both him and the sorcerer they were watching.

He had no idea where the third sorcerer might be lurking.

Desperate to fight back, Thom unslung his pack and pulled out his magician's box. If he wasn't strong enough to attack the enemy directly, maybe he could use their own arrogance against them.

Ignoring Vivien's whispered warning, he quickly mixed the powdered elements of Azure Fireflies, Meadow Dragon wings, and Glow Berries. It was one of the first enchantments he had ever learned and it came easily to him. Before releasing the magic that filled the mixing bowl at his feet, he put away his magician's box slipping it into his knapsack. He worked carefully, in spite of knowing the magic's rhythmic sound would be obvious to anyone trained in magic.

Just before making the first Wizard Light, he whispered to her, "You will need to guide me away from here because I will be concentrating on the enchantments."

He didn't wait for a response, but put his knapsack on and then reached into the mixing bowl, forming his first Wizard Light. In rapid succession, he formed four of them, sending them all to fly directly at the sorcerer, then handed her the bowl to wipe clean. She did so quickly with hastily yanked leaves, then grabbed his hand.

He looked over once before Vivien pulled him down the path and saw his bluish lights dancing around the sorcerer, even harmlessly bumping into him. They were a mere annoyance to the man, but the sorcerer had no ready enchantment to extinguish them or strike at Thom and Vivien.

Suddenly, a huge fireball roared through the sky toward them, but it wasn't aimed at the fleeing magicians. It fell on the sorcerer as he was batting away the Wizard Lights. The man died before he could scream out.

Thom stumbled as his magical connection was shattered by the explosion, but Vivien was able to keep him from falling. She led them off the path and into a copse of firs. There, in the deep shadows, she confronted him.

"You killed a full sorcerer."

Thom nodded, but he felt no pride. He could only think that two more sorcerers remained.

"Maybe your promotion to journeyman was not just for show. I could not have done that."

Thom gave her a questioning look. "Surely you can make far more Wizard Lights than I can."

"But I would never have thought to use such a simple magic to trick my enemy," she admitted.

Thom shrugged. "My shortcomings force me to be a bit more creative, that's all. You are still a far better magician than I." He wasn't trying to flatter her; he knew it to be the bare truth.

"What next?" she asked.

"Let's kill another."

Eric Loren

THIRTY-FOUR

Chasing an Enemy

They had almost crept up on another enemy magician when a trio of soldiers found them. There was no time to craft any enchantment to fight them off, even if the two had dared to try any magic so near the sorcerers. All they could was flee. The soldiers shouted out warning as they charged after them and would have caught them if the sorcerer hadn't killed them in his impatience. The fireball incinerated the soldiers then whooshed on, barely missing Thom and Vivien. Their hair and clothes were singed in the shower of sparks, but they survived.

Crinkling his nose at the smell, he yanked Vivien away from inspecting her burnt hair and away from the revealing light "We need to run or we will surely die."

As if in answer, another fireball came roaring in their direction.

They dove to the side, into the shelter of a stand of boulders, and the fire didn't harm them. Thom could feel blood trickling down his leg from scraping his knee on the stone.

Thom and Vivien rose and stumbled on, no longer trying to keep to any path. Smoke from the new fires made it almost impossible to see anything and they couldn't help but cough. They held hands to keep from losing each other and stumbled through the gardens as night settled around them. They soon lost their sense of direction.

Thom had hoped to circle around and come at the sorcerer for another direction, but missed. When he finally spotted a building through the thick growth, it wasn't the Entry Hall. He admitted to his companion that he was confused.

"That is the South Hall," remarked Vivien. She didn't mock his failure, but instead took the lead, heading back into the woods.

Soon Thomas noticed that the air had freshened and turned damp and realized that they must be near to the pool where Vivien had crafted the Cloud of Mist. When he mentioned it, she merely nodded. They walked around the pond and then followed the meandering stream that fed it, avoiding the easier paths that would probably lead them into the arms of more soldiers.

Thom could still hear fighting out in the darkness somewhere. Fireballs were still being flung, though not as often as before. So far, none of the enemy had discovered them. It took some time, but they finally came to where the stream passed between the Entry Hall and the inferno that had been the North

Hall.

It was quiet here. No battles. No magic. Thom looked in all directions, puzzled until Vivien explained, "We missed them. We are now somewhere behind the enemy."

She was right. Just then, a sorcerer crafted another fireball and the sound came from somewhere near the courtyard's center.

"What should we do?" he asked.

"We will do as you said earlier, we will sneak up and try to kill another. That might delay them a few more hours as they hunt for us."

Thom doubted it would take the sorcerers that long to find and kill them. His first attack had been a lucky one.

Vivien turned her back on the burning building. "This light robs my night vision. We need to get away from here."

"But I think this path will be quicker," argued Thom, pointing at a walkway along the hall's base. There was a danger of falling debris, but the path didn't weave around the many pools and dells.

"It would not take much for a master to pull that building down on us," she replied with a frown, "and I would not be quick enough to craft an Air Shield to deflect the burning rubble."

Thom didn't know what an Air Shield was but he could guess. Nonetheless, he still thought the path closest to North Hall would be their best route. "We need to take the risk if we want to slow their taking of Haven House. I don't think the king's knights have been able to do much against the magic."

Vivien grimaced but ceded the argument, so the pair ran off down a path brightly lit by the burning building. They had to leave the path twice to skirt fallen debris but still made good time. Nonetheless, by the time they reached the gardens' end they were too late. Judging by what they heard, the sorcerers were now inside the Great Hall.

Thom would have charged over the footbridge and into the nearest doorway, for it appeared unguarded, but Vivien stopped him. "There is magic on that door. You need to listen before rushing in like a brainless man."

He almost argued that he was a man, but wisely bit back his response. She was right, some enchantment lay on that entrance.

"Let us go around the side, to where the door opens on the path down to the Lower Gate."

They did so, keeping the stream between them and the Great Hall, but that was a mistake for there were no more bridges over to the other side. Seeing no other option, they decided to wade across, picking their way through the dark waters.

Thomas was nearly across the narrow stream when he heard a splash. He turned to see a naiad slip away among the water reeds. He turned to point her out to Vivien and found her collapsed in the stream, her face underwater.

THIRTY-FIVE

Bright Light

He yanked Vivien out of the cold water and carried her to the stream's bank, laying her among some lush grasses. She was unresponsive. Thomas turned her on her side and tried to pound out any water she had swallowed. He worried that somehow she had slipped and drowned. But as he turned her over, his hand caught on a small dart lodged in her arm.

He pulled it out as carefully as he could, but its barbed tip tore up her flesh. That was probably for the best though and he let the ripped-open wound bleed freely. It would probably not be enough, for he was suddenly sure that a poisoned dart had taken her. He just hoped it wasn't dryad poison, for that was so quick to kill.

Thom leaned close to her face to see if she even lived and felt her weak breath on his cheek. He looked around for the tiny water being that had shot her, but it was nowhere to be seen. He did notice Vivien's staff and retrieved it from the water and laid it beside her. He had no idea what else he could do.

The poison was acting so quickly; she shouldn't be unconscious already. His master or a pixie elder would probably know of a way to fight the poison, but he didn't. Tears of frustration filled his eyes as he opened his knapsack and pulled out his blanket, using it to cover her wet body in hopes of staving off the night's chill. He could think of nothing else that would help her.

He heard glass shatter and looked up to see the Great Hall looming over him. He had not realized that they were so close to it. Hungry flames came through a broken window and licked the outer wall.

Thom heard men shouting and chanting some war song and saw them exit the hall and start down the hill path toward the Lower Gate. When he saw the two darkly robed men who strode in the midst of the reveling soldiers, it caused Thom to duck down in fear of discovery. But they never noticed him and were soon out of sight. He noted that Lord Mordred was not among them and guessed that the king's bastard son still hid in the forest near the river docks, ready to ambush any who tried to flee that way.

Thomas should have struck out at them then, but the moment had been too quick for him to react. Yet he knew that he needed to do something or else the enemy would soon conquer all of Haven House and either catch the king's party or drive it into the arms of Lord Mordred waiting near the docks.

He wondered where Adele was and if the others had carried his master down to the Lower Gate. Levitanus was not a heavy man but he would still be a burden to carry. He glanced once more at the burning Great Hall and hoped that the others had not left his teacher to die in there.

He leaned close to the still Vivien and whispered a promise to return as soon as he could. He wiped away his tears as he stood, giving the journeywoman a final glance. She just lay there, no longer the fiery woman he had come to detest and respect in equal measures. He knew her death was near, but he couldn't linger. He still had to do what he could to help the others escape this trap.

Thom left Vivien and hurried after the invaders.

* * *

He ran as fast as he dared, along the dark path that meandered through the hillside gardens, for night was upon them and there were no lanterns to light the way. Thom was very aware that King Arthur was now without any magicians at his side, unless you counted Francis. He hoped the monk had confiscated Levitanus' box of elements, for he would probably need to use it.

Even as Thom thought that, he heard new magics being crafted somewhere farther down the hillside. He recognized the now-familiar mixture used to create fireballs. However, he also heard something new, something that had more to do with water elements if he heard rightly. He hoped that was some defense crafted by Francis.

Thom was just rounding a curve in the garden path and had a clear view of the lower hedge wall, when the first fireball soared through the air at the Lower Gate towers. It hit the left-hand tower with a thunderous roar, turning it into an instant torch. Even from this distance, Thom heard men scream.

But then another enchantment was released and a wave of water rose up, most likely from the garden's stream, and slammed into the flaming tower. The water kept coming, as if a waterfall had been turned upside down and now poured up, into the tower. There was an angry hiss of steam and the wooden building shook from the force. The fire died as quickly as it had been born, then the waterfall ceased too.

Thom cheered, unable to restrain his elated surprise. That must have been Francis' doing and the monk had defeated the attack so confidently.

Then another fireball roared at the Lower Gate, this time hitting the huge wooden doorway between the towers.

Somehow, Francis was able to create a second water enchantment in response, but it was weaker this time and left the gate still smoldering.

Thom began to run again, realizing that this would be too much for even Francis to withstand.

He was halfway down the hillside when someone outside of the compound created a great enchantment. The sound of it caused Thom to stumble in his run. Worried, he looked toward the sound. Were the sorcerers with Mordred finally joining the attack?

A great white light bloomed in the sky high above the hedge wall, a light so bright that it caused shadows. And then another enchantment was released and everyone heard a booming voice.

"Dalrake! I am here and I challenge you now. Come and fight me, you betrayer of our brethren. You call yourself the Great Sorcerer; let us see how great you are. Cease your hiding and slinking from me."

It was Merlin. He had finally arrived.

Someone crafted another enchantment and a white light slammed into the Lower Gate from outside and ripped the doorway open. Thom wondered if Merlin was doing all of these enchantments at the same time or if he had companions helping him, for the light still shone overhead.

Merlin's voice boomed out again. "I wait for you out here, Dalrake. Come out and face me, you coward."

Six glowing men appeared in the opening. Thom couldn't recognize them from so far away, but he was still certain at least one of them was Merlin.

Centaurs rushed through the shattered gate, swerving around the shining wizards and galloping after the enemy.

Instead of facing the powerful wizards and the charging centaurs, the invaders abandoned the fight and ran up the hillside path. Thom heard their approach and knew they would overrun him soon. He considered trying to stop them, but knew he was too weak to withstand desperate soldiers, let alone a pair of sorcerers. So Thom ran into a neighboring orchard, hiding behind one of the wider tree trunks.

The invaders fled right past without ever noticing him.

THIRTY-SIX

Dawn at Haven House

When dawn arrived, there were no more fires left in the compound. Mordred and his sorcerers had fled on the galley that had brought them. They had not even harassed the sailors hunkered in the dock fort, but had landed their galley on the shore nearby and then fled upriver.

All was quiet at Haven House as the sun rose.

A tired Thomas sat in a corner of the room where Levitanus rested. He was finally in Haven House's Wizard Wing, but he no longer had any desire to explore it. He was just too worn. According to Merlin, his master would live, as would Vivien who was sleeping in the next bedroom under the care of an elderly pixie couple. Another pixie couple regularly came to check on Levitanus. They didn't say much to Thom as they went about their business.

The king and queen had survived, as had Thom's precious Adele. Francis and the abbot lived, but the tender-yet-giant Brother Bartholomew was dead.

Thom overheard that half of the king's knights no longer lived, as well as a third of the pixies helping to defend the compound. He wasn't certain how many centaurs had been killed when they had stormed in with the seven wizards, but he doubted they came out unscathed even accompanying so many magicians.

So much had happened in one night. So many killed. It made him wonder where God was in all of this. Why hadn't the Lord at least spared Brother Bart? He had been such a gentle man. Thom was thankful that Levitanus still lived, but the losses still weighed on him.

A pixie entered Levitanus' room and Thom was surprised to recognize him.

"I bring you some food," said Dorthos the Deranged, indicating the tray he carried. "You need to replenish your body, young man. You will be of no help to your teacher if you should faint of hunger."

Thom muttered that he had no appetite.

Dorthos set the tray on a small table next to the chair and then stood in front of him with crossed arms. "I order you to eat."

Thom could not help but smile; the pixie was playing at prince again.

When Dorthos didn't move, Thom's smile faded. The pixie probably wouldn't leave until he ate. Sighing, he took a slice of cheese from the tray and nibbled it.

Dorthos still wasn't satisfied.

Thom took an apple and bit off a mouthful of the juicy fruit.

Finally, the pixie nodded and left.

Thom set the apple down and stared at his still-sleeping master and admitted that Levitanus didn't need him right now. He wanted to be of help, but the pixies were far more capable of ministering to him. Merlin had said that Levitanus would likely not wake until tomorrow.

Suddenly Thom had the desire to see Adele. He stood, leaving behind the food Dorthos had brought him, and went to find her. He hungered for her smile more than he did for any food.

* * *

Adele was with the queen and her other ladies in the fire-damaged Grand Room. They were attending the wounded. The large hall had been turned into an infirmary, with a dozen men resting on blankets along one wall.

Thom hesitated after spotting her, sudden doubt coming on him. She had asked him not to reveal their interest in each other, fearing more trouble from the other maidens who still mocked her for having had a wanton mistress before joining the queen's entourage. Adele probably wouldn't welcome his attention in such a public place.

He was about to slip away, when Adele saw him and rushed over, throwing her arms around him in a tight hug. He gladly hugged her too, though his eyes drifted up from her lovely dark hair to notice the other maidens that were watching.

"Thomas. I am so glad that you are well. I so feared that you had died last night."

He looked back just as her face turned up to his. He couldn't help but smile at her loveliness. "I worried for you too."

"How is your teacher? He was badly burned. Were they able to help him?"

"Wizard Merlin says that he will recover."

"That is good."

Queen Guinevere had noticed them and came over. Thom broke free of Adele's embrace and gave a respectful bow.

The queen touched him lightly, urging him to straighten. "It is good to see you again, Thomas. I hear that you were quite the hero last night."

He reddened as he remembered hiding in the orchard. He was no hero. "Many others were far more a hero than I. Some even gave their life to stop our enemy."

"Journeywoman Vivien tells of how you killed a sorcerer."

He hadn't known that Vivien was well enough to talk. She had been so close to death when Thom had brought Merlin and two other wizards to her side only a few hours ago. The poison had seemed well beyond treatment, but the pixies and the master magicians had done something almost miraculous by breaking her free from death's grasp. Maybe magic couldn't heal, but it could combat other magic, like neutralizing the dryad's magical poison. "Without Vivien, I would not have gotten anywhere near that enemy magician."

Queen Guinevere smiled. "Humility becomes you, young man. I see that you are fond of my Adele. I hope you have only the best of intentions toward her."

Thom nodded emphatically. "I would never harm her."

The queen raised a fine eyebrow. "I doubt you would ever hurt her intentionally, but we all cause others pain nonetheless. That is life, with its many misunderstandings and squabbles." She looked away at a new noise and Thom followed her gaze. The king and some of his knights had entered the Grand Room. The queen turned back to Thom and Adele. "Excuse me, but I must talk with my liege-husband. Do not linger in his arms too long, my dear Adele, for we need your steady hands to help change bandages. You are one of the only maidens who does not grow faint at the sight of blood or the smell of injury."

He and Adele watched for a moment as the queen gracefully crossed the room to her husband, then Thom received one more brief hug and Adele left too. He stood there, exhausted yet at peace. His focus was so honed in on Adele that he didn't notice when Sir Walton broke away from the king's entourage and was strode directly toward him. It wasn't until the knight blocked his view of Adele that Thom saw him.

Lord Walton did not stop until he stood mere inches from Thomas. He eyes blazed with anger and when he spoke, Thom could hear the barely suppressed rage. "How dare you fondle a lady, boy. If ever I see you laying another hand on one of the queen's maidens, I will cut it off. Do you understand me?"

Thom's mouth fell open with astonishment. The knight's anger was completely unexpected.

Walton poked Thom's chest with three fingers, pushing him back. "I did not hear your answer, boy. I told you to remember your place. No commoner should ever touch a noble woman, let alone embrace her. You are fortunate that the queen did not order you beheaded. But do not expect such womanly mercy from me or any other knight. Stay away from that noble maiden; you are not even worthy to gaze upon her. Do you understand me now?"

He again poked Thom in the chest.

Thom wanted to push the man back, but resisted. Instead, he glared silently, mouth clamped shut on the angry reply he wanted to shout.

Just then, King Arthur called out. "Walton, come to me. Your man Byron lies here near death and deserves a kind word from you."

Walton would have poked Thom a third time, but the journeyman stepped back, out of his easy reach. With a final glare, the knight turned his back on Thom, showing his contempt for the magician.

The king called out for Walton again and also for the abbot. The knight hurried his step.

Thom felt his face redden in anger and embarrassment as the man walked off. Walton now focused on the stricken knight, going to his side and kneeling down, but two of his companions gave Thom a cold look. He couldn't hold their stares long.

A quick glance proved that Adele had seen the exchange with Walton, as had the queen. He dared not approach either woman, which would provoke the knights' anger, so he had no choice but to leave.

THIRTY-SEVEN

Loneliness

The Great Hall was too crowded for him. Pixies and human servants were bustling about, cleaning out damaged rooms. The stench of smoke lingered everywhere even though the air was clear. He knew that some rooms were totally blackened, so he avoided those areas. Merlin and his three companion wizards had extinguished the fires quickly, creating indoor rainstorms, but much of the furnishings had already been lost in many rooms. What remained was now soot-stained and sodden. Even at this end of the hall, untouched by the initial fire, the water runoff had flowed down the hallways, soaking rugs. It offered no comfort, so Thom left the hall, avoiding as many of the muddy puddles as he could.

He wanted to search out Francis, but his master had forbidden him to talk to the monk. That angered him, even more so now in his confusion and pain. He needed someone to talk to, but all those around him were strangers.

He found his way back to the Wizard's Wing for it was no longer off-limits to him. He was glad that its hallways and rooms were nearly empty, for he didn't want any confrontations with the wizards that Merlin had brought with him.

Too restless to return to the small bedroom off Levitanus' room that had been assigned to him, he prowled the rooms and passageways, chased by a swirl of troubling thoughts.

Thom wondered why his love for Adele was considered wrong. None would have protested when she had been a mere servant of her previous lady-mistress, but now that the king had given her a title and the queen had called her as a lady-in-waiting, it had become a crime to love her. To him, she seemed no different. She was still Adele... beautiful Adele.

Unfortunately, he was still Thomas, a simple man struggling to master magic. He had some money, thanks to the king's reward for his rescuing of the queen, but he was still a commoner. He held the rank of journeyman, which was far better than being a mere apprentice, but that meant he had many years of travel ahead of him. Most spent two decades striving to reach the level of master magician and it might take him far longer since he had been moved up to journeyman earlier than most. Magicians rarely married or started a family because of the severe demands of the profession.

Thom would not be able to settle down until his hair was gray and skin wrinkled. No woman should have to wait that long.

He continued to stalk through the building, but Wizard's Wing was not that large. Downstairs were the sitting room, dining room, and Merlin's study. He didn't feel comfortable trudging through any of them, so he kept to the hallways. Upstairs were the bedrooms meant for Merlin, his guests, and any accompanying personal servants. He found himself making a circuit, marching through the bottom floor, climbing the stairway at one end, marching across the top floor, and then descending another stairway to repeat his trek across the main floor.

Thom was in an upstairs hallway when someone called for him through an open doorway. He stopped and looked in to find Vivien awake and sitting up in her bed.

"Thomas, would you pause in your striding for a moment? Come in, please."

He didn't really want to, but he stepped into her room. An elderly pixie woman sat knitting at the windowsill's bench. The diminutive woman gave him a quick glance then continued her cloth work.

Vivien looked remarkably hale, though paler than usual. Her red hair sat high on her head in an elaborate coiffure, offering a bright contrast to her pale skin, the alabaster linens, her white sleeping gown, and the bindings on her arm where the poisoned dart had torn her flesh. She had her magician's box in hand, so someone must have found it. As he entered, she slipped it back into her knapsack and set it aside.

She smiled at him and it seemed genuine.

"You have passed my door three times already. What is troubling you?" She motioned for him to take an empty chair beside her bed.

Thom sat down and looked at her, intending to share nothing. But suddenly words welled up in him and he couldn't help but tell her everything. Maybe it was from being without anyone to talk to for so long, but it was as if a dam had burst and he couldn't stop the overflow of emotions and frustrations. He told her about Adele, about his hopeless love, about his anger at being kept away from Francis. He spoke about his troubled childhood and his lonely apprenticeship, isolated at Levitanus' country cottage. He told of his fears of a future without friends or family.

Vivien listened quietly, letting him rant. It was not until the flood of words had subsided that she shared her thoughts. "We have chosen the loneliest profession. It is a high price we pay to learn how to work magic. Sometimes I am haunted by the same fears that plague you now." She straightened the bedspread that covered her stomach, looking down at it. "I am past my childbearing years and will never experience the pain and joy of having a child. Rarely, a wizard will take a young wife after attaining the level of master and start a family late in life, but I will never be able to do that. No enchantment could ever restore my womb. That is the price I have paid." She looked up at him. "Magic has cost me much, but it is worth it. I have strength now, and it will continue to grow as I master more enchantments. No one can ever rob me of that knowledge. No one can call me weak now."

Even in his own despair, Thom sensed Vivien's pain. That was something they shared.

Vivien took a deep breath and sat up straighter in her sick bed. "Did you hear that Dalrake and Lord Mordred escaped? Merlin was unable to corner them."

Thom nodded. One of the pixies had told him while he had been sitting watch over his master. "They say Mordred and two sorcerers fled upriver. Maybe they will give up this war now."

Vivien's thin lips came together in a frown of doubt. "I overheard the wizards who helped purge the poison from me. They spoke of an attack on Camelot while we were rowing down the Road of Waters. Not only did they try to retake Rowan Gate to stop the repairs on the Road of Leaves, but they nearly destroyed the magical shield that protects the whole city when an enchantment went awry. Apparently, that was part of the reason for Merlin's delay. I cannot see how he could have journeyed there and back to us in such a short time, but he somehow had a hand in stopping the city's destruction."

Thom thought of the Road of Clouds. He had never traveled it- for only master magicians could- but he knew that it was a speedy route that his own master used when the Road of Leaves was nearly severed. Maybe the Road of Waters intercepted the Road of Clouds sometimes, just as it did the Road of Leaves. He suggested that answer to her.

"Ah, that might be how he did it. There is still much I haven't learned about the greater enchantments, including the Road of Clouds. I look forward to gaining those secrets in the coming years, for such knowledge is a balm to the pains caused by the long and lonely road of being a journeywoman."

Thom wondered if that would be his future too. Maybe he was a fool, but he still hoped for more than just knowledge as a bedmate and wisdom as a companion. He hungered for friends and for Adele's love. Such pining probably meant a life of disappointment, but he couldn't deny his inner longings and doubted he could ever become as focused on merely acquiring knowledge as Vivien.

He was about to argue with her that there had to be more to life as a magician, but he saw that their conversation had taken a toll. She tried to stifle a yawn and her eyelids began to droop.

The pixie in charge of her also noticed the change and suddenly announced it was time for Vivien to sleep again.

Thom felt tired too as he left her room. He headed to the small bedroom assigned to him, a servant's quarters just off Levitanus' bedroom. He looked in on his master briefly and found him still sleeping, so he took to his own bed for some needed sleep. Yet even in his sleep he wasn't at peace, for dreams of Adele tormented him there too, dreams of chasing her but never catching her.

THIRTY-EIGHT

Confessions

Thom's stomach woke him late that afternoon, demanding to be filled. He didn't feel refreshed from sleeping through the morning. If anything, he felt more tired. Someone had been in his room while he slept, for he found a tray of food waiting and a fresh journeyman's robe. He ignored the clothes while he ate the bread, bowl of soup, and cheese. None of it tasted good; it merely satisfied the needs of his body. He would have climbed back into bed, but his body made another demand of him, so he pulled on the robe and went to find the nearest privy.

On the way back to his bedroom, Dorthos found him. "Your master is awake and asking for you."

When Thom entered Levitanus' room he was surprised to find Francis there. His teacher was propped up by numerous pillows behind his back, while the monk sat on the edge of a wooden chair at the bed's foot.

"Come in, Thomas," beckoned Levitanus. "Brother Francis and I have been talking about you."

Levitanus' voice was weak and a bit hoarse. The fire that had licked across him and burned his body had also smoked his voice. Thom already knew that his master had bandages across his chest and around both upper arms. His face was slathered with a new coating of healing balm on both cheeks and on his reddened forehead. Some of his gray hair had been singed away.

Thom came to his master's bedside, wondering why Francis was here but knowing better than to ask.

"Pull over that chair and sit down next to Francis so that I will not have to strain my neck looking up at you."

Thomas obeyed.

For a moment, Levitanus stared at him. He wanted to squirm under his intense gaze, but didn't. Finally, his master spoke. "I heard about what you did during yesterday's battle and I want you to know that I am proud of you, Thomas. You have done well and shown that your promotion was no error. Would that my last student-journeyman had been so sincere as you."

The praise was another surprise. His master was miserly with compliments, expecting much and tolerating little from his student. Thom could think of no response. He didn't feel worthy of being a journeyman. He still felt like an apprentice mis-clothed. The dark-blue robes seemed more like a deception than his proper attire.

"Where I failed to even injure any of the sorcerers, you killed one. Where I failed to stop them at the Heather Gate, you and Vivien delayed their march through Haven House long enough for the king to retreat to the Lower Gate. Your hard work allowed enough time for Merlin to arrive. If it hadn't been for you, Merlin would have come back to Arthur's corpse and an overthrown realm."

Thom protested that Vivien had done much more and that it was Francis who had protected the king when the royal party had been cornered against the Lower Gate.

"Oh, I know all of that," said Levitanus, "and, when he came here to return my magician's box, I thanked Francis for his sacrifice. I realize that doing magic was a terrible choice for him, but he placed the needs of others over his own distaste. I have not yet talked to Vivien in person, since both of us are bedridden, but I asked Wizard Ector to share with her my thanks. However, the actions of Francis and Vivien do nothing to lessen what you did. You were courageous."

"Accept the praise," encouraged Francis, speaking for the first time.

Thom gave the monk a brief smile, although he didn't feel he deserved any praise. Inside, he was even more torn. The kind words were welcome, but he still remembered Lord Walton's command, 'Stay away from that noble maiden; you are not even worthy to gaze upon her.' No praise could paint over such a harsh truth.

Levitanus shifted his weight, grimacing as the bandages pulled. He resettled on the pillows and then held a hand out to his student. Thom was gentle as he took hold of the long-fingered hand. "I must confess a mistake to you, Thomas; that I was wrong when I forbade you to talk to Brother Francis. You should seek this man's wisdom whenever you can, for he understands much. Francis is a good man, so cherish his friendship."

Levitanus' eyes focused on the monk. "I will confess something else, but only to the two of you. Francis was right to renounce our guild, for we have become twisted... soiled. We were once a band of eager learners wanting to use the magic found in the world to craft a better place. We understood that God created those elements and that we merely found creative ways to use them, just like any other craftsman used the earth's bounty- be it wood or metal or earth. But some thought themselves clever and tried to create ever greater enchantments. They even killed to find more magical elements.

"My last student chased that forbidden knowledge, the student whom I choose to no longer name. He rejected my years of training, calling the guild a flock of fearful hens. Maybe that was why I reacted so badly toward Francis, for his rejection of the guild reminded me of that old student of mine. But Francis left to serve God, while that other one selfishly chose the dark arts."

Levitanus looked at Francis. "I apologize for wrongly seeing you as walking in that man's shadow. You are a far different man, Francis. A far better man."

Thom had often wondered about Levitanus' other disciple, but his master would never talk about him.

Levitanus returned his focus to Thom, still holding his student's hand. "Francis has seen us with more clarity than anyone. The guild teaches that we expel the corrupt ones, all those named sorcerer or witch, but the truth is that many in the guild still practice the same Dark Arts. I have, though I told myself that I practiced something purer. We kill beings whenever we do any of the greater enchantments. Usually our victims are voluntary, for Merlin has wrought strong treaties with many of their kind, be it pixie or centaur or merfolk. But we still kill. Camelot was built by slaughtering hundreds, as were the Roads. We magicians have a fondness of saying that magic is costly, but the true price is paid by the magical beings butchered for their innate elements. The guild's hands are soaked in that blood."

Thom was astonished at what his master was confessing. He didn't want to believe it.

"Will you renounce the guild now?" asked Francis.

Levitanus frowned and shook his head. "I cannot. My enchantments are too entwined with those of Merlin and the others. In one way we have been different from those who follow the dark arts, we seek to offer some recompense for the blood we spill. The Roads we have wrought are now a sanctuary to much of the realm's magic. Plants, beasts, and beings all flourish within the enchantments, so I must do my part to uphold that magic."

"So you will go on killing?"

Levitanus let go of Thom and lifted his hand palm outward toward Francis. "Yes. This hand will continue to slay magical beings so that others can thrive, but I will only sacrifice those who volunteer."

"Do you want this same life for Thomas?" asked Francis. "Do you want his hands as blood-stained?"

Levitanus chose not to answer that question. Instead, he asked the monk a question in return. "Have you decided to join the Father Abbot in his plans?"

Francis didn't reply, but his tight-pressed lips showed that he was not happy.

Levitanus nodded, as if that was enough of an answer for him. "You may be wise to refuse his offer, for I don't know if the abbot's grand dream would bear any different fruit than what already rots on the guild's tree. However, Thomas may find that dream intriguing. Do what you can to make sure the abbot does not hurt my student, should Thomas choose to join." Levitanus sighed, looking worn from their intense talk. "Well, tell Justin to be even more circumspect with his plans, or else Merlin will learn of it; that wizard will not tolerate any more rogues. And if the king learns of it, he will want Justin's band to become his own- another toy for him to waste, just like the Knights of the Round Table."

"I am Thomas' friend," replied Francis. "I will not lead him to any who would abuse him."

Thom did not like how they were talking about him, as if he was some child in need of protection. He also didn't understand much of their veiled conversation and was about to demand more explanation but his master motioned for them to leave.

"I am very tired now," he stated, closing his eyes. "Depart from me."

Thom had spent too many years obeying the man to resist now. He headed for the door, as did Francis, but just before they left his master said one more thing.

"Francis, you should tell your abbot to reach out to Journeywoman Vivien. She would be a good fit to his plan- a fiery woman who will not tolerate anyone manipulating her or trying to put her to work in a kitchen. She might be able to bring Justin's dream to fruition, for she is a strong woman and a gifted magician. And yet this woman is about to go through her hardest trial. Vivien will hear devastating news soon and will need something new to put her hope in."

Thom looked over his shoulder, wondering what his master was expecting to happen to Vivien.

Levitanus gave him a slight nod. "You ought to comfort her as well, Thomas. Although she can be as prickly as a chestnut burr, there is a good woman inside that roughness. Now, close the door behind you. I need to rest."

THIRTY-NINE

News from Camelot

After leaving Levitanus' room, Thom tried to get an explanation from Francis. But as they walked down the hallway, they heard Vivien scream. The pair hurried to her open doorway and found two wizards standing over her: Merlin and Thallud. Both were scowling at her as she sat in her bed and wept into her hands.

"Calm yourself, woman," chastised Merlin. "We have already promised to find you a new teacher."

"Who?" asked Vivien, glaring up with reddened eyes and tear-stained face. "Wizardess Deandra? Wizardess Lunet? They both have apprentices; they will have no time for a new journeywoman. Will one of you take me on as your student?"

Wizard Thallud took a step back, visibly offended by her suggestion.

Merlin just shook his head. "Of course not. How would it appear for us to have a woman as a student? You will have a wizardess to guide you, as soon as one is available. That is how it will be. Just have some patience. Once another female apprentice advances to journeywoman, then that wizardess will be able to teach the pair of you."

"You demand that I wait idle until another woman advances in rank…"

"That is how it must be," pronounced Merlin, "and you will not be idle. We have graciously granted you permission to Honora's library and her notes on magic. You will spend your time studying, though you are forbidden to try any new enchantments until you have a new teacher. Studying will be enough to keep you occupied for some time, I should think."

"But it will take years until another woman reaches my rank, maybe even a decade."

Merlin lifted his hands, surrendering the point to her. "It cannot be helped, Vivien. The death of Wizardess Honora was unexpected, but she fought well to secure Rowan Gate and stop the conflagration that could have shattered Camelot's dome of magic. Take some comfort in knowing that she died bravely."

"Cold comfort, that, when I will be abandoned by the very guild she tried to defend."

Thallud glared at her, ready to protest her accusation, but Merlin forestalled him with a touch. The great wizard spoke instead. "You are distraught and do not realize what you are saying. We will leave you to your grief; we will talk again when you are more sane."

Thom hastily moved away from the bedroom door when the two wizards turned to leave, embarrassed that they had now caught him listening in. As he stepped back, he realized that Francis had already left. He looked around and saw the monk slip around a turn in the hallway. That was for the best, for Merlin would be furious if he discovered Francis here.

The two wizards walked past Thom without comment, for which he was thankful.

Once they were gone, he cautiously stepped in. He really didn't want to, but his master had just told him that Vivien would be needing comfort. Awkwardly, he came up to her bed and just stood there for a moment, uncertain what to do.

She hadn't noticed him at first, because she was crying into her hands again. When she did notice, she glared at him. "Have you come to gloat over my loss? Are you now glad that you will beat me to becoming a master magician?"

Thom was startled by her angry accusations. "No, that would be cruel. I... I just wanted to tell you that I'm sorry. Your loss is horrible, but don't let it crush you. As for which of us will reach the master level first, I think you may still win that race, although I had never thought of it as a contest. My skills in magic pale in comparison to yours. I just stepped in to offer my condolences, that is all."

She stared at him and apparently saw the sincerity in his face, for she just nodded her acceptance.

Thomas didn't know what else to say or do. She may have needed a hug, but he didn't think it proper to offer that. And yet words seemed too weak a balm. Frustrated, Thom considered who could offer the comfort he felt he couldn't and thought of Adele. "Again, I'm sorry for your loss, Vivien. May I send for one of the queen's maidens to help you?"

"I have no patience for those flighty sparrows..."

"Adele isn't like that," he hastily said. "Let me send for her. If you cannot bear her attention, then you can send her away. However, I think you will find her helpful."

Before she could refuse his offer, Thom retreated. He closed the door softly behind him and then went in search of a pixie servant. He needed to send someone to find the queen's suite and bring his message to Adele. When he found a pixie girl cleaning in a hallway, he stopped her and asked for her help. She agreed.

The message he sent to Adele was verbal, for he didn't know if she could read and had no pen or parchment scraps to use even she knew how. The pixie girl memorized his missive after just one telling, for which he was thankful. He probably would have mangled his words if forced to repeat them. He was just too nervous about asking Adele to help. He hoped she wouldn't decline, no matter that she was being discouraged from having anything to do with him. This was not about him; this was for Vivien. The journeywoman needed another human woman to comfort her. Pixie women were resourceful but he doubted they could fully understand human emotions.

He had just sent the pixie girl off, when another pixie came up to him. This one an older man.

"Are you Journeyman Thomas?"

"I am."

"Wizard Merlin requires your presence. Please follow me to his study."

Thom knew where the wizard's study was downstairs, but he still let the pixie lead. When he arrived in the large room, he found that all of the wizards except for his invalid master were gathered there, as was the king and his knight commanders- including Sir Walton. Thom suddenly feared that this was about his grievous offense of hugging Adele. He didn't want to pay his respects to the king, since Sir Walton was talking with him, so he went to Merlin instead and waited for the wizard to notice him. It didn't take long.

"There you are, Thomas. Good. You will listen in to our meeting and then report on it to your master, since his burns prevent him from being here. Do you understand your duties?"

Relieved that this was not going to be a meeting to discipline him, Thom readily acknowledged Merlin's order.

"You are to stay at the room's edge and make no comment. I will not have any journeyman's babble interrupting us. Simply listen attentively and then report on everything to your teacher. Go stand over there now, for I do not want you underfoot."

Thom gladly hurried to the far wall, thankful that he would not have to seek out the king and bring attention to himself among the nobles.

* * *

When the meeting started, the king and the wizards sat down at a large table. Three knights, including Sir Walton and Sir Lancelot, sat too. The other four stood behind their king. Thom was glad that the king's party had its back toward him, with the standing knights further sheltering him from Walton's glare. He didn't want that lord focused on him.

At first, it was only Merlin who spoke. The wizard told of why he had been delayed. After he killed the sorcerer who had sent the flood through Fog Town, he heard that Camelot had been attacked and the enchantment of Camelot dangerously fluttering. Merlin had been forced to use the Road of Clouds to hastily return, fight off the attack on Rowan Gate, and then lead the counter-attack that drove the sorcerers from the Road of Leaves again. Merlin and his companions had succeeded, but the Road of Leaves was now almost impassable. They would need to begin their repairs from scratch. The enchantment over the city was stable again, with no apparent damage or injury there.

The king was furious at the news. He interrupted Merlin and berated him for the failed schemes. Not only had he come close to losing that necessary route to his city, he had nearly died as the bait in another botched snare. Merlin sat through the verbal lashing without protest.

When the king was done, the wizard shared more bad news. "Although we have driven Mordred and Dalrake from the Road of Waters, they are fleeing toward Camelot. I fear that they may cause some mischief on their way through the city."

"That cannot be," protested Arthur. "We should have trapped him while still in this Waywater. Now we will need to chase after and make sure they are completely routed. I want that cur's head."

"We will see to it," said Lancelot. "Give us your leave, your majesty, and we will bring you that victory."

The other knights rallied to Lancelot, loudly proclaiming what they would do once they caught Mordred and his champions.

Arthur cut off their fervor. "No. I will not send others to do what must be done. I will be the one to separate Mordred's head from his shoulders, though I will expect all of you at my side."

Once again, the knights voiced their determination to bring the king a final victory. They seemed to be competing for Arthur's attention and favor, boasting of what they would accomplish when they cornered Mordred's forces. Through it all, Merlin and the other six wizards sat silently.

The king noticed their coolness and asked Merlin about it.

"Dalrake and his supporters are still strong, no matter that we killed many. You should not put yourself at risk, sire. You should instead flee downriver and seek refuge somewhere along the Thames. Let us take care of this. You are not some mere hedge knight; you are the king and you must be protected."

"I will not hide in some other lord's castle while my own is threatened. Do you take me for a coward? Let the queen and her womenfolk flee downriver. I will go to confront the bastard and end his scheming by killing him."

"But your majesty…"

"I will hear no more of it," said Arthur, interrupting the great wizard. "I have made my decision. Now, will your wizards be joining me in the chase? Or are they too frightened of battle?"

"We will go with you," declared Merlin. To Thom, he sounded displeased. "Though I will send at least one wizard to travel downriver with the queen. You will at least agree that she should be sent away from the danger?"

Arthur nodded. "That would be wise."

The conversation continued for another four hours, but it changed to one of tactics and supplies. Food and drink were brought in but none was offered to Thom. His stomach growled, but that was not important. When the king finally called an end to their gathering, Thom gladly slipped out. He was tired and hungry, but he needed to report to his master before seeing to his own needs.

FORTY

Night Conversation

Although it was near midnight, Thom found Levitanus awake. His teacher was expecting him.

"Sit down, Thomas, so that I can see you more easily." He pointed at a nearby chair.

Once seated, Thom explained why he was there and asked if his master wanted him to share now or wait until morning.

"Tell me now, for who knows what will happen by morning."

So Thom reported on that night's meeting. Levitanus shut his eyes numerous times, probably due to the pain, but he didn't drift in his attention. He interrupted regularly, asking questions that drew out more details from Thomas, things he hadn't realized that he had heard or noticed. After an hour, Thom's story was done.

Levitanus opened his eyes again. "Thank you. I needed to know their plans." He sighed and looked at the far wall, lost in some thought for a moment, then looked back at Thom. "Arthur is being rash again; even Merlin cannot always restrain him. That is one of the reasons I abhor being at court. The nobility prize brawns over brilliance. They think their arrogance is courage and they mistake foolish pride for God's blessing on their endeavors." He shook his head in disappointment. "When you spend much time at court you soon learn that nobles are no better than commoners and often have far less sense. Remember that. You are as good as any lord, if not his superior in your knowledge and abilities. It is not something to be prideful about, but you should be aware of the truth."

Thom was surprised at his master's words. Levitanus so rarely shared his thoughts on the court or the guild. He couldn't help but think of the recent rebuke from Sir Walton and wondered if Levitanus had heard about it.

"Should you ever find yourself in the role of adviser to a lord or- God spare you- the king, you will need to learn who your three best friends are, and those would be patience, integrity, and humility. When counseling fools, you will need all three at your side."

Had his master just named the king a fool? Thom dared not ask. He merely nodded his understanding.

"Dealing with the clergy can be almost as bad, for too many of them were once the younger sons of various noble houses and learned their stupidity on their father's knee. But not all are so dense. Some clergy were commoners before taking their orders; others have learned wisdom through vows of poverty and chastity. Abbot Justin is one of those good men, but he is also a cunning man. You might find him to be a good ally."

All of this talk confused Thom. So much so that he had to question his master. "Sir, why are you telling me all of this? Is this part of my training as a journeyman?"

Levitanus smiled, though Thom could tell it pained him to do so. "You can consider it that, if you want. I am just in a talkative mood tonight. Maybe it has something to do with the potion the pixies had me swallow. Perhaps it loosened my tongue as it soothed my pains."

His teacher held out his hand toward Thom. The young man scooted his chair closer and gently grasped the older man's hand. Levitanus gave him a strong squeeze in return and did not let go.

"As you may have realized by now, that the magicians' council meeting you attended was a sham. All on the council knew what Merlin and Arthur had planned and some of us had already argued against it in private. We only held that meeting to mislead the traitors in our ranks; we already knew that some in the guild were actually sorcerers, we just did not know their identities yet. I may have disagreed with Merlin about using Arthur as bait in a snare, but I concurred with that little deception of ours. I did not like deceiving you, Thomas, but it was necessary. I am sorry that you had to be lied to."

Embarrassed at having his master apologize to him, Thom simply nodded.

"There is something else that I have been meaning to share with you," continued his master. "I want you to know that everything in the hidden room at the guild house is at your disposal- the coins, the tools, and the caches of elements. The same is true with the supplies at my cottage. I only ask that you give me a report of what you have depleted so that we can make sure to replenish it. Is that understood?"

Thom nodded again. He wondered if his master was dwelling on this because he had almost died.

"Good. Good. Good." His voice faded with each repeat, sounding suddenly tired. "It is late and I know that you have not caught up on your sleep yet. Good bye, Thomas."

"Good night, sir."

As Thomas opened the door to his adjoining bedroom, Levitanus spoke again. "His name is Gweir."

Thom paused, looking back at his master with bewilderment.

"The journeyman I had before you was Gweir. He is now a sorcerer and I think he was the one who killed Wizard Bradig and took his form back at Pine Isles Waywater. Gweir was the shape-shifter who then killed Wizard Solis and left the king without a magician to protect him here at Haven House until we arrived. I wish I could confront him now."

His master sighed heavily. "I detest saying his name, but you should know it. Be wary of him, Thomas, for he is a killer. I had one other apprentice before you, a boy named Darian, whom I took on while Gweir was still a journeyman. Darian died at the age of twelve, supposedly swept away by a swift river. I was not there, but Gweir claimed that he tried his best to rescue the lad. It was not until five years later, when Gweir renounced the guild to become a sorcerer, that I learned the truth. Gweir killed Darian as part of some twisted rite and then threw the body into the river to hide his crime."

Thom didn't know what to say.

"I just wanted to be certain that you knew about him," said Levitanus, his voice little more than a raspy whisper now. "The others would probably never think to tell you. Now, go on to your bed. It is late, late for all of us."

Thom wanted to ask more about Gweir and Darian, fearing that his master's tongue might never be so loose again. He had so many other things that had troubled him over the years; topics that his teacher would never discuss. Thom wanted to ask about them now, but Levitanus had already closed his eyes. The moment of openness had passed.

Eric Loren

FORTY-ONE

Loss and Mourning

Thom woke to the sound of magic. A fire enchantment.

He sat up on his cot and smelled smoke, then realized the sound he heard in his inner ear came from the next room. He jumped to his feet and ran to Levitanus' bedroom, not even thinking to grab his magician's box or staff.

As he burst into the room, the staccato rhythm ceased. He didn't see who had crafted the enchantment but he saw the results. Fire. Fire everywhere.

Flames engulfed the bed and the window drapes behind it.

Thom stumbled as he entered, tripping over the still body of a pixie. But he kept going.

"Master! Master!"

There came no answer, not even a cry of pain.

His eyes locked on what had been the bed. He could see nothing of Levitanus among the smoke and flames.

He tried to get to his teacher, to fight through the fire, but it was too intense. He pulled back, hair singed and arms burnt. He looked around for something to smother the flames and spotted a comforter on a chair in the corner. He grabbed it and tried to beat out the roaring inferno. Instead, he just caught the blanket on fire and had to fling it away.

Thom tried to get to Levitanus again, but the flames were even higher, now licking the wooden ceiling. The smoke had thickened quickly, so that Thom could only see the flames in the thick darkness. Angry, red fire crackled and roared as it consumed the room.

His eyes watered from smoke, frustration, and fear. He yelled again, but no one responded.

Just then, Merlin burst into the room, an enchantment already prepared in his hand. He flung it and suddenly rain began to fall indoors. It was as if a storm cloud had been ripped open, pouring all of its moisture out.

The fires sputtered and died.

Thom fell to his knees under the weight of the water.

Dumbfounded, he watched the water quench the bed and then pour off the charred mess like a gray waterfall. In the middle of the blackened bed was the shape of a man under what remained of the blankets.

Thom gagged.

The rain enchantment stopped as suddenly as it had begun. In the sudden silence he could hear water trickling off the walls and furniture. He staggered to his feet and trod through black puddles to the remains on the bed. He didn't touch the body hidden under the covers that Levitanus had probably been sleeping under; he just stared at the blackened mess in shock.

Thom was still staring when Merlin came up and shook him. "Did you cause this?"

He gave the wizard a puzzled look, not comprehending.

"Did you kill your master with fire?"

Horrified, Thom shook his head emphatically. "I would never have done such a thing. Did you kill him?"

Merlin glared at him, not dignifying the accusation with an answer.

Thom asked it without thinking, but then he wondered if it was true. As far as he knew, Merlin had been the only magician nearby. But then Thom realized that one of the window shutters was ajar. The true attacker must have escaped that way, jumping down into the courtyard. Yet he didn't apologize to the wizard for accusing him, not when the wizard had so cruelly accused him.

Both of them felt a sudden ripple through the enchantment that was a constant rhythm in the background: the Road of Waters that surrounded them had shuddered. Merlin seemed to gaze far away as he listened to it. Thom just stared at the blackened blanket that covered the body.

The wizards Thallud, Cath, and Meditato barged in, demanding to know what had occurred.

"Someone has killed Levitanus," stated Merlin. "Did either of you see or hear anything on your way here?"

All three denied knowledge of any magic in use besides what had occurred here, nor had they seen anyone who looked suspicious.

"I do not like what this portends," murmured Merlin. "We never found that shape-shifter who killed Bradig and took his place days ago. Maybe he dropped his disguise and just hid in the compound somewhere. Let us hurry to our king, for I fear for his safety now. I will not have much time, for the enchantments of Camelot will soon demand all my attention. As you well know, Levitanus was part of the original crafting for all of this, but now his magic will now die off too, leaving gaps everywhere. A Founder has died; I cannot believe that someone would do such a heinous thing, for it endangers us all. How dare they attack one of us!"

The four wizards strode off, leaving Thom with his murdered master. A handful of pixies came in after they left, one of the women approaching Thomas.

"Let me see your hands and face, young man. Those burns must be tended to," she said, urging him to bend lower.

He hadn't even realized that he had been burnt. He allowed her to tend his wounds, too shocked to really notice the throbbing or the balm's cool soothing.

Levitanus was dead.

"Do you have another robe, magician?" she asked. "This one is singed and soaked." She motioned over another pixie, most likely her husband. "Oldren will help you to change and to clean your feet so you can put on your boots."

They led him back to his bedroom and the man helped Thom undress without hurting his hands more. Oldren helped him clean up and then don his original robe, which someone had already laundered and mended. The pixie packed Thom's knapsack and helped him get into his boots. Eventually, Thom had all his things, including the staff he still didn't know how to use, and was standing in the middle of the small room in shock. Gently, the pixie led him toward the only door out, through his old master's room. By the time they returned to the ruined bedroom, Levitanus' body was gone.

Oldren's wife was the only pixie still there and she was quick to reassure Thom that they had taken the body to prepare it for a proper burial, as they had with the fallen pixie. "Your master's shell will be shown the respect it deserves, so do not worry about that. Instead, come with us. You should not be here where such violence just occurred."

They led him out of the bedroom and he didn't protest. More than his arms and cheeks were numb- his whole self seemed that way.

Eric Loren

FORTY-TWO

Unsettled Enchantment

The pixie couple brought Thomas to the room assigned to Father Justin and Brother Francis, in an undamaged section of the South Hall. Upon seeing his friend, Thom staggered forward and wrapped his arms around Francis' neck. Heaving sobs burst from him as he buried his face in the monk's shoulder. Body-shaking sobs. He tried to stop, but couldn't. His teacher was dead and he felt abandoned.

The pixies told the abbot what had occurred, then left.

* * *

Thom cried for hours, realizing only now that he had loved his master despite the man's gruffness. Levitanus had been like a father to him, filling a hole in his life that his drunkard sire never was able to. Levitanus took him in as a young thief and taught him an honorable profession. His teacher might have been tight with praise, but he had been very generous with his patience and knowledge. Thom had learned so much from him, far beyond just magic.

All these truths came to him in his grief and made him mourn even more, since he could not thank Levitanus for any of it now. It was too late; his master was dead.

Francis didn't say much; he simply offered his shoulder and his brotherly embrace, letting Thomas purge the worst of the pain with tears. The abbot told Francis that he needed to check on the king and left.

An hour later, there was a knock at the door. Oldren and his wife entered, carrying a crock of soup, a pitcher of apple cider, along with bowls, cups, and spoons. They urged the two humans to eat something.

By this time, Thom was sitting in a chair, staring at nothing as memories and regrets strode through his mind, so he noticed little of the couple.

Francis thanked them politely as they withdrew. The monk tried to offer Thom a bowl of soup, but he had no hunger. Francis wisely didn't try to force it on him, but instead quietly ate the serving himself, allowing Thomas more time.

When Thom haltingly started to share his thoughts aloud, his friend listened without judgment or opinion, letting him work his pain into words. Thom shared his earliest memories of Levitanus. He spoke of the years of training and his many mistakes, which his master had patiently corrected. He told of Levitanus' demanding ways, his insistence on doing enchantments perfectly.

* * *

Another hour passed and Thom had fallen into another mournful silence. He still sat in the chair while Francis sat on a bed just keeping him company. In that silence, they both heard something that sounded odd to their inner ear, something faintly jarring. Thomas didn't react, but Francis stood up and stared first in one direction than another.

At last Thom looked up. "What is it? What are we hearing?" He hoped it wasn't another attack, for he was too tired to go on fighting.

"Something is happening to the Road of Waters," said Francis. "It is not like the attacks that happened on the Road of Leaves. This is something more subtle. It is almost as if... as if the enchantment is fading, its beat is getting slower and missing a few notes." Francis gave him a worried look. "I have never heard anything like this."

"What should we do?" asked Thom. He wondered if the sorcerers were now attacking the Road of Waters directly. "Should we warn others?"

"The wizards will already know and I expect that they have told the king. It may have to do with the death of your master because he was one of the Founders, along with Merlin and Dalrake. The three of them crafted all the original enchantments together, but now his work will fade away."

"You think that he was still maintaining those enchantment after all these years?" asked Thom. It seemed like that would have been a distracting and tedious thing, regularly having to support magic that reached across half the land.

Francis shrugged. "I'm not certain, but it is possible. The Keepers maintain and repair the enchantments, but maybe the Founders' magic is still there too. That would explain why they have never banished Sorcerer Dalrake. Maybe they still need all three Founders or the magic will have gaps or weak spots."

The words reminded Thom of what Merlin had said to the other wizards and he repeated it now to the monk.

Francis took a deep breath. "So Merlin admitted to what I just guessed. The Roads and Camelot are in danger as Levitanus' various enchantments fail to be renewed. Will you come with me to find Father Justin? I want to make sure he learns of this, for Merlin might choose to leave him ignorant. He should know since the king has named him an advisor."

Thom agreed, though he hoped they would not have to go near Levitanus' death room. As they left the abbot's assigned room, Francis raised the cowl of his robe to hide his face and Thom remembered that the other magicians would be furious if they found out that the monk was here. Levitanus may have been reconciled with Francis at the end, but the others were not.

They were halfway to the king's new assembly hall, in Merlin's study, when the abbot found them.

When told about what the pair had heard, he nodded understanding. "Merlin has just warned the king about this. Apparently, Levitanus' crafted magic was still an active part of all Camelot's enchantments. Each of those enchantments will now die off without his active care. The overall magic will become unstable until some other magician can rebuild that which Levitanus had crafted and maintained."

Francis nodded in understanding, but Thom still had a hard time believing.

"How could that be?" he asked the monk. "I spent years with the man and I know he rarely, if ever, came to the Road of Waters or any other part of Camelot. How could he be one of those maintaining the magic?"

Francis answered, revealing the depth of his knowledge. "Some of the greater enchantments- the ones demanding the blood of magical beings like pixies or merfolk- can last for months without the magician focusing his thoughts on it. That is part of the temptation of such magic." Francis looked to his superior. "Did Merlin say why Levitanus' enchantments were dissipating so soon? I would think it unusual that they are doing so."

The abbot shook his head. "Merlin is not one to be gregarious. Even with the king, he tells only as much as he deems necessary."

"Was there any talk about what will be done to stabilize the Waters?" asked Francis.

"The king asked that very question while I was in the room. Merlin's answer was rather unclear, but as far as I understood him, he intends to send another wizard to help the Keeper of the Road to stabilize everything. He did not mention who that will be."

The abbot then motioned for the two to turn back. "Let us return to our room and pack up our things. I want to get that out of the way before we hold the burial ceremonies. Everything is being done with haste, for Arthur is eager to finish off his enemies.

"The king means to leave in the morning in pursuit of Mordred and I intend to go with him. You will be coming too, Thomas."

Thom nodded understanding, but it was without enthusiasm about any more travel. The talk about burials shook him, for it seemed too soon. "Who are they burying today?"

"First, we will have a ceremony for the knights and human servants who died, then one for your old master, and then last for Brother Bartholomew. The pixies have their own rituals apart from ours."

"You are burying my master already? But he died just a few hours ago." It was much too soon. "That is unseemly. Why can't we wait and mourn him first?"

"I did not make this decision, young man. This was decided by the king and the head of your guild, so there is nothing that you or I can do to change the timing. Instead, let us go and pay proper respect to your fallen mentor." The abbot gave Thom a pitying look. The man's usually sharp gaze seemed compassionate instead. "Now, would you please help me with my packing? We only have a short time before the first funerals begin. Already, the pixies are digging the burial sites and placing the bodies next to the graves."

Thom did as asked, though he moved woodenly, his thoughts befogged.

Eric Loren

FORTY-THREE

Hasty Funerals

The burial site was located outside of the Haven House compound. The pixies had dug pits at the edge of the forest, beyond the now-destroyed Heather Gate. Twenty bodies were lined up next to the largest hole, each covered by a cloak or tapestry since there had been no time for making caskets or providing a proper burial wrap. Some were badly disfigured or burnt; others seemed to merely be sleeping. Thom tried not to look at them too closely, fearing he might recognize some.

As for the dead of those who had fought them, the warriors of Mordred and the sorcerers of Dalrake had already been buried without ceremony or mourning in an unmarked mass grave farther downslope.

The Isle of Mists lived up to its name this afternoon, with fog rolling over the meadow and dampening everything in mournful dew. It seemed that the whole island wept for the dead.

The king and his remaining knights stood close to the bodies of their fallen comrades and listened with bowed heads as Abbot Justin gave a eulogy. The queen and her ladies stood to one side, veiled in humble mourning. Thom noticed Adele and Vivien among them. The journeywoman looked worn even hidden by a veil.

The wizards Merlin, Thallud, Gildas, Ector, and Cath stood near the king, in a place of honor. Wizard Meditato was not there.

When Thom had arrived with the abbot and Francis, he hadn't been certain where to go. He doubted the wizards would want a mere journeyman nearby, especially one who was without a mentor. So he and Francis had kept to the rear of the crowd, letting the abbot go to the fore by himself.

There was another gravesite beyond the one for the fallen warriors, where the six corpses of fallen human servants lay. The rest of the human servants stood in attendance there. This was ostensibly a funeral rite for both groups, though the attention was focused on the fallen nobles. The abbot did his best to include the commoners in the eulogy, regularly looking over at them, but the separation was clear nonetheless. Thom thought that maybe he should be over there but it was too late to move without drawing attention to himself.

The pixies who had dug the holes stood farther back, watching the ceremony with a bit of curiosity since it wasn't how they honored their dead.

Thom didn't actually hear much of the ceremony. His thoughts were on the coming interment of his master.

After the king spoke of the men's bravery and the abbot offered a final prayer, the ceremony was done and they began placing the bodies into the grave. The knights worked together, respectfully lowering their fallen comrades into the pit. When all the dead lords were in their final bed, they were tucked under a blanket of dirt. Thom looked away for much of it, dreading what came next. He didn't even notice who handled the burying of the commoners.

Finally, it was time. Father Justin led some of the mourners to another grave hole, a smaller one, where only one body lay beside it. The corpse was wrapped in clean linen and a black cloth to recognize the color of a master magician. Most of the knights and commoners were still busy filling in the larger pit and placing cairn stones on top, so it was a smaller crowd who came over: the king, the wizards, along with the queen and her ladies. The pixies also came to watch. Thom was led closer to the front, since he had been Levitanus' student, and then left to stand alone. Francis dared not be so close to the wizards; Thom understood that, but he still wished his friend could be beside him. He felt abandoned.

The abbot spoke and prayed. Merlin also spoke, as did the king. Thom failed to grasp any of the words. It was all meaningless sound to him as he stared at the wrapped body. It all seemed surreal, as if it were just a dream. The weather added to that impression of unreality, masking their surroundings in a foggy uncertainty.

Thom realized that he wouldn't even have the opportunity for a final glance at his master's face and that added to his hurt. Tears of regret spilled down his cheeks, adding to the misty dew. He looked around for Francis, hoping to find at least a little comfort in his friend's sympathetic gaze, but didn't see him immediately. Instead, he noticed a hooded figure among the trees quietly watching the funeral.

Thom looked harder, wondering who this was. The dark-robed person seemed to notice Thom's attention and pulled back into the forest's shadows, vanishing from sight. Thom didn't think much of it, but kept looking for Francis and found him behind the queen's party and hidden from the wizards' sight. The monk noticed Thom's gaze and gave him an approving nod and an encouraging smile.

They never asked Thom to speak. He was both thankful and angered by that. He had no desire for such attention and would probably have stuttered over any speech, but he was the one who had known Levitanus the best. At least he had for the last decade, living with the man and serving him as his mentor instructed him on the craft of magic. He wanted to pay tribute to the man who had been like a father to him, but wasn't given the chance to say anything in front of all the others. So instead, he softly spoke his thanks to Levitanus for all he had done, hoping that God would let his master hear his words even if no one else did.

When the ceremony was done and the people began to depart, Thom went forward to help bury his master. None of the wizards stopped to help, nor did any of the nobles. The king took the queen's hand and led her back to Haven House, across the mist-soaked meadow grasses.

Thom cried freely as he started burying Levitanus.

It was the pixies who helped him lower the corpse into the hole and shovel dirt on top. Once the nobles were gone, Francis came over to help too. It was not until they were done shoveling and were placing the stones in place that Thom noticed a small group still waiting nearby. The abbot, Adele, and Vivien were watching respectfully. Everyone else was gone.

When Thom stepped back from placing the last cairn stone, Adele came up and embraced him, ignoring how muddy and soaked he was.

"I am so sorry," she whispered into his ear as she hugged him fiercely.

He hugged back, crying some more.

After a moment, Francis came near and interrupted them. "Will the two of you join us for our last funeral? We still need to lay Brother Bartholomew to rest."

Thom had forgotten that Bart had been killed too. He nodded. "Of course. Bartholomew was a good man. I wished I could have gotten to know him better."

* * *

So they held one more funeral on the Isle of Mists, as the drizzle increased to a steady rain. None of the nobles were there for the man who had been the younger son of a lord, but that seemed appropriate since Bart had renounced that heritage to become a monk. It was only the five of them who attended, and Adele had never met the man. Thom thought that a shame, for Bartholomew had been someone worth knowing.

Justin and Francis took turns sharing and praying. It was a more intimate ceremony where they shared some of their fond memories of the dead monk. Thom appreciated learning more about him and it distracted him from his pain over Levitanus.

When done with the ceremony, all three men helped the pixies bury Big Bart. Thom had the impression that Adele would have helped too, but she had to assist a still-weak Vivien back to the compound.

They buried Brother Bartholomew as the skies sorrowed.

Eric Loren

FORTY-FOUR

Travel Plans

The Road of Waters' enchantment fell out of rhythm again as Thom and the monks were trudging back to Haven House. The magic seemed to quicken, with a slight stutter to its beat. The abbot noticed the other two reacting and asked about it.

"The magic around us becomes more unstable," replied Francis. "The wizards will need to act soon or else the Road may shred apart and collapse on us."

"What would happen then?" asked the abbot, looking around as if he could see the magic surrounding them.

"For simpler enchantments, it is usually a violent ending. I would not want to be anywhere near such an unraveling of magic, let alone inside the enchantment as it comes apart," stated Francis. "But the Roads and the magic shielding Camelot have been built up over many years, with many hands involved. We have never seen such magic end. It might just sputter out, growing dim and then sputtering out like a lamp that's reached the end of its oil reserve. It might take months or years to die out, or it could just come crashing down like an old hovel pounded in a storm."

"What do you think will happen?" asked the abbot of Thom.

"I'm not certain, but when the Road of Leaves was weakened by attacks, it reacted violently. I do not think the Road of Waters is in any way more docile. The Roads react badly to wounds."

The abbot grunted. "You talk like it is a living thing."

Francis spoke up, "I have heard the river pilots say the Road will drown its enemies. It is not alive, but the Road is a complex weaving of magic that reacts to attacks."

"Can it prevent its own death?" asked Justin.

"More likely, the Keeper of the Road will bend the magic to resist," said Francis. "The other magicians will also help as soon as they realize there is a weakening, for none of them want to see any of the Roads failing. Nonetheless, some or all may fail without Levitanus' input, no matter what everyone wishes. I would think that the Road of Leaves is especially vulnerable after the damage it has already sustained, but each enchantment may react differently to the loss. I would think it would be best for us to get out of this enchantment completely until all is settled."

"But there is no way to flee the Road of Waters quickly," stated Justin.

"Everyone must either ride down to the Thames or sail back to Camelot and that will take days. Will this Road hold for another week?"

"I should think so, but I never learned the particular enchantments that are used to craft the Roads," replied Francis.

Thom just shrugged his ignorance.

They walked on a bit farther, when Justin pointed out someone else walking back toward the compound, a hooded man in a black robe escorted by a pair of centaurs. "That looks to be the Wizard Meditato. Why would he be out here alone?"

"Maybe he stood watch while the rest of us were distracted with the funerals," replied Francis. "I think the wizards have had their fill of surprises from the sorcerers and are being more cautious now."

"Does he do any magic?"

"No, Father Abbot. He most likely is just listening to make sure no one else starts an enchantment."

"You need to do the same, Francis. We cannot depend on the magicians' guild to protect us, as I have told you often enough."

Francis frowned but didn't argue with his superior.

"The League will come to be, Francis, and I hope you will join it. However, I will not force this on you."

Thom wasn't certain what the abbot meant by the "League," yet he didn't think it his place to ask. He had the impression that the abbot wanted him to hear of it, but whatever he was planning was of no interest to Thom. Not much interested him right now. He felt too numb to care.

* * *

They had made it back to the South Hall but not to the monks' room when a pixie woman caught up with them.

"Your king asks for you, Abbot Justin, and the great wizard asks for you, Journeyman Thomas. They are waiting in the wizard's study."

So the two continued on, leaving Francis behind so that he could avoid the wizards.

When they arrived, they found the room crowded with most of the knights, along with the queen and her maidens. Thom spotted Vivien sitting in a chair along the back wall, Adele at her side. Merlin was there with five of the wizards who had accompanied him. Once again, Meditato was missing.

Upon entering the study, they could hear the angry voice of the king as he confronted his chief magician. "I will not flee with the women, Merlin. I will go after Mordred and finish this once and for all."

"But your majesty, I will not be able to accompany you. I need to help Keeper Weston stabilize the enchantments here before they deteriorate any further, and then I must hurry to the Road of Leaves before it completely unravels."

"Go then, but surely you do not need all these magicians to go with you. You are the greatest wizard, are you not?"

Merlin frowned. "Your majesty, we do not know how many sorcerers accompany Lord Mordred."

"You killed four when you returned and Levitanus' boy killed another. How many more could there be? Mordred flees, knowing he is routed; I will not have him pausing to sack Camelot on his way out. I am going back to my city and my castle. If that cur is not quick enough, then I will catch him and kill him."

"So be it," stated Merlin, giving the king a slight bow of submission. However, he didn't look pleased. "I need to keep Meditato with me and we should send at least one wizard to accompany your wife downriver, in case there are any more sea serpents prowling the Waters, so that will leave you four wizards."

"That should be ample," agreed the king, "especially with Thomas and the journeywoman also coming along."

It looked like Merlin was about to protest again, but it was the queen who spoke up. "It would be unseemly for Vivien to travel upriver without a chaperon. You cannot allow that, my dear Arthur."

Her husband gave her a puzzled look.

"Do you not remember the news Merlin brought you? In the attack on Camelot, the Wizardess Honora died. She was her teacher, so Vivien has no patron or protector now. She should not travel with a large band of men. It would hurt both her reputation and yours."

"Come now, Guinevere. I will admit she is a fine-looking woman, but she is approaching a half-century in age. She is no blushing young maiden. She is also a journeywoman, used to traveling around the land to do her mistress' bidding. Besides, she is not defenseless; she knows magic."

"All of that has changed now," insisted the queen. "Her protector is dead. She should come downriver with me."

Vivien stepped up and bowed to the royal pair. "Pardon the boldness, my queen, but I must go to Camelot now if I am ever to claim my teacher's possessions. I have been promised those things so that I can study while waiting for another wizardess to take me on. But if I delay in getting there, the items may be... misplaced."

"She will go," declared the king, "for this is the business of the magicians' guild. If Merlin has no problem with her going, then we should not protest."

Guinevere lifted a dainty finger to her mouth as she pondered the situation, then she spoke. "I still do not like this. She should at least have a companion, for the sake of her virtue. I will ask one of my maidens to join her."

"I will go, my queen," said Adele suddenly, stepping up beside Vivien and bowing also.

Guinevere nodded her approval. "You are a good choice, Lady Adele. You have already proven your courage and resourcefulness. Though I will miss you, I think you are the best companion that Vivien could have. Yes, I approve."

"Well, I am glad that is resolved," said King Arthur, glancing at Merlin to make sure he had no objections, "for we have enough other things to plan. Sir

Walton, go to the docks and inform the captains that we will be sailing tomorrow at dawn. See to it that the Royal Lion and Royal Ram are ready to head upriver. Sir Lancelot, go with him. Since you will be escorting my queen downriver, I want you to make certain her boat is well-supplied for the trip. Merlin, you will have to find your own transport out of Fog Town or take your Road of Clouds once your tasks are done."

As the two knights left, the king snapped his fingers at one of his remaining attendants and the man rushed to him. "See to it that my bed is made ready. I wish to get a good night's rest before starting off again."

The servant bowed deep and then ran off to obey the king's order.

Arthur then turned to Vivien and Adele. "The two of you should go pack your belongings. Maybe Lady Adele can help you, Vivien."

The two thanked the king and accepted their dismissal.

Arthur next turned to his wife and took hold of her delicate fingers, pressing them to his lips. "You should retire too, my dearest, for you have much to get ready. I will pay you a visit once I am done here, so that we can say our longer farewells in private."

The queen kissed her husband briefly and then withdrew, her maidens going with her.

Finally, the king looked over at the abbot. "Father Justin, which party will you be joining?"

The abbot stepped forward, leaving Thom behind. He gave the king a polite bow. "I would travel with you, your majesty, if you will allow it."

Arthur nodded his acceptance. "But we will have no time to return to Fog Town for the rest of your brethren who journeyed here with you. They will have to make their own way out of the Road of Waters."

"I understand, your highness. The one monk in my company will be sufficient. I will send word to the others, telling them to return to Camelot at their own pace."

"Do so." Arthur turned to another of his knights. "Sir Kay, I am assigning you as protector to Merlin and his companions. I hear that the Keeper of the Waters has centaurs to guard him but no half-man can be as valiant as a knight of the realm. See to it that Merlin makes it to his destination and is undisturbed so that he can repair both our royal waterway and our royal road. You shall then escort him back to me. Now, tell me which knights you would want to join your party. Sir Walton, I want you to help us sort this out: who will go downriver, who will stay here, and who will join us. I do not like that we are dividing into three, but the worst of the battles are done. We only need to run off Mordred and keep him from squatting in Camelot."

The two went with the king to sit down at a table.

Thom was still standing there when Merlin finally noticed and motioned him over. "Thomas. I do not have a new master for you yet, but the council will decide on one soon. Within a year, your training will continue. For now, you will return to Camelot and help at the guild house as needed. We will find you other duties once everything calms down.

"For the trip upriver, you will serve Wizard Cath, since his journeyman is away helping repair the Road of Leaves. Do you understand?"

He nodded, glancing briefly at the rotund wizard that Merlin had mentioned. Cath was occupied talking with the Wizard Ector and didn't notice him. All that he knew about Cath was his reputation for having a temper and a passion for food.

"Go and introduce yourself and see if he has any needs this evening, then go pack your belongings. You will spend the night sleeping on his floor and seeing to his needs as a proper student."

"Yes, sir." Thom strode over to the other magician and waited for a break in the conversation so that he could introduce himself. It took some time, since Cath also enjoyed talking. It was Ector that paused and pointedly looked at Thomas as a hint to his fellow wizard.

Cath gave Thom an impatient look. "What do you want? Why are you rudely listening in on your betters?"

"Pardon me, sir, but Wizard Merlin ordered me to introduce myself and see if you had any duties for me this evening."

"Well then, introduce yourself, you up-jumped apprentice. I swear, Levitanus let you go to seed, teaching you no manners."

Thom carefully replied, trying to be respectful. "I am Thomas of York, journeyman to the late Levitanus."

He tried not to react to the criticism of his master, but it must have shown on his face, because Cath frowned. "Do not get haughty with me, youngster. Your old master had his flaws and it is best that you face that truth. Now, I want you to go to my room and pack my belongings. Not my nightshirt, for I still plan to sleep, but the rest of it. See that my dirty clothes are cleaned and ready for the trip tomorrow, even if you must do the laundering yourself."

"Yes, sir."

Thom stepped back, ready to go find the magician's bedroom, but Cath had one more comment. "And see that you leave my magician's box alone. I do not tolerate any student playing with my vials out of curiosity. If you touch my cache of elements, I will beat you. You have been warned."

He nodded understanding, although he was offended that Cath would even warn him against such stupidity. He knew better than to disturb another's supply of magical elements.

* * *

He asked a pixie on the second floor which room belonged to the Wizard Cath. The man smiled and pointed it out, explaining that the man had forbidden the house servants from cleaning in there. When Thom entered, he was appalled. Clothes were strewn everywhere, as were plates of half-eaten food. He left the plates alone for now and focused on the garments, gathering them up in a heap on the unmade bed. He used one of the wizard's voluminous robes to bundle it all and then set off to find a way to launder the pile. He hoped he could find help, or else he might be up all night scrubbing.

FORTY-FIVE

Across the Lake

Thom did find help with Cath's laundry, so it only took until midnight to wash all of it. The pixie washerwoman also helped him hang it to dry. He would have to come back before they left to retrieve and fold all of it.

After that, Thom went by the monks' room and retrieved his own belongings. Francis met him at the door, since the abbot was already asleep, and handed over a bulging knapsack. Surprised, Thom looked inside and found two magician's boxes within, along with an extra mixing bowl and pestle in a cloth sack that had a rowan tree stitched on its face. He pulled out the magician's box that had been his master's, running his fingers over the rowan tree carved into its lid.

"What is this?" he asked, his voice husky and his sight blurred by new tears.

"The pixies packed Levitanus' box among your things. I would encourage you to keep it, for you may need the additional supplies. It may be some time before you have a new master to provide any elements for your box. Although I do not like magic, I know the importance of having an ample supply of powders. I lost my master too."

Francis hadn't lost his master to death, but to the Dark Arts. Thom thought the monk's loss must have been far worse than his. At least Thom could still enjoy fond memories of his master.

He slipped the box back into his knapsack, though he wanted to linger over it. There was no time for that. "I need to go. I've been assigned a wizard for the trip upriver and I need to pack the rest of his things."

Francis nodded his understanding. "We may not see much of each other on the journey, for I will need to keep away from the wizards, but it will not be so hard to meet once we are back at Camelot. I would think that you will have an abundance of free time until they find you a new master."

Thom wasn't so sure of that, but he still agreed. He hoped that he would have time to see more of the monk. Adele came to mind too, but he realized that it might not be as easy to meet with her. Yet he still hoped for those opportunities, even though her station was now far above his. It would be a torment, but a sweet torment for however long it lasted. Someday, she would marry a lord and he would see no more of her. But for now, he could still dream of his beautiful Adele.

* * *

The king's boats didn't leave until late morning, delayed because there weren't enough servants to haul all the belongings and supplies to the docks. Thom heard numerous nobles complaining that they had to carry their own things. A half-dozen servants had died during the Battle of Haven House, but only now did it seem to bother some of these lords.

The holds of the Royal Lion and the Royal Ram were full and there were more supplies and crates stacked on deck too, even on the upper deck. Thom overheard crew members complain until a mate corrected them.

Wizard Cath carried nothing more than his own weight and a satchel containing his magician's box as he trudged down the garden hill and across the long slope of grass to the docks. Meanwhile, Thom had to make two trips to get all of the man's belongings on board. When done with the last load, he was sent to help Wizard Ector and then Wizard Gildas. He was breathing hard by the time he strode onto the dock for the fourth time. He trod onto the boat that Gildas would be riding on and delivered four bags to the cabin that the wizards Gildas and Thallud would be sharing. He was glad to see that Thallud already had his belongings in the small room. He excused himself from the wizards, neither of whom bothered to reply, and wearily crossed over to the other boat that would be sailing upriver.

He should have gone directly to the cabin assigned to Cath and Ector, but instead he sought an out-of-the-way niche on deck where he could sit on a crate and catch his breath. Vivien found him there.

"Are you ill?" she asked. "You are sweat-stained and it is a cool morning. Should I ask one of the masters to look at you?"

"Oh, please don't." Thom wiped his brow and gave her a weak smile. "I have been working as a pack mule for them all morning. Having no servants or apprentices to order about, they decided to use me as their beast of burden. But what about you? Do you need my help to get your belongings down to the boat?" He began to stand, though his muscles protested.

She smiled in return. "There is no need. Adele has already helped me with that."

He thankfully sat back down. "Good. That will give me a little longer to recover." Thom remembered the first time he had offered to help carry her things and this was a marked improvement. "I think you will find Adele to be an excellent companion, no matter that the queen forced you to this against your wishes."

Vivien nodded. "Adele is a wonderful person. I want to thank you for sending her to me the night I learned of my mistress' death. I do not know how I would have made it through all of that without her." She paused to stare into his eyes. "I misjudged you, Thomas. You are a decent fellow. Still a man, but decent nonetheless."

She gave him one more small smile and then walked off, probably to the cabin assigned to her.

He didn't know what to make of her last comment but was glad that at least she didn't see him as an enemy or clown. He rested for a few minutes longer, then went to find Wizard Cath to see what his next chores would be.

* * *

Four boats left Haven House's docks, two heading down, the others upriver. King Arthur was in the lead boat heading back to Camelot, while the abbot and Francis were on the second boat. There was a pair of wizards on each craft, along with an assortment of knights and servants. Thom was on the king's boat, as were Vivien and Adele. Unfortunately, so was Sir Walton and the man had not forgotten Thom's hug of Adele, judging by how he glared when he saw the journeyman.

Cath ordered Thom to wash the clothes that the wizard had been wearing last night, so Thom was at the rail with a wash basin, scrubbing a black robe and underclothes while the boat got underway. The crew rowed them along the length of the Isle of Mists. While pulling up a fresh pail of water, Thom looked out at the other bank they were passing. The fog had lifted enough to give him a clear view. Lake water lapped at a rocky shoreline of tangled forest. The woods were not deep, hugging a gray cliff that rose steeply into the low clouds. Thom couldn't see anything beyond the precipice, but he could hear the edge of the Waywater's enchantment just beyond.

He paused before turning back to the wash basin, listening to the magic. He heard a distinct skip in the rhythm and it wasn't temporary. He hoped it would not be much worse when they started up the Road of Waters, but he feared it might be.

When done, he hung the wizard's clothes on a wash line used by the sailors. Thom was familiar enough with the routine, since he had scrubbed his own clothes on the trip down the river. He just hoped it didn't start to drizzle.

But when Cath saw his garments displayed on deck he berated Thom. "How dare you fly my clothes like some flag? Get them down and hang them inside my cabin, you dolt. I swear, Levitanus never civilized you."

Thom gritted his teeth, but obeyed. When he entered the small room, though, the Wizard Ector looked up from where he sat reading on one of the bunks and asked what he was doing. He explained.

"I don't want Cath's clothes dripping all over the floor. Find somewhere else to hang that rug-sized robe."

When Thom hesitated, the wizard became more emphatic.

"Go. What a shame that we have no wind in the Waywater or I would tell you to hoist it up the mast. It is bad enough sharing a cabin with that man; I'll not have his clothes hanging as tapestries in here."

Thom gathered the wet laundry and stepped back out, but before he was through the low doorway the wizard said one more thing. "Do not let Cath's petty ways anger you, Thomas. You are assigned to him only for a short time. And do not assume that all other magicians are like him. I should think your new master will be more like your old one than a rude pig like Cath. My God, I wouldn't be surprised if some of those evil sorcerers are kinder than uncouth Cath. Now get out of here with those wet clothes."

Ector didn't wait for a response, but turned his attention to the book he had been reading. Thom looked at him for a moment, then stepped all the way out and closed the door behind him.

He decided to lay the garments on the out-of-the-way crate he had sat on earlier and hoped Cath didn't return to his cabin and notice the missing laundry. When he went to find Cath for his next assignment, he found the wizard with the king, the captain, and the pilot at the rudder's tiller. He dared not interrupt, so he waited until they were done. He couldn't help but overhear some of the conversation.

"But, sire, the men cannot row against the current all night. It will exhaust them to near death."

"We must gain days on Mordred. Already we are two days behind. I want us at Pine Isles Waywater by the next sunrise. If needed, my men will join them at the oars. They are a hale bunch."

"I don't mean to argue," said the captain, "but they are not used to rowing. Tis a skill, sire, and not one learned easily. A missed stroke can snap an oar or worse. I will push my men as hard as I dare, but if we do not pass Jagged Water well before midnight, I cannot risk trying to reach Pine Isle. Being caught on the Waters at sunrise is sure death."

Thom realized that the king wanted them to skip the next Waywater so that they could gain a day of travel. He wondered if it had ever been done, especially going upriver.

"I am determined that we will make up time. I will not give Mordred the chance to plunder Camelot. I want to catch and kill the cur, or at least chase him off." The king turned to Cath. "Then I must depend on you wizards. You will conjure up an extra wind to push us along."

The king wasn't asking.

Cath merely bowed his acceptance of the order.

Arthur dismissed him, so Cath lumbered off. He noticed Thomas waiting and motioned angrily for him to follow. When they were well away from the king, the wizard turned on Thom.

"Why were you eavesdropping on us? Have you no manners, you uncouth wildling?"

"I was simply awaiting your pleasure, sir."

"I have no pleasure with you around. Merlin must dislike me to saddle me with you. I think you are beyond correcting, conceited by your early promotion, and I will be sure to let Merlin know that. So far you have done nothing to prove to me that you are worthy of the rank of journeyman. Maybe you should be moved back to apprentice or simply released from the guild."

Cath glared at him, daring Thom to argue.

Thom knew better, for that would just confirm the man's opinion that he was too forward.

"You will need to work hard to change my opinion while on this trip," stated Cath after a moment, "and so far you have failed miserably. Now get out of my sight until this evening. I plan to study the currents and devise a way to make the king's wishes a reality and I'll not have you bothering me."

* * *

The crew rowed the Royal Lion past the end of the Isle of Mists and across the lake toward the triple set of archways. The Royal Ram followed in its wake, but not too closely since the clouds had dropped down again, kissing the water. Both boats rang their fog bells to make sure they didn't collide.

Even with slowing down due to the fog, they reached the gateway well before evening. Thom could barely make out the bluish glow to the fog ahead, marking where the archway spanned the narrowed waterway. They had a few more hours to wait before the Road of Waters came into being for the night. The crew used the time to rest, laying here and there on the deck and ignoring both the drizzle and the activities of those who still had tasks to do. Thom used the time to gather up Wizard Cath's garments and return them to his room, a bit damp but carefully folded.

It promised to be a hectic night.

Eric Loren

FORTY-SIX

Troubled Waters

Cath assured the captain and the pilot that the sun had set or else they would not have already started the men rowing through the archways. It was hard to tell when sunset happened beyond the gloomy fog, so they would have hesitated a while longer without the magician's confident statement. Thom heard the exchange because he was standing nearby, tasked with listening for any anomalies in the enchantment once they passed through the glowing curtain of mist. He didn't know how the wizard could know the time of day so accurately in the gloom, but apparently he could.

The captain yelled his orders and they carried over the calm waters, easily heard by the other craft. Both boats began to move forward. They passed under the triple archways, and soon were in the canal that led to the Waters' main flow.

The first thing Thom noticed was the lack of fog on this side. He saw stars already winking overhead, for it was just after sunset on a clear summer evening. The waters already glowed blue, softly lighting up the sides of the boats, but too weak to touch the darkened trees on either bank. The boat's lanterns had already been lit, giving the crew and passengers enough light to see their way around the deck. And everyone was on deck, for not even the knights would be allowed to sleep through what promised to be a hard night of sailing and rowing.

It looked normal, but Thom's inner ear picked up an oddity. There were no missing sounds in the enchantment's rhythm this time or any fading, but somehow it still grated on his magic-attuned ears.

He was trying to puzzle it out when Wizard Ector stepped up beside him and put a hand on his shoulder. "The enchantment's beat has sped up significantly. Do you hear it?"

He realized the truth in what the magician said. "What does that signify?"

Ector shrugged. "Trouble, I would suspect, but it is something new to me. You had better warn Cath, for he seems too distracted in his mixing to have noticed the change."

That was true. Wizard Cath had opened his satchel and laid his ornate magician's box on top of a crate. Thom suspected the man would have had trouble bending down all the way to the deck.

Thom hurried over to catch the man before he started mixing. Already he had four vials laid out next to a fine mixing bowl.

"Wizard Cath, there is trouble with the Waters," he said, louder than he intended, but he wanted to get his attention before the magician unstopped a vial.

Several crewmen overheard and gave Thom a worried look. The captain also heard and stepped closer to find out what Thom had to say.

Cath stopped what he was doing and looked up with a frown. "Must you yell like some wretch at the market shouting about the carrots he has for sale? Come here and talk in a dignified tone."

Thom reported on the change in the magic.

"What does that mean?" asked the captain.

"Most likely the Waters will be sped up," said Cath grudgingly. "Expect stronger currents and a greater breeze. We shall know for certain soon enough. This canal is not that long. Maybe you should go back to your place next to the pilot, captain, and be ready for rough sailing."

The man strode off, not pleased with the dismissal.

Cath frowned at Thom. "You should stop neglecting your post, journeyman. By this stage in your training, you should know better than to interrupt a magician while he is mixing an enchantment. Get back to the railing and your duties."

Thom wanted to argue that he had called out so that he wouldn't be interrupting Cath's work, but he doubted that the wizard would see it that way.

* * *

When the Royal Lion came to the main flow, it shivered and danced, fighting against the pilot's chosen direction. Cath had insisted that they had to be at the center of the river before he could release his enchantment of wind, so the crew labored to row through choppy waters that raced downriver, while a strong wind howled in the other direction.

The boat rolled and shook as the oarsmen fought to get it across the current. Even as the pilot straightened them out at the Waters' center and the captain ordered the sails up, the boat began racing backwards downriver. It was too fast a current for the rowers to stop the Waters' push.

There was a strong wind howling upriver and it snapped the extended sails, almost ripping them. The Royal Lion slowed and then stopped its downriver plunge, as wind and current fought. The boat hung in one place, heaving up and down as the current slammed into its prow and sent spray airborne, most of it lost to the screaming wind.

Cath finally released his enchantment and the winds increased. Slowly, the Royal Lion began to make headway. The captain ordered the oarsmen to double their pace.

The boat sped up.

They made it back to where the canal led to the Lake Waywater and passed the Royal Ram waiting its turn to plunge into the stormy flow. Thom noticed it as he was leaning over the railing to vomit. It was a good thing that the second boat had waited or else they would surely have collided.

Thom wiped his chin and tried to focus on the magic around him again, but his stomach roiled almost as much as the river around them. Stuck on the upper deck, he had been forced to vomit down on the walkway below. Fortunately, the fierce wind had flung the worst of his mess away from the galley, but he would probably need to go down to clean the walkway planks nonetheless.

Thom could sense Cath struggling to keep his enchantment centered on the sails as the boat continued to heave. If the magician lost control, his magic could collide with the enchantment that enfolded them. That would result in disaster.

He could also sense the Road of Waters, still beating over-fast, but now with a slight arrhythmia to it, like a heart missing a beat. Not wanting to disturb Cath, he made his way carefully across the deck to where Ector stood next to a frowning king.

"Sir," he yelled into the wind, "the Waters becomes more erratic."

Ector nodded and said something into the king's ear, which brought a deepening of the frown.

"Go back to your post, Thomas, and keep listening, but go down to the lower deck, so that your weak stomach does not sicken others," ordered the wizard. He smiled to take some of the bite off his rebuke. "A weak stomach is not something anyone can control, but I would suggest a change of clothes once we reach a waywater. Magician robes are impractical on ship anyways. Now get back to your duties. You are doing well."

Thom staggered off, taking the ladder down to the main deck and then hurried to the railing.

Eric Loren

FORTY-SEVEN

Exhausting Storm

The Road of Waters worsened as the hours passed. Even though the skies were clear overhead, it was a freakish storm within the enchantment's watery passage. The next change in the magic around them was first noticed by Adele. She told Vivien and then the two of them came over to Thomas.

"Have you noticed the color of the waters?" asked Vivien.

Thom had just retched over the side and had then pulled up a bucket-full of water to wash off the splatter, but he hadn't noticed any change. At the moment, he was surreptitiously wiping his chin to make sure it was clean. "What changes are you talking about?" He tried to isolate the magic that made up the flow of the Waters, but couldn't separate its sound from that of its walls.

"The color has deepened," said Adele. "It is now a darker blue."

Thom didn't want to look out on the churning flow, but forced himself. It did seem darker, almost a glowing indigo. "Maybe it is caused by the faster flow. Do you want to mention it to the wizards or shall I?"

"You should," stated Vivien. "They seemed to get a sour stomach just from seeing me."

Thom's own stomach started to protest. He was afraid that he would embarrass himself in front of the women, so he just nodded and stumbled off to find Ector. Wizard Cath would be too busy to have any conversation. The fat magician was having difficulty just standing on the heaving deck as he concentrated on maintaining his enchantment. King Arthur had assigned two burly knights to stand beside the wizard and keep him from tumbling.

Thom had no such help, so he fell twice just getting around to the front of the deckhouse so that he could climb up to the pilot's deck. The second time, he bumped against the last row of oarsmen, receiving a curse in response. Thom apologized and struggled on, grabbing hold of the ladder to the pilot's deck and climbing its wet rungs. He was halfway up when the Waters decided to shift. The warning bell sounded and the boat shivered even more.

The captain leaned over the rail above Thom's head and yelled to his crew. "Starboard, ease up on my count, but just a bit. The pilot needs to turn us to keep her in the middle of the flow. My count: three, two, one, hold starboard now." He paused for just a second. The galley pulled sideways with only one bank of oars fighting the current. "Now get ready to drop back into that crazed river, starboard. On my count: three, two, one, back into it."

Thom just clung to the ladder during the change in course. He feared that if he fell off he might fall on the oarsmen. When he finally made it up to the pilot's deck, he looked around for Ector and spotted him with the king, the captain, and Sir Walton. They were yelling as they tried to discuss their plans. Thom heard snippets of it as he staggered closer.

"I want... Pine... tonight," yelled the king, half his words lost in the wind.

"We can't... too slow... die," argued the captain.

The king turned to Ector. "Help Cath... faster... must... for... Camelot."

Ector bobbed his head in submission. "I... try..."

Thom attempted a bow to the king but nearly fell over as the boat lifted and dropped hard.

Ector caught his arm and yelled into his ear. "What do you want?"

"The Waters is changing colors. It darkens to an indigo," Thom yelled back to him.

The wizard paused to listen to the magic with his inner ear. Thom wasn't sure how he could do that with the wind howling so loudly. He was finding it ever harder to discern the enchantment's sound.

"I cannot hear any new danger. However, I want... to stay... near."

A sudden gust caught a few of the words, but Thom thought he understood the wizard's instructions. "You want me to stay on the upper deck?"

Ector nodded, pointing him toward the railing so that he wouldn't be in the way.

Thom obeyed. He tried to concentrate on the enchantments around him, listening for any more anomalies, but his stomach kept distracting him. He retched twice more and was unable to clean up afterward. He felt and looked horrible.

The boat hit a wave, the prow lifting high and then slamming down. Suddenly the sails lost their extra wind. Thom looked over and saw that Wizard Cath had stumbled against one of the men holding him up. From what Thom could hear, the man had not lost his enchantment, but the stagger had taken the wind's focus off the sails.

As Cath straightened himself and redirected his magical wind, it caught one side of the sail more than the other. The cloth began to tear and a few guide ropes snapped before the wizard could get the extra rush of air centered. Two of the crew scrambled up the mast in response to the damage as the boat shuddered under the strain. One of the climbers lost his hold and fell, the wind catching him and flinging him past the deck and into the roiling river.

There was no time to throw a rescue line after him; he was gone before an oarsman could stand up and look over the side.

Thom swallowed the bile in his mouth and this time it wasn't from seasickness. He looked around the upper deck and realized that Wizard Ector was motioning for Thom to come to him near the tiller. King Arthur stood next to him, his anger apparent even in this faint light.

Thom made his way over by following the deck's rail, always keeping at least one hand on the highly polished wood. He didn't want to follow that sailor over the side. He finally let go when the tiller was right in front of him. A grunting captain was bracing himself against the side to help the pilot keep the rudder straight. He stepped around the struggling men and went to Ector.

The wizard leaned close. "I need to add more wind to the sails, for the king wants us to sail to Pine Isles Waywater, but I fear the stress will snap the mast. Can you craft a Root of Power to anchor it?"

"I have no idea how to make such an enchantment," confessed Thom, practically yelling in the wizard's ear, "but Vivien may know how."

"No!" replied Ector. "We cannot have a woman mixing her magic with men. Cath would be livid and the idea even makes me uncomfortable. We need to find another answer."

"What did he say?" asked the king, having missed their exchange.

"The boy is too ignorant to help," yelled Ector, "and if we try to increase the winds without anchoring the mast it will shear off and we would likely sink the boat. I see no other way to push the Royal Lion through this flood. We ought to turn around and try returning to Isles Waywater."

Thom had a horrible thought. "But isn't the Royal Ram behind us somewhere? If we go hurling down the river, we will surely collide."

This time the king heard Thom, for he pointed a finger at Ector's chest. "Wizard, we cannot abandon... now or... collide with... find a way or..."

Thom's stomach rebelled at that moment. Unable to control it, he staggered to the stern and threw up over the side. He heaved and heaved again, though there wasn't much left inside. The wind threw it right back at him.

Exhausted from the effort, he hung over the rail. It was then he had an idea of how they might get out of here.

Excited, Thom turned back to Ector and the king, not bothering to wipe the trickle from his mouth. "Can't you just push the boat with your wind?" he asked as loud as he could. "If the sails can't handle more, why not shove the boat's backside? Send the wind into the stern, above the waterline. It would be like pushing a wagon to help the horses pull it free from a rut."

Ector frowned. "But we are on the boat. I wouldn't be pushing the wind into sails; I would have to call the wind to me and then turn it to catch the stern."

"Do it," ordered King Arthur.

Eric Loren

FORTY-EIGHT

Dangerous Waters

Thom had to assist Wizard Ector by holding his mixing bowl to keep it from sliding away on the rocking deck. The king also helped by steadying the magician as he concentrated on crafting his enchantment. When Ector finished and released the magic, Thom was able to follow its sound with his inner ear. The enchantment, slightly different from Cath's, called the wind to Ector. As a stream of wind responded, the wizard redirected it to slam into the boat's stern, directly below him.

The Royal Lion bucked and skittered, but Ector kept going and soon the wind became steady and strong, washing over the back of the boat and giving it a firm push upriver. Thom stood next to Ector at the back rail, ready to steady the wizard should he lose his balance.

The only one not occupied on the deck was Arthur. He glared northward as if he could see his rebel son just ahead. It was for their king that everyone strove so hard to get upriver.

They made great progress with both wizards using magic to push the boat but they still didn't reach the side canal to Jagged Lake Waywater until well after midnight. The pilot and captain prepared to turn the galley, but Arthur protested.

"We must go on," he yelled to them. "I want to confront Mordred once and for all."

"We cannot, sire," protested the captain. "We will surely die if we try to bypass the Waywater."

"We are making good progress now. At this pace we can easily reach Pine Isles or even Quiet Reed," argued the king.

Ector spoke up, haltingly due to his split attention but still loud enough to be heard over the wind's roar. "We... must... rest. Cath... is... near... exhaustion."

Thom saw that it was true. The other wizard's arms shook from the strain, his hair and face sweat-soaked. He was sitting on a crate and the accompanying knights were now holding his arms up to keep his enchantment going in the right direction.

"I want Mordred's head!" yelled Arthur, venting his frustration.

"You... will... have... to... wait... for... another... day."

Arthur glared at Ector. For a moment, Thom thought the king would still order them to keep going, but then he relented. Biting off each word in disgust, he gave the order. "Take. Us. In."

King Arthur then lumbered across the pilot deck and looked over the front rail, ignoring the others.

The captain and the pilot began to argue about how to get them out of the Waters' raging current. They knew better than to try turning the boat, for that would surely capsize it.

It was Ector who told them how it would have to happen. "You... will... need... to... back... her... into... the... canal... as... I... let... up... on... the... wind."

And so they went past the canal for a way, then Wizard Ector slowly lessened the wind in his enchantment, slowing the vessel and then bringing her to a standstill in the current. He was better able to talk now and gave the captain more orders. "Tell the rowers to ship their oars until it is time to turn into the canal. We will tell Cath to lighten up on his enchantment too, but not yet. I fear he might just collapse and let it completely falter."

Even as he was talking, Ector lessened the wind pressing on the stern even more. Thom could hear the magic fade and then die completely from him. The rowers had also stopped. The Royal Lion surrendered to the current and started racing downriver backwards, in spite of the magical wind Cath still strained to enhance.

"Get ready," yelled Ector. "Turn us hard when I signal, pilot. Thomas, you help him to wrestle the tiller."

Ector strode off to help the captain direct the oarsmen. He ignored the laboring Cath, walking right past him.

Thom stepped closer to the pilot, not daring to touch the worn wooden rudder arm until the man told him to.

The Royal Lion picked up speed quickly. Thom heard a faltering in Cath's magic but he had no way to help the magician or shout warning to Ector. The strain finally overwhelmed the fat magician and he lost his enchantment.

The boat sped up even more, with only the Road of Water's unenhanced winds to combat the current. From what Thom could see across the deck, Ector wasn't distracted by Cath's collapse. Instead, the wizard was bent over his mixing bowl, preparing some new enchantment.

"He prepares some new magic," Thom shouted to the pilot.

Just before releasing the enchantment, the wizard yelled something to the captain and waved to the pilot.

"Grab hold!" ordered the pilot to Thom as he began wrestling the galley into a turn.

Thomas lost track of everything else occurring. His attention was solely on the rudder's tiller, which fought back as they tried to yank it over. Ector did something to give the galley a final push out of the terrible current.

It was hard fought, but they succeeded in getting the Royal Lion backed into the waterway and suddenly they were out of the current and wind. The men let out a ragged cheer. Thom would have too, but he and the pilot had to get the galley straightened quickly before they ran aground.

The captain must have ordered the anchors dropped, because they slowed to a crawl and then to a full stop.

Thom laughed, wiping tears off his face that he hadn't realized he'd cried. They were still alive.

Eric Loren

FORTY-NINE

Break in the Storm

They lingered in that canal, too exhausted to continue. Thom dropped to the wooden deck next to the rudder arm, glad to rest. He closed his eyes but then had to reopen them to verify that they were no longer moving. After such a harrowing trip, his body imagined that it was still getting thrown about. It made his stomach protest, but there was nothing to vomit. He repressed the desire to gag and sought comfort in the dark trees to either side of the canal, shadows that did not sway or pass by. They had made it.

After a while, Thom remembered his duty to Wizard Cath. The big man and the two knights that had been helping him were strewn on the deck; Thom wasn't certain whether the wizard still lived. One of the knights was now getting to his hands and knees and crawling over to check on Cath.

Thom turned to grab the rail and pulled himself up. He heard a loud slap. When he turned back, the knight was shaking Cath, trying to get a response. Thom trudged over. "Sir, is he alive?"

"He breathes," replied the knight, "but he won't respond to any words or prods."

Thom wasn't certain in the faint lighting, but it looked like one of Cath's cheeks had reddened. He bent over the man and tried to get a reaction, but the wizard was unresponsive. The man was too big to carry back to his cabin, so Thom sought to ease his rest where he lay. The wizard's satchel was jammed between two crates, so Thom yanked it free and then put it under Cath's head as a pillow, then straightened akimbo legs into a more comfortable position. There was not much else he could do until the wizard awoke, so he went to find Ector.

He found the wizard with the king at the upper deck's fore rail, looking down on the groaning oarsmen. They turned at Thom's approach. Thomas remembered to bow to his king and waited to be acknowledged.

"What is your need, journeyman?" asked Arthur.

"I have come to ask for help with Wizard Cath. He is unresponsive."

"Most likely he has passed out from exhaustion," said Ector, "but I will go to him now and make certain of that. Meanwhile, you should go down and assist the women as they care for the injured sailors."

"Yes, do that," echoed the king. He seemed angry and preoccupied, most likely because they had failed to reach Pine Isles Waywater.

Thomas bowed again and headed down the ladder to the main deck. He found Vivien and Adele ministering among the wounded oarsmen, putting salve on their bloody hands and bandaging worse wounds. Though very tired, Thom knew he was in far better shape than these men who had been rowing all night. He did what he could to help.

* * *

An hour later, the captain roused as many of the crew as were able and had them row the boat onward, after turning it in the canal. The Royal Lion limped through the shimmering veil of fog and came out on Jagged Lake. Instead of trying to cross the Waywater to one of the Day Docks, they lingered next to the archway in hopes of meeting the Royal Ram when it came through. They waited for two more hours as the night grew old, but the second galley never showed.

King Arthur started pacing the upper deck, his aggravation obvious. He ordered Ector to use his magic to find out where the boat was. When the wizard explained that he knew of no enchantment that could do that, Arthur became more agitated.

He demanded that the captain send a skiff through the archway to see if the Royal Ram was just outside. The master of the galley tried to comply, but the men were fearful about going through, afraid that the storm might have affected the canal too.

"Send young Thomas with them," suggested Ector. "They will have more confidence with a magician on board."

So it was, that Thom had to sit in the middle of a rowboat as four sailors rowed them back through. He and the sailors saw nothing of the missing galley on the other side. What Thom saw was a trio of pixie boats.

Each small craft was being pulled by a line of swans that called out as they flew. Upon seeing the humans, the pixies had their birds land on the water and that slowed their approach to almost a stop.

"Thomas!"

He was surprised to recognize one of the men. "Dorthos? How did you get here?"

The deranged pixie laughed. "How do you think? We came up the Waters."

"Did you see the Royal Ram? Is it near?"

"The other galley that left with the king's? They gave up the fight hours ago, their sail shredded and mast snapped. They missed the upriver entrance to Isles Waywater, but they most likely found a way to swerve into the downriver entrance. At least, I hope so, and that they were not swamped or dashed against some bend in the river. Surely, the wizards on board would find some way to keep the boat together and bring them to safety."

Thom felt even more concerned now. Francis was on that boat.

"Why are you here, pixies?" asked one of the sailors. "Have you come to still the Waters or to help our king?"

"I may be a prince, but I am no magician," replied Dorthos. The other pixies let him talk for them, apparently not offended at his claim to nobility. "Ask the magician in your skiff to fix the enchantment, for he is more likely to know how. As for helping the human king, that is indeed why we are here. We have come to make sure Arthur makes it to his city. Wizard Merlin asked us to do so when he realized how terrible the Waters had become."

"Is Merlin on his way, too?" asked another sailor.

Dorthos shrugged. "The last I saw of him, he was marching across the Isle of Mists, looking for the Keeper of the Waters. I would guess that he will come along this way eventually, but I was led to understand he had more pressing responsibilities. But you need not fear, humans, for we have come to save you and your king."

The pixie held up his small bow and waved it overhead.

Thom heard the sailors mutter at the prospect, apparently not impressed by the small man. He doubted that Dorthos heard, for the pretend prince bragged some more.

"We will see to it that your king makes it safely to his stone house. You have the word of Dorthos the Daring on that. Now, let us get inside the Waywater before dawn catches us."

The swans tethered to the pixie boats had been paddling lazily about, but now they burst into the air. The three pixie boats leaped forward and were soon out-of-sight, gone through the archway's mist curtain.

The sailors were slower turning their skiff and getting it moving, but they soon followed, leaving behind the raging Waters. Thom looked back up the canal and he listened to the hectic rhythm of the magic. It hadn't slowed any. He wondered what would happen when sunrise arrived. Usually, the magical route dissipated for the day, but would that happen now? More importantly, would the Road of Waters reappear tomorrow night? Without the Waters, their refuge would be cut off from everything.

Thom hoped they weren't rowing into their tomb.

Eric Loren

FIFTY

Jagged Lake Again

The Royal Lion, escorted by three pixie boats, prowled across Jagged Lake to the Day Dock meant for those vessels traveling upriver. As they drew near, Thom saw wreckage along the shoreline and remembered the two sea serpents from the last time. He listened carefully and caught the sound of them, for they hadn't fully healed from their earlier wounds. The pair were somewhere at the head of the lake, as far away as they could be. That wasn't a comfort to him, though, for he remembered how fast the monsters had raced through the water.

He told Ector and a now-conscious Cath about the beasts. They thanked him for the warning but didn't seem very concerned.

Since they gave him no other duties, Thom decided he would try to get some sleep as soon as they were tied up. He went to the lower deck to see if he could find a shady place to sleep. It promised to be a calm and sunny day in Jagged Lake Waywater. He found a spot on the far side of the deckhouse that would remain out of the sun until late morning and lay down. It was the narrow walkway just beyond the cabin doors, where no one would have a need to step over him.

Within minutes he was asleep, his back pressed against the wall and his feet against a railing post.

* * *

The late afternoon sun woke him. Thom moaned and tried to stretch, but winced as muscles complained. He sat up and felt more aches. It was then that he noticed Vivien and Adele standing at the rail close by.

Adele looked over and smiled. "You look cute when you wake, Thomas, no matter that your hair points in all directions."

He hurriedly ran his fingers through his oily hair, embarrassed at his appearance. He didn't look down at his robe but was sure that it was stained from last night's numerous bouts of vomiting. He had been using his knapsack as a pillow, but now he grasped it to his chest as he sat there, hoping to hide the stains. "You should be keeping your distance from me, Adele. Sir Walton hates it when commoners and nobility mix."

"That brute is still asleep. Besides, I doubt he could best you, Thomas."

Thom smiled at her confidence in him, though he knew he could never hold his own against a knight.

Vivien interrupted them. "I need your advice, Thomas."

He blinked, surprised by her blunt statement. He struggled to his feet and then joined the two women leaning against the galley's railing. He kept his body turned toward the water, hoping to hide the worst of the soiled garment. "What can I help you with?"

"What do you know about the League of Barnabas?"

He was at a loss for a moment, then remembered some hints about a secretive League. "Is that something we should be talking about so openly?" He looked over his shoulder at the upper deck to see if anyone might have overhead from up there.

"The wizards sleep, after putting me on duty to listen for any trouble," she said, "and I trust Adele to hold any secrets she might overhear. From your response, I see that you do know about the League."

"Not much. It is something that Father Justin is involved in. I know none of the details, but my master knew something about it. He suggested to Brother Francis that the abbot ask you to join."

"Levitanus knew? And he suggested that I join? That is encouraging. How well do you know the abbot?"

"I met him the first time on this trip. He seems humble about himself, sincere in his beliefs and intentions. Though he also has a stubborn streak when it comes to things he feels must be done. I would say that he is intelligent yet temperamental. He is used to getting what he wants. However, Francis respects him, which speaks highly of the abbot."

"You are close to Brother Francis?"

Thom smiled. "I consider him a true friend. We survived the Road of Leaves and that brought us close."

Vivien nodded her understanding, sharing a look with Adele. Thom wondered if the two had been talking about those adventures.

"What have they told you about this League?" asked Thom.

She met his look. "They want to form a band of magicians and warriors to protect the realm. More than that I haven't been told, for the details are only for those who are members."

"Will you join their ranks?" he asked bluntly.

Vivien shrugged. "I haven't decided. What would you counsel?"

He found it humorous that she would ask his advice. When they first met, she wouldn't even let him help carry her bags onto the boat. "I trust Francis, but I do not think he is part of this League yet, if ever. He resists the abbot's urging, probably out of his hatred for magic." He paused as he gave her question more serious consideration. "I would have my doubts too, for who will direct the League? What will keep it from going over to the dark arts or lusting to take the throne for its favorite? You should ask many questions. However, I also heard Levitanus say that the League might be a good fit for you."

Thom looked out over the still Waywater and wondered where Francis was now. Had the second boat capsized and all its passengers drowned? He refused to accept that possibility. Francis had to be alive. He wondered what the monk would tell Vivien, and then smiled as he realized what he would have said. "I think my friend Francis would tell you to pray and ask God for wisdom."

One of Vivien's fine eyebrows rose. "Pray? I would not have expected that advice from you."

Thom gave a crooked grin. "Francis would say that, not I. I doubt God would listen to my prayers. You should try it though."

"Maybe I will, Thomas. Maybe I will."

Mentioning Levitanus reminded Thom that he had his master's box in his knapsack. His master had only allowed him to study its contents once and that had been when Thom was seven years old and a new apprentice needing a lesson on humility. After that he had only caught quick glimpses of the contents. It was time for him to look at and listen to what he was carrying. "Are you certain the wizards are sleeping?"

"I passed their cabin on my way to find you and heard two distinct snores."

Thom set his knapsack on the deck and opened it, pulling out the magician's box that had belonged to Levitanus. It was a dark wood box with a rowan tree carved into its lid. Thom had seen it often enough over the years when his mentor crafted enchantments. He ran his fingers over the rich wood as he remembered the many lessons that had begun with Levitanus opening this box.

"Your box is more ornate than I would have expected," stated Vivien.

"It was my master's." Thom opened the lead-lined lid and heard the intricate sounds of the trove of elements.

Vivien looked over his shoulder, as intrigued as he was. "Every slot is filled with a vial. Even my mistress had a half-dozen openings in her box, but not your master's. I am envious."

Adele quietly listened to their exchange. Her face showed her curiosity but she didn't interrupt them. Where Vivien crowded in on Thom, Adele watched from a few steps back.

He ran his fingers lightly across the cork stoppers and chose one vial at random, holding it up to the sun. The powder inside was blue, with a green shimmer. He had no idea what magical thing had been distilled to make it.

"Is that Merfolk Glamor?" Vivien asked. "My mistress told me that it had a green shine to it but I have never seen any before. That is very rare."

Thom grimaced, re-inserting the vial in its velvet-lined slot. To make Merfolk Glamor, a pair of merfolk had probably been killed. He wanted to wash his hands just because he had touched the vial; he couldn't imagine actually working with such a powder.

He quickly shut the lid and stowed the magician's box inside his knapsack, shoving it next to his own cache.

"Do the masters know you have that?" asked Vivien.

Thom shook his head. "Please don't tell them. It is the only thing I have of his. Besides, I will not likely get a fresh supply of elements until they find a new master for me and that could take years."

Vivien frowned. "I will say nothing if you are willing to share with me. It will probably be much longer until I get a new mentor."

It felt like she was coercing him, but he understood her desperation. Besides, there was his master's large cache back at Clas Myrddin that he hoped to somehow reclaim. "I will share, but only those elements that you have already been allowed to have in your magician's box. If you were found with something that only a master should have, there would be too many questions."

"You will not be experimenting with those elements, will you?" she asked.

"Of course not. I will stow Levitanus' box somewhere safe and only use it to replenish what I already have." He didn't mention that he already had powders beyond his level of training, for it had been Wizard Cruthen who had forced those on him during his adventure on the Road of Leaves.

"Then we have a bargain," stated Vivien.

Adele spoke up then. "I will keep your secret too."

He appreciated that she gave her word without any conditions. He smiled at her and then looked back at Vivien.

"Do you need anything now?" He didn't want to take any of Levitanus' powders yet, but he thought that he should make the offer.

"No, not yet."

He swung the pack over his shoulder and went to stand at the railing. He didn't know what else to say. The two women leaned on the rail next to him and they all stared out at the lake in silence for a while.

They were still standing there when the two magicians heard something. Magic.

Someone, somewhere else on the lake, was crafting an enchantment.

FIFTY-ONE

Fire Attack

Vivien and Adele hurried for the wizards' cabin to warn them, while Thom climbed the ladder to the upper deck. He rushed to the mate, who stood near the tiller. All the rest of the crew was asleep.

"Rouse the men!" Thomas yelled. "We are about to be attacked."

The mate demanded to know more but Thom ignored him. Instead, Thom took off his knapsack and pulled out his magician's box this time, along with his mixing bowl. He set his tools out on the deck and opened the case, debating which vials to pull. What enchantment could he use to fight this? A Twist of Air was the only one that came to mind, so he quickly selected the vials of powdered Snow Hummingbird feathers, Saber Leaf Dandelion seeds, and powdered Midnight Petrel wings. As he mixed the elements with water, he could hear the fireball released by its maker. It sounded huge, but he dared not look.

Thom crafted a small whirlwind, and then sent it out over the lake. Only then did he search the skies for the fireball. It came arching over a headland and across the waters, racing toward the Royal Lion. Thom wanted to intercept it with his enchantment and so deflect the fire, but he realized he wouldn't have enough time. The fireball was too fast. He positioned the whirlwind between the boat and the fireball, but it was only a few hundred feet away.

The two enchantments collided in a loud explosion that shook the galley. Flames peppered the boat, setting fire to clothes and cloth. Some just-roused men shouted in pain as they tried to extinguish burning shirts.

The explosion had tumbled Thom. He scrambled back to his box and knelt over it, ready to begin another enchantment.

Wizard Ector strode over and put a restraining hand on Thom's shoulder. "Stop. Quickly close your magician's box."

He looked up at the man, puzzled.

"Do it," he ordered with more force.

Thom shut the lid, cutting off the whispers of the various elements.

Ector nodded. "They use that sound to aim their fireballs. Your actions provided them a target."

Abashed, Thom realized the truth of it. The sorcerers weren't even in view, so how else could they have found the Royal Lion? They had known that a magician was there when Thom had opened his master's box. They had continued to know where the boat was because Thom had opened his own box when he heard someone starting an enchantment. He apologized, embarrassed by his error, but said nothing about having his master's box.

"Do not be too hard on yourself," said Ector. "You deflected the attack and you also told the mate to ready the boat. Cath is ordering the sailors to get us away from the Day Dock. The attackers will not be able to find us then, unless they come out of hiding."

Whoever was crafting the next fireball seemed to pause in finishing the enchantment, waiting for someone to react and reveal his target. When no one on the Royal Lion did so, the sorcerer lofted the firestorm over a nearby headland toward their general direction. The aim was not as good this time, and it splashed in the lake well away from the boat, sending up a furious geyser of water and steam.

The galley kept moving, with the trio of pixie boats following close behind.

They all headed toward the hidden attackers at the king's orders. Arthur gathered the magicians to him- all four of them. Included in their small group was Sir Walton, who frowned at both Thomas and Vivien. Adele stood a few steps back, fulfilling her role as Vivien's escort.

Thom had the impression that Walton didn't think either journeyman should be there.

"Can you tell how many sorcerers are attacking us?" asked the king. "Is it just one or many?"

"Two," stated Cath. "Only two have been sending fireballs at us."

Just then another fireball soared overhead, landing near the Day Dock that they had left behind.

"Then we have them outnumbered," noted the king.

"We know that there are at least two, but there may be more," tempered Ector. "Only two have been crafting magic, but there could be others in their party."

"Is Mordred with them?"

Ector shrugged and looked to Cath for an answer.

The fat man replied, "He may be there, but I counsel caution."

"We are trapped in here until sunset, even if the Road of Waters calms down," said Walton. "How cautious can we be on a small lake? We cannot flee or hide for long. There are many coves, but they would only need to row the lake's length to find us. I say we need to press near, to attack."

King Arthur nodded agreement to the nobleman's words. "That is my thought too. Can you magicians offer some better alternative? Maybe some way to draw the sorcerers away from Mordred? I would rather face him in combat and behead the bastard, without having to deal with magical attacks."

"I would presume that our enemies are all on one galley," said Wizard Cath, sounding peeved. "So how could the sorcerers leave Mordred? It is not like they can walk off."

"Freeze the lake, then the sorcerers can walk off," said Sir Walton.

Cath gave him a credulous look. "I am not God, but a wizard. No magician can freeze this entire lake."

"Isn't this whole place a wizard's creation?" argued Sir Walton. "Magic made all of this, so surely magic can alter it."

"Walton makes a good point." Arthur looked over the galley's railing at the nearest pixie boat. "What kind of magic could you craft if you had the proper elements?"

Thom wondered if the king was implying that they should kill pixies to gain their innate magic, but then reconsidered. Surely, Arthur wouldn't be so callous.

"Do not get your hopes up, sire. Being inside another's enchantment limits us," explained Ector. "Besides, the Road of Waters and its Waywaters are a weaving of over a dozen enchantments crafted over a span of months and then reinforced for many years. We have no time for such elaborate magic, even if we weren't within the confines of another's enchantment."

"Then you will have to kill the sorcerers," stated Arthur. "Eliminate them, but leave Mordred to me. I will mete out justice to that one."

Both Cath and Ector nodded acceptance of the king's order.

Another fireball soared past them.

Eric Loren

FIFTY-TWO

Eagle's Spying

The galley made it to the tip of the headland unharmed and apparently unnoticed. As they drew closer, the captain ordered sailors to fill all the wash buckets and place them back on their various hooks around the boat, just to be ready in case more fire peppered the galley.

When the crew rowed the Royal Lion around to the next cove, they finally saw their enemy's boat, the same galley that had fled Haven House. While half of the bay was already in the tall headland's shadow, the galley rested at the far end, still surrounded by sunshine. Standing on the upper deck near Cath, Thom could see the other boat clearly, men racing to get its oars into the water. He could hear two different enchantments being prepared over there and recognized them as the elements that went into crafting a fireball.

He expected Cath to begin an enchantment in response, but the wizard just stood there, staring and listening to their enemy.

Wizard Ector, who had gone to the prow with Vivien and Adele, finally began mixing some elements while Vivien held his bowl steady. Thom recognized the rhythms of only two of the four elements that went into the bowl.

Nervous about the coming attack, he wanted to start an enchantment too, but he had been told to do only what Cath ordered. And Cath was still doing nothing. Waiting.

A fireball came at the Royal Lion, exact in its aim.

When it was almost on them, Ector threw up a wall of water that caught and extinguished the flames.

The other sorcerer released his enchantment, but Thom was unsure of its purpose. Apparently, Cath recognized the magic and was waiting for something to occur. The fat man turned to look away from the enemy's galley, gazing up the long, narrow lake. Thom couldn't hear anything distinct in that direction, not with all the magical noise occurring in this cove, but Cath must have.

"Thomas, hail the pixies. They need to help chase off this coming attack."

"What attack?" he asked, confused.

"Surely you heard the call sent out for the serpents. You cannot be that deaf to magic. Now, tell the pixies that two sea monsters are racing toward us. The beasts are injured but still strong, so we will need the pixies to help fight them off."

Thom ran to obey. He looked over the railing and motioned to the nearest pixie boat. "There are sea serpents coming our way. Both monsters are wounded but they are still moving fast." He could finally hear them himself.

"Where are they?" asked the female of the hunting couple.

Thom pointed up the lake. "The pair race toward us, side-by-side. They are about halfway up the lake."

"They will separate when they get near," she stated. "All hunters do. Yell to us when they pass that headland with the steep cliff of granite."

Her husband signaled for the swans to pull their small boat closer to the other two skiffs and the great birds did his bidding. The pixies talked while their swans paddled lazily nearby, keeping their pull lines slack and untangled. They were intelligent birds.

Thom listened and watched for the serpents. When the monsters passed the designated headland, he shouted to the pixies. They motioned that they had heard and then ordered their swans into motion. They positioned themselves in a wedge formation between the Royal Lion and the onrushing serpents. Thom would have lingered to watch how they planned to protect the Royal Lion, but Cath was calling for him. He hurried back to the wizard.

"You must watch over me while I am linked to my next enchantment. I will be crafting an Eagle's Spying. I need to look down on the enemy's vessel and see who we are facing. The king wants to know if his bastard son is over there and I want to know how many sorcerers we face."

Thom had never witnessed the creation of an Eagle's Spying but he knew it was used to see things at a distance. His master had used it to find him a few times when he had been much younger and more prone to scamper off into the wilderness around their cottage.

Cath mixed the magic, attuning it to himself with a drop of blood from a pricked finger. A tiny, purple-glowing sphere rose from the mixing bowl, like a floating eyeball to settle at the head of Cath's staff, the crystal embedded there reacted to take on the same hue. Then the sphere shot away from the galley, heading toward the enemy's boat. It had a very distinct click to its fast beat and Thom wondered how long it would take before the sorcerers noticed it and reacted. Cath sat down on a crate and just stared at nothing, his vision somehow linked with the enchantment he had just created. He held his staff with both hands, somehow using it to help guide his enchantment.

Thom lost sight of the small sphere, its shimmer lost in the bright sunlight, but he could follow it by the sound. It made it two-thirds of the way to the other galley before a sorcerer reacted. Someone threw a fireball at it. Either Cath was able to swerve the sphere or the enemy's aim was bad, for Thom could hear it still going on. Another fireball soared at Cath's enchantment and this time they connected in a spectacular explosion of orange and violet.

Cath gasped, his head snapping back as the enchantment exploded. Thom stared at him, concerned. The man's eyes were dilated, his face dripping with sudden sweat.

Thom approached, worried for the wizard's health, but Cath waved him off. "Listen for any counter-attack, you fool."

Chagrined, Thom did so, listening for any response. Someone did toss another fireball their way, but Ector and Vivien handled it easily.

"What have you learned?"

Thom turned, surprised to find the king now standing over Cath. The wizard wiped a sweaty brow with the sleeve of his robe and then rubbed his eyes.

"Out with it, wizard. Is Mordred on that galley?"

Cath looked up at the king, his eyes still seemingly out of focus. "He is there, your majesty, but so is the Sorcerer Dalrake."

"How many other magicians?"

"I saw only Gweir on the upper deck…"

"Then he has only two magicians," interrupted Arthur. "I have him outnumbered four to his two. That is good."

Cath tried to protest, muttering something about Dalrake being as powerful as three others, but Arthur had already gone to where the captain and the pilot stood at the boat's tiller.

Soon orders went out to the rowers and the Royal Lion leaped forward, charging at its prey.

The sudden acceleration brought Ector and Vivien hurrying back from the prow. Adele had to put her arm around the journeywoman to help her to make it past the oarsmen without bumping any of them. She also helped a drained Vivien climbed the ladder to the upper deck.

Wizard Ector confronted Cath. "What is the meaning of this? What did you find with your spying?"

Cath told him, concluding with his assessment of the king's plan. "He means to grapple onto Mordred's galley and send his knights leaping over. We will need to prepare for close combat."

"What of the serpents? Has Arthur forgotten that those monsters are racing our way?"

"Most likely he means to let the pixies take the brunt of that attack. He thinks only of killing the rebel."

"And you are certain that you saw Dalrake? I would have thought him too cunning to allow himself to get trapped in a Waywater."

"It is Dalrake. When I was a journeyman, I saw him at the guild house, striding the halls as confidently as Merlin. And that was after his fall."

"They let him in?"

Cath smirked. "They couldn't keep him out, until Merlin interfered. Dalrake is that powerful."

"And that is what I fear. We can overpower Gweir, but I'm not so certain that the two of us can take on Dalrake. Arthur is foolish to force us into battle against Dalrake and Gweir at the same time, with only a pair of fledglings to help." Ector looked over at Thom and Vivien. "I intend no insult to the two of you, but you are no match for a master."

Thom knew that to be true, but he still hoped he would have the chance to slay Gweir, for that one most likely killed Levitanus. The sorcerer deserved death for such a horrible crime.

Thom considered how he could overwhelm a master. He had done it before and was determined to do it again. Let the wizards concentrate on this Dalrake; he would hunt down Gweir and bring justice down on his head. Yet he said nothing about his desire for vengeance. He feared that the wizards would forbid him the honor if they learned of his plans. Instead, he quietly considered what enchantments he could use against a master that might catch the man off guard.

FIFTY-THREE

Contrary Winds

As the rowers on the king's galley sped up, Mordred's boat turned away and a magical wind filled its sail. At the same time, an Eagle's Spying sphere came soaring over to look down on the king's vessel. Ector destroyed the sphere and then Vivien crafted a wind enchantment to fill their sail as well. Cath and Thom did nothing to reveal their magical skills so that their enemy wouldn't realize how many magicians were on board.

The enemy's boat raced behind the fast-approaching serpents, which had now parted to come at the Royal Lion from two directions. The pixies were able to strike at the one but the other passed beyond their reach. Thom heard the first serpent's mortal wound as its innate magic poured from it as quickly as its blood flooded the bay. The thing thrashed in agony and tried to upend the pixies' skiffs, but failed. The swans were too quick, pulling the boats so swiftly that at times the boats were airborne. The pixies pulled away to a safe distance and watched their foe die.

The second serpent came at the Royal Lion head-on, forcing the magicians to respond to it. Cath slammed a fireball into the lake, where it exploded with such force that the serpent recoiled. The boat was also turned by the resulting waves.

Thom could hear that the sea serpent was gravely hurt now, as it dove to get away from its attackers.

Ector followed up with a huge fireball of his own, heaving it at the fleeing monster. The fireball was so bright that, when it plunged into the depths, Thom could follow it with his eyes as well as his inner ear. The light went deeper, to where the beast was lurking near the bottom of the lake, and then exploded with such force that water shot skyward. Both serpents were dead now.

Thom looked around and noticed that their enemy had used the distraction to slip away, cutting close to the tall headland and then sailing boldly out into the middle of Jagged Lake. As the galley left the headland's shadow the late sun lit the craft, bringing a golden glow to its full sail. It looked deceivingly serene.

The pilot turned the Royal Lion and Vivien filled its sail with an even stronger wind as they raced after their prey.

Mordred's galley headed toward the archway out, even though it would be useless until the Road of Waters reappeared after sunset. The king's galley raced after it, with the trio of pixie boats following. The wind that was magically filling the enemy's sail suddenly turned and the sail went slack, letting the boat coast the last of the distance to the archway.

Thom was puzzled, for he still heard the enchantment blowing. He couldn't tell why the sorcerer kept it going, until Cath yelled.

"He sends the wind at us! Vivien, let go of your enchantment. If their magics clash it will shred our sail." The wizard hurriedly began crafting a magical response, but it would be too late.

Vivien let her enchantment die. Thom moved near to Cath, expecting that he would need help when the wind hit. The boat quickly slowed and the sailors hurried to lower the sail, then the great wind struck them from the other direction.

The Royal Lion floundered. The sail, not yet completely folded, caught the wind and whipped out, tearing. The boat began to move backwards as the pushing wind continued. Cath almost fell over from the rocking, but Thom steadied him. The wizard completed his mixing but didn't release the new enchantment yet. Thom suspected he waited for a break in the wind, concerned that the enchantments would clash.

Cath yelled to Ector. "Can you direct the boat out of this enchantment? I cannot release my magic in the middle of this."

Thom could hear the tension in Cath's almost-enchantment; it wasn't easy to restrain it at the cusp of release. Cath's forehead and temples ran with sweat even with the wind buffeting him, and his hands shook as one clung to the bowl while the other covered its contents to prevent any spill or other accidental release. The rhythms inside the bowl were building and Thom wondered if they would coalesce even without Cath's final touch.

He heard Ector ordering the captain to get the rowers working and the pilot to turn them out of the windstorm. Even without looking, Thom could tell that they were still getting pushed backwards across the lake. He didn't dare take his eyes off the struggling Cath, though he didn't know what he could do to stop the wizard's enchantment from completing.

Cath's face was red from strain, his teeth bared. The almost-there enchantment was getting louder in Thom's inner ear.

Through clenched teeth, Cath gave an order. "Help me to the side. Now."

Not fully understanding, Thom helped the wizard toward the boat's railing. Cath staggered when a swirl of wind gave him an extra hard shove. Thom tried to brace him but succeeded in only bumping the wizard's elbow. The bowl tipped, its contents seeping between Cath's covering fingers. The enchantment came closer to coalescing on its own.

Cath hurried his steps, while Thom did what he could to brace him against the wind's constant shoving.

Finally, they reached the boat's side. With an angry scream, Cath threw his mixing bowl and its contents into the lake. Thom winced as his inner ear filled with a screech of strained magic. Sparks flew as the bowl spun through the windstorm, but then it plunged under the water, quickly dispersing the magical elements.

Cath cursed and backhanded Thom across the face. "Your bumbling almost killed us."

The wizard didn't wait for Thom's reply, but stalked off to join Ector.

Thom thought the fault lay with the wizard's slowness in crafting an enchantment, but he dared not talk back to a master.

* * *

The wizards could do nothing against the magical wind, not without risking the boat and their king, so they had to depend on the crew to get them out of danger. In the end, the captain was able to escape the windstorm by cutting close to a headland. The steep hillside caught the worst of the wind and gave the pilot a chance to turn the galley so that they were no longer being pushed backwards.

Thom was glad to hear the enchantment die off, but he noticed that they were dangerously close to the rocky shoreline. They were so close that he could see centaurs racing toward them, down the shadowy slope. Nearly two dozen of them charged the shoreline, sure-footed even on that steep hillside. Thom saw them lift their bows and realized that they meant to attack the boat for getting too near to their lands.

He yelled out warning just before a hail of arrows rained down on the deck.

Eric Loren

FIFTY-FOUR

Enemies Meet

The arrows dropped so swiftly that no one could avoid them. Thom saw the king fall and the pilot collapse. He heard Adele cry out and saw her kneeling over a stricken Vivien. The captain grabbed the tiller and turned them away from shore; he yelled for the mate to get the men rowing faster.

Ector hurried to Vivien while Cath went to the king, yelling for Thom to come also. "Give me your mixing bowl and pestle, for I must prepare a remedy to the poison."

Thom handed over the items demanded. He looked down at the moaning king, who lay on his side and had two arrows protruding from his arm. Sir Walton, who was cushioning the king's head in his lap, was yelling at the wizard to heal Arthur.

Cath ignored the noble, instead grabbing the bowl and pestle from Thom and ordering him to pull the arrows out.

Thom tore the king's shirt away from the arrows and then worked each out as carefully and quickly as he could. The wounds bled profusely, but the blood was almost black in color. The flesh around the wounds was already darkening in reaction to the poison.

Cath, done with his mixing, shoved Thom aside and bowed over the king. He slathered a magical poultice on the wounds.

"Will he live? Will he live?" demanded Walton.

Cath was too focused on what he was doing to respond.

Frustrated, Walton grabbed Thom's shoulder. "What happens?"

Thom pulled free. "Wizard Cath's potion works against the poison, drawing it out of the king's body. Let us pray it leeches all of it."

He noticed that the king was looking up at him, his expression pained and his eyes wide. Thom thought he should comfort him. "You will be well, your highness. Wizard Cath has made a poultice to draw out the poison."

Arthur gave a weak smile and tried to reply but it came out as a pained cough.

"Rest, sire," urged Sir Walton, stroking the king's hair. "Do not strain to talk, but let the magic work."

The knight glared up at Thom, as if he had been the cause of the king's pain. Thom tried to ignore the accusatory look, but it still hurt.

Cath stood, pressing his hand against the deck to steady himself.

"What now?" asked Walton.

"Now we wait. It is a quick poison, but I seemed to have stopped it in time. The king should come back to his senses soon." The wizard held out the dirty mixing bowl and pestle to Thom. "Clean these and then bring them back to me. I will need a replacement for those I had to fling overboard. And throw those arrows over the side before someone brushes against the poison still on their tips."

Thom obeyed. The wizard's demand of his bowl and pestle was outrageous; no magician could take another's instruments or supplies, but still he would do as told. Cath was the greater magician and he had need of them. Thom also found comfort in knowing that he still had his master's tools hidden in his knapsack.

Vivien also survived and she recovered faster, since the arrow that grazed her had not embedded in her flesh, limiting the amount of poison released in her body. Ector's poultice had worked, but she was obviously weak. The journeywoman needed Adele's help even more. Thom doubted that she would be strong enough to craft any more enchantments today.

Others were less fortunate. The pilot died, as did two oarsmen and one knight.

* * *

It was almost an hour later when the king was finally able to struggle to a sitting position. Though others wanted to carry him to his stateroom, he insisted on sitting on a crate near the tiller. "I will not go to bed while my enemy lingers nearby. We must charge at them again, and this time we will grapple their galley and send my knights over to slaughter the traitor's crew. Just remember that Mordred is mine."

Ector objected. "But your majesty, you are still too weak for battle. We should be glad to be alive and choose a better day to fight our enemies."

Arthur looked up at the hillsides cupping the bay in which they sheltered. One side was in shadow while the other side was gold-lit by the low sun. "If we do not confront them soon, they will escape on the Road of Waters. I want Mordred dead and this rebellion over before the sun sets."

"We shall do it, my king," pronounced Sir Walton. "Captain, ready your crew. If you need any knights to replace your lost oarsmen, tell me."

Thom overheard all of this even though he stood off to the side, next to where Vivien and Adele shared another crate. He looked over at the two wizards to see how they would react to the king's order. Both were frowning but they didn't try to argue the king out of his decision. Thom wanted to object, but knew that no one would listen to him. As much as he wanted to avenge his master's death by killing Gweir, he didn't think they had the strength to face two sorcerers.

* * *

When the Royal Lion sprang around the headland, its hastily patched sail was full of Cath's magical wind. Before it rose Ector's Wall of Water, geysering up from the lake and providing the lion's roar. The boat ran toward Mordred's galley which sat still in the water, just outside the archway exit. Overhead, the sky was beginning to darken in the east as sunset arrived. Ector's water wall stayed ahead of them, its top edge feathering back from the speed at which it moved.

Thom simply watched, for the wizards were crafting enchantments well beyond his abilities. He did have his magician's box out, though, as well as the bowl and pestle from his master; he wanted to be ready to help should either magician's enchantment falter.

The captain stood at the tiller, now acting as the pilot too. Because he was forced to stay in one place as the wind howled around him, he was yelling his orders as loudly as he could. He had sailors climbing the rigging to reef sails as needed. He ordered others to sit at the oars, ready to row.

Next to the captain sat King Arthur on a crate his men had set up. The king sat stoically through all the yelling, ignoring all the noise and clamor; his focus was solely on the other river galley.

Thom noticed that the trio of pixie boats that had been scattered by the sorcerer's wind was now heading toward Mordred's boat too. The pixies did not have a helping wind, but their powerful swans pulled the skiffs so fast that whitewater broke over the prows.

Thom could hear new elements being mixed on the enemy's boat, although he didn't recognize the enchantment. Whatever it was that the sorcerer released, it collided with Ector's water wall. Instead of breaking through, the wall bulged out as it engulfed the other enchantment and then both exploded.

The Royal Lion charged through the downpour of water, heading toward Mordred's galley.

He heard another enchantment being crafted on the other boat and hurriedly started mixing a Twist of Air to replace Ector's Wall of Water. It wouldn't be as impressive as the wizard's magic, but hopefully it would be strong enough to interfere with whatever the enemy was making.

He sent the whirlwind spinning off over the lake. It wobbled as he sped it up and brought it in front of the speeding boat and he was able to maintain the necessary speed to keep it well ahead of the king's galley.

A sorcerer threw a fireball at them, so Thom swerved his whirlwind into its path. The enchantments exploded when wind and fire met, spewing flames all over that end of the lake. Both boats were sprinkled with fire. Thom staggered from the destruction of his enchantment; he had lingered too long in his connection to the magic and now his inner ear rang from the explosion.

Thom leaned against a barrel to catch his balance and his breath. The noises around him seemed muted after the explosion, but he heard the king yell out for the captain to keep them heading for Mordred.

Knights hurried to smother the few fires that had kindled while the sailors now started rowing. Cath's wind still filled the sail. Ector was starting another enchantment. Thom shook his head to clear the ringing and then set out his magician's box again, wanting to be ready with another enchantment. He heard

Vivien's box open as well and he wanted to protest that she hadn't recovered enough strength yet, but there was no time to do so.

Ector flung a fireball, as did one of the sorcerers on the other galley. The burning missiles missed each other in mid-flight. Thom mixed another whirlwind to stop it, but Vivien was quicker. Her whirlwind caught the fireball and then both exploded, splashing the Royal Lion with sparks. Sailors hurried up the rigging to douse a bit of smoldering sail but other than that the boat and crew made it through unharmed.

Cath finally stopped his wind, whether from exhaustion or to keep from fanning the fire Thom wasn't sure, but the galley continued on its own inertia, bearing down on the enemy's boat.

Meanwhile, Thom had a whirlwind without an obvious target. He turned it and guided the winds toward Mordred's galley. One of the sorcerers had deflected Ector's fireball, but neither was ready to intervene with Thom's miniature tornado. The spinning winds struck the boat broadside and caused it to wallow and turn to the right. The sail tore and some of the men were knocked over. It didn't do much damage, but it forced the sorcerers to pause in the enchantment making just long enough for Cath to create a fireball and heave it into their sail.

Mordred's boat burned.

The Royal Lion closed the rest of the distance. The two galleys rubbed sides and sailors jumped over to Mordred's boat to tie lines, so that they wouldn't slip apart. Arthur's knights followed, jumping the gap and wreaking havoc among the enemy's sailors. Thom saw Sir Walton leading the men.

One of the sorcerers wrought a wind and pushed on Mordred's galley, trying to break free, but instead it just sent both boats moving, drifting toward the archway.

The other sorcerer crafted a Siren Call and his voice filled the ears of everyone on both galleys. He lured them to cease fighting and go to sleep. Knights and sailors dropped weapons on both boats and lay down on the decks. The wizards weren't fast enough to respond and became trapped in the enchantment with all of the others.

Thom yawned, trying to fight off the urge to close his eyes, but the magically enhanced voice kept urging him to sleep. For just a moment he remembered fighting off a similar enchantment on the Road of Leaves when others covered his ears, but his mind was too fogged and his reactions too sluggish. The moment passed and Thom could think of nothing except sleep.

As Thom looked around for a soft place to lie down, he saw the lone man standing on the other boat's upper deck. The only one not lulled to slumber was the sorcerer who had crafted the enchantment.

Dalrake.

FIFTY-FIVE

Through the Archway

As everyone fell asleep, the two boats drifted through the archway exit. However, as they passed into the glowing curtain of mist, the sorcerer had to release his magic or else cause a fatal explosion. Without the constant whisper to sleep, some began to recover.

Thom struggled to open his eyes, knowing his life depended on it. He was having trouble fighting the magic's residue, for he was indeed tired. He sat up as the chill dew settled on him. It was then that he heard his magician's box, its lid wide open and its contents exposed. The magical elements whispered to him.

He was glad that he hadn't fallen asleep in the middle of making an enchantment or else it might have destroyed the gateway and all of them. He still reached over and shut the lid as a precaution, for the various rhythms seemed to be speeding up in response to the magic they were passing through.

The boats drifted into the side canal that led to the Road of Waters and suddenly he could hear the Waters' magic, still over-fast though not as hectic as last night. He knew that he should be starting another enchantment to defend himself, but his mind was still clouded from the Siren Call. He stood, clutching his magician's box, and looked around. Men were rousing on both boats and returning to their fighting. The other boat was still on fire, the sail and mast fully engulfed and dropping globs of fire on the deck. And then Thom saw three men jump across to the Royal Lion, Mordred and his two sorcerers. A group of ten black-clad soldiers of Castle Crow also jumped over and began hacking at the lines holding the two boats together.

Thom yelled out warning, but none heard him over the sound of renewed fighting. Suddenly, the boats were apart and almost all of Arthur's knights were on the wrong boat.

Mordred and his sorcerers ignored the sailors, rushing up onto the upper deck where Arthur still sat on a crate and the wizards were hastily trying to craft enchantments. The ten Crow soldiers were right behind them.

The wizards were stopped at sword point, in the middle of their mixing. Gweir seized their mixing bowls and pestles, throwing them into the canal with no consideration of the half-crafted contents. He then took their magicians' boxes too, but those he wasn't about to wastefully throw away. Thom's box was also taken, as well as the sword dangling at his side. Their magician staffs were also taken away and all of their belongings were placed into a pile in front of Dalrake. They missed the second box stashed in Thom's knapsack, for no magician ever carried two.

Vivien hid hers as well as her magician's staff, so they overlooked it at first; they probably weren't expecting a female magician. But the sorcerers knew that four magicians were on board and demanded to know where the fourth one was. When no one spoke, Dalrake ordered Ector brought near. The threat he whispered must have been dire, for the older man began to shake and then suddenly point out Vivien.

Dalrake pushed Ector aside and marched over to her and retrieved her magician's box, easily overpowering Vivien without using any magic. She was just too weak from the poison. The great sorcerer then tossed the four cases into a heap, well away from their owners.

During all of this, Mordred had walked up to his father and backhanded him, sending the weakened king sprawling on the deck. He kicked Arthur twice as he struggled to get up. The king curled up, trying to protect his head and chest. Mordred stood over him, staring down contemptuously at his moaning father.

Dalrake strode up to the captain as the man clutched the tiller. "Order the men to the oars. I want us to stop before we drift out into the Waters' maelstrom."

The captain did as told and soon the Royal Lion stood still on the canal. The other boat was still burning and drifting toward the raging river, but that wasn't good enough for Dalrake.

"Gweir, shove that boat out of our way. I will not have Arthur's pets trying to swim back over here."

The sorcerer crafted a simple Teasing of Air and gave the other craft a push. The burning galley floated down the canal and seemed to linger for a breath, but then the Road of Waters caught it and whipped it away.

Neither Dalrake nor Mordred showed any remorse over the lost galley and crew.

FIFTY-SIX

Captured

Thom stood there, uncertain what he could do. He still had his master's box, but there was no time to get it out and create an enchantment, not with the soldiers watching. He tried to move closer to Vivien and Adele, but a soldier noticed and stopped him with a sword point.

Dalrake noticed him too and came over, motioning for the knight to continue on with his comrades that were going down to the main deck. The sorcerer smiled at Thom, but it was a cold smile. "So you are the youngster who defeated Sorceress Narissa? Maybe you should reconsider her offer to join us. I would see that you are fully trained and I would not keep secrets from you, Thomas. You would not be neglected among us or without a master."

Thom couldn't help but glare at Gweir, the one who had killed Levitanus.

Dalrake laughed. "It need not be him, if you so dislike your teacher's old student. Would you like me as your new mentor? There is no magician greater than I. Even much-praised Merlin fears me. I will teach you the greater magics, those enchantments that can alter time and reality."

Thom felt no temptation to such a life, for it meant killing magical beings. "Your hands are soaked in blood."

Dalrake held up his hands, turning them in front of Thomas to show their cleanliness. "Blood washes off, but the power remains. Give my offer some careful thought, Thomas. The guild will soon be destroyed and then what will you have?"

The sorcerer walked away, showing no fear in turning his back. Thomas glared after him as the magician went over to where Mordred was once again kicking Arthur.

Most of the soldiers had climbed down to the main deck to make sure the sailors stayed at their rowing stations and behaved. Only two remained up here with the sorcerers and Mordred, but it was enough. One stood watch over the two sorcerers while another kept watch on the captain to make sure he did nothing rash with the rudder. They didn't bother to set guards on Thom or the women.

Thom heard a muffled disturbance on the main deck. He glanced that way, but he wasn't close enough to the railing to look down. He was uncertain if the soldiers were abusing one of the sailors or if one of them had taken revenge. So far, there was no outcry. Then the sound of a skirmish arose. Sailors and soldiers yelled out, but no voice was clear enough to understand in the sudden uproar.

"Gweir, find out what is happening," ordered Dalrake, "while I protect Lord Mordred."

The great sorcerer crafted an opaque shield around himself and Mordred. Arthur, splayed at his son's feet, was also inside.

Gweir quickly crafted an enchantment unlike any Thom had ever seen or heard. He completed his crafting by plunging his hand into the mixing bowl. When he lifted it up, lightning sparked off each fingertip. Then he strode toward the railing.

At that moment, Cath ran for the magician's boxes, surprisingly fleet for such a large man. The guarding soldier yelled and ran after him.

Gweir noticed and pointed his pinky at the wizard. A flash of lightning shot out and hit Cath, sending him sprawling on the deck. The wizard screamed as he writhed in agony.

Thom moved closer to Gweir. Somehow, he wanted to stop him and get revenge for his dead master.

When the sorcerer turned back, Thom stopped advancing. He forced himself to be patient, to wait for an opportunity to bring justice to the killer.

Ector and Vivien, who had both started toward the stash of boxes, stopped.

But before the guard could kill either, a tiny arrow caught him in the neck and another in his side. He staggered and fell. Another pair of arrows, in quick succession, struck the shield around Mordred and Dalrake. The tiny shafts fell harmlessly to the deck, shattered against the enchantment.

Gweir spun toward the ladder and released two more blasts of lightning. In the brief flash, Thom saw two pixies thrown back by the lightning bursts, surely dead.

Thom moved again, still not certain what he could do. There would be no time to craft any magic, not when the sorcerer was so near. He had no sword, since the soldier had disarmed him, but he did have a knife. He decided that he would tackle Gweir and then stab him.

This time, Gweir saw Thom moving and he smiled. He stepped away from the railing and actually came closer to Thomas. "What are you planning, little whelp? The only reason you are not yet dead is that Dalrake hopes you will join our ranks. I, on the other hand, would rather see you as a pile of ashes. You are pathetic in your scheming, almost as pathetic as your weak master."

Thom glared at the smug man. "Levitanus was a far greater man than you."

Gweir chuckled, stepping a little closer. "Then why is he dead? I am only sorry that I was not the one who killed him. I would have enjoyed seeing him writhe in agony. I heard that he burned to death. He must have screamed greatly, the weakling."

Rage for his master rose in Thom and he hurled himself at Gweir. He made it only four steps when the lightning hit him in the chest and threw him across the deck. He screamed as his body trembled and shook. Lightning coursed through him, making everything twitch. Even in his agony, he wanted to get up, to attack the sorcerer. But his body would no longer respond. Even as the shock wore off, he remained limp, no longer able to move his arms or legs.

Eric Loren

FIFTY-SEVEN

Back to the Waters

As Thomas lay there against a row of crates, unable to move, he heard the mate bark an order to the sailors who still lived. The boat began to move toward the Road of Waters. When Thom saw Gweir angrily stride back to the railing, he wanted to shout out a warning but he had no control of his voice. All that came out was just an incoherent gurgle.

Only one of Gweir's fingers still held lightning. He pointed it at the lower deck and the lightning blazed. Someone screamed and the oarsmen fell out of sync, but the boat was already moving. Gweir looked at the captain still clinging to the tiller and ordered him to turn the galley at the canal's shore.

The captain ignored him.

The Royal Lion kept moving toward the raging Road of Waters.

Gweir's magic ended with that last lightning strike, so he had nothing to throw at the captain. He had been a magician too long to even think of confronting the man physically. Instead, the sorcerer pulled out his magician's box and quickly prepared another enchantment.

The captain bravely held the tiller steady, aiming them into the furious flow.

Thom was able to sit up, resting against the crates, but his body was still weak and twitching at times. He saw Ector and Vivien run for their magician's boxes. Somehow, the wizard bumped into her and sent the weak journeywoman sprawling. Ector didn't stop to aid her, but grabbed his magician's box and opened it, starting his own enchantment. Adele rushed to Vivien and tried to help her to her feet.

Thom saw that Cath was now crawling toward the pile of magicians' boxes, unsteady even on his hands and knees.

He looked over as he heard Gweir complete his enchantment. His fingers dripped with lightning again.

The sorcerer pointed one finger at the captain and the lightning strike threw the man hard against the tiller, knocking him unconscious. The Royal Lion finally turned, but it was too late. Instead of catching the side canal's bank, it merely angled as it dove into the Road of Waters' flow. The galley whipped around as the current caught it, the tiller arm wavering without anyone fighting it into line. Suddenly, they were racing downriver, a piece of flotsam in the flood.

Thom heard a loud honking protest from over the side and realized that the Night Swans were still following the boat, struggling to stay close for their pixie masters.

The galley shivered, heaving up and down. Gweir staggered but kept his feet. Thom expected the sorcerer to blast Ector next, but he withheld. Instead, he smiled and yelled out across the deck as the wind howled around them. "What now, Ector?"

The wizard rose, lightning in his hand as well. "We ride this wild flood to the Isles Waywater, or even all the way down to the Thames. There is no way we can fight upriver to Camelot now, not with a hostile crew and a torn sail."

Gweir smirked and yelled back. "True. Conquering Camelot will have to wait, but we have the king. That is more important."

Apparently, Dalrake and Mordred could hear the comments from within the opaque shield, for the noble gave Arthur another kick when he heard him mentioned.

Cath, in his staggering crawl, had almost made it to the cache of boxes when Ector turned toward him and pointed two fingers. The double lightning struck the weakened wizard and threw him against the railing to move no more.

"Did you kill him?" asked Gweir.

Ector shrugged. "I hope so. I can't stand that fat pig." He walked over to the rail and yelled down at the crew, demanding that someone take the tiller. He reinforced his order with another lightning strike.

Two burly men hurried up the ladders and made their way to the back, grabbing the tiller and fighting it so that the galley pointed squarely down the center of the swift current. The galley still bucked and shook like a wild stallion fighting the saddle, but now it didn't wallow.

As this was happening, Thom finally realized that Ector was a traitor; that he had been a practitioner of the dark arts while pretending to still be loyal to the guild. His heart sank, for now it was three sorcerers against Thom and Vivien. He gave in to his protesting stomach and vomited onto the deck beside him.

FIFTY-EIGHT

Traitor

"How many pixies have you killed?" asked Dalrake from within his shield.

"Four," replied Gweir.

"Then find the last two. I will not end this shield enchantment until you do."

Gweir and Ector moved to the rail and gazed down on the lower deck, trying to spot the pixies among the shadows and the milling crew. Gweir ordered the men to reveal where the pixies hid, but apparently no one spoke up because he sent two lightning bursts to crash among the sailors. Men screamed in pain.

Meanwhile, Mordred had started abusing his father again, now kicking his head. Dalrake ordered him to stop before he killed the king, saying something about sparing him for the trial.

Thom took that moment of distraction to pull himself behind some crates and sacks, sitting up in that shelter and taking off his knapsack. He found Levitanus' box and set it on his lap. He then pulled a half-full water bucket off its hook at the rail, and took a ladle full to wash his mouth of the taste of vomit and to make sure his spit was pure. He ladled a bit more water into the mixing bowl as a base for an enchantment. He replaced the ladle and took a deep breath. It was time.

Thom ran his hands over his master's richly carved box, worried that he wasn't strong enough to do this but certain that he wouldn't have much longer to try. He knew that as soon as he opened it the others would hear, so he had to be ready to create an enchantment as fast as he could. With bowl and pestle ready in his lap, he unlatched and lifted the lead-lined lid. The elements sang out, a jumble of raw rhythms.

He chose three vials by sound, quickly closing the box, and then poured each vial's contents into his bowl, stirring them into the water to form a paste. There was no time for careful measuring. The mixture sloshed over the rim when the boat rocked. As Thom stirred it, he added his spittle to attune the magic to himself.

Lightning struck the crates hiding him, setting them on fire and raining splinters at Thom. He had bent over and covered the bowl when he heard the magic release, so none of the debris contaminated his mix. It did hit his back and head though. Two more lightning bolts hit his shelter as he smeared the thin paste on his hands and lips.

His shelter was now gone, burning debris scattered all around him. Only smoke hid him from sight, but the magic's sound told the sorcerers right where he was.

A small whirlwind rose from Thom's hands, the Waters' wind tugging at it, trying to break it up. He had to concentrate on the enchantment, no matter that an attack was imminent. He sent the whirlwind dancing across the deck, toward the two sorcerers. One of them responded with a lightning flash that caught the whirlwind and whipped around it. For just a moment the two enchantments seemed to merge, creating a swirling light, and then they exploded, throwing sparks and gusts of wind in all directions.

Thom tumbled from the concussion, still clinging to his mixing bowl. When he came aright, he realized that he still had enough mixture to try to form another whirlwind. It came out weak and unstable, but it formed.

The explosion had blown out the fires and the steady wind of the Waters cleared the smoke. He was now completely exposed. As Thom struggled to hold his flawed enchantment together, he looked for a target. That is when he saw Adele, knife in hand, stalking Ector. He almost lost his enchantment then, out of fear for her, but refocused on it, sending the wobbling windstorm to crash into the sorcerers. Both stumbled but the whirlwind wasn't strong enough the knock them over. Gweir, who had been kneeling over his magician's box, lost hold of it as he steadied himself and it skittered away. The sorcerer had to hurry after it.

Unplanned on Thom's part, the wind shoved Ector toward Adele.

She grabbed his billowing robe and pulled him even closer, thrusting her knife into him, just below his ribs. She lost her grip when the traitorous wizard pulled away. Ector grabbed his side and then stared at the blood that already stained his hand. In a rage, he pulled the blade free and lunged at her.

Adele would have died then, but a pixie arrow came out of nowhere and caught Ector in the eye, stopping his knife thrust. The traitor stumbled and fell.

FIFTY-NINE

Lightning Strikes

Thom saw Dorthos the Deranged step off the ladder, another arrow already notched. The crazy pixie had used the wind to rush his arrow right into its target.

The Waters' strong wind turned Thom's enchantment and it started back across the deck, right at Dalrake's magical shield. Gritting his teeth, Thom fought to turn it away. As much as he wanted to destroy that shield and shock the sorcerer, he couldn't risk killing the king.

When Dalrake saw and heard his effort, he smiled at Thomas. It was a cold, calculating smile.

The whirlwind swept off the back of the galley, missing the men at the tiller too.

Thom let the enchantment die off. There was no time for him to relax; he had to get his tools ready for another enchantment. He scooped water from the bucket into his mixing bowl, swishing it about to loosen the residue, and then pouring the mess onto the deck. He used a garment from his knapsack to wipe the pestle and bowl clean.

Without looking up, he could hear that Gweir had opened his magician's box and begun a new enchantment.

Thom hurried to do the same. He opened his master's case, but then hesitated over the many vials. What to make? A half-dozen enchantments came to mind, but nothing seemed a good answer. Fire was too dangerous, and the constant wind made any air enchantments risky. He couldn't settle on anything that he could use to fight against a sorcerer.

Gweir's magic was forming, its rhythmic beat growing stronger.

Desperate, Thom snatched vials of powdered Azure Fireflies, powdered Meadow Dragon wings, and dried and crushed Glow Berries. He quickly mixed the elements and added his spit. He formed small balls of the resulting paste, balls that started glowing as he worked them. They were Wizard Lights, which would provide a soft light but no heat. Touch them and your finger might tingle, but they certainly caused no harm. Thom felt foolish, but it was too late to create some other enchantment.

As he stood from his crafting, Thom held a small, bluish-glowing sphere in each hand, with enough left in the bowl to form another pair. He tossed the glowing balls at Gweir, more in hopes of distracting the sorcerer than of actually stopping him. He guided them with his thoughts even as bent to form two more. The Wizard Lights dipped and weaved as the wind battered them, but Thom guided them expertly. He had mastered this particular enchantment many years ago. But he wasn't fast enough. Gweir finished his enchantment and released it as well, a roaring fireball.

Thom's tiny Wizard Lights were swallowed with barely a slowing of the fireball, too weak to disrupt the other magic. He dove to the side and the fireball soared past, curving as the Waters' winds caught it.

Gweir let go of the enchantment and it sputtered out before it could hit the Road of Waters' boundary of magic.

Thom pushed off the deck and hustled back to his bowl, scooping out the last of his mixture and forming two more Wizard Lights. Raising both hands over his head, he threw them at Gweir, willing them to keep straight even as the wind yanked at them.

The sorcerer showed no fear of the attack. He stood there and grinned, knowing that a Wizard Light was harmless.

But at the last minute, Thom turned the lights, sending them diving at the planks in front of Gweir. One hit the rim of the sorcerer's mixing bowl, flipping it into the air where a particularly strong gust of wind caught it and sent it sailing over the rail and into the river. It was almost as if the Waters' wind had strengthened just to carry it off. The other Wizard Light collided with the corner of the man's closed magician's box, sending it spinning across the deck.

Thom hurriedly rinsed his bowl, for he needed a stronger enchantment if he hoped to stop Gweir.

Gweir must have recovered his stash of elements, because Thom suddenly heard them whispering their peculiar rhythms.

Worried, Thom open Levitanus' box and began crafting another enchantment, choosing a Twist of Air this time.

Gweir finished before Thomas, lifting a handful of lightning again, but instead of striking out at Thom he pointed at the ladder that came up from the lower deck, sending two sailors crashing backwards.

"Behind you, Gweir," yelled Dalrake in warning, his voice muffled by the shield he still maintained.

Gweir spun and shot a flash of lightning into Vivien, who had just opened a magician's box. It knocked her over and left her twitching on the deck.

Adele had been sneaking toward him with a sword she had grabbed from a dead soldier, but now realized that Gweir saw her. Instead of trying to hide, she ran at him.

She didn't make it.

Gweir pointed a finger at her and the lightning shot out, catching her in the chest and spinning her around.

Thom saw Adele collapse. Her body shook violently and then went still.

"No!" He stood and almost ran from his nearly completed enchantment, but then caught himself. His master had lectured him too often about the danger of leaving an enchantment unfinished.

Choking back his anger and fear, he finished the mixing and added his spit.

He formed a whirlwind, small but sound in its beat.

Just then, Gweir turned toward Thom and raised his hand, lightning flickering along his fingers.

Eric Loren

SIXTY

Over the Side

Thom would have died in an explosion of clashing magic, but he sent his whirlwind skyward just before Gweir pointed a finger at him. A blast sizzled toward him, but his enchantment was out of the lightning's path. Instead of striking the whirlwind, the lightning hit Thomas.

The impact tossed him backward and over the side railing, his body shaking violently. Thom tried to catch himself, but he couldn't control his limbs. His arms and legs flailed as he dropped. He landed hard on the rail of the lower deck and would have kept falling, into the Waters' torrent, but two small yet calloused hands grabbed him at that instant and yanked hard to bring him onto the narrow walk.

As Thom lay convulsing on the walkway, his eyes still blinded from the flash of lightning, he heard Dorthos' deep voice.

"Not a night to go swimming, lad."

He said nothing. Thom wouldn't have replied even if his teeth weren't chattering from the after-effects, for he had just realized that he hadn't lost his enchantment. Somehow, through it all, he had maintained his link to the magic. His inner ear cleared before his sight or normal hearing and he could hear the elemental rhythms again. He knew where Gweir stood, hearing the last of the lightning enchantment in the sorcerer's hand. Thom called the Twist of Air back down, rushing it at Gweir.

The sorcerer must have released his last lightning burst, for Thom's enchantment exploded.

"Are you still playing with magic even while shaking?" asked Dorthos, trying to see what happened on the upper deck. "Or was that from the woman magician?"

Thom was too weak to reply. The worst of the shaking had ceased, but his whole body was sore and exhausted. He was able to give the pixie a slight nod. He wanted to get up. He wanted to know what Gweir was doing. He wanted to know if Adele still lived.

Adele.

He tried to express his rage and fear, but all that came out was a groan.

Dorthos patted his head. "You have done well so far, Thomas. Rest for a moment to recover from the shock. If the sorcerer peeks over the side, I will feather him in the forehead."

The pixie stood watch over Thom, allowing him to catch his breath and regain control of his body.

Thomas tried to ignore the tingling numbness, concentrating on moving his limbs. Finally, he was able to pull himself to a sitting position, resting against the deckhouse. So far, he could hear no new magic, just Dalrake's shield. And he heard the Road of Waters, of course. The complex enchantment was a constant music in his inner ear, still racing like the heart of a messenger after running to the top of a tower.

"Do you know what they are doing up there?" he asked Dorthos, raising his voice to be heard over the constant wind.

"I have heard some arguing but cannot make out the words."

Thom struggled to stand, leaning heavily against the deckhouse for support.

Dorthos stepped close. The tiny man was able to get face-to-face with him because Thom was still bent over somewhat. "What are your intentions, Thomas? Are you after the younger sorcerer for revenge? If so, then know that is not the honorable thing to do, not when others are still at risk. Think of the king."

"Gweir killed my master. I think he killed Adele too."

"I know that pain," replied the pixie, "but you must resist embracing vengeance; there is no comfort in those cold arms. When I lost my beloved Daria, I sought only revenge on her killer. That is what drove me to madness. Do you really want to follow in my footsteps?"

Surprised, Thom looked deep into the pixie's clear eyes. Dorthos the Deranged was right. Although Thom's heart hurt even more than his bruised body, he needed to deny it. He needed to focus on saving the king.

"Will you help me?" he asked of the pixie.

"Of course I will. How could I deny the Road Saver? In truth, I am still disappointed that I missed your adventure on the Road of Leaves."

Thom smiled through his pain, thankful to have this small man at his side. "Are any others of your kind still alive?"

Dorthos grimaced. "Gorsen, Hiltara, Yirsard, and Tivolla have all perished. Olzo still lives, but his leg is broken. The sailors hide him under one of the rowing benches. Although the sailors are willing to help, they are needed at the oars. I think they are struggling to keep the boat centered on the Waters in this terrible flood."

The mere mention of the Waters caused Thom's stomach to protest; it wanted to remind him that it detested this rocking galley. He strove to ignore his unruly innards and decided that he needed to prepare another enchantment before seasickness distracted him too much. He could still hear no magic from Gweir but he was certain the sorcerer would react as soon as Thom opened the magician's box. He just hoped to craft his enchantment faster.

SIXTY-ONE

Death by Drowning

Thom opened his master's box and quickly grabbed the vials he wanted. He had decided to make another whirlwind, hoping to use it as a distraction so that he and Dorthos could climb to the upper deck. It seemed an impossible task, but he would have to get Dalrake to drop that shield so that they could free the king.

As he expected, he heard a reaction on the upper deck. Gweir was crafting an enchantment too. He recognized its rhythms by now- more lightning.

Thomas completed his Twist of Air and sent it high into the air above the boat, fighting to keep it from getting shredded by the Road's wind. For now he was successful, keeping it in place without ripping into the rigging nearby. Dorthos helped him pack his box and bowl so that they could get going. They made their way around to the main deck where the sailors labored at the oars. Thom kept the whirlwind in the air well above the deck in case Gweir tried to destroy it, but so far the sorcerer hadn't thrown any of his handful of lightning bursts.

Thom and the pixie stopped at the foot of the ladder. Even without seeing his opponent, Thom could tell where Gweir stood by following the sound in his inner ear. He moved the whirlwind, bringing it down to touch the upper deck so that it was between them and Gweir, then he and Dorthos hustled up the ladder.

Gweir struck. Two lightning blasts hit the whirlwind. Thom stopped at the head of the ladder so that he could concentrate on his straining enchantment, laboring to keep it intact as it fought with the sorcerer's magic. Lightning crackled throughout the spinning winds. The whirlwind became erratic, lopsided, but it held. Dorthos was able to get up and notch his bow.

As Thom strained to keep the whirlwind intact, he heard two more enchantments being created. A quick glance told him it was Vivien and Dalrake. It frightened Thom that the sorcerer was able to start a new enchantment while still maintaining the shield.

The boat shivered. Thom had spent enough nights on the magical river to recognize that feeling. The Road of Waters was about to shift. The two sailors manning the tiller started turning the rudder in response, heaving it larboard. The Royal Lion responded, turning left. The boat shook from one end to the other, an intense shiver as it sought the new center of the Road.

Thom's stomach reacted to the change and started its own heaving. He lost

273

his concentration on the whirlwind just as Gweir hit it with a third lightning bolt and it shredded violently. Thom staggered from the force but didn't fall.

Dorthos took that moment to shoot, his tiny arrow aimed right at Gweir, but the Waters' wind betrayed him. A stronger gust caught the poisoned arrow and nudged it off target. Gweir didn't flinch as it flew past. His concentration was on Thomas as he raised his last two fingers that had lightning chasing up and down their length. It would be a killing blow.

The Royal Lion shook again and the sailors on the main deck screamed out. Even in the roaring wind, everyone on the upper deck heard the splintering of numerous oars. The two at the rudder tried to react, but they were too late. The river galley's left side hit the edge of the Road of Waters, colliding with the magic wall that separated it from the normal river that flowed beside it.

Just before Gweir flung lightning at Thom, the galley pushed off the enchantment's edge, leaning sharply starboard as the magic repelled it. Thom fell to his hands and knees and the lightning sizzled past, well over his head.

The boat tipped further and Thom heard Vivien's budding enchantment collapse as she lost her balance. Thom saw Adele grab her and then both of them slid down the tilted deck until they hit Dalrake's shield.

For just a moment, Thom felt a bit of relief, realizing that Adele was not dead.

A pair of barrels tipped over and also collided with the shield. Dalrake's concentration was already divided, since he was just completing his second enchantment, so the shield became unstable, bending in from the weight on its side and becoming lopsided.

Lord Mordred lost his balance and fell against the inside of the shield, putting even more strain on it. Suddenly, the shield collapsed.

Mordred stumbled across the deck, catching himself at the rail.

Dalrake also staggered but kept his feet. He was able to avoid the barrels that rolled past and he sidestepped Vivien and Adele as they slid against the unconscious king. Dalrake glared about him, exposed but not defenseless, for he held lightning in one hand.

The cargo on the deck shifted more. A trio of crates slid starboard and crashed into the railing, ripping through and plunging into the raging Waters. Dorthos lost his balance and tumbled right through that same gap. Thom saw no splash, not in those already-stormy waters.

The bow dug into the river then heaved up, shooting into the center of the flow as it rocked upright and then leaned larboard. The barrels rolled back across the deck, distracting Dalrake. Thom used the tilt to his advantage and suddenly ran at Gweir. He crashed into the older man and they both staggered down the slanting deck until Gweir's back slammed into the railing.

Thom pummeled Gweir with his bare hands. The sorcerer fought back viciously, biting Thom's shoulder.

A bolt of lightning from Dalrake just missed the grappling pair; it was because Adele had grabbed Dalrake's ankle and yanked him off balance. He paid her back by stomping on her hand, not even wasting his lightning on her. He ignored Vivien, who was slowly crawling to where her magician's box lay, probably seeing her as no threat.

Unnoticed by the chief of sorcerers, Dorthos pulled himself back up on deck. The pixie hadn't fallen into the river after all. He had lost his bow but he had an arrow in hand. He ran down the tilted deck and jabbed the poisoned arrow tip into Dalrake's side.

In reaction, Dalrake flung the pixie from him, releasing another lightning bolt but missing.

Thom continued wrestling with Gweir, not getting anywhere until the galley careened against the River of Waters' other side. The boat leaned hard to the left as it bounced off. Thom took the opportunity to push Gweir over the rail, but the sorcerer grabbed Thom's right arm as he fell and both tumbled off the upper deck.

Thom fell onto the side walkway, while Gweir hit the lower railing. The sorcerer would have slipped over and plunged into the raging river, but he held tight to Thom's arm. His weight began to pull the journeyman after him.

Thom braced against the railing, trying to use his left hand to break the sorcerer's grip.

Gweir reached up with other hand and grabbed Thom's robe. "Wait! Pull me up and you will be richly rewarded. Money. Power…"

"Save your words!" yelled Thom, tears of pain and anger running down his cheeks. "You will die tonight, Gweir. This is for Levitanus, the apprentice you murdered, the pixies, and all the others you've killed."

"I did not kill our master!" he yelled back. "No one would dare kill a Founder. What will the guild think if you kill me for something I am innocent of doing? They will exile you too!"

Thom paused in his struggled to break free. He wasn't thinking about the judgment of the guild, but about whether Gweir was innocent of killing Levitanus. If he wasn't the one, then who had destroyed his master with fire? Maybe the others, like Merlin, should question the sorcerer and find out the truth of it all. But could he capture Gweir rather than kill him? Yet he couldn't waste time on this sorcerer while Dalrake still needed to be stopped.

At that moment, the galley bobbed upright and then its prow dug into the Waters. The whole boat shivered and shook, throwing Thom to the side and he almost went over the railing with the sorcerer.

It was too much for Thom's stomach. He tried to stop it, but the vomit spewed all over Gweir. The sorcerer tried turning his face away and lost his grip on Thom's robe in consequence, but he still held Thom's arm.

Thom grabbed hold of his wrist and tried to keep him above the raging water, but the boat tipped the other way and Gweir's feet caught one of the waves, pulling hard. Gweir grabbed Thom's robe again, but this time the fabric betrayed him. It ripped, causing the sorcerer to swing outward. With the sudden shift of weight, Thom's grip slipped and suddenly Gweir lost his hold on Thom's arm. His eyes widened as he realized that he was about to fall. He grabbed desperately with his free hand but succeeded only in clawing the back of Thom's hand.

Thom yanked bank to keep from tumbling over the railing himself, crashing against the deckhouse as Gweir fell. The sorcerer plunged deep into the River of Waters, never to resurface.

SIXTY-TWO

Enemies Flee

Thom would have collapsed on that walkway, relieved to have vanquished Gweir, but he couldn't. There was still one more sorcerer on board and the king was still in danger.

He ignored all the chaos with the crew, who were trying to regain control of the Royal Lion, as he stumbled to the ladder. When he climbed to the upper deck, he saw Dalrake bent over his mixing bowl, creating a new magic one-handed. His other hand still crackled with lightning as he held it away from the exposed elements. Thom recognized some of the magical elements he mixed, powders often used in healing.

Thom was shocked that Dalrake could handle two spells at the same time, even while poison was racing through his body.

Thom staggered across the heaving deck toward the sorcerer, ignoring Mordred and the women. Adele was scurrying across the deck, probably trying to get out of the way, but he had no time to focus on her. He needed to get to Dalrake while the powerful magician was distracted.

Dalrake had torn his robe to expose his wounded side. When the greatest of sorcerers finished his newest enchantment, a glowing paste of healing, he slathered it on his weeping wound.

It must have stung, for he sucked in his breath and gritted his teeth.

Adele returned, bringing something to Vivien. Thom wished she had kept farther back, for Dalrake still had four bursts of lightning left.

He ran at the sorcerer as he heard Vivien starting an enchantment. He wished that he had thought of doing the same, but all that he could think to do was to try pushing Dalrake over the side as he had done to Gweir.

Dalrake finally noticed Thom running toward him and pointed one finger at him. Thom tried to dive out of the way, but the instant burst still brushed his shoulder and spun him as he flew to the side. That burst probably saved him though, for he hadn't noticed Lord Mordred charging at him with a bare sword.

The nobleman swerved, even though the lightning had already passed, and then glared at the sorcerer. "You almost struck me."

If the sorcerer replied, Thom didn't hear it in the constant wind.

Thom shook from the shock, even though the lightning had barely touched him. He knew he needed to move or else Dalrake would strike him again or Mordred would slay him. He knew he had to move, but the urgency wasn't understood by his sluggish limbs. He labored to get up on his hands-and-knees and then couldn't move any further. He knelt there, shaking in his weakness.

When he looked up, he saw that Dalrake was motioning Mordred over to him. The sorcerer swayed as the constant wind buffeted him. Thom also noticed Vivien behind the men, sitting up with a magician's box in her lap. If she opened that case, Dalrake would hear it instantly.

Thom began to crawl toward Dalrake and Mordred. He wanted to hide, to find some corner and collapse in exhaustion, but he couldn't. He needed to keep them distracted from whatever Vivien was planning. So far she hadn't opened it, but she would soon.

He wasn't thinking clearly, but he remembered that King Arthur needed to be rescued. And Adele. If anyone survived, he hoped she would. He actually muttered a prayer for their protection.

Dalrake was arguing with Mordred about something, but their voices were too low to hear over the rushing wind.

Thom looked over at Vivien and she motioned emphatically at her back and at him.

He stopped crawling, confused at what she meant.

She again pointed at her back and at him.

Finally, he understood. She wanted him to take off his knapsack.

When he did, she pointed at the box in her lap, pointed at him, and then made an opening motion with her hands.

Thom sat and opened his pack, pulling out Levitanus' box and a bowl. It was his food bowl, but he didn't have the time to rummage for a proper mixing bowl or to find a pestle among his pack's contents. He looked up at Vivien and nodded, then both of them opened their cases, revealing the rhythms of the magical elements they contained.

Thom stared at the box's contents, his thoughts too scrambled to think clearly. He grabbed a few vials, at first not even aware what his tired mind had chosen. Only when he closed the lid, did he realize that he held the elements for making Wizard Lights, the most basic of spells. He frowned at the choice, but he had no time to pick something else. He mixed powders into the bowl with his finger, quickly added his spit, and then formed a Wizard Light. He didn't think he could control more than one at a time. He sent the light to bob between him and Dalrake, struggling to keep the wind from carrying it away.

Surprisingly, Vivien had also crafted Wizard Lights and she now had three of them in the air around where she sat with Adele, next to the unconscious king. Dalrake still held his lightning, so far not responding to their little lights. He was still arguing with Mordred.

When Mordred finally noticed the glowing spheres, he pointed to them angrily and raised his voice to the chief sorcerer. "See? Their magic is practically useless now. Kill them while I slay Arthur."

He moved toward the king, but Vivien swerved one of her globes in front of him and he stopped.

"Help me now!" yelled back Dalrake, his voice sounding strained. "If I do not get aid soon, I will die."

"Heal yourself, old man. You keep saying that you are the greatest of all magicians. Surely you can fight off a drop of that midget's poison."

"We must leave now, Lord Mordred. I have only four lightning bolts left. Not enough to kill all of your opponents. Do you think you can stand against all the rest by yourself? Especially after I die?"

Mordred frowned at the comment but his eyes were on Vivien's light. She sent another one close to him.

"Come to me, Mordred," ordered the sorcerer. "Flee with me or we both die on this cursed galley."

Mordred made one more attempt to get at his father, but Vivien cut him off with one of her glowing globes. No matter what the noble said, he showed that he was still afraid of the magic. Angrily, Mordred returned to the sorcerer's side and took hold of the magician's box Dalrake held out. The sorcerer then grasped Mordred's arm for support and the two of them crossed the deck to the ladder.

Thom watched them go, uncertain what to do. As he struggled to stand, he moved the Wizard Light so that it was between him and the two who were fleeing. He was doubtful that he would be quick enough to move it into the path of any lightning bolt, but it was the only defense he had.

He soon lost sight of Mordred and Dalrake as they descended to the lower deck. He staggered after them, fearful and weak, but determined to do his best to stop them.

It took some time for Thom to reach the deck's edge, for he often stumbled as the boat continued to heave. He was almost there when he heard Dalrake starting another enchantment. Thom hesitated before looking over the side, for it was unsettling to hear that the sorcerer still held lightning and the magic of the poultice while crafting a third enchantment.

When the sorcerer finished his third enchantment and released it, Thom recognized it as some kind of calling. He almost panicked, remembering how the sorceress almost overpowered him on the Road of Leaves with a similar Siren's Call. Dalrake was calling someone or something to him. When it didn't affect Thom, he looked over his shoulder to see if it was meant for the women or the king, but none of them seemed to be responding to the wooing either. Thom crept the last few feet and peeked over the edge.

The sorcerer concentrated on something in the water, while Mordred stood watch with a bared sword to make sure the sailors kept well back.

Thom moved to look over the boat's side and finally saw what Dalrake was calling to him. The three lines of Night Swans were paddling toward the galley, pixie boats in tow. Thom saw them more as a shadow against the glowing water, but he could still see that the boats weren't manned. These were the crafts that Dorthos and his companions had used. The huge birds were coming to Dalrake's call, though they struggled to keep ahead of the skiffs as the current pulled and tossed all of them.

He realized that Dalrake and Mordred planned to flee that way, but he couldn't think of any way to stop them. He wasn't certain that he wanted to stop them, for his greater concern was protecting the king and Adele.

As Thom dawdled in his uncertainty, Mordred tossed the galley's rope ladder over the side and then helped a distracted Dalrake to climb over the rail. It was Thom's last chance to retaliate and he sent his Wizard Light racing toward them. He hoped to hit Dalrake's handful of lightning and cause an explosion.

Unfortunately, Mordred happened to step into the light's path and the globe bounced harmlessly off the noble. Mordred stumbled against the boat's railing and then glared over his shoulder at Thom.

Thom tried to maintain his connection to his enchantment, to bring it back at Dalrake, but the storm caught it and the Wizard Light shot away in the strong wind, quickly falling behind the galley.

Thom tried to call it back, but it was too hard to fight against the wind once away from the boat's slight shelter. Frustrated, he let the enchantment dissipate.

Dalrake was too distracted with the balancing of three enchantments to notice any of it; he just kept climbing down to the pixie boats that were now alongside the Royal Lion.

Thom took off his knapsack and knelt. He pulled out Levitanus' box and opened its lid. The various elements whispered to him. He was more purposeful this time, not wanting to create another useless Wizard Light. As he considered what he should make, he dug around to find that misplaced mixing bowl and found it. He set it in on the deck and then pulled three vials, closing the magician's box and stowing it. He took out his water skin and squirted what was left into the bowl, adding the last of the powders in the glass vials. He added his spittle and mixed the enchantment quickly yet thoroughly. He listened to make sure the rhythm was right and then finished crafting another Twist of Air.

But he was too slow. Dalrake and Mordred had already climbed into the one of the pixie boats. Somehow, they were able to harness all three swan teams to one craft and now they pulled away from the galley.

Thom tried to send his whirlwind after them, but it shredded before he was able to get it close. Instead, he could only watch as the pair fled.

The twelve swans took flight, letting the strong wind help lift them. The boat strained as the current tried yanking it in the other direction, then the skiff started bouncing along the top of the rough surface. With a mighty heave, the birds yanked the pixie boat out of the waters and carried it skyward.

Instead of dangling beneath the birds, the pixie boat kept behind them, suspended in some new enchantment from Dalrake. Galley and skiff were quickly growing farther apart, but the sorcerer wasn't done with them yet. He threw the last of his lightning bolts at them, perfect in his aim. All four struck the furled sail with bright flashes, setting the cloth on fire.

It was Vivien who saved the galley from burning to the waterline. She crafted some water enchantment and sent a rain on the flames, dousing them completely. In all the confusion, Thom neither saw nor heard how Dalrake broke through the Road of Waters' enchantment, but somehow the sorcerer did, for Thom could no longer hear his magic nor see anything of them. He assumed they had passed up and out, for the enchantment was weakest there, letting in sunlight and rain, but he wasn't sure of it. He knew too little about such complex enchantments.

Exhausted, he turned to look over the deck to where Vivien now tried to minister to Arthur. Adele was watching her work.

Beautiful Adele.

Thom staggered to them, intending to give Adele a strong hug. Instead, she caught him before he tripped. They still hugged, however, and it felt wonderful.

Eric Loren

SIXTY-THREE

Camelot at Sunrise

The Royal Lion limped back to the Isles Waywater, making it by the determination of its remnant crew and the magical help of two exhausted student magicians. They found the Royal Ram waiting just inside the archway, where it had been waiting for a break in the storm. The other galley escorted them to Fog Town, where Wizard Weston and a party of pixie elders met them. The wounded were quickly tended to, especially the king. From the galley's railing, they watched as the king's condition was accessed. He was then carried off, while Weston turned to the Royal Lion.

The Keeper of the Waters came aboard and walked up to the remaining magicians. They met him with two magicians' boxes. Earlier, Thom and Vivien had scavenged through the caches of Cath and Ector, taking whatever they needed to refill their own boxes. They would both need the extra supplies now that they were without mentors to advocate for their restocking. In addition, Thom took Ector's mixing bowl and pestle to replace the ones the sorcerer had thrown overboard. It seemed only fair and he didn't want to use his old master's tools. Thom now had two boxes in his knapsack again, along with two bowls and two pestles, for he still had the supplies that had belonged to Levitanus and he wasn't about to turn those over because they were his inheritance according to guild tradition. Vivien had made sure that he understood that, for she suspected that some of the guild might try to break that tradition since a Founder's belongings would be something of a prize among the lesser wizards. Vivien had kept only her own box, but it was now fully replenished. So the magician boxes they turned over to Weston were only those of the two magicians who had died on the boat and those caches were not as full as they had been.

Weston took the boxes that Vivien handed him and gave the contents a brief inspection but said nothing about missing or empty vials. From Thomas he accepted Cath's staff, for they never found Ector's and assumed it had been washed overboard.

"You did well," said the Keeper, "although I wish we hadn't lost so many and that the Road of Waters wasn't so stirred up. Now I must go check on King Arthur and make sure he is comfortable."

He said no more, but turned and left. Thom thought he looked rather haggard, but then he had been fighting his own battles, trying to tame the enchantments around them.

Thom gladly disembarked too, walking down the gangplank with an arm across Adele's shoulders. Vivien walked behind them, helped by one of the sailors. Behind them came Dorthos the Daring, who helped a hobbling fellow pixie.

Thom smiled when he saw who awaited them on the dock: Francis. The monk embraced both Thom and Adele, then took over for the sailor helping Vivien. The two pixies went to join their kind, while the four humans went to the nearest inn. The common room was lightly patronized, so they had no trouble finding an unoccupied trestle table.

Thom sighed as he sat down on a polished wooden bench, setting his knapsack between his feet for safekeeping.

Now it was just the four of them, without any wizards or sorcerers about. Thom took a moment to listen for any crafting or active enchantments, but there was none. For once, all that he heard was the background sound of the Road of Waters and nothing else.

The common room's fire seemed cheerful and its heat was welcome as he scooted over a bit so that Adele could sit down.

She offered him a shy smile. "You could buy me a drink, journeyman, if your purse can afford it."

He smiled back, remembering when she had said something similar at the Root and Bough Inn. She had run off that time while he had been trying to call over a pixie maid to take his order. This time he put his hand on hers before looking around; he didn't want her getting away.

* * *

It took a month for the Road of Waters to settle down enough so that the galleys could once again ply the waterway. Apparently, the lower half of the Waters had never been as stormy as the upper half, so the queen and her entourage had made it safely to the Thames and then on to the castle of a loyal supporter. Yet river traffic had come to an end for weeks along the whole course, stranding galleys at Fog Town and at some of the various Waywaters. As soon as the river calmed enough, Merlin sent pixies and merfolk to visit the Waywaters and help any who might be in dire need of food or other provisions.

The first convoy upriver included the Royal Lion and Royal Ram, both having been repaired by pixie shipwrights. King Arthur insisted that his galley be the first back to Camelot and that he should be on its deck. This time, Merlin joined him, as well as the wizards Gildas and Thallud.

Thomas, Adele, and Vivien traveled on the second boat, along with the abbot and his monks. All the noblemen went on the Royal Lion with Arthur, so Thom didn't have to worry about being seen near Adele and took advantage of the opportunity. During the trip upriver he spent many hours with his arm around her waist or holding her hand. He tried to hide his seasickness but she was aware of it and offered him sympathy. He was embarrassed by it all, but appreciated her compassion. He had abandoned his journeyman's robe for regular traveling clothes, including a cloak to ward off the regular mists. In all the fighting, he had lost the ribbon that had held his now-long hair back, so it now hung down to his shoulders. Maybe this time he would get that haircut he had considered while on the Road of Leaves.

It was near the end of their fourth night of travel and they were nearing the Royal Waywater, which would be the terminus of their boat ride. Thom stood at the prow with Adele, trying to control his unruly stomach. He wanted a quiet moment with her, but his belly was not being cooperative. He was almost glad when Vivien interrupted them.

"There you are," she said, more to Adele than to him. "I talked with Father Justin again and I am even more convinced that the League is where I belong."

Adele smiled. "I am so glad. He seems an honorable man and his cause is just." She gave the older woman a strong hug. "This will be good for you. In truth, I have been weighing whether I should join too."

"What are you two talking about?" Thom asked.

"The League of Saint Barnabas," replied Vivien. "Is your seasickness making you dense?"

"But what do you have to offer this league?" he asked Adele, ignoring Vivien's barb. "You aren't a magician."

"The abbot wants to include warriors as well as magicians. It is meant to be a band of people who will protect the realm and its citizens."

Thom knew that she was skilled at bow and blade, but she had no warrior's build. He wanted to object, but before he could say anything, Vivien added another barb.

"Besides, she could become a wizardess if she wants to," stated the journeywoman, raising an eyebrow at Thom's frown. "Her inner ear is a sensitive one; she only needs to be trained."

Thom gaped at Vivien and then Adele. "You can hear magic?"

She smiled shyly and nodded. "At first I thought I was just imagining things, but it became obvious during this trip. I can hear the enchantments and even the elements before you mix them."

He was amazed and glad for her. Now he could talk about magic to her and she would understand what he was talking about. But then Thom considered the other part that Vivien had said and he looked at the journeywoman again. "You want to see Adele actually trained in the craft? But she's ten years older than any starting apprentice and you are no wizardess."

"I have been told that the league has master magicians that are willing to train any who can hear magic, no matter how old the person is." Vivien looked at Adele. "She has ear for it, she's very intelligent, and she's willing to learn. I would think that would be enough."

Thom almost shook his head in disapproval of all this wild talk. This crazy idea might be good for a journeywoman who had lost her mentor and had no real prospects of finishing her training, but dragging Adele into it as well? He didn't like this.

"You should join the league too," suggested Adele. In her excitement she apparently didn't notice Thom's disapproval. "Father Justin wants to recruit more trained magicians."

He almost blurted out 'never,' but stopped himself. Instead, he merely asked, "Has Francis agreed to be a part of this?"

Her excitement dampened a little. "No, Brother Francis still objects to any magic."

"Francis objects to magic but still encourages others to use it when he sees the need," said Vivien. "I overheard that he was the one who saved the Royal Ram when it was swept off by the Waters when the two wizards exhausted themselves trying to chase after the king's boat. He did no crafting himself, but he ordered them in their final enchantments when they were too weary to think straight, timing it just right to push the galley into the lower canal to the Waywater."

Thom didn't like the implication that Francis still did magic through proxy. His friend had been faithful to his vow to leave magic behind. "I don't know what Francis did when the Waters went berserk, but he has always acted with integrity around me. Even though he has renounced magic, he is a man I respect. If he is still hesitant about this League, don't expect me to embrace it."

He stared at Vivien, daring her to disagree, but she merely arched an eyebrow and then directed her next question at Adele. "Will you go with me to visit the convent when we get back to Camelot? The abbot says that any women in the League will be trained there, so as not to offend the brothers at the monastery."

Adele nodded. "I would like that. I want to hear more about how the abbot intends for this to work."

Thom was about to protest, but noticed the galley in front of theirs, the Royal Lion, was starting to sail through the final archway. He decided to wait until they had passed through before trying to talk them out of this folly.

As their boat vanished into the curtain of glowing mist, everyone on board became quiet. Once on the other side, the crew gave a great shout, relieved to see this hard journey come to an end. Thom didn't join in, still upset at what he had just learned. Vivien was wooing Adele to join her in this foolish endeavor.

He looked at Adele and tried to think of a way to convince her to keep away from this League, but she radiated with excitement at the prospect. At a loss for words and feeling a bit hurt, he looked away and didn't notice that Vivien had stepped close.

"One more thing Thomas," she said, startling him. "The secret to lighting your staff is not trying to light it from outside. You cannot put a fire into it. Instead, look into the jewel and bring out the sparkle that is deep inside the gem. Just like a person's character reflects on their continence, so a magician's staff reflects outward the light inside it and the skill inside the magician."

With that she turned and walked away, heading toward the cabin assigned to the women.

Thom watched after her a moment and then looked more closely at his staff. What she said, suddenly made sense and he was able to kindle the jewel finally, a greenish light in the darkness.

"You did it!" laughed Adele, happy for him.

He grinned back at her, enjoying her smile almost as much as he did the glowing staff. It had been surprisingly easy once he understood how to light the gem. He left it burning as he moved to the railing and looked out over the waters, holding his staff in one hand and Adele's hand in his other. He did not let go of either the light or the hand until they were ready to enter the archway to King's Harbor. He let go of the magic then, for it was a kind of crafting even if it didn't involve other magical powders or mixing, because the jewel itself was an element.

"I should go pack my things," said Adele, giving him a brief kiss on the cheek. "I want to get off this boat as soon as we dock. I've had enough of Road adventures."

"Go ahead. I'll be waiting here."

He watched her leave, then turned back to the dark waters. He already had all his belongings strapped to his back, so there was nothing for him to do. It gave him a quiet moment to reflect and to worry. What would happen to him now? He no longer had a master and he wasn't known at Clas Myrddin. What wizard would be willing to take him on? Would a new master be as understanding or as free with his knowledge? He wondered if anyone would want him since he was such a young journeyman and more like an overly glorified apprentice. Maybe he could finally kindle the jewel in his magician's staff, but there was so much more about which he was ignorant.

* * *

They came through the last archway into King's Harbor just as night ended. As their boat lingered in the harbor to allow the king's galley to dock, Thom watched the first light of dawn touch the billowy highway of the Road of Clouds that shot over the city to touch the unbelievably tall Sky Tower. Although he couldn't see the rest of it, that was where the guild house waited his return. He stood alone because they had decided it would best if he kept his distance from the women and also from the monks because now they were back in the city and anyone might be watching them.

Fairly soon the golden light of dawn touched everything around Thom as a fresh breeze picked up and caused his cloak and long hair to blow to the side. For some reason he had rekindled his staff upon entering the enchantment of the king's city and now the green light contrasted with the golden hues all around him. He was glad that the magic shield covering all of Camelot seemed hale and in rhythm, so at least that was at least one enchantment that wouldn't need repairing.

Finally, the king's boat was secured, so it was their turn to dock. The sailors bustled to the oars while the pilot expertly guided the galley to its assigned place near the king's galley. There were men rushing everywhere, with shouts and laughter and curses. But even with all the men bustling around him, Thomas suddenly felt alone. Longingly, he looked over to where Adele stood with Vivien, but they were watching the piers. He looked past them to the group of monks and Francis caught his gaze.

The monk gave a nod of acknowledgment and a smile and he realized that he wasn't alone after all. He smiled back but resisted the temptation to wave or walk over. It was best for Francis that Thom kept some distance from him. So much possible intrigue now that he was drawing close to the guild house and the king's court. Camelot would not be as simple a place as traveling on the Roads. That thought caused him to chuckle.

"Why do you laugh?"

The question surprised him and he looked over to find a small man approaching, his clothes bright enough to make the dawn seem subdued. He had forgotten that some of the pixies had chosen to come back to Camelot.

"It is good to see you, Dorthos. I was just considering how complicated it was to be in the king's city. Camelot might make the Roads seem tame in comparison."

The self-claimed pixie prince came to stand next to him, although he could barely see over the top rail. "Arthur's city does have its share of intrigue, but let us hope it will be much calmer than our last few days. There is so much to rebuild if we want the Roads restored. We need a time of peace."

Thom nodded his agreement but he wondered how much calm they would have, for there was so much that was still unsettled, so much that was being plotted in secret for good and for ill.

WAYS OF CAMELOT
4-Book Arthurian Fantasy Series

1- Road of Leaves
First Book of the 4-Book Ways of Camelot Series.. Available in paperback and e-book.

2- Road of Waters
Available in paperback and e-book

3- Camelot of the Roads
Available **September 15, 2023** in paperback and e-book.

4- Road of Clouds
Available **October 15, 2023** in paperback and e-book.

Eric Loren

About the Author
Eric Loren

Eric is an American author of fantasy, science fiction, and dystopian novels.

His writings include the Ways of Camelot series, the upcoming Tag Warren series, and the Cirian War saga.

The son of immigrants, he can speak his parents' tongue, though with a decidedly American accent. He studied our collective past and our present (holding a degree in both History and Religious Studies), and still enjoys learning about the world's diverse cultures and beliefs.

Eric currently lives in California, enjoying the sunshine and natural wonders of that unique state. He is married to his beloved Amy and has two wonderful sons.

Learn more about Eric at his website:
http://ericloren.com